GHOST TARGET

By Andy McDermott and available from Headline

Featuring Alex Reeve
Operative 66
Rogue Asset
Ghost Target

Featuring Nina Wilde and Eddie Chase
The Hunt for Atlantis
The Tomb of Hercules
The Secret of Excalibur
The Covenant of Genesis
The Cult of Osiris
The Sacred Vault
Empire of Gold
Temple of the Gods
The Valhalla Prophecy
Kingdom of Darkness
The Last Survivor (A Digital Short Story)
The Revelation Code
The Midas Legacy
King Solomon's Curse
The Spear of Atlantis
The Resurrection Key
The Temple of Skulls

Standalone Thriller
The Persona Protocol

ANDY McDERMOTT
GHOST
TARGET

HEADLINE

First published in 2023 by
HEADLINE PUBLISHING GROUP

1

Cataloguing in Publication Data is available from the British Library

Hardback ISBN 978 1 4722 8502 7
Trade paperback ISBN 978 1 4722 8503 4

Typeset in Sabon by Avon DataSet Ltd, Alcester, Warwickshire

Printed and bound in Great Britain by Clays Ltd, Elcograf S.p.A.

Headline's policy is to use papers that are natural, renewable and recyclable products and made from wood grown in well-managed forests and other controlled sources. The logging and manufacturing processes are expected to conform to the environmental regulations of the country of origin.

HEADLINE PUBLISHING GROUP
An Hachette UK Company
Carmelite House
50 Victoria Embankment
London EC4Y 0DZ

www.headline.co.uk
www.hachette.co.uk

For Kat and Sebastian

CHAPTER 1

The Munich hospital's staff knew the blond-haired surgeon as 'Herr Doktor Holke'. It was not his real name.

Harrison Locke contemplated his patient. Paul Telemann had visited his *Hausarzt* – general practitioner – with several symptoms. Shortness of breath, ripping chest and back pains, difficulty walking. The doctor immediately referred him to the hospital for a full check-up. The alarming truth did not take long to find. Telemann was suffering from an aortic dissection, in imminent danger of aneurism. Emergency surgery was needed to save his life.

'Doktor Holke' – Locke – was the duty surgeon. The first stage of the operation was routine to him. With the anaesthetised patient lying on his right, an incision was made down the chest. The ribs were cracked open and spread. The major organs were moved aside for access to the heart. Then, with blood-thinning medication administered, the aorta and its major branches were clamped.

Locke examined the distended blood vessel. Would it require repair, or reconstruction? The latter was far more difficult, and risky. The chance of death during the extensive surgery was high.

The thought sent a familiar frisson of excitement through him.

Telemann's life was literally in his hands. And not merely as an outcome of his surgical skills. He could kill the German on a *whim*. The tiniest deliberate slip of the scalpel, just a millimetre or two, and Telemann would die. The perfect murder.

If Locke chose that route, it would not be for the first time.

His explorations of mortality had begun in his teens, with animals. A pet mouse first piqued his curiosity. He had dissected animals in biology class at school. But they had all been dead. He'd wanted to see what it looked like inside while still alive. The bloody results intrigued him; he was keen to learn more. The mouse, he'd informed his parents, had escaped. He was told off for his carelessness. There would be no more pets on which to practise.

No pets of his own, at least.

Squirrels, birds, a couple of local cats had been lured into traps for vivisection. He'd begun with knives, then advanced to a scalpel bought for 'crafting'. His skills advanced with each new subject. He started to borrow veterinary and medical texts from the library. His pleased parents had taken that as an interest in medicine in general. Their prompting on whether he'd considered it as a career made him think: *Why not?* He'd enjoyed what he had done so far. The focus required; the need for precision; the visceral sensation of cutting into living flesh. They appealed to the very core of his being.

His crowning teenage achievement had been the

dismantling of a stray dog persuaded to follow him. After that, he'd forced himself to restrict his activities. There was a greater goal ahead; being caught killing animals could threaten it. He dedicated himself to the task of obtaining his medical degree.

He succeeded. Any number of options in the world of medicine opened up to him.

Instead, he had chosen to join the British army.

Why? was a question he still couldn't quite answer. An urge for adventure? Avoidance of the stifling bureaucracy and tedious cliques of hospital life? Perhaps both. But also, perhaps another reason.

It would allow him to kill, legally and with impunity.

At the time, the army was embroiled in Afghanistan and Iraq. He'd made it clear he was ready and willing to serve on the front line. As a result, he saw violence and the deaths resulting from it on a regular basis.

The first human he killed was a wounded prisoner in Afghanistan. A young member of the Taliban, shot in the abdomen and leg. Locke could have saved him; the surgery would have been simple enough. But on the drive back to base, an urge overtook him. The man was an enemy, who would kill him given the chance. He wasn't worth saving. So why not do what he had always wanted to do?

The prisoner was restrained for transport. The other soldiers in the Foxhound patrol vehicle were occupied with more pressing matters. Locke had pretended to work on the man's wounds. While doing so, he cut his femoral artery and let him bleed to death.

The Afghan's helpless realisation that he was being

3

murdered thrilled Locke far beyond his imaginings. The *power* he held! The sheer *charge* of watching life vanish from another's eyes . . . and knowing he was responsible. No other feeling he'd ever experienced came remotely close in intensity. He wanted more.

Carefully, diligently, he had worked to get it.

The prisoner's death was given only a perfunctory investigation. Locke had made sure it looked accidental, a result of the bullet wound. Besides, nobody cared.

He dealt with three more Afghans in similar ways. Still no one was bothered. But he knew he needed to be wary. Too many deaths at his hands would make him look incompetent. For a man who sought perfection in all things, the idea was . . . *insulting*. So he became more fastidious in choosing his victims, looking for borderline cases. Those who would die without surgery . . . but could easily die during it. The choice was Locke's. The power over life and death was his alone. To use as he wished.

The next person he'd killed had been a British soldier. He'd felt no qualms about doing so even when the man was on his side. There were no nations beyond death. Another two Afghans after that . . .

Then, for the first time, Locke killed out of emotion.

It had been for the most trivial reason. His victim was a British officer, a major. Locke was a captain. The man had annoyed him a few months earlier, pulling rank, inconveniencing him. The major later ended up under Locke's knife. He did not leave it alive.

This time, though, the case was not borderline. Locke had actively needed to work to end his life. He still did so carefully. But not quite carefully enough. The death of an officer brought a full investigation. Locke had performed countless similar procedures with no fatalities. Why this time?

He'd covered his tracks. Had explanations and justifications for every point raised against him. But for the first time since his teens, his parents asking about the mouse . . .

He'd felt the sweat of fear on his brow.

Locke had been cleared. But it had been a narrow thing – and now others would be suspicious. He would be watched closely, his future options limited. What to do? He'd considered leaving the army, but civilian practice would be even more restrictive. He needed another alternative . . .

And then, as if in answer, he was approached by SC9.

The most deadly of Britain's spears, as it had been put to him. SC9 was an agency so covert, not even the Prime Minister knew it existed. An assassination bureau, functioning under total deniability. Doing what needed to be done while keeping politicians' hands clean.

Sometimes, it even dealt with politicians themselves. The interests of the British state as a whole came above any individual within it. Anyone who threatened it in any way was a target for SC9. At home or abroad, British or foreign. No nations beyond death.

Locke was approached because someone at SC9 had realised what his investigators hadn't. He was a murderer, a psychopath, who had killed without being detected. For most agencies, that would have been not merely disqualifying, but cause for imprisonment.

For SC9, it was a *requirement*. Nobody was recruited to it

without having killed at least once during service. Whether that killing had been sanctioned or not was irrelevant.

So he had willingly joined. Gone through the most demanding training of his life. Successfully become a member of SC9. He had been given two new identities. One was his name: Harrison Locke. His birth name was gone, all but forgotten. His past was no longer relevant. The other was his code within SC9: Operative 61.

Now, almost two years later, Operative 61 had another assignment. Like most SC9 missions, the goal was simple – kill the target.

Telemann was not that target. He would be merely a bonus.

If Locke decided to kill him.

He examined the aorta more closely. Ultrasound imaging had been performed, but in a rush once the case's urgency was realised. The result was inconclusive. His own experience would now determine the course of action. Fenestration, or open reconstruction? The wrong choice, and Telemann would die whether he wanted him to or not . . .

Locke made the decision. He raised his scalpel to open the aorta and begin a repair. Paul Telemann would live today. The German would go the rest of his life unaware of the truth. He was alive only because Locke had permitted it.

That choice had been made for two reasons. The first was that a successful operation would be beneficial to Locke's cover. The second . . .

There was no way to see the fear in an unconscious man's eyes.

* * *

It was evening by the time the surgery was concluded. Successfully, of course; Locke had not expected any other outcome. He knew his skills were exceptional. That part of Dr Holke's résumé had not been forged.

There was a real Dr Holke in Denmark. As far as Locke knew, he was alive and well. The Dane had no idea another man was using his name. SC9 had put Locke forward for the surgeon's position some months earlier. Britain's electronic spy agency GCHQ monitored all communications from the hospital. Phone calls and emails regarding Holke were intercepted, redirected. Internet search results were amended. When Holke's employers were contacted for references, those responding were actually in England.

There was a small risk that the deception might be uncovered. Someone in Munich could have encountered the real Holke at a medical conference. But SC9 had done its homework. Holke had been chosen specifically because that risk was minimal.

When Locke arrived for his first interview, he'd been certain he would get the position. His résumé had been tailored for it. He was fluent in German, charming when needed. His interviewers accepted him as who he claimed to be. With his surgical record and excellent references, his appointment was all but inevitable.

Once he was in place . . . his mission could begin.

Another stage of that mission would be carried out that night. Locke checked his watch as he removed his scrubs. There should be plenty of time, but his target would not follow a set timetable. He had to be in position well in advance.

He changed into his suit and donned his glasses, then departed. He was heading for the lifts when someone called 'Stef!' behind him. After four months in character, Locke responded at once to the name. He turned to see his immediate superior, Dr Rudolf Emmerich, approaching. 'There you are,' said Emmerich. 'I'm glad I caught you. I wanted to say well done on the Telemann procedure.'

'It was straightforward enough,' Locke replied. He was not being performatively modest, simply stating a fact.

'And that's why we're glad to have coaxed you out of Denmark. From what I hear, the aorta was in imminent danger of rupture. A very difficult operation. But you didn't even break a sweat.'

Locke gave the other surgeon a brief smile. 'Perhaps one drop.'

'Ah, so you *are* as human as the rest of us.' A chuckle from Emmerich. 'I've invited the team for a celebratory drink. Will you join us?'

'Normally, I'd love to,' Locke lied. 'Unfortunately, I have a prior engagement.'

'Oh, I see. A pity. But there'll be plenty more successful procedures to celebrate, I'm sure.' Another small laugh. 'Then I won't detain you. See you on Monday.'

'I'll see you then, Rudolf,' said Locke, continuing on his way.

He took the elevator down to the underground parking lot. Heading for his car, he was surprised to hear his cover name called again. Another doctor angled towards him. 'Working late?' asked Gerhard Hitzfeld. The other surgeon was a few years younger than Locke, in his mid-thirties.

The Operative found him irksomely pushy.

'A long procedure,' Locke told him. 'Emergency aortic reconstruction.'

'Successful?'

'Of course.'

A twitch in Hitzfeld's expression told Locke he had taken the factual statement as arrogance. He didn't care. 'We should swap shifts sometime,' said the German. 'You deal with the Friday night broken-bottle gashes for a change.' A hint of challenge behind the too-broad smile.

Again, Locke didn't care. 'I will have to check my diary, but we could do that. Work is work.'

It was not the answer the other man had expected. 'Oh. Good, that would be good, yes.' His veiled attitude vanished. 'Hey, you should come round to my place for another drink one evening.'

Locke had endured various social engagements with his new colleagues. Establishing Holke as open, friendly and popular aided his cover, however tedious the task. 'I'd enjoy that, thank you.' He wouldn't. 'We will have to arrange a time. Speaking of time, you don't want to be late for your shift.'

Hitzfeld checked his watch. 'Oops, no, I don't. Okay, I'll see you later. Have a good evening!'

Locke continued towards his car. 'I will.'

Locke sat unmoving in the dark, waiting.

He had broken into the apartment two hours earlier. That gave him more than adequate time to prepare. He wore medical coveralls, paper booties over his shoes, latex gloves, a facemask, even goggles. An all-encompassing disposable protective sheath, to minimise shedded DNA evidence. The Covid-19 pandemic had made such items far more widely available. That they were hospital-issue would no longer point towards him.

He had set out everything else he needed on the bed. All that was missing now was his target.

Said target went on social media by the name Franka Jannings. Mild irony that both hunter and prey hid behind false identities. 'Franka' was actually a man – a transvestite. On his Facebook profile he claimed to be a pre-op transsexual. To Locke, the difference was academic. Any surgery would be merely cosmetic, a façade over genetic reality. And he was the expert in surgical matters, after all.

Jannings' real name was not relevant. What mattered was that he matched the profile. The right age range, a regular at the nightclub, a cross-dresser, lived alone. Another victim for the Bondage Killer.

That was not the name Locke would have chosen, but it was perhaps inevitable. The German tabloid media was as salacious and sensationalist as its British counterpart. Three identical murders in four weeks? Obviously the work of a serial killer. With the sexual and fetishistic overtones, the newspapers were delighted.

After tonight, they would be ecstatic. The total would rise to four identical murders in six weeks. The pattern behind the killings would be absolutely unmissable.

Which was exactly what Locke and SC9 wanted.

A glance at his watch. The nightclub had now closed, so Jannings would be on his way home. There was a chance he might spend the night at someone else's place. That would disrupt the pattern, but it was an unavoidable risk. However, GCHQ had tracked Jannings' phone back home on the two previous club nights. A more likely issue would be that he did not return alone.

Locke was unconcerned. He'd carried out three supposed serial killings, but there had actually been four deaths. The second victim came home with another man. Locke ambushed him, stabbing his heart, before overpowering his target. The mission then proceeded as planned. The extra death was to Locke's benefit. Establishing that the Bondage Killer murdered others as collateral damage foreshadowed his ultimate objective.

He waited, a spider unmoving in its web. Eventually he heard a sound outside the apartment. Footsteps: high heels on the hallway's hard-wearing linoleum. He moved into position behind the bathroom door. Was anyone with his target?

No other footfalls. Good. That simplified matters.

A rattle as a key was pushed unsteadily into the lock. Jannings was probably drunk. Again, good: an intoxicated victim was easier to subdue. The door opened. The footsteps became louder, sharper, as heels clacked on the wooden floor. The hall light came on. A stumble, followed by mumbled obscenities in German. A thump as shoes or boots were kicked off. Would the target enter the bedroom to undress, or visit the bathroom first?

The bedroom. Locke heard the door open and readied himself. Jannings entered the room – then stopped in surprise. He had seen the items on the bed. A confused exclamation—

Locke stepped out silently from the bathroom. His target was right before him. A long blonde wig obscured Jannings' shoulders. That didn't matter. The surgeon knew exactly where to strike. The edge of his right hand chopped hard against the base of the German's neck. Such a blow to the vagus nerve could be fatal. But Locke was precise. He intended only to stun, and was successful. Jannings fell forward on to the bed as if his bones had liquefied.

The Operative moved quickly. His victim would soon recover. But everything had been prepared. He dragged the limp figure up the bed and rolled it on to its back. The limbs were spread, and cuffed at the wrists and ankles. A large ballgag was forced into Jannings' mouth and buckled in place. Then the ropes attached to the cuffs were pulled and knotted tight. His prisoner was now completely immobilised.

Completely helpless.

Locke switched on the light, then regarded his bound victim. At first glance, Jannings could pass for a woman. But a few seconds' observation revealed the truth. Visible larynx despite the costume jewellery trying to cover it, wide shoulders, narrow hips. Unmistakeable signifiers of masculinity. Locke's lips curled in disapproval. Why deny what you were?

No time for further musings. Jannings was starting to recover. Locke stood at the head of the bed, looking down as his victim's eyes focused. Bewilderment became shock, then panic. Jannings struggled against the bonds. No use. Locke had secured them well. A muffled cry came from behind the gag.

'Be quiet,' said Locke firmly. He knew the sound would

not be audible outside the apartment. The command was merely to establish his authority. Jannings looked up in terror at the masked figure. Another strained yell. Locke pushed his palm down on Jannings' throat. The noise became a choked rattle, then stopped.

The prisoner stared at him, wide-eyed. The unspoken questions were obvious. *Who are you? What do you want?* Then, a deeper fear manifested in the trapped gaze. Jannings had just realised the intruder's identity. Locke had monitored his social media posts over the past few days. Their tone was mocking detachment. *Sure, there's a serial killer targeting Munich's trans community. But I'm not scared. I'm still going to the club on Friday. Nothing will happen to me.*

Wrong.

Locke opened the leather bag he had placed beside the bed. He took out a large pair of scissors. 'This is nothing personal,' he told Jannings. He brought the scissors to the neck of his victim's dress and began to cut. Jannings struggled against the ropes as the blades snipped downwards. He tried to cry out again as cold metal brushed his skin. Locke returned a hand to his throat; the sound stopped. One last cut, and the dress was opened. He peeled the two sides apart. Beneath it, Jannings wore a red bra containing silicone breast forms, and matching satin underwear. Male genitalia were tucked within.

Locke contained his distaste. There was work to do. More snips, and both undergarments were sliced in half. Jannings' body was now fully exposed. He shivered in terror. Locke regarded the expanse of flesh with surgical professionalism.

Then he returned the scissors to his bag – and drew out a scalpel.

Jannings' eyes again went wide in fear as the blade was held over his genitals. Castration while still alive was the first stage of the procedure. 'I assure you,' said Locke, 'I am not doing this for any kind of personal pleasure.'

But, tingling anticipation rising as the scalpel lowered, he knew that was not entirely true.

The task was done. Then came the follow-up.

It was tedious, thought Locke, but essential. The removal and careful positioning of the victim's organs added a ritualistic element. Catnip for the media – and a distraction from his true objective. The authorities, he knew, were already concentrating on that aspect. GCHQ was monitoring the Munich police's communications on behalf of SC9. Was there a secret meaning to the act? A clue to the killer's identity? A warning of the next victim?

There was, in reality, nothing. It was all nonsense, devised by Locke and his superior. More diversions and distractions to occupy investigators, and conceal the true objective.

Which would be his next, and final, target.

One final review of the grim tableau. Was everything as it should be? There had been an unexpected interruption. A noise at the door while he was extracting the victim's liver. He froze – was someone coming in? But then the unseen person moved on to another flat. Locke waited for a full minute before resuming his task. Had the disturbance affected it?

Unlikely. He knew what he was doing. Remove each

organ surgically, then lacerate the cuts to appear less skilled. He could have simply hacked out each organ in the first place, but . . .

An involuntary sneer. The very idea was offensive. Perfection in all things. Words he did his best to live by. He was sure his work met the necessary standards.

Locke collected his belongings and left the bedroom. There was still blood on his gloved hands. He went to the front door and checked through the peephole. Nobody in the hallway. He opened the door and smeared a bloody runic symbol above the handle. That would ensure the murder was quickly discovered. He closed the door and went back into the flat.

He had entered via a narrow French door in the living room. He opened it and peered outside. A small third-floor balcony overlooked a snow-covered courtyard between apartment blocks. Few lights were on. No movement, no sound. He carefully stepped out, snow crumping underfoot. He would leave footprints, but was unconcerned. His shoes were a size larger than he normally wore, padded out with tissue paper. They would be incinerated with the rest of his coverings.

Locke took a plastic sack from his bag. All his shroud, bar the gloves, went into it. He dropped it to the ground below. Then he donned a coat he had left outside and closed the door. The bag had a strap; he shouldered it, then began to climb down. He took his time, minimising noise. At last he was on the ground. Fresh snow had already covered the footprints he'd left on arriving. More was falling; the new set would soon also be obliterated.

The gloves went into the sack, which he tied up tightly. He checked for nearby activity. Nothing. He was clear.

His objective completed, the Operative vanished into the night.

CHAPTER 2

Angry shouts woke Alex Reeve.

He jerked upright in his bed, instantly ready to fight. Had SC9 found him? Or were the Slovenian police carrying out a raid?

Neither. He recognised the voice. Daxner, as usual yelling when something wasn't to his liking. He calmed, but didn't lower his guard. He was a hunted man, on the run. Any potential threat had to be treated as a real one. If SC9 caught him, they would kill him. If he was arrested for any reason, the same would soon happen. He had burned through the last of his fake IDs in Italy four months earlier. Now he was technically an undocumented immigrant, his presence in the European Union illegal. If caught, he would be photographed, fingerprinted, detained.

And SC9, watching for him via Britain's extensive intelligence networks, would be alerted.

He had evaded the assassination agency for nearly two years. Once, he had been part of it. SC9 had recruited him from the British army's Special Reconnaissance Regiment. He became Operative 66 – newly qualified, ready to serve his country. Then his colleagues turned on him. Another Operative, a mole backed by Russia, had framed him for his own espionage actions. Reeve was declared *Fox Red*: a traitor, to be killed on sight. It was a status that could not be rescinded. Even though he eventually exposed the spy, he was still marked for death. He knew too much.

Alone, wounded, he ran. Then, unexpectedly, he met someone who helped him. Connie Jones, a nurse. She tended his injuries, gave him a place in which to recover. He told her what had happened; she believed him. Trusted him. Fell in love with him. And he fell in love with her. They escaped as one, the perfect couple, together for ever . . .

Until he left her. Abandoned her. *Betrayed* her. Every day since had felt like a jagged spike through his heart.

At the time, he'd thought he was doing the right thing. SC9 had found him again. Sooner or later, they would catch him. Kill him. If Connie was with him, they would kill her too. So he did what he believed was necessary to keep her safe. He walked away. Left her behind. Alone.

Regret had been almost immediate, overwhelming. He returned to Venice to look for her. But she was gone. He had no way to find her. She had given up everything to be with him. He repaid her sacrifice by leaving her when she needed him the most.

She was gone. And though his wounded heart still held the hope of finding her again . . .

Deep down, he knew that would never happen.

He had lost the most important person in his life. As much as he tried to blame SC9, the decision had been entirely his.

The greatest mistake he had ever made.

And now he was here. A tiny room in a run-down house on the periphery of Bled, Slovenia. Living with other undocumented immigrants, runaways and criminals. Chopping down trees deep in the surrounding forests in the dead of winter. Everything about the work was illegal. No forestry permits, wages paid in cash to dodge tax. But it was work he had to do, because . . . he had no choice.

He had exhausted his remaining resources in the months after leaving Connie. Winter came, so he needed shelter. Which cost money. Without ID, real or fake, he couldn't get any kind of legal job. The lumberjack work was all he could find. He knew he was being exploited. But it was that or nothing.

He checked his watch. Just before seven. Time to get up. His employers collected their workers at eight. He got out of the clammy, creaking bed. It was a single. He missed having a big bed.

But he missed sharing it with Connie even more.

Reeve made his own breakfast. He generally kept himself isolated from the four other men in the house. Enough time was spent in their company during the long working day. He only interacted with them when there was no other choice.

This was one of those times. The kitchen was cramped, but Marko Daxner was holding court at the table. The crop-haired Slovene was large in body and voice. Reeve only got the general gist of the conversation; his grasp of Slovenian was limited. The two men in Daxner's entourage listened, laughing sycophantically. The dynamic around the table reminded Reeve unpleasantly of his bullying father. He too had had his own posse of hangers-on and bootlickers. Little fish, hoping for scraps from the shark.

Reeve brought his plate to the table and sat at the opposite end from Daxner. The big man pointedly did not acknowledge him. On his arrival, Daxner had tried to demonstrate the house's pecking order through physical intimidation. Reeve effortlessly overpowered him and flattened him face-first on the table. After that, Daxner left him alone.

The house's last occupant entered, looking agitated. Like Daxner, Hedeon Pinsker was large, but his timorous attitude seemed to halve his size. He regarded the other men, twitched when he noticed something about Daxner, then hesitantly approached. Daxner smirked dismissively. He knew exactly what Pinsker was concerned about.

Reeve quickly worked it out for himself. Daxner was wearing a thick fleece with a distinctive orange collar over his other clothing. Reeve recognised it as Pinsker's. The Belarusian hesitantly asked for it back. Daxner refused with a laugh, his sidekicks joining in.

Pinsker's cheeks flushed with anger and humiliation. He seemed about to protest, but quailed at Daxner's menacing gaze. Instead he turned to Reeve. 'He's stolen my fleece,' he said – in Russian. Both men were fluent speakers. 'I'll freeze today if I don't have it. Can you make him give it back? Please?'

Reeve's eyes flicked towards Daxner. The Slovene suddenly paled. Pinsker's expression became hopeful . . .

Then collapsed as Reeve replied. 'Not my business,' he said – in English. Pinsker and Daxner knew the language. The Slovene laughed again. Face burning red, Pinsker scurried from the room.

'That guy's such a loser,' said one of Daxner's clique, in Italian. The comment was aimed at Reeve, who was passing himself off as that nationality. The youthful Sergio Mangano claimed to have fled Italy after getting a powerful man's daughter pregnant. Whether her father was in the mafia or a politician varied in the telling.

'Yeah, yeah,' the other man agreed. Otakar Antal was another Slovene, but in this region Italian was a common second language. 'Pathetic, utterly pathetic. I don't know why he's here. He can hardly lift an axe!' He laughed, glancing at Daxner as if hoping he would join in. When he didn't, the sound quickly stopped.

Daxner's gaze finally turned towards Reeve. 'Surprised at you, Martin,' he said. Reeve currently went by the name 'Leo Martin'. It was generic enough to have come from any of several countries. 'Thought you'd be the sort to play the hero.'

'Like I said,' Reeve replied flatly, 'not my business.'

The battered old minibus ground uphill into the forests above the Radovna Valley. Twelve men were squeezed inside. Reeve and the others from his house worked alongside another, similarly indigent group. Conversation was muted. The dirt track was bumpy, the day snowy and grey and cold.

Pinsker in particular felt that latter. Even with a coat on he was shivering, hands clenched tight for warmth. He glared angrily at Daxner, two rows ahead. The Slovene had made sure the stolen fleece's orange collar was in prominent view.

Why didn't you help him?

The inner voice was Connie's. Reeve's conscience had adopted it some time before. *You would have done while we were together. You could have made Daxner give it back with no trouble . . .*

I don't care any more, was his unspoken reply. That wasn't strictly true, he knew. Rather, he didn't *want* to care any more. Without Connie, nothing mattered.

Any willingness to express feelings had been beaten out of him as a child. Then further forced down by his military and SC9 training. He was an assassin, after all. But in their time together, Connie had reawakened his long-dormant empathy. He had *started* to care, first for her, then for others . . .

But now it was too painful. All it did was remind him of what he had lost.

The wound in his heart ached again. He angrily shut down the thought. The only thing that should be on his mind was survival.

There were three basic options. The first was *hide*: as he was doing now. Stay well out of the way, below the radar. Avoid being noticed. So far, the tactic was succeeding. But without money or resources, it was a miserable, stressful existence.

Less stressful than the second option, though: *run*. Keep moving faster than he could be tracked. Again, a tactic that became increasingly difficult without money. Lacking a passport, he was effectively trapped in Europe's Schengen travel zone. A big arena in which to run, sure. But even after Brexit, British Intelligence still had eyes everywhere. One unwitting appearance in a facial-recognition database would ring alarm bells. And then SC9 would come after him.

The anger returned at the thought of his former employers. That led to the third option.

Attack.

He had tried that before. His mentor during training, Tony Maxwell, surreptitiously provided help after realising Reeve had been framed. The aid was information: the name and location of SC9's boss. Sir Simon Scott had headed the agency since its creation three decades earlier. Reeve confronted him twice. The first time, at Scott's vacation home in France, was to plead his innocence. Scott rejected his appeal out of hand. The second time, Reeve escalated to threats. He infiltrated SC9's London headquarters to deliver an ultimatum. *Leave me and Connie alone, or I'll expose SC9 to the world.*

He had the power to do that. The mole had hacked into SC9's servers and copied hundreds of files: assassination records. Encrypted copies were released to the media around the world. All that was needed to decode them was the password.

Reeve had obtained it. But . . .

He couldn't bring himself to reveal it. The Operatives had killed in allied countries as well as hostile ones. Even within the UK itself. Politicians, officials, businesspeople, journalists . . . if Scott decided they harmed British interests, they were declared targets. And his definition of British interests was extremely broad.

Releasing the password would damage Britain diplomatically and economically. The fallout would hurt ordinary people more than the Establishment elites Scott worked to shield. Whatever SC9's head asserted, Reeve was no traitor. He couldn't do it. He'd signed up to SC9 to protect the country, and all its people. His motives had been honest – and hadn't changed.

The stolen files were too blunt an instrument. To release one, he would have to release them all. He'd had another option. Craig Parker, the mole, had copies on his phone. Reeve had taken it from him, gained access. He'd used a few selectively, to persuade Maxwell to help him. He could have continued to do so, drip-feeding chosen files to the media. That would have raised questions, drawn outrage – and bogged down SC9 into inoperability.

But the phone was at the bottom of the Venetian Lagoon, lost in his escape. The only way he could now attack SC9 was to expose an operation in progress. And the chances of doing so were slim. Secrecy and deniability were the Operatives' raison d'être. Scott had trained his people well.

A vision of Scott's face flashed through his mind. A plump, smug bureaucrat, who had taken the power of life and death upon himself. If Reeve had only been dealing with Maxwell, his offer of détente would have worked. But compromise was not in Scott's nature.

His fists clenched involuntarily. Scott had been at his mercy, twice. If he had killed him, he and Connie would be safe – and together.

Despite the cold, that knowledge stoked a furious fire inside him.

CHAPTER 3

Tony Maxwell had delivered the speech to SC9 recruits-in-training before. But this was the first time he would do so as the head of the agency.

He regarded the current batch as they stood at attention in the training facility's gymnasium. Men and women, ranging from their mid-twenties to late thirties. All came from various arms of the British security state: the military; intelligence services; police. Their records and profiles showed them to be loyal and extremely capable. SC9's training in the Scottish Highlands had made them even more so.

And all had killed in the line of duty. Whether authorised to do so or not. That was what had first brought each to SC9's attention.

For the early months of training, the recruits were known simply by numbers. Now, they had adopted their new identities. Maxwell regarded each in turn. Patrick Steele. Jake Wells. Lynn Powell. Chris Franks. Ella Brand. Paul Taylor. Bland, generic monikers; nothing memorable. Even an Operative's name would be lost in a crowd.

If they *became* Operatives. That was why he was here, why he had endured the tedious journey from London. Sir Simon Scott, his predecessor, had always remained a distant leader. He'd preferred to stay hands-off, an isolated, some-what threatening figure behind the curtain.

That was not Maxwell's style. He had trained most of the currently active Operatives. He knew their strengths person-ally, not just as bullet points in a file.

Now he was the director of SC9, though, he had to rely on those files. This was the first time he had met the recruits. He hoped all would still be here by the end of the day.

He suspected, however, that some would not.

Time to find out. 'Good afternoon,' he said. 'My name is Tony Maxwell. I'm the director of SC9. My predecessor, the man in charge when you first arrived, wouldn't have made this visit. But I'm not my predecessor.' Maxwell had actually *killed* his predecessor. The justification was that Scott let an operation get out of control, threatening SC9's security. That was true, as far as it went. Maxwell even went so far as to obtain approval from the other intelligence chiefs. But Scott's removal, by retirement or other means, had always been part of his plan. 'If you complete your training and become Operatives, I'll be your boss,' he continued. 'But I'm here today . . . to give you one last chance to drop out.'

Confusion from the line of men and women. Their thoughts were obvious: *Why would we want to do that?* There had originally been nine. Three had failed to meet the gruelling physical requirements. But the remainder had pushed hard to get this far. Why leave now?

Maxwell began his explanation. 'You've been training for six months to be the most deadly agents in the world. But so far, you haven't been told the exact reason *why*. It's now time to answer that question. But there's a question each of *you* has to answer first.' He paused, letting expectation rise, before continuing. 'It's this. Is there a limit to how far you'll go to protect and serve your country?'

He let them take in his words before elaborating. 'Are you willing to break national and international law in the performance of your duty? Are you willing to sacrifice your freedom, or even your life, if that's what's required? This is the point of no return. If the answer is anything less than an unequivocal yes, SC9 doesn't need you.'

He assessed the recruits' reactions. The instructors, watching from nearby, did the same. Based on the profiles they had compiled, Maxwell thought one, perhaps two, would drop out. He might be wrong; he hoped he was. Scott's rash actions had cost the lives of several Operatives. The agency needed to rebuild. But reliability, *total* reliability, was infinitely more valuable than raw numbers. Most of all, he needed people who would obey orders – and would not break.

'I'll give you five minutes to make your decisions,' he said. 'If your answer is yes, then you'll learn SC9's full nature and purpose. If your answer is no . . . you'll be leaving with me.' Maxwell turned and marched from the gym, leaving the recruits to make their fateful choices.

He returned, as promised, exactly five minutes later. An instructor barked a command; the recruits lined up again.

Maxwell stood before them once more. 'So. Have you all made your decisions?' The six responses were in the affirmative. 'Good. Then, if your answer is an unequivocal yes . . . step forward.'

Four members of the line advanced. Two men, two

women. The two men who did not move were the ones he had expected. Franks had seemed resistant to the idea of breaking the law. His refusal was not a surprise. Taylor had been borderline, though; a shame.

Maxwell nodded. 'Okay. The four who said yes, wait over there with Mr Kane.' He gestured towards one of the instructors. The recruits went to him, leaving Taylor and Franks behind. 'Mr Franks, Mr Taylor . . . Chris, Paul. I'm sorry to lose you – you're both exceptionally capable. Your assessment results prove that. But I understand and support your decision. SC9 needs total dedication, with zero room for doubts. If you have any, better we know now than when they might compromise the agency. For security, I'll need you to leave while I carry on.' He nodded to two other instructors. 'If you'll go with Mr Stone and Ms Flynn to collect your belongings? I'll see you in the head instructor's office when I'm finished here.'

Mark Stone and Deirdre Flynn escorted the dropouts from the gym. Both Operatives gave Maxwell brief, knowing glances as they left. Maxwell's own face was utterly impassive.

Stone and Flynn had been at Mordencroft Hall, the training facility, for two weeks. Their roles were specialist instructors. Flynn, a former MI5 officer, was a world-class sniper. Stone had been a Metropolitan Police officer, telling the recruits how to impersonate a cop. Their teachings were a genuine part of the training regime. But they had a secondary purpose for being there.

'All right, lads,' said Stone as they reached the trainees'

spartan bedrooms. 'Grab your stuff.' Franks and Taylor entered their rooms to gather their possessions. It did not take long.

'Sorry to see you go,' Flynn offered as the two men emerged. 'You're a good shot, Chris. Seems a shame to waste it. Can't see you'll find much use for that talent as a civvie.' There was no going back to service in whatever branch they had left. Part of SC9's recruitment process was to tarnish the recruits' prior records. Should they be caught or killed as Operatives, they could be officially disavowed. Written off as disgruntled washouts turned mercenary, criminal or mentally unstable.

'Sure I'll find something,' Franks replied. He seemed stunned, shell-shocked at the abrupt end to his training.

'Plenty of work for blokes who know how to fuck people up,' Stone said jovially. 'If you know where to look for it.'

'Any tips?' asked Taylor.

'Tell you on the plane,' said Flynn. 'Okay, let's wait in the office until the boss finishes.'

They trooped downstairs. The office had, when Maxwell was stationed here, been his. It was a functional space, one wall lined with box files. Matthew Green, the new head instructor, had not changed much since taking over. There was not much *to* change; the only major difference was a new desk. The old one had been wrecked on the day Flynn and Stone graduated as Operatives.

'Take a seat,' said Flynn, pulling out two stacking chairs for the recruits. She positioned them facing the desk. 'The boss won't be long. His spiel takes maybe half an hour.'

Franks and Taylor sat. 'I just wanted to thank you both,'

said Taylor. 'For the training. I learned a lot.'

'No problem,' Stone replied. He went to a cabinet behind the seated men. 'Hey, while you're waiting, you want a drink?' The big Londoner opened the cabinet. Amongst other items inside were some bottles of spirits, and glasses. 'Green's secret stash.'

Taylor looked around at him. 'Are you serious? You're going to steal the head's booze?'

'Thought alcohol was strictly a no-no at Mordencroft?' added Franks.

Stone snorted dismissively. 'If I stuck to the rules, I wouldn't be an Operative.'

'Go on,' Flynn added. 'Live dangerously.'

Before either recruit could object, Stone started to pour out drinks. 'Here you go. It's . . .' He examined the label. 'Ten-year-old Ardbeg. Nice.' He passed a glass to each of the seated men, then poured two more. 'Here, Deirdre.' He leaned over Taylor and Franks to give one to Flynn.

'Thank you, Mark,' she replied. Stone straightened and stepped back behind the men. 'Just wanted to say to you both, it's been a pleasure. Best of luck for the future.' She held out her glass towards the recruits. 'Cheers.'

'Cheers,' they echoed, raising their own glasses to clink them against hers—

Stone drew a suppressed pistol from his jacket and shot both men in the head.

Their bodies instantly slumped to the floor. Franks's glass fell and shattered, Taylor's somehow surviving and rolling across the floorboards. Flynn had been between the pair, avoiding the bullet fragments from their exit wounds. The splatter of blood and brain matter was another matter. She looked down at her ruined clothes, then back at her partner. 'You stupid fucking *shite*, Stone!' she exclaimed. Training had softened her Northern Irish accent, but now it returned with full force. 'These were clean on!' She banged her glass down on the desk.

Stone shrugged and swallowed his own whisky. 'Just get changed.'

'All my stuff's packed for when we leave! Fucking idiot.'

'You were going to get dirty anyway. We've got to clean this up before Maxwell can finish.' The fate of dropouts was not something the other recruits learned until graduation, if ever. He opened a cupboard, revealing cleaning equipment. 'I'll bag these cunts up; you do the floor.'

'Fuck's sake,' Flynn muttered, collecting a mop.

Maxwell glanced at a clock on the gym wall as he continued his speech. Flynn and Stone had left thirty minutes earlier. They would hopefully soon complete their grim task. 'So that's SC9's purpose, in a nutshell,' he went on. 'We do what needs to be done, before the politicians even know it needs doing. At home, or abroad, it makes no difference. We take out threats to the state, to Britain, to the people. And we do it without anyone ever knowing. Now, I assume you're all still okay with that? Because after telling you, if you back out now, I'd have to kill you.' A pause, taking in his audience's uncertain faces – then he grinned. Relief blossomed, followed by a few nervous chuckles. 'Trust me. I look after my Operatives. You're the most valuable assets this country has. I have no intention of wasting you – pardon the pun.'

More laughter, slightly more confident. But Maxwell's gaze snapped to the gym's door as it opened. Stone leaned in and nodded to him, then disappeared again. 'Okay, I'm done for now. You still have a few more months of training. But you've passed the point of no return, and I'm confident you'll make it. The next time I see you? You'll all be Operatives.'

He was slightly taken aback when the recruits broke into spontaneous applause. But he accepted it, smiling. 'Thank you. All right, Matthew, if you'll take over? I have to get back to London.' Green gave an order, his charges quieting as Maxwell headed for the exit.

Stone was waiting in the hallway outside. 'All done, guv,' the Londoner told him. 'Bags are in the boot.'

'Any problems?'

'Flynn fucking whining about getting blood on her jeans, but apart from that, no. Straightforward clean-up.'

'Good. Where is Deirdre?'

'Getting changed. She'll meet us at the car.'

'All right.' Maxwell started for an exterior door. 'Let's get moving. We've got a long trip ahead.'

Stone drove Maxwell and Flynn the sixty-plus miles from Mordencroft to Oban airport. Conversation was subdued. The corpses in the boot made the drive tense, especially when a police car passed. On home soil, such matters could be covered up, but it required time and effort.

The first leg of the journey was completed without incident, though. A twin-prop plane awaited them at Oban. Permission had been obtained to bring the car right to the aircraft. Shielded from onlookers by the fuselage, the bodies were quickly loaded. The three living passengers boarded, and the pilot soon had them airborne.

By the time they reached cruising altitude, it was dark. The plane's destination was London, but it was not flying a direct course. It instead followed a dogleg route over the Irish Sea. The North Channel separated mainland Britain and Northern Ireland. Within it was Beaufort's Dyke, a trench in places more than a thousand feet deep. Over a century, the British military had dumped a million tons of surplus munitions there.

That practice had long stopped, but the area still had its uses. The pilot checked waypoints on a navigation screen. 'We're over the Dyke now,' he announced.

Stone smirked. 'We all like being over a dyke, don't we?' he said, looking at Flynn.

She rolled her eyes. 'You fucking child.'

'That reminds me, Tony. Which of the new batch'll be Operative 69? Powell or Brand, I hope.' A lecherous chuckle.

Maxwell contained his disapproval. 'Mark, open the rear door. Time to drop off the cargo.'

Stone unbuckled his seatbelt and lumbered to the cabin's aft end. Two body bags lay there, wrapped in chains. Heavy pieces of scrap metal were padlocked to their feet. He leaned over them to unlock the hatch and forced it open against the wind. A freezing gale rushed inside. Stone winced, but crouched and shoved the first weight through the door. The slipstream dragged it backwards, pulling the body with it. It disappeared into the blackness below. 'Bye, shithead,' he said. The second corpse soon followed. He peered out of the hatchway as if hoping to see it hit the water.

'Don't fall out,' Flynn called sardonically.

Stone retorted with an obscenity that was obscured by the gale, then closed the hatch. He returned to his seat. 'Least we got rid of them this time. Remember that balls-up in Italy, with the woman from Reeve's house?'

'Christ, don't remind me,' sighed Flynn. 'Driving around Tuscany with a body in the boot. I'm just glad it wasn't our car.'

'MI6 had to clean up after you,' Maxwell informed them. 'They weren't happy.'

A dismissive huff from Stone. 'Fuck what Six think. We don't answer to them.'

Maxwell made a sound of agreement. That covered the truth, though. To protect himself when removing Scott, he'd had to make a deal with the Devil. Several devils, in fact, one heading each of Britain's intelligence services. But MI6 was the most troublesome. SC9 relied upon the Special Intelligence Service's resources when operating abroad. By virtue of seniority, Scott had been able to bully other agencies into cooperating. Maxwell very quickly found that his voice didn't carry nearly as much weight. That was a problem he needed to address . . .

His companions did not pick up on his concerns. 'Can't believe Reeve still got away,' said Flynn. 'Do we know where he's gone, Tony? I mean, he's still Fox Red, surely?'

'He is.' That was no longer technically true, though Maxwell kept it to himself. 'But right now, he's low priority. If he wanted to expose SC9, he would have done it already. He showed Scott proof that he'd decrypted the files on Craig Parker's phone.' That was a straightforward lie. Reeve had shown *Maxwell* proof, to blackmail him into helping. Maxwell had agreed – because it served his own purposes.

The Operatives were shocked. 'He did?' said Stone. 'Fucking hell, Tony, why isn't he SC9's *top* priority?'

'Because I don't want another cluster-fuck like Venice,' Maxwell replied firmly. '*That* was the closest SC9's come to being exposed. Four dead Operatives, in the hands of foreign authorities. I am not prepared to have that happen again.'

Stone reluctantly nodded. 'Point taken. But even so . . .'

'I know. Alex Reeve is still a threat. But if he's hiding, which he seems to be, he's not an immediate one. Seems we've reached a state of détente. As long as he doesn't mess with us, we won't mess with him.'

'And if he does?' asked Flynn.

'Like I said,' said Maxwell, 'he's still Fox Red.'

CHAPTER 4

Muscles aching, Reeve clambered from the minibus. Snow was falling, but more lightly than during the day. His housemates followed him out, stretching and grumbling. They headed for their front door as the bus drove away.

Reeve waited on the road, though, checking his surroundings. Force of habit. The last time he'd become sloppy, in Italy, SC9 found him. And also because . . . faint alarm bells were ringing in his mind.

It wasn't that something had changed. More that something *hadn't*.

He'd been in Bled for over a month. In that time, he'd explored every possible escape route from the house. His military training had also taught him to note vehicles, spot anything out of place. There were no streetlamps, only spill from nearby buildings. But one car stood out as if pinned by a searchlight.

In itself, it was nothing unusual. A silver Opel Insignia saloon, a couple of years old, about thirty metres downhill. An anonymous vehicle. But compared to the smaller, older hatchbacks common in the area, it stood out. He hadn't seen it before today.

Then there was the plate. Bled was in the Gorenjska region

of Slovenia. The regional capital of Kranj provided the KR prefix to locally registered cars. The Insignia's prefix, however, was LJ – the national capital, Ljubljana. The car had been in the same place this morning . . . except facing the other way. It had left after the loggers departed, then returned before they came back. Why?

'Leo?' Reeve glanced around to see Pinsker at the house. 'You coming in?'

'I'm . . . going into town,' Reeve replied. 'Can't be bothered to cook tonight. Might get a pizza.'

'Oh. Okay.' The Belarusian hesitated, clearly wanting to join him, before deciding to save money. 'I'll see you later.'

Reeve nodded noncommittally, then tugged up his coat's hood and set off downhill. He already suspected the car had an occupant, and was right. As he drew closer, he saw it was tilted towards the driver's side, windows misted. But part of the windscreen had been wiped clear from within.

Tension rose. Had SC9 tracked him down? He had minimised his electronic footprint to evade GCHQ's eyes. No laptop of his own, no smartphone, using only cash. But old-fashioned detective work still had its place. All it took was one pointer to his location, then doggedness.

The road had been ploughed. Piled snow forced him closer to the parked Opel than he liked. He had no gun, only a small folding knife used for cutting wood. If the person in the car was armed, he could be dead within seconds. But he had to know. His hand closed around the knife, thumb ready to flick open the blade . . .

He reached the Insignia. Its occupant was visible through the clear patch of windscreen. Male, older, thick-rimmed spectacles. The man stared straight ahead, as if deliberately not looking at him. Then Reeve's view was obscured by condensation as he passed.

No movement, no clunk of the door unlatching. Reeve cleared the boot, and kept walking. Five metres, ten. Nothing. At twenty metres, he glanced back. The man inside hadn't reacted to him.

But he *was* watching for him, if only indirectly. The car faced Reeve's house. The other homes nearby were widely spaced, fields and woodland beyond. There was nothing else he might be observing.

Probably not SC9, then – but a different kind of threat. Police? Immigration? The man had the pinch-faced look of officialdom. If he was gathering evidence on illegal workers, a raid could follow. Time to think about moving on.

But to where? Despite his work, he still had very little money. A good chunk of his wages went straight back to his paymasters as rent. And deeper into Slovenia, the language barrier would become more of a problem. Could he risk returning to Italy? The police there might still be actively searching for him . . .

For now, though, he was hungry after a hard day. He trudged on through the snow towards the centre of Bled.

Carrying a pizza box and soft-drink cup, Reeve returned the way he had come. The Insignia was still there, an hour and a half later.

He walked past it. A glow inside the cabin; the man was reading something on his phone. Reeve checked him as he passed. His flabby physique confirmed he was not an

Operative. On the passenger seat were a clipboard, notebook – and a small pair of binoculars.

That settled it. He was an official of some kind. Reeve's freedom was definitely under threat. Could a raid come tomorrow morning? Should he leave right now?

If he did, he would be at a major disadvantage. Tomorrow, Tuesday, was payday. He would need as much money as he could get. But could he risk staying in Bled for one more day?

The result of his mental threat assessment was *probably*. Not the most helpful answer. But the observer was still here, late in the evening. He would need to return home, file his report, await a decision. A few illegal workers were unlikely to be a high priority for an urgent dawn raid.

Probably.

He would have to take the chance. But if there *was* a raid tomorrow morning, he needed to be prepared for it.

He reached the house. Behind, a car's engine started. A glance back. Headlights came on, and the Insignia pulled out. The snoop had waited for him to return home before leaving. A bad sign, that he'd waited until everyone was corralled, or just coincidence?

Either way, he took it as further proof that he needed to be ready to leave.

Antal peered from the lounge as he entered, relaxing when he saw who it was. He relayed Reeve's assumed name to someone in the front room. Probably Daxner. The Slovenian generally took residence in there of an evening, monopolising the television. Reeve headed upstairs. The house originally had three bedrooms. The two largest had been crudely divided by drywall panels to create extra rooms. The spaces created were barely wide enough for a bed, but he appreciated the privacy.

Pinsker's room was opposite his, at the house's rear. The door opened as he reached it. 'You're back,' said Pinsker, in Russian. A hopeful look at the pizza box. 'Any left over?'

Reeve flipped the box open. It was empty. 'Sorry. Didn't want to drop any litter.'

The other man was disappointed. 'Oh. Okay. But why did you bring it up here? The bin's downstairs.'

Reeve waggled his cup. 'Haven't finished yet.' He opened his door – then paused. 'By the way . . . can you move out fast if you need to?'

'What do you mean?'

'Is all your stuff in a bag that you can grab in a hurry?'

Owlish bewilderment – then nervousness. 'No, but – I can pack, I suppose. Why?'

'Just some helpful advice. You might need it.' Was that enough to assuage Connie's voice in his head? He didn't know, but there were more pressing matters. He entered his room and closed the door.

Like the pizza box, his cup was actually empty. He had brought them home as cover to appear innocuous to the observer. In reality, he only needed the plastic straw. The EU had banned single-use plastics, but the pizza place seemingly had a stockpile. That observation, made weeks before, had determined his evening's meal choice. He extracted the straw, then opened his backpack. His scissors were in a pocket with other tools. He retrieved them and set to work.

CHAPTER 5

Tony Maxwell was not looking forward to the meeting.

He had been summoned – there was no other word for it – to MI6's headquarters. SC9's infinitely less conspicuous HQ was only three miles away. But the drive through the morning traffic took almost forty minutes. By the time he arrived at Vauxhall Cross, Maxwell was frustrated and tense.

He doubted he would feel any better when he left.

SC9 had been founded by Sir Simon Scott, then a senior officer at MI6. Its entire purpose was to be deniable; to do what other intelligence agencies couldn't. Or wouldn't. They were ultimately accountable to politicians. And no politician was *completely* immune to the pressure of public outrage, whatever they maintained. They were also subject, however loosely, to the rule of law. Even in the post-truth era, scandals could still end a career. So SC9 was created to operate in the shadows cast by its larger cousins. They, in turn, pretended it did not exist.

Until it suited them.

Maxwell passed through several security checks, then was escorted to a meeting room. Waiting for him were the men whom Scott had regarded as little more than quartermasters.

MI6, MI5 and GCHQ had previously given SC9 almost free rein to do its job.

With its founder gone, the balance of power had shifted.

The three men sat on one side of an oval table, facing him as he entered. His own chair was isolated opposite them. Basic, blunt intimidation tactics: *We are in charge, you are a supplicant.* He tried not to show his annoyance. Instead, he remembered Scott's own advice for dealing with the intelligence chiefs. *Be firm. Be resolute. Be ruthless.*

It was an approach he had ended up using against Scott himself.

Such blunt-force methods of dealing with opposition wouldn't work here, he thought wryly. He couldn't have brought a weapon into the MI6 building undetected. He would need to get his way using words rather than bullets. What that way *was*, he didn't yet know. The meeting's subject had not been revealed; only that it was of national importance. Most likely, they wanted SC9 to eliminate someone to keep their own hands clean. A mental shrug. That was SC9's purpose, after all. But why did the request need the Big Three of British Intelligence to ask it?

'Good morning, Tony,' said one of the trio. Aubrey Ryford-Croft was the Chief of the Secret Intelligence Service: MI6. Maxwell had dealt with him before. Scott hadn't liked him, and nor did his replacement. He was a bureaucrat by nature, not a former field officer. Protecting his own turf was prioritised over larger issues. 'Glad you could join us.' A hint of sarcasm? His visitor was perhaps two minutes late. He gestured at the empty chair.

Maxwell sat down. 'Aubrey,' he said with a nod. 'Justin,

Michael. What can I do for you?'

'It concerns one of your current operations.' The speaker was Michael Barwell, Director of GCHQ. Government Communications Headquarters: Britain's electronic spy agency.

Maxwell gave Barwell a look of studious implacability. 'Well, as you know, I have no comment to make regarding any of SC9's operations.' Scott's standard reply to questions from the intelligence heads.

It may have worked for Scott. For Maxwell, it did not. 'Cut the crap, Tony,' said the third man. Justin Stockley, Director General of MI5, was the youngest in the room by some margin. His relative youth did not translate to deference. 'You requested that GCHQ monitor someone in Germany. That kind of surveillance from SC9 is invariably the precursor to a hit. Is it one of Simon's leftovers, or someone you've taken it upon yourself to target?'

Any air of geniality in the room had already evaporated. 'I have no comment,' Maxwell replied tersely.

'Well, you'll need to make *some* comment,' said Ryford-Croft. 'Because your target is also one of *our* targets. There is, shall we say, a jurisdictional dispute. That's why we asked you here: to ensure we're all working towards the same goal.'

'My goal is the protection of Britain and its interests.'

'So is ours,' said Barwell. 'We just want to be sure we're in agreement *on* those interests.'

Maxwell leaned back in his seat, regarding the three men coldly. 'Then tell me what they are, and we'll see how they intersect SC9's.'

'Very well,' Ryford-Croft said. 'Your target is a figure of importance in the German arms industry. Correct?' Maxwell said nothing, but gave the smallest nod. 'The driving force of a proposed merger between several smaller European arms manufacturers. Such a merger would create, I believe, the fourth-largest in Western Europe. I'm sure we all agree that represents a challenge to our own arms industry. Yes?'

Stockley and Barwell both replied in the affirmative. 'Yes,' Maxwell added reluctantly.

'Excellent. So we are all on the same page, at least.'

Stockley took over the discussion. 'Now, if this individual suffered some . . . mishap, the merger would probably collapse. The worth and share prices of the separate companies would suffer as a result. Which would leave them open to takeover by, *hypothetically*, one of our own arms giants.'

That was exactly Maxwell's thinking, and Scott's before him. But he was still unwilling to give anything away. 'A logical chain of events,' was all he would offer.

'And therein lies the problem,' said Ryford-Croft. 'You see, we know something that you don't.'

Maxwell stiffened. 'I was under the impression SC9's charter required sharing of *all* pooled intelligence. Not just a cherry-picked selection.'

'This is a new development,' said Barwell, without apology. 'Have you heard of Roger Glennmore?'

'Yes. The head of Xeneon.' It was a recent corporate agglomeration of several UK arms manufacturers. The name had doubtless been focus-grouped to be as meaningless as possible.

Ryford-Croft nodded. 'Xeneon would be in a prime position to buy controlling interests in these European companies. Unfortunately . . .' He exchanged faintly aggrieved looks with his companions. 'Mr Glennmore has been some-what indiscreet. In a way that would jeopardise any such deals – and thus harm British interests.'

Maxwell was intrigued despite himself. 'What's he done?'

'He had a meeting with our mutual target,' said Stockley. 'It was meant to be private and secure – no recording devices of any kind. The room was swept for bugs, phones were left outside. They were even checked for wires by a third-party security firm. Everything they said should have remained utterly confidential.'

'Except it didn't,' said Maxwell, drawing the obvious conclusion.

'No,' said Barwell, shaking his head as if to say: *That idiot.* 'Mr Glennmore was rather too open about his future plans. He implied – no, that's far too weak a word. He *stated* that, should the merger go ahead, he would sabotage it. Evidence of sanction violations by the target's company would be planted. That such evidence doesn't exist was not, for him, an issue.'

'He was going to fake it?'

'Admitted, loud and proud,' Stockley said, turning up his hands in disdain. 'Presumably he thought such a blatant blackmail threat would scare the opposition into backing down. But that doesn't really work when someone records you making it!'

'How did they manage to record the meeting?' Maxwell asked.

'We don't know,' Barwell told him. 'But the target emailed Glennmore a clip from it. The most incriminating part, of course, but the whole discussion was presumably captured.'

GCHQ would have discovered the recording. All electronic communications within the UK were routinely intercepted and analysed by the agency's supercomputers. Such an intrusive policy was officially denied by the government, of course. 'The implication that it would be publicly released was clear.'

'And that would kill any takeover attempts by Xeneon stone dead,' said Stockley. 'The EU would never allow it, and nor would the individual national governments. Arms manufacturers are companies of national security importance. The buyouts would be blocked on that basis. Xeneon is run by a liar and a blackmailer – hardly a suitable new owner. Now, if Glennmore were to resign, that would get Xeneon as a whole off the hook. But it would also damage its share value – making it harder to carry out the takeovers.'

'So you see the problem, Tony,' said Ryford-Croft. 'If the target suffered some mishap, as Justin put it, the recording might be released. We need to make sure all copies of it are found and erased.'

Maxwell glanced towards Barwell. 'Can't you just hack their computer to find it?'

'We did,' came the glum response. 'And their phone. And every other gadget we could access. It's not on any of them.'

'They must have had it there to email it, though.'

'It was copied from some other device. One we haven't identified yet.'

'Which brings us to your operation.' Ryford-Croft's tone hardened. *Here it comes*, Maxwell knew. *The demand.* 'We know SC9 is targeting this individual. Their removal is in the national interest, to scupper this merger. However,' his tone

hardened, 'we *must* have the recording. All copies. They need
to be recovered, or destroyed. Before the target is eliminated,
your Operative needs to ascertain their locations. If they're
on a physical device, obtain it. If they're stored electronically,
find out where.'

'GCHQ can do the rest to delete them,' added Barwell.

Maxwell said nothing for a moment. Then: 'By "ascertain
their locations", you mean, "extract that information from
the target". Yes?'

Stockley gave him a somewhat mocking nod. 'Got it in
one.'

'SC9 aren't torturers. I believe that's more MI6's department.'

Ryford-Croft frowned. 'It's a simple request, Tony. I'm
sure your Operative is up to the task. Simon did enjoy
lecturing us about how his people were the best of the best.'

'They are,' Maxwell replied, 'at what they do. But what
they do is not espionage.'

'They've been trained with all the necessary skills,' said
Stockley. 'And many of them probably had those skills
already. You recruit from both MI5 *and* MI6. Is your
Operative in Germany originally one of our people?'

'I have no comment,' said Maxwell curtly. 'But what
you're *requesting*,' his tone suggested *demanding*, 'isn't SC9's
job.'

Ryford-Croft leaned forward, steepling his fingers. 'The
fact of the matter is, Tony,' he said, 'you have someone in
place already. I know how thorough your Operatives are.
They will have performed surveillance, identified routines,
familiarised themselves with the target. So they are in the

best position to act, quickly and effectively. This will merely be a slight extension of their objective.'

'I'm not going to go into operational details,' said Maxwell, annoyed. 'But we're following a plan that ensures the job cannot be connected to Britain. Interfering with that could do more than just jeopardise my Operative. It could blow back to damage the country as a whole.'

'A plan that can't adapt to changing circumstances is more of an epitaph,' Stockley announced. He seemed smugly proud of the aphorism. 'And the circumstances *have* changed, Tony. Failing to act will also damage Britain. If the recording goes public, Xeneon will take a big hit. In the time it takes to recover, our competitors will take advantage. We can't let that happen. *You* can't let that happen. For the good of the country, Tony.'

Maxwell shook his head. 'It's still not SC9's job.'

'It is now.' Ryford-Croft's voice abruptly hardened. 'This is a matter we touched upon with Simon, before his . . . departure. SC9 has had several high-profile failures in the past few years. The business in Italy. Craig Parker's attempted assassination of an MP.'

'There's no evidence that Craig Parker was ever a member of SC9,' said Maxwell sharply.

The head of SIS raised an eyebrow. 'Indeed. But there are also matters like SC9's reprisals against Russian assets. The Russians retaliated – against *our* assets. And before you deny any knowledge or involvement, spare us. Simon said the same, but his actions were painfully transparent. Which brings me to our point. SC9's activities have begun to affect our own, in a negative way. Too often, you've made a mess that we've had to clean up. Like the body of an Italian civilian left in one of our cars in Florence. This situation is, frankly, becoming untenable. SC9 needs to work *with* us – or find its own way.'

Maxwell felt a coldness in the pit of his stomach at the unmistakeable threat. 'Meaning what, exactly?'

'Meaning,' said Stockley, 'the other intelligence agencies will withdraw support. No more computer hacks or wire-tapping. No more cars full of guns waiting for your Operatives at foreign airports. And,' he added pointedly, 'no more covering for SC9's actions on home soil. You want fake IDs, or to get someone out of police custody? You'll have to arrange that on your own.'

'SC9's charter guarantees all those things,' Maxwell protested, voice rising. 'Do you really want to risk getting your hands dirty doing our job yourselves?'

'We did it before SC9 was founded,' said Ryford-Croft. 'We can do it again. Times are changing. There is far greater tolerance of the state taking any actions necessary to protect itself. Call it patriotism, populism, nationalism, what you will. The fact remains that it is happening. The Covert Human Intelligence Sources Act now gives us greater leeway. Any minister can grant immunity to undercover officers or assets for crimes they commit. And for all practical purposes, you could replace most ministers with a rubber-stamp machine.' He chuckled at his own joke.

Maxwell was anything but amused. 'So you're no longer willing to accept SC9's existence as an independent agency?'

'Oh, you'll still have your independence,' Stockley told him airily. 'In the same way that the former Crown Colonies have theirs. You do your own thing. But just remember who shields you from the rest of the world. Sometimes, that shielding will come with strings attached.'

'This is one of those times,' said Ryford-Croft. 'Xeneon, and Roger Glennmore, need to be protected. That means obtaining the recording. Your Operative will need to do so. It's as simple as that.'

Maxwell sat in silence under the three men's stares, anger rising inside him.

The feeling of fury had only grown by the time he left the MI6 building. Everything he'd worked towards for several years was under threat. He'd removed Scott, gained control of SC9 . . . but that control was about to be stolen. He needed to fight the attempt – and quickly. The nature of power in a bureaucracy meant that once it was lost, it was never regained. If he failed, SC9 would be reduced to a mere adjunct of the other services. No, worse than that. A disposable *contractor*, the Deliveroo of assassinations.

His personal plans depended upon SC9 maintaining its independence. If he had someone watching over his shoulder, he would be restricted – trapped.

But Ryford-Croft and the others were right. SC9 couldn't operate without the support of the other agencies. A share of their black-book assets was funnelled into an even blacker book. Money was the lifeblood of every country's intelligence operations. Without it, SC9 would wither and die in short order. Even withdrawal of something as basic as MI5's ability to forge credentials would be crippling.

There had to be a way to prevent it. What that might be, though, he didn't know.

He needed time to think. The answer would come to him. It had to. If he couldn't carry out SC9's operations with impunity . . .

His secret backers would no longer have any use for him.

CHAPTER 6

Tuesday's work in the depths of the forest had been tough. Reeve's paymasters plundered different areas each day, making it harder for authorities to catch them. The terrain today had been more difficult than usual. It was too steep to drive up, necessitating a long walk in thick snow. The cut logs then had to be dragged back to where they could be loaded. A slow, time-wasting process; not good when you were paid by quota. On top of that, a near-blizzard sprang up in the afternoon. The minibus became stuck in a snowdrift on the return journey. There were no shovels; Reeve and the others had to dig it free by hand.

At least he'd been paid. His bosses might be criminals, but so were some of their employees. Daxner, for one. His reaction to any mention of the police suggested he was a wanted man. The casual, factual way he discussed violence implied he was happy to use it. Their employers doubtless reasoned that withholding promised payments could see such violence turned against them. That even Daxner was wary of Reeve was something they wouldn't have missed either.

A modest wad of euros in his pocket, Reeve exited the minibus. He looked around, wind-driven snowflakes spiking into his face. No sign of the Opel Insignia. Was that a good or bad sign? The house was no longer under observation. But did that mean the snoop had everything he needed?

He had already decided to move on. His plan had been to eat, gather his belongings, then slip out. But the weather showed no sign of improving. Leaving in a blizzard at night wouldn't be smart.

Instead, he made plans for the next morning while he cooked his dinner. Pinsker was in the kitchen with him, on the laptop. The machine was his, but he'd been browbeaten into letting it become the house's computer. The text on screen was Cyrillic. Checking what was happening in his homeland? The young man had fled Belarus for the European Union. Reeve had never asked why, though escaping Europe's last dictatorship seemed an understandable decision. However, the EU had since sanctioned Belarus for aiding Russia's invasion of Ukraine. Pinsker had no rights of residency in the EU, or even a visa. Lacking the necessary paperwork, he'd found himself a criminal by default.

He had that much in common with Reeve, then. But it was not a life he was suited to. Timid, shy, struggling with the language barrier, he was a natural target for predators. Men like Daxner.

Or his entourage. Mangano entered, swaggering to the table. 'Hey, hey,' he said in Italian, rapping his knuckles against the back of the screen. 'I need to use that. Get off it.'

Pinsker looked up at him in nervous confusion. He replied in Belarusian. Mangano was unimpressed. 'I don't speak your retarded language. Go on, fuck off.'

'He says he wants to use the laptop,' Reeve told Pinsker in Russian.

'But – I'm in the middle of something,' Pinsker protested. 'I'm talking to somebody.'

Reeve relayed the message back to Mangano in Italian. 'So?' Mangano exclaimed. 'He can do that later.'

Daxner lumbered in from the other room. 'Something wrong?'

'I need to use the laptop,' Mangano told him.

The big man gave Reeve a cautious glance. Seeing no sign that he was taking sides, he jabbed a finger at Pinsker. 'Go on. Go.' The finger indicated the door.

Pinsker got the message. A helpless look at Reeve, but the Englishman turned back to his cooking. With a despairing sigh, Pinsker closed the window, then reluctantly pushed the laptop to Mangano. He left the room without looking back.

'Ha. Thanks, Marko.' Mangano sat at the machine and started typing.

'What's so important?' Daxner asked him.

'Weren't you listening to the news? The Bondage Killer's murdered another transvestite.'

'Oh.' The Slovene's response radiated disinterest.

Mangano, though, was unsettlingly enthusiastic. 'That's four victims now. One every two weeks.'

'The who?' Reeve had only been half listening.

'The Bondage Killer. He's a serial killer, in Munich. In Germany.'

'Yeah, I know where Munich is.'

The Italian ignored his sarcasm. 'There's a website, gets leaks from inside the police about the case.' He regarded the screen. 'It's in German, so let me just translate it . . . there.'

Daxner shrugged and started back towards the living room. 'Some guy goes around killing trannies? Sounds more like a public service.' He paused at the door, giving Mangano a mocking look. 'Why are you so keen? You into them? Like girls with something extra, do you?'

'No!' said Mangano with urgent vehemence. 'I'm just interested in serial killers.'

The Slovene shook his head. '*Prekleti čudak*,' he muttered, leaving the kitchen.

'I'm not into trannies,' the Italian told the empty air behind him. He turned back to the laptop. 'You know why he's called the Bondage Killer?'

As the only other person present, Reeve presumed he was being addressed. 'I can take a wild guess,' he said, sarcasm deepening.

'He waits for these girls to come home – well, not girls, but anyway. Has all this bondage gear set up on their beds. Chains, handcuffs, ropes, all that kind of stuff.' Mangano's speech became faster, more excitable. Reeve doubted he even realised. 'Knocks them out with some sort of karate chop and ties them up. Then he slices off their dick and balls before cutting them open. Takes out all their organs and uses them in a satanic ritual.'

Reeve was unimpressed. 'You know I'm about to eat, right?'

'Sorry, sorry,' was the non-apology. 'But there's some new stuff here, about the latest killing.' He read in silence until the information became too much to contain. 'Yeah, it's definitely the same guy! Four victims now, plus some random dude who came home with one of them. Not his lucky night.'

He sniggered. 'Got part of the coroner's report on the newest one here.' Another pause as he read on. 'Yeah, same routine,' he said, almost to himself. 'This is new, though. Normally the organs he takes out are a bit hacked up. But the coroner says the liver was removed with surgical precision. Like the hacking was done to cover it. Everything else was the same, though. All the organs were arranged around—'

Reeve belatedly registered Mangano's words. He whipped around. 'What did you say?'

The Italian blinked in surprise. 'What, about the coroner's report?'

Leaving his half-cooked food, Reeve came to the table. 'Let me see.' He looked over Mangano's shoulder. A blood-spattered logo, *DieGelbePresse*, greeted him. The website was designed to resemble an old-fashioned sensationalist newspaper on yellowed paper. Its text was in Italian, machine-translated from German. 'Where's the bit about cutting out the organs?'

Mangano pointed out a paragraph. Reeve read it – and immediately realised he needed to learn more. 'Move,' he ordered. When the confused Italian didn't respond immediately, he pushed him off the chair.

'Hey!' Mangano cried as Reeve took his place. 'What the fuck are you doing?'

Reeve gave him a cold, warning look. 'Shut up,' he said, before returning his attention to the laptop.

Flustered, Mangano complained again, then headed into the living room. He returned soon after with Daxner. 'What's going on?' demanded the Slovene. 'Sergio was using that. There a problem?'

The only emotion in Reeve's stare was chill menace. 'Not yet.'

Daxner was first to look away. He covered his unease with a dismissive shrug and walked out again. Mangano hesitated, then followed.

Reeve scrolled to the top of the page and started reading. The translation was at times clumsy, but the details were clear enough. The so-called Bondage Killer had committed his first murder just over six weeks ago. Another killing took place every second Friday night thereafter, the latest four days prior. Five deaths, but as Mangano had said, one was essentially collateral. Four were ritualistic.

Appeared ritualistic. But Mangano's words had tripped a mental alarm. Something didn't quite fit.

He speed-read on until he found the specifics. Someone in Munich was clearly leaking information to the sensationalist website. There were sections of crime-scene reports, autopsy findings. A few photographs from the murder scenes confirmed their authenticity. They showed the victims. Reeve shot a disgusted look after Mangano. The Italian had been gleefully thrilled by the gruesome images. Sick bastard.

SC9's training had included desensitisation to death in all its forms. Reeve had seen photos of human bodies that had suffered countless forms of destruction. He had moved and dismembered corpses in various states of decay. But there was something about these pictures that affected even him. It wasn't merely that they had been brutally butchered, cut open while still alive. There was a mechanical *coldness* to it. Organs had been removed and placed around the body, connecting lines drawn in blood. It was clearly meant to represent some kind of occult symbol. He didn't know what, but no doubt the website's followers would have opinions.

It was irrelevant, though. Two things Mangano had mentioned now coalesced in his mind. The 'karate chop'; the concealment of precise surgical work beneath cruder cuts. He found the relevant sections of text. A faint bruise had been found at the base of each victim's neck. Reeve knew what had caused it.

A vagus strike. A precise blow with the edge of the hand to a particular nerve. The impact interrupted the body's autonomic control of breathing and heartbeat. Properly executed, a light attack could stun or even knock the victim unconscious. A heavy attack could kill.

Reeve was skilled in the technique. Part of his SC9 training. As it was for all Operatives.

The other aspect that had caught his attention was the attempt to hide precision behind crudity. More SC9 training. Make an assassination look like an accident, or panicked violence. One precise stab wound could kill in seconds. A dozen frenzied hacks at the same spot would conceal that the killer knew that. A mugging gone wrong; a desperate attempt at self-defence. The authorities would be unlikely to suspect the victim had been premeditatively murdered. They would *definitely* not suspect outright assassination by a state agency.

Reeve knew he had the ability to carry out such a killing. But it would not have been the best use of his talents. His speciality was more in line with his military career in the Special Reconnaissance Regiment. Undercover work: survival, infiltration, deep-cover espionage using a false identity. He did, however, know another Operative who would have been the ideal choice.

Harrison Locke – Operative 61 – had been a military surgeon before joining the agency. Reeve knew that much about him. He was also a perfectionist. His *need* for absolute precision had once saved Reeve's life. Locke had hesitated while locating the perfect spot to stab his throat. Only for a split-second – but that was enough for Reeve to turn the tables.

Despite that, Locke was an ideal choice to act as a serial killer. He had the necessary combat and surgical skills to overpower and vivisect his victims. He was cool, calm, efficient – and knew how to cover his tracks. The truth, that the murders were not some madman's work, would be impossible to detect.

Almost impossible.

Had Locke made a mistake? One slip revealing a surgeon's hand behind the apparent butchery?

Maybe. But why would he be posing as a serial killer in the first place?

To Reeve, the answer was obvious, and chilling. The victims were *ghost targets*.

Like the raw cuts hiding the surgical incision, they were cover for the true objective. SC9 wanted someone in Munich dead. But they also wanted no possible suspicion of British involvement. Would SC9 – would Scott – go that far? Would they murder innocent people to disguise an assassination?

Yes. SC9's methods ranged from brutally blunt to insidiously cunning. An unsubtle warning to others was a job for someone like Mark Stone. Crack heads, leave a very visible corpse. The implication: *You can't stop us. You can't even touch us.* But if SC9 wanted to remove a target without anyone even realising they had been assassinated . . .

Then an Operative like Locke would be used.

He resumed his study of the leaked information, memorising details. The names and addresses of the victims. Any common factors that linked them. The obvious one was that they were all transvestites, or transsexuals. Reeve wasn't sure of the difference. It was not a subject he'd ever given much thought. All were in their twenties. All regularly visited a particular nightclub. Whether they had attended on the nights they died was uncertain, but seemed likely.

They were not people SC9 would normally consider enemies of the British state. Which meant the real target was somebody connected to one – or to a future victim. Who?

That wasn't something he could find out here. For that matter, he had no proof of SC9's involvement, only suspicion . . .

'Leo? Is something burning?'

Reeve snapped back to the present, seeing Pinsker peering through the kitchen door. He suddenly realised smoke was rising from his pan. 'Shit,' he said, rushing to the cooker. Blackened beans greeted him. He hurriedly scraped at the mass with a wooden spoon. It remained stuck to the metal. He sighed. So much for a last hot meal before he left. One last fruitless attempt to salvage anything, then he filled the pan with water.

Pinsker entered and opened the window to let out the smoke. 'Oh, no. What are you going to eat now?' His nervousness suggested he thought Reeve would help himself to his own supplies.

Reeve had no intention of doing so, though. 'Sandwiches, I suppose. You can have your laptop back.' He closed the website's window before handing the machine over. The young man didn't need to see graphic murder imagery.

Pinsker accepted the machine with relief and sat down. Annoyed at his own carelessness, Reeve made a couple of sandwiches. He sat opposite the Belarusian and ate them quickly. The other man paid him no attention, typing messages. Half-hidden smiles came to his face every so often. 'Who are you talking to?' Reeve asked out of polite curiosity. 'Family?'

'A friend,' came the reply, his cheeks flushing faintly.

'Girlfriend?'

The answer was a nervous, non-committal sound. Did he mean a boyfriend? That would explain why he had fled Belarus. It was not known for its tolerance of anything other than strict, macho heterosexuality. Reeve decided not to enquire any further. It wasn't his business – and again, not something he'd ever given much consideration. Where he'd grown up, attitudes to sexuality were little different from those in Belarus. Merely being perceived as anything other than normal was an invitation to a beating.

He finished his food and headed to his room. All his belongings were now in a single backpack, ready to go. He took off his boots and lay back on the bed, thinking.

Was SC9 behind the apparent serial killings? It was certainly possible. But his suspicions didn't amount to proof. To get that, he would have to visit Munich, in person.

Which would be extremely dangerous. Surveillance in Germany was both more intensive and more extensive than in Slovenia. SC9, via GCHQ, had ways to access it. The odds were vastly higher that he would be noticed, especially in a major city. He also had no ID, no papers. Any encounter with the authorities could end in his arrest. And that would lead, before too long, to his death.

But, if Locke *was* the killer, and Reeve could deduce his target . . .

He could catch him. Expose him. More importantly, he could expose SC9. And do so without bringing international retribution on the country as a whole. A targeted strike, rather than an all-out nuclear apocalypse.

Then, with SC9 crippled, he could find Connie.

A deep breath. He was getting ahead of himself. He had already decided to move on from Bled. But his plan had been to move deeper into hiding, somewhere more rural. Going to Munich would put him at far greater risk of exposure. What should he do?

He didn't know. The answer, he decided, would have to wait until tomorrow.

CHAPTER 7

Reeve did not sleep well.

His dreams were intense, confusing, chilling. Thinking about SC9 had stirred up unpleasant things from the sludge of his subconscious. He was running, running after Connie as fast as he could. But it was not fast enough. He could never quite see her face. She drew ever further away from him – and his enemies were catching up from behind—

He snapped awake. A noise outside, engines. His enemies weren't just catching up.

They were here.

He sprang from the bed and went to the window, twitching back the curtain. Falling snow swirled in the headlamp beams of four approaching vehicles. One car, two vans, another car following. He recognised the last. An Opel Insignia.

Reeve was dressed in moments. Donning his boots took longer. He swore as he knotted the laces. Then he jumped up and grabbed his bug-out pack. A quick glance from the window. The convoy had stopped outside. The lead car and vans were white with blue and yellow markings. Police.

A raid.

He snatched up his coat and hurried out. Pinsker's room was across the landing. No time for politeness. He shoulder-barged the door. Wood splintered around the flimsy lock. He barrelled into the cramped bedroom. Pinsker jumped up in his bed, shocked. 'What – what are—'

'It's a raid,' Reeve told him brusquely, going to the window. He pulled the curtain aside. No lights at the house's rear. It hadn't been surrounded – yet. 'They just arrived at the front. If you don't want to be arrested, come with me.' He unlatched the window and strained to raise the ill-fitting sash.

Pinsker hurriedly got up. Reeve pulled harder, and the sash rasped fully open. He ducked through. A freezing wind hit him as he stepped onto a sloping roof. The half-dressed Belarusian gasped at the sudden cold.

'Hurry up,' said Reeve. 'I can't wait for you.' The roof covered an extension at the house's rear. Its slope was only shallow, but several inches of snow made it treacherous. He slithered clumsily down it, heels finding the gutter at the bottom. A brief glance back. Pinsker was struggling to put on his clothes. Still no movement behind the house. He jumped down. A snowdrift below cushioned his landing. He rose and donned the coat and backpack, then yomped towards the fence. 'Hedeon! Last chance! Come on!'

'I haven't got all my stuff!' The young man scrabbled to gather his belongings. 'My laptop—'

Reeve paused at the fence. 'You need to move. *Now!*' He had already heard activity from the house's front. Vehicle doors slamming, urgent voices. A torch beam swept across the snow at the building's side. He vaulted the fence into the property beyond. Coat bundled under one arm, a bag in the other hand, Pinsker climbed outside.

Reeve didn't have time to wait for him. He concentrated on his own escape. Even in the darkness, he knew where he was going. There was a small barn a hundred metres to the northwest. That would shield him from view – at least until the cops spotted his trail. Past that were woods. Cutting west through them would bring him to a narrow lane. In turn, that would lead him to an industrial estate. Beyond its parking lot was a railway line. Crossing it on foot would force any vehicles following him to make a long diversion. That would give him time to get clear.

In theory. He was about to learn whether it worked in practice.

Shouts rose behind. A loud crack of wood told him the cops had smashed open the front door. He glimpsed figures holding torches at both sides of the house. Pinsker slid down the roof, falling into the snowdrift with a frightened cry.

Reeve ran on. His eyes adjusted to the pre-dawn gloom. There was the barn, a black block in the slate-grey of the snow. He angled towards it. Slow going; in places, the drifts reached almost to his knees. A stern voice called out. He looked back. A cop had seen Pinsker as he clumsily scaled the fence. Torch beams locked on to him. The Belarusian threw himself over and fled, following Reeve's path.

One cop came after him, climbing the barrier. Another hurried back towards the vehicles. The remaining police closed their net around the building. A window opened, Antal leaning out – only to yelp and retreat as lights found him.

Reeve kept going. He passed the barn, heading for the woods. A siren echoed across the farmland as the police car set off. The driver would try to intercept the runners on the far side of the trees. In normal conditions, he might make it. In the thick snow, the Operative fancied his own chances—

'Leo! Leo, wait!'

Pinsker, near panic. His lead over the cop was twenty metres, if that. And his pursuer was gaining.

Reeve had told Pinsker to hurry. Warned him that if he didn't, he would be on his own. But—

Not even sure why, he turned and ran back to the barn.

The Belarusian lumbered through the snow towards it, the cop closing. Reeve ducked around the structure's side, stopped. Pinsker's heavy, fearful panting grew louder. Then he ran past without looking, following Reeve's tracks in his blind panic. Reeve waited. Thudding footsteps, a torch beam skittering past—

Reeve darted out and swung his arm, clotheslining the cop to the ground. His torch landed in the snow, the beam reduced to a faint glow. The man tried to rise. Reeve kicked him in the chest, pounding him back down.

Pinsker halted, turned. 'Leo? Oh my God! You attacked a cop! They'll—'

'Just run,' Reeve growled. Pinsker took the hint and set off again. The two men hared through the drifts towards the woods. Reeve looked back as they reached the trees. The cop's torch was still in the snow; he hadn't got up.

'Did you *kill* him?' Pinsker was on the edge of terror.

'No. Just knocked him down. He'll be okay.' Reeve picked his way through the trees. 'Keep moving. There's a car coming after us – we've got to get to the road before it does.'

The wood was deciduous, leaves lost for winter. But thick

snow piled on the bare branches made the darkness beneath almost total. Trunks loomed with startling suddenness from the murk ahead. Reeve was forced to slow. How much further? The woods were not large, maybe a hundred metres deep. But all the local roads were ploughed at least semi-regularly. The police car could be halfway around by now . . .

Lighter ground ahead. They were nearing the wood's edge. Arm shielding his eyes from low branches, Reeve increased speed. He emerged more or less where he had intended. Ahead was open grassland near a small church, a couple of houses beyond. The road was just past them. Brighter lights shone downhill: the industrial estate. His escape route.

If he could reach it.

He hurried down the slope, kicking up snow. Pinsker followed. 'Leo!' he gasped. 'Slow down!'

'If I slow down we'll get caught,' Reeve shot back. The siren's warble had faded as they traversed the woods. Now it was rising again. He passed between the houses, arms raised for balance as he descended a steeper slope. The road was just ahead—

Lights off to his right. Pulsing blue strobes above headlights. The police car came around a bend. Less than a hundred metres away. Even in the snow, it would catch up in moments.

They had him—

More headlights – to his left. Bigger. A truck. Both vehicles slowed as they saw each other. With ploughed snow piled at the roadside, there wasn't enough room for them to pass. 'Hedeon!' he shouted, angling towards the now-stationary truck. It would have to reverse some distance to let the car past. Would the cop stay in his vehicle, or pursue on foot?

The answer came a moment later. The siren's tone changed to warning shrills: *Get out of my way.* Reeve reached the truck, which juddered as its driver put it into reverse. By the time it started moving, he was past the trailer. Pinsker followed him. A sprint, and he reached a junction. He went right, heading for the industrial estate. The truck lumbered backwards towards the intersection. The police car urged it onwards, strobes turning the snow blue.

Down a narrow lane, past a warehouse and an industrial products store. Reeve's destination was ahead. A large car park – with a barrier at its gate. He rounded the obstacle, hurrying into the snow-covered expanse beyond. Between trees across it, he made out a long, elevated embankment: the railway line.

He looked back. Pinsker was struggling to keep up. The police car had cleared the truck and was coming after them. It entered the short road to the gate – then the cop realised his mistake. He braked hard, the car skidding on the snow and almost hitting the barrier.

This time, the officer got out. He hurried after the fugitives. By now, Reeve was at the foot of the embankment. He scrambled up it, using his hands for extra purchase—

A new noise, quickly growing louder. The metallic thunder of an approaching train.

He looked right as he neared the top. Headlights in a triangular pattern were approaching. He felt the rising vibration through the ground. Reeve could easily cross the single track before it reached him. But Pinsker was still hauling himself up the slope. The cop was halfway across the car park. He wouldn't beat the train – but nor would Pinsker if he didn't speed up. 'Come on!' Reeve shouted, stopping beside the line. 'Move!'

The urgency in his voice spurred the Belarusian. Gasping, he dragged himself up the last few metres. The cop neared the embankment, shouting in Slovenian. The train's horn blared as its driver saw the figure beside the track. Pinsker finally reached the top. Reeve grabbed his hand—

And pulled him across the line as the locomotive rushed at them.

Both men dived flat on the far side. Another nerve-shattering blast from the horn – then the loco snarled past. Heavy freight wagons screeched and thunked along behind it.

Reeve shielded his face from the snow whirling in its slipstream. 'Hedeon, come on!' he shouted over the hammer-blow cacophony.

Grimacing, Pinsker followed as he crawled clear of the line. 'What do we do now?' he asked. A road ran parallel to the railway. 'Run along there?'

'Not yet. Get into those bushes.' The Englishman scrabbled down the steep slope into concealment. He looked back up at the line as the last wagon thundered by. Had the cop followed them this far? He waited for a dark figure to appear against the grey clouds overhead . . .

The only movement was falling snow.

Reeve kept watching. Ten seconds passed, twenty. Still nothing. If the cop were there, he should have reached the track by now. 'Wait here,' he told Pinsker. He retraced his steps up the slope, then peered over the embankment's summit.

The cop was almost back at his car, picked out by the industrial estate's floodlights.

Reeve watched as he got in. The car reversed, then started along a road running around the car park's side. It would lead it through a bridge under the railway line. 'Come back up here,' he called to Pinsker.

'I thought we were running?' came the confused reply.

'We are. But that cop's coming around to try to find us on the road. We're doubling back.'

The Belarusian started up the embankment. 'Where are we going?'

'Away from here,' said Reeve firmly.

Bled Jezero railway station was far grander than the single-track line it served. It was only a kilometre away, but Reeve took a roundabout route, avoiding main roads. By the time he and Pinsker arrived, it was daytime. The snow-laden clouds gave everything a funereal, twilight air. It seemed appropriate for a departure.

'Will the police still be looking for us?' Pinsker asked, surveying the street nervously.

'Yeah,' Reeve told him. 'They get quite pissed off if someone knocks one of them down. But it was dark, so they wouldn't have got a good look at us.'

'That cop you hit kept shining his flashlight at me. He'll have seen my coat.' The garment was a distinctive two-tone red and purple.

Reeve regarded him for a moment, then shrugged off his

pack. 'He didn't see me. Here. Take mine.' He removed his deliberately anonymous blue-grey coat.

Pinsker was startled. 'Are you sure?'

'Yes.'

'Okay.' He was about to remove his own coat when Reeve shook his head: *No need.* 'But you'll freeze!' The hoodie that was now Reeve's top layer was not weatherproof.

'I won't need it on the train. Go on, put it on.'

Hesitantly, as if expecting some trick, Pinsker donned the coat. Reeve was more muscular than him; it fitted over his own, albeit tightly. 'Thank you.' He examined his new garment, then looked back at Reeve. 'Where are you going on the train?'

'Better that you don't know.'

He was taken aback by Reeve's bluntness. 'Can I . . . come with you?'

'No. We need to split up. The cops are looking for two people.' He checked the street again. Still no police presence. 'Don't go into the station yet. Stay out of sight until eleven twenty-five. Then buy a ticket to Nova Gorica.' The town's station was mere metres from the border with Italy. Pinsker could decide whether to stay in Slovenia, or move further afield. 'The train should arrive at eleven thirty-one, so get on it.'

'You've memorised the timetable?'

Reeve gave him a small, humourless smile. 'Why do you think I'm here now? One's due in six minutes.' He took out his pay from the previous day and peeled off a few notes. Slovenian train journeys were not expensive, but Daxner had probably stolen more than clothing.

Pinsker accepted the money with surprise, then gratitude. 'Thanks. So . . . will I see you again?'

'I doubt it. Stay safe.' He hesitated, then extended his hand.

Pinsker took it, shaking it – then embraced him. Reeve awkwardly returned the gesture. 'You saved me, Leo. You know that? You saved me! Nobody's ever done that for me before.'

The Operative withdrew. 'Just trying to do the right thing.'

The younger man laughed. 'Well, keep on doing it!'

Reeve nodded. 'I've got to go. Remember, stay off the main street until it's time to leave.' With that, he turned and headed for the station.

'Bye, Leo,' Pinsker called out behind him. He didn't look back.

He crossed the road. One last check for police, then he entered the station. It was not busy; it took only a minute to buy a ticket to Jesenice. The town was on a main line to the north. He would find another train there.

His current train was on time, according to the information board. He went to the platform. It was cold, but a canopy sheltered him from the snow. Being outside also gave him more opportunities for escape.

The wait was tense. He feigned bored apathy, standing in plain sight. The cops would be looking for someone trying to hide. The man he'd attacked wouldn't have seen his face. In darkness, wearing a thick coat, his build would have been hard to determine accurately. But if they arrived and demanded ID from every man they found at the station . . .

He checked his watch. Two minutes. Bled was on a secondary, unelectrified line; the train would be diesel. He looked southwards, listening for the sound of an approaching engine.

Nothing on the track – but he heard one on the street behind him. It grew louder . . . then stopped. A glance through the station building's door. Two burly silhouettes in baseball caps and heavy coats came through the main entrance.

Police.

Reeve controlled his rising tension. There was nowhere to hide on the platform. That left two choices: run, or bluff. The first would leave him where he'd started, with the added disadvantage of being identifiable. So . . .

He had a phone in one pocket. A basic, disposable burner on the cheapest credit plan. He couldn't remember the last time he'd made a call with it. Another look inside. One cop was out of sight. The other was questioning a man in the waiting area. They would soon come to him. He took out the phone—

And started talking.

There was nobody on the other end of the line; the phone wasn't even on. That didn't deter him. 'Yeah, mate, I know,' he said, his natural Manchester accent resurfacing. 'Fucking freezing here. Still, my own fucking fault, eh? I should have come here in summer. Teach me to come when it's cheap, won't it?' He laughed. 'Yeah, yeah. Could have gone to Ibiza, would have – hold on, someone here.'

One of the cops had come on to the platform, looking him over. He spoke in Slovenian. Reeve blinked, then put a hand over the phone. 'Sorry, mate. I'm English.' He lifted his palm. 'Some copper, wants something. Hang on.'

The policeman spoke again. Reeve gave him a helpless shrug. 'Pass-port,' the man said, holding out a hand.

'Oh, for fuck's sake,' Reeve muttered. 'Really? My train'll be here any minute.' He gestured down the line.

The cop merely stared at him, hand still outstretched. Reeve let out an aggrieved sound and made a show of removing his backpack. 'I keep it in here so I don't get pickpocketed. Someone nicked my iPhone in Lub-jubjana, you know?' He waggled the burner. 'Had to buy this piece of crap.'

'Ljubljana,' said the cop: *Loo-bee-ah-nuh*.

'Yeah, whatever it's called.' He squatted, opened the pack and began to dig through its contents. Most was clothing. 'Great welcome to Slovakia. Here one day and get my phone swiped.' The man reacted with confusion, then faint offence, at the wrong country name. 'So I hid my passport in a sock. It's all the way at the bottom.' He took out clothes, piling them carefully on his thighs.

'Slovenija,' the cop told him firmly. *Slah-ven-ee-ah*.

Reeve gave him a blank look. 'What?' He saw something beyond the officer. 'Oh, come on!' he said, gesturing. 'My train's here! I'm going to miss it!' A white and red diesel multiple unit was approaching the station. 'I'm meeting my mate in Salzburg. Germany, Deutschland? If I miss the connection, I'll have to wait for hours. Please?'

'Slovenija,' the cop repeated, pointing at the ground. A small shake of the head. '*Ne Slovaška*.'

Reeve's eyes widened. 'Oh, balls, shit, did I get your

country's name wrong? Sorry, sorry!' Abject apology in his tone. 'Slovenia, Slovakia. No wonder everyone gave me weird looks! Sorry!' The train was almost at the platform. 'Look, please don't make me miss my train, okay?' He gazed up at the cop with helpless, pleading eyes.

The man stared back, emotionless. Reeve tensed, ready to fight for his escape—

'Ehh,' the cop sighed, with tired disdain. '*Pojdi*. Go.' He stepped back as the train came to a stop.

Reeve hurriedly stuffed the clothes back into his pack. 'Oh, magic, mate! Cheers.' Nodding in thanks, he hurried to the nearest carriage door.

His expression of gormless gratitude vanished the moment his back was turned. Closing his pack, he boarded and found a seat. Outside, the second cop came onto the platform, talking to his partner. The first man waved mockingly in Reeve's general direction. *Some idiot English tourist. Didn't even know which country he was in.* The other man laughed.

Reeve didn't care. The ploy had worked. He was free to go.

The train set off. Reeve's tension eased as the station, then Bled, rolled away behind him. *You did a good thing for Hedeon*, Connie's voice told him.

Well, yeah, was his unspoken, sardonic response. *Makes up for letting Daxner steal his stuff and not doing anything to help him.*

You made things right. That's what matters.

He frowned. Would the real Connie have been so forgiving? Or was even his own conscience trying to find excuses for his actions? He didn't know.

Reeve pushed the thought aside. He had to plan his next move. He could still travel on to anywhere within Slovenia, or any eastern EU state. The further he was from Britain, the safer he would be.

But circumstances had aimed him in another direction. He had to move, no matter what. So why not take advantage? If the so-called Bondage Killer really was an SC9 Operative, was Locke . . .

He could catch him.

And bring his hunters down.

CHAPTER 8

After Alex Reeve – the one-time Operative 66 – infiltrated its headquarters, SC9 had moved. It gave up a corner of one anonymous government building for a basement in another. Its home was now Bartleby House, a bureaucratic records facility – a glorified warehouse for paperwork. 'Security through obscurity' had been a tenet of its former director. Tony Maxwell didn't necessarily agree, but now he was stuck with it. Besides, he mused, the dour surroundings were entirely his own fault. He had told Reeve how to find SC9 in the first place.

No point in regrets, though. That act had eventually led to his ascension as SC9's new boss. Not entirely planned, despite his ego's best attempts to claim credit. Nevertheless, he was now in charge. Power over life and death was his. If he wanted someone eliminated, anywhere in the world . . . they would be gone. Scott had created a very efficient killing machine. It was solely up to him how it would now be used.

In theory. Reality, it turned out, was more restrictive.

He was still fuming about the previous day's meeting. Whatever Scott's failings, he had always imposed his authority over the other intelligence chiefs. He had once been Ryford-Croft's superior at MI6, and received a degree of deference. That was not the case with Maxwell. His first meeting with Ryford-Croft, months before, had made their relative positions very clear. Maxwell had been forced to kowtow to him to get the support he needed. Now, Ryford-Croft was taking advantage in a way he would never have dared with Scott. If he had his way, SC9 would end up as MI6's stooge.

The situation had to be rectified. The question was: how?

An answer would come, he was certain. He just hadn't found it yet.

In the meantime, he had to play along with his would-be superiors' demands. He gazed at his desk phone for a moment, then picked it up. He tapped in a number and waited. It was entirely possible that he would have to leave a message. Operative 61's cover could leave him occupied for long periods.

But Locke soon answered. 'Yes?'

'It's me,' Maxwell replied. The call was unencrypted. Locke's phone was equipped with a scrambler, but it was rarely used. Scrambled calls could, perversely, draw more attention from spy agencies than open ones.

'How are you?' Locke spoke in English, but maintained his Danish accent.

'Fine, thanks. Listen, something's come up. I need you to do me a favour.'

'What is it?' Locke's tone became wary. Understandably so. The plan the two men had devised was precise. Changes at this late stage would introduce risky, unpredictable variables.

'Seems your patient,' a codeword for *the target*, 'recorded a business associate saying something stupid. My partners here want to make sure there's no . . . embarrassment.'

'Your partners,' Locke echoed with cold disdain. No explanation was needed.

'I didn't want them involved, but they insisted.' Maxwell made his own disapproval plain. 'So you need to obtain the recording. We don't want their business deal to collapse because some idiot had a big mouth.'

'I see.' A pause followed. Maxwell could almost hear the other man's displeasure bubbling up. 'Listen,' Locke said at last, 'what you're asking is not my job.'

'I'm aware of that. But my partners are pushing for it.'

'Added complications before an operation increase the risk of failure.'

Maxwell frowned. Locke was right, but . . . 'It needs to be done.' An unmistakeable command.

The Operative did not take it with good grace. 'I would remind you that I have a particular skillset. What you want is not part of it. Your partners should take care of their own problems.'

'Agreed,' said Maxwell, with growing impatience. 'But the situation is what it is. So find that recording – all copies of it. You'll have to ask where it is before the operation.'

'Or perhaps during.' There was no humour in Locke's voice.

'Whatever needs to be done. I'll email the details to you.' That would be encrypted, at least. No need for woolly euphemisms and codes there.

'Understood.' The call ended sharply.

Maxwell let out an annoyed breath, then hung up. Locke,

he suspected, did not approve of the change in SC9's leadership – or its circumstances. There were definitely Scott loyalists amongst the Operatives. The more overt ones, he had either sidelined or kept too busy to cause difficulties. But Locke kept his feelings under tight control. Those feelings he had, at least. Maxwell had trained him, knew his profile. He was the perfect choice to play an ice-cold serial killer. The role required very little acting.

So where did Locke's loyalties lie? Maxwell decided to keep a closer eye on events in Munich.

Reeve had never been to Munich before. Or anywhere else in Germany, for that matter. The language was alien to him, overheard conversations mostly gibberish. Not even his fluency in French and Italian helped him. German was closer to English than either, yet he still understood only the occasional word.

He left the train at its terminus, Munich Central station. *München Hbf*, a platform sign corrected him. Was 'Hbf' an abbreviation for 'Central', or an actual German word? He had no idea. Here less than a minute, and he was already out of his depth.

He headed for the exit, looking for an information bureau. Somewhere he could get a free, reasonably detailed map. He had memorised the address of the Bondage Killer's most recent victim. Now he needed to find it.

It didn't take long to find someone who spoke English and get directions. There was a tourist office not far away. Reeve left the concourse, stepping out into falling snow. The weather here was no better than in Bled. His six-hour train journey, with two changes, had at least been warm. Now, he was already missing his coat.

The tourist office was on a side street, the bare trees along it laden with white. A perky woman at the counter was keen to show off her English skills. He soon had a map, and a list of local hostels and cheap hotels. The next thing he needed was an internet café. The friendly lady told him there was one nearby.

He went to it and paid for an hour's access. His first visit was to Google Maps. Munich was a city where the buildings were mapped in 3D, which would be helpful. He could get a general idea of what to expect before visiting.

The victim's flat was in an area called Glockenbachviertel. He put in the address, and examined the building in 3D mode. A six-storey block on a corner. There was a school across the road – he knew what *schule* meant, at least. Did German schools have CCTV cameras? If so, the killer had probably avoided that street.

He swept the virtual viewpoint to the block's rear. More apartment buildings formed a castle-like wall around a long rectangular courtyard. Lower structures stood within it. Garages and small businesses, he guessed. The murder had taken place in the middle of the night. Nobody would have been around.

Did the block have a rear entrance? Not that he could see. The flats at the back of the block had balconies, though. That meant exterior access, if an intruder could climb up to them. Reeve knew he could – as could Locke.

He continued to survey the area. Familiarising himself with it – and finding escape routes. There was a river not far away. That would limit his options. He looked for other alternatives. Eventually, his hour was up. He cleared the browser history, then left.

The sky was already darkening, snow still falling. Go to Glockenbachviertel now, or find a room for the night? He chose the latter. His task would be easier without hauling his backpack around. Especially if he had to run.

There were several cheap places near the station. The first hotel he tried was full; the second wanted his passport. He found a vacancy at the third, a hostel. The room was no bigger than the one in Bled. But it was private, warm, and appeared clean enough. That was all he needed.

He unpacked his clothes, wanting extra layers for what would be a very cold night. Once changed, he headed back out. His destination was just over two kilometres to the south. The streets had been largely cleared of snow, but the walk still took forty minutes. Reeve was in no rush. He was also avoiding CCTV cameras. Even with a baseball cap shielding his face, he still diverted to bypass them.

The school did indeed have cameras, he saw on arriving. One, high on a wall, overlooked the street opposite the victim's building. Head down, he continued on. Snow ploughed from the road was piled along the side of the pavement. Someone came out of the apartment block as he passed. A glance inside. Another camera watched the entrance from within. Newly installed following the murder, or a permanent fixture? Whichever, it meant he couldn't get to the flat that way.

He rounded the block. The central courtyard was accessed via an alley. He went down it, pretending to be checking an address on his phone. The precaution was unnecessary. Nobody was watching. By now, the businesses here had closed for the day.

He turned towards the victim's building. It was instantly obvious where they had lived. A third-floor balcony was marked off with police tape. No lights were on inside. Reeve cautiously moved for a closer look. Could he climb up?

Yes. The route up the balconies seemed straightforward enough. He checked for cameras covering the rear, saw none. As long as he made no noise, he would be fine.

He had done all he could for the moment. Now, he had to wait.

It was close to midnight when Reeve returned to the apartment block.

He had spent the evening eking out time in a coffee shop and tapas bar. The streets were now quiet. Munich on a cold Wednesday night was not exactly buzzing. All the same, he made sure the road was empty before going down the alley.

A sodium lamp cast a sickly orange glow over the snow. He regarded the balconies above. One flat on the top floor still had lights on. The others were dark.

He moved a wheelie bin and clambered on to it. The balcony was now in easy reach. He pulled himself up as quietly as he could. His hands were gloved; no need to worry about fingerprints. The balcony was shallow, just enough room for a small chair. A glazed door gave access to the apartment. The curtains were drawn. He paused, listening. All he heard was the wind blowing the snow around him.

His climb continued. A worrying moment when the metal

83

railing creaked under his weight. He froze. But no lights came on. Still, he waited for several extra seconds before resuming.

Before long he reached his destination. A strand of police tape flapped and crackled in the wind. Reeve peered through the railing. More tape was stretched across the closed door. The curtains weren't closed, blackness beyond the glass.

He clambered on to the balcony and took out a small torch, examining the door. Stress marks in the frame near the handle. It had been forced open, without the lock being broken. Locke – if it was him – had used a pry bar or similar to gain entry.

Reeve didn't have the luxury of tools. Instead he hit the glass sharply with an elbow. In the snowbound silence, the crack felt as loud as a gunshot. He tensed, then struck again. A large shard fell into the flat, broken pieces tinkling.

Too loud. He would have been more surprised if a neighbour *hadn't* heard. He needed to work quickly.

He reached through the hole and turned the inner handle. The door opened. He broke the tape and stepped inside. A freezing wind hissed through the ragged void in the glass.

He was here. Now to work out who else had been.

If the killer *was* Locke . . . what would he have done?

What would *Reeve* have done?

A flick of a mental switch. He was an Operative again. He'd gained access via the balcony. What then?

He thought back to what he'd seen on the sensationalist website. The bloody image of the victim, bound spreadeagled to the bed, came vividly to mind.

Find the bedroom.

He used his torch to survey the flat. A lounge, two doors. The nearest was ajar, kitchen beyond. He went to the other. A hallway. The bedroom was off it. He entered. The double bed was before him. It had been stripped, bedding removed to analyse for evidence. Only the mattress remained, stained with dried blood. He stared at the grisly sight for a long moment, then closed his eyes.

His mind took him back on to the balcony. The killer had climbed up as he had. Footprints in the snow would have been unavoidable. But an old trick was to wear shoes a size larger, thick socks padding them. An Operative would incinerate them afterwards anyway. Force open the door silently. Once inside, then what?

So far, the police apparently had no trace DNA evidence from the Bondage Killer. That suggested full-body coverage. Gloves, overalls, facemask, something over the hair. All that would have to be brought, along with the restraints and surgical instruments. The killer would need a reasonably large bag to carry everything. They would have changed at the balcony door, possibly even outside, again to limit DNA traces.

Reeve updated his mental image. He was now fully covered, latex gloves replacing winter ones. What would the killer's next step have been?

The victim had gone to a nightclub. The killer knew that. They would have broken in well in advance to give themselves time to set up. Once done, they would wait, for hours if necessary. Where?

Reeve turned. The bathroom was across the hall from the bedroom. The toilet's lid was down. The victim hadn't used

85

it before being attacked. The killer had probably waited there. Then they rose at the sound of a key in the front door. He looked back into the bedroom. The wardrobe was ajar. Showy, flamboyant female garments on one side; more mundane and unisex ones on the other. The victim had entered to undress on returning home. Turn on the light – freeze at the sight of the bondage gear on the bed—

Then the killer attacked from behind.

A vagus strike to the unprotected neck. The victim collapsed on to the bed. Drag them into position and secure them before they recovered. Then – start work. Scalpel in one gloved hand, lowering it to their exposed abdomen . . .

Reeve realised his own hand was raised, as if holding an invisible surgical instrument. He hurriedly lowered it. He already knew what had happened next. But who was the murderer? A serial killer driven by madness to perform a sick ritual, or . . .

He turned back to the bathroom. The killer was there, seated. A faceless, spectral figure. Waiting patiently and emotionlessly in the dark. Ready to kill, hiding surgical skill behind deliberate butchery. The blank face took on form.

Harrison Locke.

Certainty in Reeve's mind. The one small mistake, precision accidentally left uncamouflaged, solidified it. Maybe there had been a noise outside, momentarily distracting him—

There *was* a noise outside.

CHAPTER 9

Reeve snapped back to full alertness. A car idling; German voices. The sounds reached him through the broken window. He quickly returned to the lounge. Pulsing blue strobe lights danced over the ceiling from below. He went to the balcony door. A police car was in the courtyard. A cop, flashlight in hand, checked the rear of the apartment block. His partner at the car raised his own torch – shining it up at the flat.

Reeve ducked back. He didn't know if he'd been seen or not. It didn't matter. The broken glass was enough warning of an intruder. An urgent shout from outside.

Breaking into a crime scene was a serious offence. If he was caught—

Reeve was already moving. He threw open the front door and rushed out, breaking police tape across it. He was in a narrow corridor. Which way? An illuminated fire exit sign above one door. He ran for it. Behind, an apartment door opened, a man calling out after him. Probably the person who had reported the breaking window. He ignored him, barging the exit door open. It led into a stairwell.

He pounded down the steps two at a time. His map of escape routes was already visible in his mind. Heading north-west, towards the city's heart, would give him the most options.

But he had to get out of the building first. An insistent buzz from below – the release for the street entrance. The man above was letting the cops in. Pre-emptively – the door hadn't opened yet. He should reach it before they could round the building—

They weren't alone. A loud bang as the exterior door was thrown open. Boots clattered on tile. Reeve glanced over the banister. More cops were hurrying up the stairs.

He reached the first floor and charged through the fire door. The building's rear was to his left. He went right, running to the last apartment door – and shoulder-slamming it open. The lock broke, splintered wood hitting his cheek. A woman screamed in a nearby room, a man yelping in alarm. Reeve ran down the hall into a lounge. The flats at the block's front were bigger than the rear, but lacked balconies. Streetlights backlit the curtains. He made out a sofa, grabbed one of its seat cushions—

Then sprinted at a window.

He held the cushion up like a shield as he jumped through it. The curtains tore loose, glass smashing – then he fell. He twisted as he dropped to bring the cushion underneath him—

Even with padding, landing in the piled snow, his landing was still punishing. He cried out, bowling off the cushion. Glass clinked down around him. His right shoulder had taken the brunt of the blow. He sat up, pain spiking through his joints. Nothing broken, though. He would be badly bruised, but could still function.

He would need to. A shout from above. A cop looked down at him from the broken window. Reeve scrambled upright and ran.

He was at the building's corner. He rounded it to head northwest—

The police car backed at speed from the alley, turning to face him.

Reeve instantly reversed direction and charged diagonally across the street. Most of his escape routes were now useless. Change of plan. He passed the main school building, heading for a high wall beyond it. The police car's siren howled as it came around the corner after him. Its engine roared, gaining with a terrifying burst of speed—

He reached the graffiti-covered wall. Jumped, grabbed its top – and swung himself over. The school's playground was on the other side. He dropped down into the snow. There was a gate across the grounds.

He didn't head for it. Instead he angled around an outbuilding towards the playground's far corner.

The siren moved away at speed. The car would try to intercept him on the next road. More shouts from the street behind. The cops had come out of the building after him.

He reached the corner of the grounds and hauled himself up the wall. The tree-lined street beyond ran parallel to the river. The police car hadn't yet come around the block. He rolled over the wall and darted to some nearby parked cars, hunching down between them.

A burst from the siren heralded the police car's arrival, about a hundred metres to his right. It sped towards him—

And passed. The driver had assumed he would head for the gate. Reeve broke from cover and rushed across the road. He reached the far side, then kept going, slipping into trees and bushes on the riverbank. The police car stopped near the gate. He went in the opposite direction. The bank was steep, slippery and treacherous with snow. He grabbed at branches to keep his footing as he moved. How long before he could risk emerging? The police would soon realise where he had gone. All they had to do was find his footprints . . .

A couple of people passed on the path. Even at midnight, the city was not completely dead. He could justify his presence. He pushed back up through the bushes, stopping just before reaching the footpath. A rapid change of clothes. The baseball cap came off, replaced by a woollen beanie hat. He shrugged off his outer hoodie, and the sweater beneath it. Then he put them back on: hoodie first, covering it with the sweater. The colours were different – no longer matching what the cops had seen.

He looked back along the street. The police car had stopped, its driver getting out. Another cop climbed clumsily over the school's wall. They would soon find his trail. He emerged from the bushes, slumping his shoulders to look smaller. He was not far from a bridge spanning the river. More traffic; people milling near a taxi rank. He headed for it, his footprints lost amongst others. Another siren sounded ahead, but he kept walking, disappearing into the snowy city.

Reeve took a circuitous route back to his hostel. Once there, he peeled off his snow-dampened clothes, draping them on the little radiator. Only when he felt secure did he allow his body to process its adrenalin surge. It had been a close escape, his investigation almost over at the start.

But he'd evaded the police. And now, he was certain that

Locke was the Bondage Killer. Somebody connected to his victims was SC9's real target. He had to find out who that person was – before Locke eliminated them.

Then he could catch Locke. Expose SC9. End their hunt for him.

And resume his search for Connie.

CHAPTER 10

The next morning, Reeve found another internet café and began his research.

His first port of call was *DieGelbePresse*, running the website through a translator. Its name in English was revealed as *The Yellow Press*. He needed as much background information as he could get about the killings. He'd bought a notebook and pen; he started writing.

One dead man did not fit the serial killer's profile. He was, Reeve learned, a friend of the second victim. Witnesses had seen them together at a nightclub. The club was called Legbite; presumably there was some meaning to the odd name. The second and fourth victims had definitely attended on the nights they were killed. Whether the first and third had was uncertain, but both had visited in the past. All but the third victim were followers of the club's Facebook page.

He found what information had been leaked about the collateral victim. Stabbed several times in the chest. The deepest wound had passed cleanly between the ribs to puncture the heart. Reeve expected it was also the first wound, the others for show. Locke, precise as always.

Back to the intended victims. What were the common factors? All in their twenties. Men dressed as women. No male clothing in the fourth victim's flat, Reeve mused, so having a sex change? Either way, the serial killer's apparent motive was obvious. He was killing male-to-female trans clubbers in their twenties.

They were the ghost targets. So who was the real one? What interests did SC9 have in Munich?

Next stop: Facebook. He found the Legbite club's page. He'd hoped to find a list of followers, but the link was greyed out. Private: presumably you had to be a member of the group. The rigmarole of signing up would waste time. Instead, he found a link to Visitor Photos. An album came up with over three hundred pictures. Many were posters or memes, or didn't show any faces. Yet he had to check each one. He needed the names of the people who had posted them.

He set to work. Each name was written down in turn. Whenever a clubber was tagged in a picture, he noted their name as well. They were recorded in blocks of ten. After some time, he had one hundred and forty-seven.

A fair number were obvious pseudonyms. They were a secondary priority. He concentrated on real names – specifically, female ones. The four victims had all called themselves by women's first names. It wasn't those he was interested in, though. The surnames were what mattered.

SC9's target would be somebody important in Munich. Almost certainly someone in business, government or politics. He looked up the German names for various official bodies. This in turn formed a long string of search terms, separated by AND/OR operators. Then, laboriously, he appended each surname and ran many, many searches.

It was a tedious process. Some surnames were common

enough to produce dozens, even hundreds of results. All had to be checked. Hours crept by; he paid for an extension to his internet time. After a while, he began to get paranoid. He was, after all, collating a long list of German citizens. That some could work for the government, intelligence services or military was also an issue. Germany's electronic spies were as capable as Britain's, if less intrusive globally. He cleared the browser history and moved on.

A fast-food lunch, then he returned to the tourist office. The woman at the desk was not the same as yesterday; he wouldn't be remembered. He got addresses for more internet cafés. The nearest was southeast of the station. He passed the terminus, now hyper-aware of how many police were patrolling nearby. Had the cop seen his face after he jumped through the window? Had his description been circulated? He kept his head low as he walked. Luckily, the ever-falling snow meant others were doing the same. He didn't stand out from the crowd.

His search resumed at the next internet café. It was no less tedious than before. He was starting to narrow things down, though. Munich was home to some German government departments, and an intelligence outpost. The BND – *Bundesnachrichtendienst*, Germany's foreign intelligence service – had a GCHQ equivalent on the city's outskirts. But he found no obvious links between it and Legbite's patrons.

He did find potential connections to businesses, however. Several surnames from the club matched important local figures; Munich was a major industrial centre. BMW, Siemens, warplane manufacturer Panavia and the global financial group Allianz were all based there. A faint smile.

SC9 probably wasn't engaged in operations to protect Britain's car industry. That had been sold off to foreign corporations decades ago.

The *weapons* industry, though . . .

He knew from Parker's stolen files that SC9 had killed to aid Britain's oil industry. There were doubtless other fields where Scott had interfered. The arms trade, perhaps? The country was one of the world's largest exporters of weapons and associated systems. Germany, though, ranked above it. Post-Brexit, the UK had been isolated from the European market. Shut out from lucrative deals, collaborations and mergers. Was Scott targeting the competition?

The thought was enough for him to open a tab for a new search. Were there other arms manufacturers based in Munich? Yes, several. None were major players, but—

One name suddenly leapt out. *Foss Präzisionsmetall, GmbH*. There had been someone in his list called Foss . . .

He flicked back through his notes, found the name. Avelina Foss. A connection? He drilled deeper into the search results. Foss originally made metal parts for others, but now had a major arms division. It was a member of a consortium manufacturing point-defence systems for warships. It also, he now remembered, produced handguns. He'd never used one; they were expensive, specialist weapons. But they had a good reputation for accuracy and reliability.

Who was in charge of the company? One Idonia Foss, another search revealed. From her photo: late fifties, stern, businesslike. Short dark hair and an unsmiling mouth. He put her profile through a translator. Foss Präzisionsmetall was a family business, founded by her father. She had taken it over on his death in the early nineties. It had gone from strength to strength under her leadership. Now, she was spearheading a merger of several European arms companies. It would create the fourth largest in Europe. Globally, that would make it a major player. A threat to Britain's own conglomerates – if the merger went ahead.

He went back to the search results. A German magazine profile came up. He speed-read the translation. She was divorced, with one child. A son, Theodore. It mentioned that he was at university – but the article was five years old. If he'd graduated, he would now be in his mid-twenties . . .

New search: Theodore Foss, former student at Munich Technical University. It got results. Theodore had studied mechanical engineering, graduating with a Grade 1 classification – a First. He had been active in drama, sport and progressive politics. There were a few pictures of him. The clearest showed him skiing, what Reeve recognised as the Matterhorn in the distance.

He regarded the picture more closely, examining Theodore's features. He didn't know the face – yet something about it jogged a memory. He opened the nightclub's Facebook page in a new tab and found the photo album. What had he seen earlier? He scrolled through the thumbnails. That one – a group of clubbers posing. He clicked on it. The image expanded.

Five people. Four women, at least dressed as such. Was one of them Theodore?

Three people were tagged – but he'd already identified Foss before the pointer revealed the name. Reeve was trained to see through disguises. Some things, like eye spacing or mouth shape, couldn't be altered. Not even makeup and a long, punkish wig could hide his target.

Locke's target, he corrected himself. 'Avelina' – Theodore – Foss was the Operative's ghost target. SC9's plan came together. The Bondage Killer would make Theodore his victim . . . and also kill his mother. Collateral damage, in the wrong place at the wrong time. The police and press would focus only on the serial killer cover story. Who would believe it was a political assassination? Only the most unhinged of conspiracy theorists.

But Reeve knew that was exactly how SC9 operated. How *he* had been taught to operate. Make a politically motivated, state-sanctioned murder look like anything but . . .

Despite his apparent breakthrough, he kept checking the names. Idonia Foss was *probably* Locke's target, but he had to rule out all other possibilities.

After a few hours, he had. Eyes tired from staring at the screen, he leaned back, thinking. Any further links between his list and people of potential interest to SC9 remained hidden. He went back to Legbite's Facebook page. He'd noted that Theodore/Avelina Foss had posted several photos. He checked them in more detail. He, or she – which to use? He chose the former – only appeared in a few. Usually he was behind the camera. But his look was different every time. Colourful cyberpunk with dreadlocks; spiky-haired goth in black; fetishist in PVC or rubber. Always as 'Avelina', though. Some of the pictures had captions, in German. He copied them into the translator. The club was a favourite. 'Fridays alternate between goth and trans nights', read one caption. 'So I get to go every week!'

That was the link. That was how SC9 and Locke had chosen their ghost targets. Theodore Foss had provided the profile of the Bondage Killer's victims. They were marked for death because of their similarities to him. He – and his mother – would soon meet the same fate.

Unless Reeve intervened.

The last victim had been killed on the previous Friday. He checked the club's page again. That had been trans night. The next such event was a week tomorrow. Theodore Foss would probably attend this Friday's goth night. Would Locke be there, stalking his target? It seemed unlikely – but he might still observe the club itself. It could be worth checking out.

First, though, he needed to investigate Idonia Foss herself.

CHAPTER 11

Foss Präzisionsmetall's headquarters were in northern Munich, near the Olympic Park. A tram took Reeve most of the way. He walked the remainder, snow caking his clothing. He needed a new coat, but didn't want to spend the money. It might be required for more important things.

Evening was coming as he reached the building. A low-rise block of glass and pale brick, on a small campus of similar structures. Unassuming, anonymous. Even the company's sign was modest in size, bland in design. It didn't seem industrial; presumably the actual factory facilities were elsewhere. There was nothing to suggest the company was involved in arms manufacturing. Which was perhaps exactly the intent.

He was here. What to do now? Part of his mind – the part that spoke with Connie's voice – had a suggestion. Warn Foss that her life was in danger. That was the obvious course of action. But . . .

If Foss became aware she was an assassination target, she would take precautions. Change her routine, hire body-guards – even leave Munich. Such options were easily available to the wealthy. But if she did, SC9 would be forced to change their plans. They might even withdraw Locke entirely, bringing in a different Operative with a new approach. Someone Reeve didn't know. The chances of his intercepting them would be reduced almost to zero.

So, as much as his conscience objected, he couldn't afford to interfere. Foss was his live bait. Without her, he had no chance of catching Locke.

Then why did you come here? A familiar voice, not his, accusing. He didn't have an answer. Had he subconsciously wanted to warn her?

The moment the idea entered his conscious thoughts, it took root. It wasn't going to leave, however hard he tried. He muttered an obscenity. He wouldn't have had such doubts as an Operative. Connie had changed him. A sudden surge of loneliness. He missed her. He wanted to be back with her. There was only one way to do that. He had to catch Locke, expose SC9 . . .

People had been leaving the Foss building, cars emerging from an underground parking area. One caught his attention as it neared the exit barrier. A long-wheelbase BMW 7 Series – an expensive luxury vehicle. One for senior executives, company bosses. The rear windows were tinted. Was Idonia Foss inside?

Before even realising what he was doing, Reeve ran across the road towards it. The barrier rose. The BMW set off – then stopped abruptly as its driver saw the approaching man. One of the rear doors opened. A tall, black-haired man in an expensive suit jumped out. He moved to intercept Reeve, shouting in German.

Reeve slowed, raising his hands. The Foss building's lobby had a glass front. He saw two uniformed men inside racing for the door. 'Idonia Foss! Is Idonia Foss in there?'

The tall man switched instantly to English. 'Move away from the car!' He advanced, fists clenched. Behind him, Reeve glimpsed movement inside the 7 Series. A woman peered warily back at him: Idonia Foss. 'If you don't leave now, the police will be called.'

'I don't want trouble,' Reeve replied. 'But I need to talk to Mrs Foss. Her life's in danger.'

The suited man spoke sharply over his shoulder. Reeve understood one word clearly enough: *polizei*. The driver jabbed at a touchscreen. 'Not from me,' Reeve quickly added. 'But she needs to take precautions. Her and her son.'

'Why?' the man demanded. 'Who is endangering them?'

The security guards were now outside and charging towards him. Reeve backed into the road. 'Just tell them they need to be careful. Okay?'

The tall man responded by snapping out an order to the guards. They closed on Reeve. He turned and ran. A passing car braked hard to avoid him; he swerved around it and sprinted on. The two men maintained their pursuit, but Reeve quickly drew ahead. Even in hiding, he had kept up his running whenever he could. A frustrated shout from their boss, and they withdrew.

Reeve turned down a side street. The police had been called. He couldn't afford to be caught.

'Sorry, sir,' said one of the guards. 'He was too fast.'

'That's okay.' The tall man, Reynold Netz, was Foss's head of security. It was normally a bureaucratic role. But if protecting his boss required intervening personally, he would do so. 'Give his description to the police when they get here. And see if we got his face on the security cameras.' The guards acknowledged and returned to the lobby.

Netz got back into the car. 'What was all that about?' asked Idonia Foss. She was merely surprised by the encounter, not scared. It wasn't the first time someone had threatened her. 'I only heard part of it. What else did he say?'

'Not much,' said Netz, closing the BMW's door. 'That your life's in danger – he claimed not from him – and you should take precautions. You and . . .' Brief hesitation. 'Your son.'

Alarm flicked across Foss's face. 'That was all? He didn't say from whom?'

'No. What do you want to do?'

'I don't know. Do you think he was a real threat? Or just some crazy guy? He looked like a tramp, after all.'

'That he did. But it's not as if you haven't made enemies, so . . .' Netz opened the door again. 'I'll talk to the police when they arrive. You go home. Make sure the house's security is on, just in case.'

'All right,' said Foss. 'I'll see you tomorrow.'

Netz nodded, then exited the car. Foss gave an order to the driver, and the BMW set off. She sat back, perturbed. Her hand went semi-consciously to her watch, brushing its face. She belatedly realised what she was doing. A moment of thought, mulling over what had just happened. Then she withdrew her hand and gazed out at the snowy streets, frowning in concern.

* * *

Reeve kept running until he reached a residential street. He ducked into a recessed garage entrance, out of sight of the road. A rapid swap of hoodies and hats, and he set off again, walking unhurriedly through the snow.

He headed back towards the tram line. A police car drove past before he reached it. The officers inside looked him over. No reaction: his clothes didn't match the description they'd been given. The car continued on.

He calmed. The part of him concerned with escape, at least. Another part of his mind was fuming. What the hell was he doing? No sooner had he thought he shouldn't warn Foss than he'd gone and done it! The act may have soothed his conscience, but it didn't help him achieve his goal.

But . . . it hadn't actively *harmed* it either. He hadn't given away any specifics. It was just a warning of impending danger, that was all. If Foss increased her security, Locke wouldn't know why. In her business, she had probably faced threats before. All he'd done was—

He abruptly terminated that whole line of thought, realising what he was doing. He was *justifying* his actions, rationalising his bad decision. To whom? Himself? Connie? She wasn't with him. Nor would she ever be if he failed to catch SC9 in the act. Idiot!

Enough. He had to keep that part of himself under control until his mission was accomplished. He couldn't afford another mistake. First and foremost, he had to become an Operative again. Cold. Rational. Unemotional. He had an objective: stop Locke. If doing so saved the Fosses, that was just a side benefit. Beyond being Locke's targets, they were of no importance to him at all.

Newly resolute, jaw set, he marched back towards the centre of the city.

CHAPTER 12

Avelina Foss hesitated at the house's gate.

At first, she didn't know why. She had grown up here; until fairly recently, lived here. But then the answer came. When she'd lived here, she had been 'he'. Her mother not only didn't understand why she'd changed, she didn't *want* to understand. Never warm, their relationship had finally been frozen by Avelina's decision. Moving out had been unpleasant. But at least her mother was too emotionally restrained to display her fury. Or worse, disgust.

She took a breath, then opened the gate. 'Come on, Peppo,' she said, tugging the lead. Her dog was a wire-haired rescue she'd adopted not long after moving out. One of the many things she had never been allowed at home. Her *old* home, she corrected. Even after several months, she hadn't transferred her sense of belonging to her new place.

Or, for that matter, some of her *actual* belongings. Which was why she was here. There were lights on inside, so Mother was home. Time to get it over with.

Avelina walked up the path to the front door, Peppo following. She still had a key. She unlocked the door, walked in—

And jumped as the alarm warbled.

'Shit, what the fuck, shit!' she gasped. Peppo tried to run back outside, claws scrabbling on the polished floor. The alarm panel was hidden behind a wooden flap in a nearby arched recess. She opened it and hurriedly tapped in the code.

It didn't work. She tried again. The noise still didn't stop. If the alarm wasn't shut off within a minute, the police would be called. 'Oh come *on*, what—'

A door opened. Avelina looked around. Her mother hurried from her study. She appeared startled to see her visitor – then angry. 'What are you doing? Turn it off!'

'I'm trying!' Avelina shot back. 'Have you changed the code?'

A flicker of embarrassment in her mother's eyes, quickly covered. 'Yes, yes. Four-six-two-seven. Quickly, come on.'

Avelina tapped in the new code. This time, to her relief, it worked. 'Why did you change the code? Actually, why is the alarm even *on*?'

'Reynold's recommendation,' came the reply. 'There was a minor security issue at the office. Just a precaution.'

'What kind of issue?' Avelina asked, but her voice trailed off. She recognised her mother's disapproving expression. 'What?'

'I didn't say anything.'

'Not with your mouth, but I could still hear you thinking.' Her voice became higher-pitched, mocking. '"What *are* you wearing?" I'm wearing what I want, thank you. What I feel comfortable in.'

'Comfortable' included a bright red Puffa jacket, short leather skirt and rainbow-striped leggings. Idonia's gaze moved down the ensemble to her boots. 'You're wearing high heels in snow?'

'They've got rubber soles, with grips. They're fine.' She walked to her mother, chunky heels thudding on the floorboards.

Idonia looked across at Peppo, who was sniffing at a corner. He raised his head and shook off snow and water. Her lips tightened. 'Did you have to bring that in here?'

'I can't leave him outside, it's freezing.' Avelina let out a sarcastic tut. 'You know, it's *nice* coming home to someone who's always happy to see you.' She pulled down her hood to reveal a feminine bleach-blonde hairdo with coloured streaks. 'It makes a change.'

Idonia eyed it dismissively. 'I *am* always happy to see you, Theo. But I would have appreciated some notice. I'm in the middle of a Zoom call.'

Avelina frowned. 'That's not my name.'

'It's the name I gave you.'

'And Avelina is the name I gave myself. It would be nice if you would respect my decision and not deadname me, *Mother*.'

Idonia glanced back into the study. 'Other people don't need to hear our personal issues,' she hissed. 'Excuse me for a moment.' She went back in to mute the video call.

'Oh, I'm sorry, am I embarrassing you?' Avelina called loudly before she could reach the controls.

Idonia apologised to her caller, then muted the mic before turning in exasperation. 'Frankly, yes, you are. After that news article, all I had for weeks afterwards were questions about you.'

The newspaper *Süddeutsche Zeitung* had run a story

about Munich's transgender community. Avelina, as the child of an important local figure, had featured prominently. 'People were asking you about your daughter? Oh no, how terrible for you.'

Idonia drew in an angry breath. 'I don't care if you're dressed like some, some . . .' She struggled to find a comparison. 'Punk scarecrow. You are not my daughter – you are my son!'

'You don't define who I am, Mother,' said Avelina, her own anger turning cold. 'Not any more. This isn't just a fad, and I'm not doing it to annoy you. This is entirely about me. This is who I am. Who *I* choose to be, nobody else. If you don't like it . . . that's your problem, not mine.'

There was a long and awkward silence. Avelina finally broke it. 'I came to get some more of my books. I'll go and find them.' She shrugged off a pink backpack adorned with unicorn decals. Her mother's disapproval, though silent, somehow became louder. 'Don't let me interrupt you making even more money from killing people.'

Even as she said it, she knew she had gone too far. But it was too late to backtrack. Idonia tensed, then without a word turned and returned to the computer.

Avelina closed the study door. 'Fuck,' she muttered, now angry at herself as well as her mother. Still, it proved that her freedom had changed her. *Theo* Foss would never have dared challenge his mother like that. 'Come on, Peppo. Let's get my things, then go home.'

Perhaps, if nothing else, the uncomfortable visit would cement that this no longer *was* home. She headed up the stairs, the damp dog trotting inquisitively alongside her.

* * *

Idonia ended her discussion with one of her intended future partners, the screen going blank. She immediately released her pent-up growl of anger. Of all the times for Theo to turn up and pick a fight! Especially looking like . . . *that*. She was just glad he hadn't come into the view of her laptop's camera. That would have taken the conversation down a path she didn't want to follow.

She heard the thud of the ridiculous boots and clattering claws in the hall. Should she acknowledge him? *Wait and see if he does first*, she decided. But there was no call of goodbye. All she heard was the front door closing. If that was how he wanted to treat his own mother, then let him go. See how he managed without her.

She rose and went into the hall to make sure the door was locked. It was, but she slid the bolt across for extra security. The encounter with the homeless-looking man had unsettled her. Netz was probably right. Best to be safe. Especially with the merger in its final stages. Her security chief was correct about her making enemies. Not least Roger Glennmore. The head of Xeneon had tried to threaten her into ending the deal. Her response had doubtless shaken him to the core. Well, it was his own fault. Play with fire, as the saying went . . .

She checked her watch. Getting late. Time to set the alarm fully. She entered the code. The doors and windows were now all secured. The motion sensors would activate in five minutes, giving her time to reach her bedroom. Another reason not to have a dog; imagine the thing constantly setting them off! She started upstairs. A twinge in her wrist; she brought her hand to the watch. Consideration for a moment, then she tapped it.

The past hour was one she didn't need to relive.

CHAPTER 13

Reeve spent part of the next morning at another internet café. This time, his research was relatively quick. He needed to learn as much as he could about Theodore/Avelina Foss.

Some social-media trawling revealed that Foss worked in a clothes shop. He checked the address. Glockenbachviertel – not too far from the fourth victim's flat. Since Foss was something of a chameleon, it was worth establishing his current appearance. He wiped the browser history and set off. Would it ever stop snowing? It felt like all he could remember was winter.

The shop was called Zwei Zwei. *Two two*; he knew that much German, at least. Its street address, he wasn't surprised to find, was twenty-two. From the outfits in the window, it sold counterculture fashions: goth, punk, metal, fetish. Not somewhere he would normally have visited. Nor was he dressed like the typical patron. It didn't matter. In this weather, coats and hats were universal, whatever was under them.

He entered, keeping his head down. Shops often had cameras covering the door. Loud music greeted him, a pounding electronic beat with a singer growling in German. He looked around. Was Foss here? A tall, skinny man with a beaky nose stood behind the counter. Not him; the facial shape was completely wrong. But the shop extended deeper into the building. He pretended to look over the clothes as he moved deeper.

Voices became audible over the music. He reached the threshold of a back room and peered in. A chubby woman in a long coat was talking animatedly to someone he couldn't see. Reeve made his way around the racks. The other person became visible. Their back was to him; he only saw a mane of spiky bright red hair. Either a wig, or the product of an entire can of hairspray. Was it Foss? He needed to see their face.

He sidled along a display of t-shirts towards them. Someone laughed. Even through the music, it sounded too deep to be a woman's voice. Probably Foss, but he wanted to be sure. He reached the end of the display, about to glance sidelong—

'Hey, *was haltet Ihr von diesem Lied?*'

He realised the question was aimed at him and turned. Foss was indeed the person under the expansive wig, looking at him. Full makeup, women's clothes. What had he said? Probably asking if he needed help with anything. '*Nein, nein,*' he replied, with a small shrug.

Foss's reaction told him his guess was wrong. Confusion for a moment, then a faintly mocking grin. '*Ah, wirklich nicht dein Ding, okay,*' came the reply. The woman suppressed a giggle. Reeve suddenly felt embarrassed. He turned away, briefly perusing the clothes again before heading for the exit. A look back. Foss was watching him with an amused expression.

Snow blew into his face as he reached the street. Damn it!

He hadn't intended to interact with Foss, only observe. That might cause problems later. His plan was to stake out the nightclub that night. Foss had said he attended every week; tonight was goth night. The Bondage Killer wasn't due to strike again for another seven days. But there was a chance Locke might be surveilling his target.

If he was, Reeve would find him.

He had to get through the rest of the day first. His money was running low. He had already booked a few extra nights in the hostel. It gave him a base, and somewhere to stash his belongings. But even though it was relatively inexpensive, Munich as a whole was not cheap. His money might not last another week. Running out would complicate his mission enormously. Crime was an option, but he couldn't afford any more brushes with the police . . .

The cold wind bit at his exposed skin. He needed shelter. Somewhere with cheap food that he could nurse for an extended period. He was at least apparently in the right part of the city for that. He checked his map, then set off through the snow.

The day passed slowly. Reeve was used to long periods of forced inactivity. His undercover missions in the Special Reconnaissance Regiment had often demanded it. But the grey, cutting coldness was wearing him down. His inability to understand the language only made matters worse. He felt isolated, more alone than ever. The company in Slovenia of people he didn't especially like had become a comforting memory.

He passed the time with long, slow drinks of hot chocolate

and coffee. His mind he kept occupied with thoughts of Locke. Operative 61 would be operating under a cover identity. But what, and where? He tried to remember which languages Locke had studied during training. Russian, definitely. They had both undergone the same intensive course. German, surely, because of the nature of the mission. Two others, but which? He had a feeling one of the Scandinavian languages, but wasn't certain.

Would he be posing as German, or someone from another European country? The latter would have definite advantages. There was less chance of being confused by some triviality that any German would know. It also reduced the odds of running into someone with an ostensibly shared background. Reeve knew an SRR operator who'd had to abort a mission for that reason. SC9's research would be exhaustive, but couldn't handle every eventuality.

As for Locke's cover . . . it could be anything. But his prior skillset was medical rather than engineering or business. It would be easier for him to infiltrate a hospital than, say, a bank. An angle worth investigating? He had a week before the Bondage Killer was due to strike again, after all.

For now, though, his priority was surveillance. He had to find out the Fosses' address. The previous victims had been murdered in their own homes. If Idonia was SC9's true target, presumably Theodore lived with her. So first, he had to intercept the younger Foss himself.

That meant going to the nightclub. Not his natural environment. Even in his youthful days in the army, Reeve had never enjoyed clubbing. He disliked the crowds, the noise, the inability to communicate without yelling. Nights out with his squaddie comrades had been more to fit in than for pleasure. But he knew he could handle it. He'd endured far worse.

Night came. He ate a cheap dinner of noodles and vegetables, then set out. The club was about halfway between Foss's shop and the railway terminus. He arrived not long before it opened. There was already a small queue. A short distance down the street was a bar. A few people braved the elements beneath a canopy. He went in and bought a drink, then took up unobtrusive position outside to observe.

'Legbite', the club's name, turned out to be a visual pun. The letters LGBT were capitalised. Reeve got the reference: lesbian, gay, bi, trans. A faint, unwelcome twinge of discomfort. He had grown up in an impoverished, working-class part of Manchester. The worst insult that could be aimed at a teenage boy there was 'gay'. It was practically a demand for a fight. His father had regularly belittled him with similar terms. *Queer. Faggot. Sissy. Poof.* The army had been little different. Homophobia and its variants were drilled in at almost the genetic level.

Connie, on the other hand, had been the exact opposite. She'd had gay friends of both sexes. That he found the idea uncomfortable came as a big surprise to her. The discovery had caused tension between them for a few days.

Yet now here he was, watching a gay bar for a transvestite. A half-smile. Maybe she would think he'd made progress.

The club's doors finally opened, a couple of bouncers emerging. The clubbers outside were looked over, the younger ones showing ID, then allowed in. More people turned up as the evening went on. He'd expected goth night's dress code to be black leather and velvet. His image of the scene was apparently outdated, at least in Germany. Or – equally likely – goth night was just an excuse to dress outrageously. Hair in vivid colours was as common as vampiric *schwarz*.

No sign of Foss, though. But Reeve was thirty metres away, and his target effectively in disguise. Would he spot him in the snowy dark from that distance? Foss had a different look and outfit in every photo on the club's page. He couldn't rely on recognising his clothes, or even wig. All he could do was scrutinise every woman, or person dressed as one. It might not be enough.

As the evening wore on, Reeve got the horrible feeling that was the case. The number of people entering the club dwindled. One of the bouncers went inside. Anyone going to Legbite tonight was likely in there already. Reeve mouthed a curse. He had probably overlooked Foss on the way in. If he missed him coming out as well, his whole plan was in jeopardy.

He would have to go inside to look for him.

He'd earlier seen several people turned away. Conventional attire seemed a disqualifying factor. A look down at himself. His clothing was as un-goth, unshowy, unglamorous as it could be. He looked like what he was – one step above homeless. The bouncer wouldn't let him in.

Not without . . . encouragement.

He left his long-nursed drink and headed for the club. The remaining bouncer blocked his way. He said something in German. Reeve had no idea what.

'*Nein sprechen Deutsch*,' Reeve told him. The bouncer's incomprehension proved it. '*Sprechen . . . euro*.' He held up a small wad of banknotes.

The man hesitated, then shook his head. Painfully aware of his limited cash reserves, Reeve added another twenty. The bouncer glanced inside to check he wasn't being watched – then took the money. '*Los,*' he muttered.

Reeve entered a narrow, dimly lit lobby. The bass thud of music had been audible from outside. Its volume rose considerably. Corrugated metal and grillwork were the theme of the club's décor. A long-haired woman sat in a booth to one side. She called out to him as he headed for the inner doors. 'Hey. *Zehn euro.*'

Zehn – ten? More money gone. He suppressed a sigh and handed over a banknote. He now definitely couldn't afford the hostel for a full week.

Worry about that later. His priority was finding Theodore Foss.

He entered the club proper. Pounding music assaulted his ears. Lights pulsed, briefly disorienting him. He stopped, getting his bearings. A bar in a corner to the left. Dance floor and a small stage on the right. Booth seating near the bar, smaller tables scattered elsewhere. How many people? Over a hundred, he estimated. The place seemed busy, but not full. The weather had probably deterred some of the regulars.

Had it put off Foss?

He started his patrol, slipping around the room's perimeter to check the booths. Slightly more women than men – though some of the women, well, weren't. He surreptitiously compared facial features to his mental image of Foss. No matches yet. He kept moving. His discomfort returned. This was absolutely not somewhere he fitted in. There was an overt sexual charge in the air, clubbers dressed to excite. Lots of couples: same-sex, opposite, indeterminate. Groups too, people huddled together very closely. He was checked out several times as he continued through the crowd. He was six feet tall and athletic, and Connie had certainly considered him good-looking. His clothes, though, clearly didn't make the grade. He drew a couple of *what* are *you wearing?* sneers.

Reeve ignored them and kept searching. If Foss was here, he wasn't near the bar. He began to check the other tables. They were small, tall, with only a couple of high stools at each. The seats were mostly for those in high heels, others leaning on the tables. He followed a slow, weaving course between them.

The music changed. The new song mixed aggressive synth beats with what sounded like an industrial hydraulic press. He immediately disliked it; so, it seemed, did most of the clubbers. There was an exodus from the dance floor. Reeve stopped, surveying the incoming patrons. Was one of them—

There. Theodore Foss.

Heavy makeup and a spiky white wig could only camouflage his features, not change them. Reeve watched as he went to one of the tall tables. Several people were crowded around it. A young man in leather trousers gave up his stool to the new arrival.

Foss had embraced the goth look, wearing a short leather skirt and fishnets. Knee-high boots with roughly a dozen buckles and chunky high heels. Not exactly suited to the snow outside, Reeve thought.

But he had found his target. Now, his mission became to observe. Follow home.

And see if Locke was doing the same.

He went to the bar and bought a non-alcoholic lager. Drink in hand, he retreated to a corner to begin his surveillance.

CHAPTER 14

'Oh, thank God,' said Avelina Foss as the music changed again. 'I hate that song.'

'You're just getting old,' said one of her friends with a broad grin.

'Ha ha. Fuck you.' Avelina gave her the finger, topped by a pointed black nail.

'Hey, Avi – want another drink?' Uli had offered his stool to her. He had also bought her all her earlier drinks. Avelina knew full well what he wanted in return. Well, maybe he would get it. She was in the mood for some company that spoke rather than barked. He was a fun enough guy – and looked good in leather, so . . .

She nodded. 'Sure! Thanks.' Uli smiled, then headed for the bar.

Avelina watched him go, admiring his butt, then looked around. The club was less crowded than usual. The cold weather was partly to blame. But Legbite itself had gained an unwanted reputation. Some of the recent murder victims had attended the club on the nights they died. Avelina had known one in passing, recognised another. The thought that they were now dead was disturbing. A serial killer, targeting trans women? That made her a potential target.

But she could take care of herself. As Theo, she had practised martial arts for a few years. And on trans night, she rarely went home alone. As for tonight, it didn't fit the killer's timetable. Nothing to worry about.

All the same, she surveyed the crowd with more attention than usual. As a regular, she recognised quite a few of the clubbers. And goth night drew a very specific scene. For all the airs of doom and gloom, almost everyone was friendly. Anyone who didn't fit would stand out clearly . . .

Like the guy in the corner.

He was hard to see, cloaked in shadow, lit by occasional flashes of blue light. Definitely not dressed for the evening, though. The club was hot, people peeling off their outer layers. This man was still wearing a hoodie – a grubby one, at that. He looked like a vagrant. Why come to a goth night if you weren't going to make some effort?

Before she could give him any more thought, a bottle clinked down in front of her. 'Here,' said Uli. He tapped his own drink against hers. '*Prost!*'

'*Prost,*' said Avelina, returning the gesture. 'Thanks, Uli.'

'My pleasure.' They struck up new conversation, the man in the corner already forgotten.

A while later, Avelina remembered him again. Someone leaned past her to greet one of her friends. She turned her head – and spotted the man. He was in the same place, holding quite possibly the same drink. She frowned, giving him a closer look. Not dressed for the event, not with anyone, not into the music. His age was hard to judge, but . . . older than most. And—

His eyes met hers. His gaze was intense, focused. Then it flicked away, finding something fascinating off to one side. But his body didn't change position by even the tiniest amount.

Avelina kept watching, until Uli nudged her. 'What's up? You with us?'

'Yeah, yeah.' She turned back to him. 'There's a weird guy over there.'

'He's in the right place, then.'

She laughed. 'Not that kind of weird. He just looks like he should be drinking in a *Kneipe* by the station.'

Uli looked around. 'Where is he?'

'Over in the corner.'

He peered through the crowd. 'Which one? What's he wearing?'

Avelina looked again. 'A hoodie.' The man was watching her once more, quickly redirecting his gaze.

'Ah, yes, a hoodie,' said Uli sarcastically. 'The universal symbol of weirdness.'

'Oh, piss off.'

'Just kidding.' He put a hand on her back. The move felt faintly possessive.

Normally she would have reacted to it, whether positively or negatively. This time, though, she was concerned with other things. 'He keeps looking at me.'

'Well, who wouldn't?' Uli proclaimed. 'Have you seen yourself? You look super-sexy tonight, Avi.'

The praise was blatant in its purpose. But . . . it was also working. She smiled at him. 'Why, thank you, Uli. You can keep that up.' She regarded the man again. He had turned his head, actively looking away from her. 'He just seems a bit creepy.'

'Maybe he's the Bondage Killer.'

'Not funny, Uli.'

'Sorry. But he's not going to do anything in here, so don't worry about him. You want another drink?'

She considered the question, not wanting to get *too* drunk. She still had to walk home through the snow. But . . . she was sure everything would be fine. 'Okay. Why not.'

'I'll go get them.' Uli stood.

'Thanks. I'm just going to pee.'

Normally she would have headed directly for the toilets. But this time, she took a roundabout route – past the creepy guy. He had realised she was moving, looking down at his drink – but glancing towards her. A shiver of tension as she walked past him. He was taller than she'd thought, strong build obvious despite his loose clothing. An indefinable air of *hardness* about him, a familiarity with violence. But he didn't move. She walked on with relief.

Another glance back as she neared the toilets. He was surreptitiously watching her again. And now she had an uncomfortable feeling that she had seen him before.

The chilling answer came while she sat on the toilet. He'd been at the shop! 'Shit!' she said out loud. The same man who'd given her a weird answer and then left in a hurry. She was certain it was him.

The fun of the evening rapidly drained away. Uli had joked that the guy might be the Bondage Killer. The joke now felt even less funny. First he was at the shop, then here.

Watching her. What if the serial killer was scouting for victims tonight?

The man was gone when she emerged from the toilets. But she suspected he was still in the club. She hurriedly rejoined her friends, then looked around, trying to spot him. Uli regarded her curiously as he returned, two bottles in hand. 'What's the matter?'

'I want to go home.'

'But I just bought you another drink.'

'No, I'm going.' She became awfully aware of how unsuited her platform heels were to running. 'Can you walk me home, Uli?'

He glanced at the untouched drinks, then decided potential sex was worth wasting ten euros. 'Sure!' Five euros, as he hurriedly glugged one bottle down. 'Okay, let's go.'

They headed for the exit. Avelina scanned the room again as she went.

The man in the hoodie was in a different corner, still watching her. Despite the heat, she felt suddenly cold.

CHAPTER 15

Reeve watched Foss and his friend exit. Foss had spotted him, he knew. In this place, looking anonymous made him more visible. Foss had pointedly walked past him on the way to the toilets. Then after returning, a hurried departure. Had he been remembered from the shop?

Even if he had, he still needed to tail Foss home. Locke, he was now sure, was not in the club. But he might still be watching for Foss outside. Reeve would need to avoid being recognised, just in case. If SC9 realised he was here, he would become their new priority target.

He waited thirty seconds, then followed his target out. A brief pause at the inner doors to check the lobby. Smart move: Foss and his companion were collecting their coats. He hung back, giving them time to leave. Once sure they were outside, he went after them.

The freezing January air hit hard as he reached the street. He donned his beanie hat, for warmth as much as disguise. Which way had Foss gone, left or right? There: left. About forty metres away. He crossed the road, then followed, head lowered.

After a couple of blocks, Foss turned down a narrow side street. Reeve drew level and paused to check it. It was darker than the main road, snowflakes swirling through intermittent pools of light. A plough had cleared it, but some time ago, snow building up again. Foss and the other man stayed in the middle where it was shallowest.

Figures appeared in a more distant light pool. Four men, young, shambling. Drunk. They neared the couple, who edged towards the street's side.

It made no difference. The men moved to intercept them. Voices reached Reeve, loud, leering – aggressive. Foss was drawing most of their attention. They hadn't yet realised his true nature.

When they did . . . he suspected more than voices would be raised.

'Oh, shit,' Avelina whispered, slowing. The four young men emerged from the shadows. Crop-haired, glassy-eyed, several drinks the worse for wear. They might well have come from a rough bar by the station. Her earlier joke suddenly seemed a lot less amusing.

'It's okay,' Uli assured her. He moved to put himself between her and the approaching group.

It made no difference. 'Oi, oi,' drawled one man, pointing at her. 'Aren't you cold in that skirt?' Avelina self-consciously tugged it lower.

'That's all right,' said one of his friends. 'I've got something to warm her up. My *fat cock*!' He and another man, the biggest, let out lecherous roars.

Avelina backed away. Uli maintained his protective position. The men still drew closer. 'That a wig?' the first man asked. He had a jutting lower jaw that made him resemble a bulldog. 'Come on, show us your real hair. Take it off, let's see. Come on.' He stretched out an arm towards her. She withdrew, fear rising. Maybe she could protect herself against one person. Not four.

'Hey,' Uli snapped. 'It's cold; let's all get home and warm up, okay?'

The man's eyes widened in offence. 'Don't fucking tell me what to do, you fucking freak. I just want to see what she really looks like. I like girls who look natural. Come on.' His tone became demanding, harder. 'Take it off.'

'Okay,' Uli repeated, stepping in front of him. 'Leave her alone, or I'm calling the cops. Let's all just—'

The man suddenly burst into motion. A fist slammed into Uli's stomach. He folded, crumpling into the snow. Avelina jumped back in shock, thumping against the wall. The man exhaled deeply, breath steaming in the cold air, then faced her. 'All right. I asked nicely. Take off the wig. Take it off.' His friends closed in around him, blocking her escape.

Avelina looked in horror at Uli, too scared to respond at once. Before she could, the man snatched her wig from her head. The cold abruptly hit her where she had been sweating beneath it. But that wasn't the only chill she felt as she was exposed—

'Oh *ho*!' crowed one of the others, a chunky man in a Bayern München shirt. 'It's a trannie! Elias, you fag! You just got a hard-on for a man!'

Elias whirled towards him. 'Fuck off! You calling me a faggot? I'll put your fucking eyes out, you—'

Uli scrambled to his feet. Avelina's heart filled with new hope—

Which instantly vaporised as he ran the way he had come – not looking back. 'Uli!' she yelled after him.

Elias turned sharply back to her. He held up the wig. 'That what you do? You trick people into thinking you're a real girl? You fucking queer! Trying to make me look like a fag too?'

'That – that's not—' Avelina tried to protest. But the others shouted over her, a cacophony of abuse. She shrank back—

Her phone. In her bag. Call the police. She grabbed it and thumbed at the side button. Five presses would start an emergency call—

She only reached three. One of the men yanked her arm upwards. Elias saw the phone – and angrily swatted it from her hand. It hit the wall with a crack of breaking glass and fell into the snow.

Elias rounded on her, face filled with drunken fury. 'Calling the fucking cops on me?' His expression changed, mouth clenching tight. Avelina knew he was about to attack her. She struggled to recall any of her martial arts training—

His fist was faster than her memory.

Reeve watched from the wider street. One of the men punched Foss in the stomach, the others cheering him on. He should intervene—

Cold reason halted him. Helping could wreck his whole plan. If Locke or anyone working for SC9 saw him, they would abort their operation. He would never catch Locke – and never see Connie again . . .

But Connie was already there with him. He knew what

she would want him to do. What she would *expect* him to do.

He ran into the side street. 'Hey!' Sometimes a mere warning that someone else was there could scare off attackers.

Not this time. All four men turned towards him. Foss was on the snowy ground, curled in a ball. Probably just winded. The attacker hadn't had time to inflict more damage.

He assessed the threats as he neared the group. Four men. In their twenties. Drunk to varying degrees. The biggest also seemed the least steady on his feet. Close facial resemblance to one of the other men: brothers? The one who had hit Foss appeared to be the ringleader. Wide, intense eyes beneath a deep scowl: he was in an alcohol-fuelled rage. Reeve knew the look. He had seen it on his father many times as a child.

'Leave him alone,' he ordered. The only response was incomprehension. He didn't know enough German to translate the command. '*Raus, raus,*' was the best he could manage.

The ringleader barked a harsh stream of syllables at him. Reeve guessed he was being told to fuck off. Or challenged. The men's stances changed, ready for a fight.

If that was what they wanted, they would have it. He'd given them a chance to leave. They hadn't taken it.

Their mistake.

Two of the men rushed at him. The smaller brother, and a guy in a football shirt. Little Brother was first to reach him. Reeve easily jinked aside, spinning to deliver an axe-hand strike to his temple. The man stumbled, stunned. Reeve continued his whirl and kicked Football Shirt square in the balls. He collapsed with a breathless squeal. The Operative completed his turn by hitting Little Brother with a kidney punch. This time, he went down. The fight was three seconds old.

The other two were briefly frozen in disbelief. Then the bigger brother reacted to the assault on his sibling. An outraged shout – and he charged.

Reeve was ready. The guy was lumbering drunkenly, telegraphing his movements. He reached out to grab him. Reeve ducked beneath his outstretched arms and punched him in the gut.

It would have dropped most men. But the combination of fat, muscle and booze meant Big Brother just grunted. He wobbled back, anger flaring. Another charge, hands becoming claws. Reeve dodged – but the snow was slippery underfoot. He caught himself before falling.

Too late. Big Brother grabbed his sleeve. Reeve attempted to twist free, but the claw gripped tight. A sharp pull, and the Englishman was yanked towards him.

The ringleader saw his chance. A fist rushed at Reeve's face. He saw it coming and tried to pull clear. The big guy's grip didn't loosen. Knuckles clipped his temple, jarring him. His hat came off. He swung around to drive an elbow into the big man's side. Another grunt, Big Brother lurching, but he kept his hold.

A second strike by the ringleader. This time it connected solidly. Reeve flinched as a balled fist smacked into his abdomen. That was enough for the big man to snag him with his other hand. The German hauled him closer, restraining his arms.

Triumph in the ringleader's eyes. His opponent was trapped; he was going to take full advantage. He lashed out with a kick at his groin. Reeve twisted just enough to catch it on his hip. But the fierce impact still made him stagger back against his captor.

His attacker was about to deliver another blow – then paused. He pulled something from a pocket. Metal clicked. A flick-knife. The ringleader's arm drew back, about to drive the blade into Reeve's stomach—

Reeve moved again. A rapid side-to-side twist, slamming both elbows against Big Brother's gut. The other man convulsed as pain penetrated flab and alcohol numbness. One hand came off Reeve's arm. The Operative instantly spun, dropping low – grabbing him. He bent forward, thrusting upwards with the full strength of his legs. The hefty German came with him. Reeve turned his upper body and hurled him over his shoulder. Big Brother crashed into his companion with a startled yell. Both men fell to the street.

Reeve wasn't finished. Before Big Brother could recover, he kicked him hard in the face. Blood squirted across the snow. The ringleader was pinned face-down under the bigger man's legs. Reeve stamped on the back of his head. Teeth and cartilage snapped against concrete with a wet crunch.

Breathing heavily, he stepped back. Had the first two men recovered? No; they remained writhing on the ground. He turned to find Foss still slumped against the wall. His head was now raised – he'd seen the brief, brutal fight. Heavily mascaraed eyes wide, he looked up at Reeve as he approached. Fear on his face—

Reeve extended a hand. 'You need to get out of here.'

Surprise, then comprehension. Foss understood English. He hesitated, then took the proffered hand. Reeve hauled him upright. The movement brought him into the light. His real hair was covered by a gauzy nylon cap. That plus the stark illumination now made him look masculine, Reeve thought. But anyone not knowing his real identity would easily have been fooled beforehand. No wonder the ringleader had been so shocked. 'Are you okay?' he asked.

Foss stammered before answering, switching gears to speak in English. 'Ah – yes, yes.'

'All right. Go on, then.' He released Foss's hand. 'You need to move before they get up.'

Foss looked around in sudden alarm. 'My phone!' It had disappeared into the piled snow. '*Scheisse! Wo ist es?* Hey, Siri! *Mach die Taschenlampe an!*' But there was no reply from the digital assistant.

Impatient, Reeve set off. 'I'll make sure you get home safe. How far away do you live?'

An alarmed look at the fallen men, then Foss snatched up his wig and followed. 'Not far, a few streets.'

'Okay. Show me the way.'

Foss caught up. In his chunky platform heels, he was as tall as Reeve. They left the narrow street and headed quickly through the city. 'Thank you for helping me.'

'No problem.'

'I . . . I think a lot of men wouldn't have. Once they realised.'

'That you're not a woman?'

'I *am* a woman.' Sharpness in Foss's voice. 'A trans woman. But some people have a big problem with that. Like those assholes back there.' A burst of angry German. 'I can't believe Uli ran off and left me!'

'Lucky I was passing,' said Reeve.

Foss eyed him. 'Yes. Lucky.'

Reeve didn't meet his gaze. 'How much further?'

It was not far. A couple more streets, and they reached an apartment building. Foss fumbled in his handbag for the keys. 'Will you be okay?' Reeve asked.

'Yes. Thank you.'

Reeve nodded, then turned to go—

Foss spoke again. Calm, light in tone – but unmistakeably an accusation. 'Why were you following me?'

CHAPTER 16

Reeve stopped, facing away from Foss. 'I wasn't.'

'Yes, you were,' Foss insisted. 'You were at the shop today. I asked what you thought of a song, but you freaked out and left.'

Reeve turned towards him again. 'I don't speak German,' he admitted. 'I thought you were asking if I needed any help.'

'Oh, I see. But . . .' Foss cocked his head. 'You *were* following me. You were at the shop, then the club – then you followed me out. Why?' Reeve said nothing. 'Do I need to call the police? That would be a pity after you rescued me.'

Reeve concealed his alarm. Foss had now seen his face. He could give a clear description. The police actively searching for him would hugely complicate his mission. 'Okay,' he said with reluctance. 'I *was* following you. Somebody's going to try to hurt you, and I want to catch them.'

Foss glanced back the way they had come. 'But you stopped those guys.'

'I didn't mean them.'

'Wait – you mean somebody *else* wants to hurt me?' Before Reeve could reply, the sound of a distant siren echoed down the street. His instant reaction, head snapping around to look for its source, was not misinterpreted. 'You don't want the cops to find you?'

'I just beat up four guys, so no,' Reeve replied.

'But you were saving me. It was self-defence.' A pause, then: 'Here. Come inside.' He unlocked the building's outer door.

Reeve shook his head. 'No. I need to go.'

'Are you crazy? They won't find you indoors.' A pitying glance at his clothes. 'And I think you have spent a lot of time on the street, yes? Do you need food?'

Reeve was about to tell him he had a room at a hostel. But he *did* need food; the gnawing in his stomach made that undeniable. Especially after an unexpected burst of adrenalin. 'Okay,' he said.

Foss ushered him inside and led the way to the second floor. 'This is it,' he said, opening a door. 'Come in.'

Reeve entered – to be greeted by excited barking. A dog with wiry brown fur jumped at Foss. 'Peppo, shush, shush!' he said in a loud whisper. '*Ruhig sein! Es ist spät!*' He crouched to hug the animal, which manically wagged its tail.

Reeve closed the door. 'Boy or girl?'

'Peppo? A boy,' Foss told him, taking off his boots. Reeve followed suit with his own damp footwear. 'He was going to be put to sleep at the pound. I rescued him. He loves everyone – I don't know how he could have been abandoned. The rules of the building say no pets, but . . .' An exaggerated shrug. 'Between following a rule to protect someone else's money, or doing the right thing? I do the right thing. Don't I, Peppo?' The dog wagged his tail even harder.

Reeve looked around. He had come directly into the flat's lounge. It was messy, the home of a young, rebellious person. Posters on the walls, books and magazines strewn about, a PlayStation under a large TV. The battered furniture all looked second-hand. The windows overlooked the street, lights shining in from outside.

An arched opening led to a small kitchen. 'I don't know what there is to eat,' said Foss, going into it. 'I need to go shopping in the morning.' He opened cupboards, then the fridge. 'I have bread, and . . . cheese. Sorry.'

'That's fine,' said Reeve. He looked for a place to sit, pushing books aside on the sofa. The moment his backside touched the cushion, Peppo jumped up next to him.

'Okay, good. I'll get some for you.' Foss returned, pulling off the wig cap. His real hair spilled out. It was blond with purple and lilac streaks, in a feminine shoulder-length cut. 'I'll get changed first. Ah, Peppo likes you.' The dog wagged his tail. 'Do you have any pets?'

'I used to have a cat.'

'I like cats. But I like dogs too. And Peppo was here first, so I'll stick with dogs for now.' He disappeared into another room, leaving the door open. 'What did you mean when you said someone wants to hurt me?'

Reeve frowned. How to answer? His plan would have to change now he had met Locke's ghost target. Since he couldn't lurk any more, the truth might be the best option. As long as he didn't reveal the *whole* truth . . . 'Do you know about the serial killings in Munich?'

'The Bondage Killer? Of course. It's scary, because he's targeting people like me. I knew one of the victims.'

'You did?'

'Only a little. I met them at the club once. But it's still . . .' A lengthy pause, then: 'It frightens me,' Foss finally said. 'And ordinary life is already frightening enough for people like me.'

'What do you mean?'

A snort of sardonic anger. 'You saw what happened when that guy pulled off my wig. It's like that *every day*. Most people are okay with me – or if they're not, they hide it. But there are always assholes, men and women. These sorts just cannot mind their own business. Maybe I get a *look*.' He leaned back around the door, demonstrating with a disgusted sneer. 'Maybe they insult me, or pull their kids away like I'm a monster. Sometimes they bump into me, on purpose. I've been punched in the back, knocked over, had things slapped from my hands. And sometimes, like tonight . . . they start a fight.' Foss fell silent again, expression pensive as if reliving the encounter. Then he blinked and retreated into the room again. 'So yes – I know about the Bondage Killer.' A small, forced laugh. 'It's not you, is it?'

'No,' Reeve replied. 'But I think I know who it is.'

Foss hurriedly returned to the doorway. 'What? You do? Why haven't you told the police?'

'They won't find him. But I might be able to.' A breath, wondering if he was doing the right thing. 'The person carrying out the murders isn't a serial killer. He's a British agent called Harrison Locke. The victims are what are called ghost targets. They're decoys, to disguise the *real* target.'

His host stared at him in disbelief. A gradual upwards turn of the mouth; Foss thought he was joking. Reeve's expression remained deadly serious. 'Who is the real target?' Foss said at last.

'Your mother,' was the blunt reply. 'You're the ghost target he'll use to get to her.'

Any trace of Foss's smile vanished. He came back into the lounge, now wearing an oversized t-shirt. It had a picture of a colourful cartoon unicorn on the chest. An unexpected, painful memory hit Reeve. Connie had worn a similar garment as a nightshirt. 'Why would a British spy want to kill me and my mother?'

'He's not a spy. He's an assassin. He works for a covert agency called SC9. Officially, it doesn't exist. But its job is to eliminate enemies of the British state. And it has a very broad definition of who those enemies are.'

Foss perched on the sofa's far arm, hesitant to get closer. Peppo moved over to him. 'I don't understand. Why am *I* an enemy of Britain? Why kill trans women?'

'If you were a real woman, the ghost targets would be real women.' A startled, then affronted reaction to the term. Reeve ignored it and pressed on. 'If you were . . . a red-haired man, the ghost targets would be red-haired men. To the police, you'd fit the pattern – you would be the intended victim. Your mother would look like collateral damage. But she's the one SC9 are really after.'

'*Why?*' The word exploded out in a mixture of fear and outrage.

'She's working on a corporate merger.' Foss's reaction told Reeve he was aware of it. 'That's a threat to Britain's arms manufacturers. Competition. So SC9's boss has decided the best way to stop it is to kill her. Without her, the whole deal will fall apart.'

When Foss spoke again, it was in a hesitant whisper. 'That's probably true. She's been working on the merger for over a year. But . . .' He shook his head. 'An agent acting as a *serial killer*? Murdering innocent people? That's crazy! Wouldn't it be easier just to – to shoot her?'

'If she was obviously assassinated, it would mean there was a political motive. The German government and the EU would investigate on that basis. They'd look at Britain as very obviously having something to gain. But this way, the serial killings act as a distraction. Everyone looks at them – nobody sees the real target. There's no way to connect it to Britain.'

'So why not just run her over or something?' Foss sounded close to panic, hands flitting as he spoke. 'Make it look like an accident?'

'The boss of SC9 decided to do it this way, so it gets done. And the guy they sent to do the job would enjoy it.'

'How do you know about all this?'

'I used to be in SC9.'

Shock – then Foss recoiled, uncertain, fearful. 'You're . . . an assassin?'

'No,' Reeve said firmly. 'The day I finished my training, they tried to kill me. They thought I was a traitor. I wasn't, but because I ran, they didn't care. I've been on the run from them ever since.'

'So why are you here? Why are you helping me?'

'I want to expose them – to stop them from killing anyone

else. The best way to do that is to catch one of their Operatives.'

'And then what?'

'Make him talk. Get a confession. Show the world that SC9 exists, and what it does.'

Foss nodded, eyes wide. 'Am I in danger right now?' he asked quietly.

'Not at the moment. The killings follow a pattern – every second Friday. The next one won't be for another week.'

Another nod. 'Trans night at Legbite. Is that when I would be a target?'

'Probably. There have been enough murders now to solidify the serial-killer cover.'

'I – I could leave town. Go somewhere this guy won't be able to follow—'

'If you change your plans, SC9 will change theirs,' Reeve told him. 'Locke could have a secondary ghost target while he waits for you to come back. Another innocent person. Or if they think their cover's blown, SC9 will abort. Locke would be replaced by someone else – with a different approach. They always have a backup plan. Your mother's the target, however they do it. They might not go after you any more. But they *will* go after her. They'll get her, whatever it takes.'

Foss sagged, as if the revelation had drawn the air from his lungs. 'We have to warn her.'

'I tried. Her security weren't happy. She might listen to you, though.'

A sarcastic noise. 'It's been a long time since my mother

listened to me about anything. I can try, though.' He looked towards a phone charger by the sofa, then huffed in exasperation. 'I'll have to do it in person. I've lost my phone.'

'I wouldn't do it by phone anyway,' said Reeve. 'Her calls will be monitored.'

'What – bugged?'

'Yeah. Yours probably were as well. GCHQ can take control of any smartphone remotely and use it to spy on you.'

'Oh my God.' Foss's eyes went wide. 'Wow. If they did, then . . . they will have seen some stuff.' He glanced towards the bedroom.

Reeve decided not to enquire further. 'When you talk to her, or we do, her phone can't be in the room. SC9 can't know I'm here. They still want to kill me.'

'I see. Wow,' Foss said again, shaking his head. 'This is . . . unreal. But either you are so insane you believe everything you say, or it's true. Either way, you saved me tonight, so thank you again.' A small frown. 'By the way – what's your name?'

'Alex Reeve.'

'Alex. Hi. And I'm—' Foss paused, a faint smile forming. 'I bet you know already.'

'Yeah. Theodore Foss.'

Reeve's answer did not produce the reaction he expected. '*Gott!*' Foss erupted. '*Du bist so schlimm wie meine Mutter*. My name is *Avelina*. Theodore Foss is in the past, and he's not coming back. Whatever my mother might want. So I'm Avelina. I'm a woman. Please – treat me as one.

141

And call me by the name *I* chose, not my mother. Okay?'

'Okay,' Reeve agreed, taken aback by the intensity of Avelina's feelings. 'If that's what you want.'

'It *is* what I want. Thank you.' She stood. 'I was going to get you some food, wasn't I? Sorry. Finding out someone wants to assassinate you is quite a distraction.' A half-hearted attempt at a grin, then she headed into the kitchen. Peppo followed, hoping for scraps. She put bread into the toaster. That done, she looked back into the lounge. 'After you've eaten . . .' she asked tentatively.

'What?'

'Could you stay here tonight? I . . . I don't feel safe. And not just from what you told me. I'm – I'm still shaking after what happened on the way home.'

'Yeah, I can,' said Reeve.

'You can share the bed if you want.'

'No thanks.' The words came out with more force than he'd intended.

Avelina narrowed her eyes, but managed to reply with humour. 'You don't need to worry. I don't go for trannie chasers. Unless they're cute.' Her smile disappeared at Reeve's determinedly stoic lack of response. 'Do you have a problem with me being trans? Is that why you absolutely refused to be in the same bed as me?'

'That's not it,' Reeve replied awkwardly. 'It's because . . . I'm with someone.' The half-truth of his statement was like a punch to his soul. He *had been* with someone. Despite his best efforts, emotion entered his voice.

Avelina was about to make a sarcastic comment, but held back. 'Who is she?' A thought, then: '*Where* is she?'

'I had to leave her behind,' Reeve confessed. 'To protect her from SC9.'

She was about to ask more, but then the toaster popped, distracting her. 'Oh, there. I'll get your food.'

Reeve replied from the heart – and the stomach. 'Thank you.'

CHAPTER 17

Reeve was woken by a tongue in his face.

He jerked upright, startled – to find Peppo on the sofa with him. 'All right, come on,' he said, gently pushing the dog away. He checked his watch: just after seven in the morning. Still dark outside.

Hunger stirred him from the couch. Late-night toast and cheese hadn't filled him. Peppo followed him into the kitchen as he searched cupboards. Theodore Foss – Avelina, he corrected – hadn't been joking. There was almost no food. He made himself a sandwich with what little he could find. Was there any coffee? A jar with a few remaining scrapings of instant granules. He did the best he could, then returned to the sofa.

What to do now? He had told Locke's ghost target about SC9. The next step would be to tell Idonia Foss herself. The question then was: how to prevent her from wrecking his plan? The obvious thing for her to do would be leave Munich on some pretext. Zoom calls or similar could replace face-to-face meetings regarding the merger. But if she did that, Locke might withdraw. How to keep his live bait?

He mulled the problem for a while, not coming up with a solution. Eventually, he heard movement. Peppo jumped from the sofa and trotted into the bedroom. Reeve heard Avelina greet him. He waited, expecting her to get up, but nothing happened. It was quite some time later before she finally emerged. 'Hello,' she said.

'Morning,' Reeve replied. Without makeup, hair unkempt, Avelina looked somewhat androgenous. She had a faintly pained expression. 'Are you okay?'

'I'm bruised.' She tugged up the unicorn t-shirt to reveal her stomach. Mottled green and purple patches stood out against her pale skin. 'That guy hit me really hard.'

'I don't think he'll be hitting anyone else for a while.'

'No, probably not. Thank you.' She noticed his empty plate and mug. 'Oh, you had breakfast. Is there anything left?'

'Afraid not.'

She sighed. 'I did say I needed to go to the supermarket, so . . . What is the time?'

'Nearly nine.'

'Oh. Early for me on a Saturday.' A small smile. 'But last night was not a normal Friday.' She petted Peppo, then started back to the bedroom. 'There is a coffee house near the supermarket. They do a good breakfast. Do you want to come with me?'

'Sure.'

'All right.'

When she returned, she was dressed. Her daytime outfit was far less outrageous than her club clothing. Even so, it was still almost exaggeratedly feminine, despite its punk-ishness, Reeve thought. Short skirt, patterned leggings, cherry red Dr Martens-style boots with heels. Avelina definitely wanted to be noticed. Which might be why she also drew the negative kind of attention. But he kept that observation to himself.

'Are you ready?' she asked.

Reeve stood. 'Yeah.'

She opened the curtains. It was now light. Still snowing, though, falling flakes whipped along by a strong wind. 'It's going to be cold,' Avelina warned. 'Do you have a coat?'

'I gave it away.'

A look of mild surprise, as if she hadn't thought him capable of generosity. 'I've got a spare one. Don't worry,' she added with a smirk, 'it's unisex.'

'Thanks.'

'What about a hat?'

'A baseball cap.' His woollen beanie was probably not far from her lost phone.

'Your ears will freeze! I think I've got something.'

It turned out to be as noticeable as Avelina's own clothing. Reeve could only think of it as a winterised jester's hat, just lacking bells. Long flaps in a patchwork of colours hung down to protect the wearer's ears. 'I think I'll stick with the baseball cap,' he said.

'I'm not joking about you freezing,' she insisted. 'We're near the Alps. Munich is super-cold in winter.'

'I'd noticed.'

'Then put it on. Please? You saved me; I should at least save your ears.'

Reeve admitted defeat. 'All right,' he said, donning the ridiculous garment.

Avelina smiled. 'It suits you. Okay, let's go.'

* * *

Harrison Locke sat in his car down the street from his ghost target's flat.

His surveillance mission was unplanned. Theodore Foss's routine had been observed and analysed, by himself and GCHQ. His phone had been implanted with spyware, turning it into a tracking device and bug. Earlier hacks required a call or text to the device; not any more. The latest software could do it from across the globe while the user remained oblivious.

Something had gone wrong, though. GCHQ had been monitoring the phone the previous night when contact was lost. Computers first, then a human officer checked the last few minutes of recordings. Foss had apparently been assaulted. He attempted to make an emergency call – then the link cut off. His phone had presumably been broken.

He hadn't been admitted to any hospital in Munich. Nor was he reported dead. But not knowing his exact location and status concerned Locke. Theodore Foss was key to the entire mission. If SC9 lost track of him, the whole thing could collapse. Months of work would be wasted. Locke disliked waste. It was inefficient.

And he prided himself on his efficiency.

So now Locke was waiting for Foss to show his face. He was normally a late riser, especially on Saturdays after going clubbing. But he had left the nightclub earlier than usual. Why, Locke didn't know. The cacophonous music made it impossible for the phone to pick out speech. Foss had left with someone else. Probably with the intention of having sex. But Foss had still sounded concerned about something, or someone. Again, Locke didn't know what. Foss's phone had been in a bag, muffling the audio. But then came drunken shouts, a confrontation – and silence.

No doubt he had aroused the ire of a transphobe or homophobe. It wasn't the first time it had happened. But this had clearly been a physical assault. Phones didn't break themselves. Foss might have been hurt, traumatised. The experience could deter him from attending the club on the coming Friday. That would be a problem—

Locke sat up as he saw Foss emerge from the building. He recognised the coloured hair flowing from beneath a hat. His target was with someone. Another man, taller, wearing an idiotic jester's cap. Presumably his companion from the club. The dangling flaps blocked any view of his face as the pair walked away.

The Operative dismissed him as unimportant. Foss was no stranger to one-night stands. For the most part, he lived alone apart from his dog. Locke waited until his ghost target and the other man passed from sight. Foss was following his Saturday routine, albeit earlier than normal. Breakfast at a local café, often followed by grocery shopping, then walking the dog. He would be gone for at least an hour.

That gave Locke ample time to carry out the next stage of the plan.

He waited another few minutes to ensure Foss was clear. Then he picked up a carrier bag and headed for the apartments.

CHAPTER 18

The coffee shop was just off a road called Fraunhofer-strasse. Reeve was starting to get a feel for Munich's layout. He was not far from the shop where Avelina worked. Or from the flat of the Bondage Killer's previous victim. *Final* victim, he corrected. He would stop Locke from killing anyone else.

'Do you like the place?' asked Avelina.

'Yeah, it's nice,' Reeve told her. In truth, he thought the café was trying too hard to be quirky. Random junk hanging from the walls and ceiling didn't ensure a genuine atmosphere. He suspected the pride flag in the window was the main reason she came here. But the coffee was decent enough. Overpriced, but Avelina was paying. He was relieved, and also vaguely embarrassed. The cost of breakfast for them both would have severely depleted his remaining cash. 'Is this the trendy part of town?'

'Yes, I suppose so.'

He nodded. 'It's a lot cleaner than the trendy bits of where I'm from.' That applied to Munich as a whole, from what he'd seen of it.

'So where *are* you from? You are English, yes?'

'Yeah. I'm from Manchester.'

Avelina's face lit up. 'Ah! Manchester United! Do you support them?'

He shrugged. 'I'm not really into football.' His father had been, aggressively and sometimes violently so. That had left Reeve with an antipathy towards the sport.

'Oh, that's a shame. United are a great team. Not as good as Bayern Munich, of course. We always beat them. Well, apart from in 1999 . . .' She grinned.

'You a big football fan, then?'

She nodded. 'It's maybe not very feminine. But there are some things about yourself you can't change.'

'Unlike your body, I suppose.'

Avelina gave him a faintly confused look. 'What?'

'Your sex change operation.'

'I haven't *had* a sex change operation.'

Now it was Reeve's turn to feel confusion. 'But I thought you had. You know, when you said Theodore Foss was gone and you were Avelina now.'

Her expression became one of caution: was he mocking her? But then she realised his bewilderment was genuine. 'I don't need surgery to change my gender,' she said. 'Maybe I will some day, I don't know. But right now I'm living as the person I want to be. What else matters?'

'So . . . you're still really a man?'

Anger flared in her eyes, but she controlled it. 'I'm going to decide you are being ignorant rather than deliberately insulting.' Her voice became lecturing, about to deliver a well-practised statement. 'Sex and gender are two different things. Sex is biological, physical. Gender is in your mind, and is fluid. You get it?'

Reeve struggled with the concept, then decided he would rather not think about it. 'Okay,' he said, hoping to change the subject.

She leaned towards him. 'Does it make you uncomfortable?'

'A bit, yeah,' he admitted.

'And is that my problem, or yours?'

'Sorry. It's not something I've dealt with before.'

'Okay. Let me explain it in a way you'll understand, Mr Assassin.'

Reeve gave her a warning look. Had anyone overheard? Nobody nearby appeared to be paying attention. 'I'm not an assassin any more,' he said in a low voice.

Avelina dropped her own voice to match. 'And I'm not a man any more. I suppose you know how to use disguises, yes? You make yourself look like someone else, but you're not really them?' He nodded. 'Theo, the boy version of me . . . he was the disguise. This, Avelina,' she tapped her chest, 'is the *real* me. Now do you get it?'

Another nod. 'Yeah.' He did, he thought, but he also wanted the discussion to end.

'This is who I really am,' she continued. 'Who I always was, inside. Whatever my mother thinks.'

'She doesn't approve?'

'My God, no. She won't even call me by my name. She thinks it's just a . . .' A pause, searching for the right English word. 'A *fad*, something I'll grow out of. She's wrong. But she's never admitted to being wrong in her entire life.'

'There's a lot of people like that,' Reeve agreed. 'By the way, your English is really good. About a million times better than my German.'

151

'We learn it at school,' Avelina told him. 'And films, television, the internet . . . all in English. I learned the term "trannie chaser" on Discord,' she added. 'If you don't know English, you miss out on a lot of things. But I also travelled with my mother, when she went away for work. More people in foreign countries speak English than German. It's useful for business. And I spent a year at university in America.'

'I'd like to go to America.' Reeve had not often left Europe in his military career, and never crossed the Atlantic.

'It's overrated.' She giggled. 'It's fun to visit, but I wouldn't want to live there.'

'I still want to go sometime. So what did you do over there?'

'I was studying engineering. Either I was trying to please my mother, or she pushed me into it. I don't remember. She wanted me to be ready to take over the company when she retires.' She laughed. 'She never will, as long as she's alive. But that's fine. I don't want to do it anyway.'

'You don't want to take over? Why not?'

'We make weapons!' On the surface her reply was sarcastic, but there was real chagrin behind it. 'The company has other divisions, but weapons are the biggest thing we do.' Reeve noticed her repeated use of 'we', but didn't comment. 'That's why I left.'

'You worked for your mum?'

'After getting my degree. I actually patented a process for metal casting. But we used it to make guns. To kill people. And this merger . . . It'll make the company part of an even bigger weapons maker. I don't want to be involved in that.' Mention of the merger sparked an alarming memory. 'Would the British government *really* kill me and my mother to stop it? Is it that big a threat to them?'

'It's not the British government,' said Reeve. 'Not directly. The politicians don't know SC9 even exists. Completely plausible deniability. SC9's boss chooses the targets by himself. Including me and Connie.'

'Connie?' Avelina's tone became one of genuine curiosity. 'Is she your girlfriend?'

'Yes.' The word felt such an inadequate description of what she was to him. 'She saved my life when I first ran from SC9. Helped me escape. I thought we'd got away from them, but . . . I made a mistake. They found us again. So we had to run.'

'And you left her behind to protect her? Where is she now?'

'I don't know.'

She was startled. 'What? How can you not know?'

'If I knew, and SC9 caught me, they'd get it out of me. Eventually. And then they'd kill her.' His fists unconsciously clenched. 'I can't let that happen.'

'Did you love her?'

'Yes, of course I did.'

'Then how could you leave her like that?'

'I didn't *want* to,' Reeve snapped. The conversation had taken a painful turn, and he didn't like it. 'I *had* to.'

'But you could have protected her if you'd stayed with her. You're protecting me, and you don't even know me!'

'I'm protecting you to protect her. If I catch Locke, I can expose SC9. *Destroy* them.'

'And then you'll find her again? You'll go back to her?'

He didn't answer that. Instead, he said: 'Once I've taken SC9 down, Connie will be safe. That's all that matters to me.'

That last was said with a firmness that he hoped would end the discussion. But Avelina's expression slowly changed. Deduction – dawning comprehension – and finally, dismay. 'So . . . you're not trying to stop this man to protect me and my mother. You don't actually care about us, or any of the women who were killed. You're doing it for – for *revenge*? Because you want to get back together with your girlfriend? Why – because you feel guilty that you abandoned her?'

'That's not it,' Reeve insisted.

'Oh, but I think it is,' she shot back. 'And your plan is, what? To *use* us? You told me not to leave Munich, even though you know I'm a target.' Further realisation, this time horrified. 'You want me to be your fucking *bait*?' Her voice rose enough to draw curious glances from other patrons. 'You can go to hell!'

'I can protect you.'

'I don't *want* your protection! Would you even have helped me yesterday if you hadn't needed me for your plan?' She didn't give him time to answer. 'You wouldn't, would you? You would have let them beat me up, or worse. Just so you could carry on with your little mission!' She stood. 'I'm leaving town. And I'm going to tell my mother to do the same, and why. Maybe she'll believe me, or not – but she will still increase her security.'

Reeve rose as well. 'It won't make any difference,' he said, following her to the exit. 'They won't be able to handle Locke. Only I can.'

'Who are you, Superman? James Bond? No! Leave me alone.'

She left the coffee house and started down the street. Reeve went with her. The cold bit his ears; he realised he had forgotten the ridiculous hat. 'I'm not joking,' he said. 'Locke's what's called an Operative. They're an elite unit, best of the best. And what they're the best at is killing people.'

Avelina didn't look around at him as she strode onwards. 'And you're one of them.'

'*Was* one of them. Now I want to stop them. I can do that. But I need your help.'

'Oh, *now* you're asking for my help?' she said with bitter sarcasm. 'Now that I don't want to act as bait?'

'It'll save your life. And your mother's. And maybe a lot of other people's. If I expose SC9, it'll—' He broke off at the sound of a siren, looking around in alarm. A police car was powering towards them. He hunted for an escape route. But he was hemmed in by buildings, nowhere to run—

The car hurtled past, braking hard to round a corner. But Avelina had seen his switch to fight-or-flight. 'You have a problem with the police? They went towards my flat – maybe I should tell them you are bothering me.'

'I'd rather you didn't.' Reeve didn't want to threaten her, but used more emphasis than the mild phrase justified. 'I'm trying to *help* you. I can save you, and your mother. And anyone else Locke might use as a ghost target.' They reached the corner. 'But you have to—'

He broke off. The police car had stopped ahead, outside Avelina's building. Fear – were they looking for him there? But then he saw *why* the car had stopped—

'*Oh mein Gott!*' Avelina cried. '*Das ist meine Wohnung!*'

Smoke swirled from a window of the apartment building. One of Avelina's windows, Reeve realised. Her flat was on fire. They both broke into a run.

Two police officers jumped from the car. One shooed onlookers back to a safe distance across the street. The other went to the building's entrance. People were already spilling from it, the cop directing them clear.

'Peppo!' wailed Avelina. 'He's still inside!' She reached the entrance. The officer shouted for her to go back. '*Mein Hund, mein Hund ist drin!*' He was unmoved, trying to block her. But then an elderly man tripped as he exited. The cop turned to help him up – and Avelina rushed in.

Reeve hesitated. A small crowd was watching. The fire was almost certainly Locke's doing. If the Operative was nearby, observing, he was screwed: SC9 would know he was here. But there was no sign of him. No one else he recognised either.

If he'd been identified, there was nothing he could do about it now. He followed Avelina inside.

A shrill bell clamoured in the lobby. More people hurried down the stairs. Avelina pushed past them. A woman called out after her, but she continued upwards. 'Avelina!' Reeve shouted. 'Wait!' She didn't stop. He pounded after her, squeezing past fleeing residents.

The sharp smell of smoke hit him as he reached the second floor. Avelina was already at her door, fumbling with keys. Terrified barks came from inside the flat. 'No, wait!' he yelled in warning—

She opened the door – and ducked with a shriek as flames

gushed out. Reeve caught up and pulled her away, shielding her. The rush of fresh air had fanned the fire inside. He moved to slam the door shut—

Then heard Peppo crying fearfully inside. Avelina had left him in the living room. He was now trapped in the bedroom. Locke had been in the flat, and deliberately left him to die. A flash of anger. The cruelty reminded him of his father.

The surge of flames through the door subsided. Smoke was heavy in the room beyond, but he could make out details through it. Reeve buried his mouth and nose in the crook of his elbow and darted inside. His eyes stung; he squinted. The bedroom door was across the lounge to his left. The fire was strongest in the other direction. He glanced into the kitchen. A pillar of fire whirled from a frying pan on the hob. More flames rose from the floor in a wide splatter pattern. He saw the melted remains of a plastic bottle – cooking oil. Not an item he'd noticed while searching the kitchen for food.

A staged 'accident'. Exactly as he would have set it up himself. All part of SC9's training. Fire investigators would come to the obvious conclusion: carelessness by the flat's occupant. The hob accidentally left on, the pan catching fire, the oil bottle melting and falling. The target would insist that wasn't what happened. They would be ignored. The evidence was clear; they just couldn't admit to their mistake . . .

The blaze was too big to extinguish with anything available. Instead, he ran to the bedroom door and threw it open. 'Peppo!' he shouted. No movement. Where was the dog?

To his alarm, Avelina hurried up beside him. 'Peppo!' A whimper – from beneath the bed. The dog was scared, hiding.

She dropped to her hands and knees, trying to coax him out.

No time for that. Reeve bodily lifted the bed, tipping it on its side. Peppo was revealed cowering against the wall. Avelina pushed past to grab him.

Reeve backed to the door. Tears ran from his stinging eyes as the smoke thickened. He turned – and saw the fire had spread between him and the exit. Avelina, carrying Peppo, reached him. She froze at the sight of the barrier of flames. 'Come on!' he shouted.

But she didn't move. Her instinctive fear of fire was overriding all other thoughts—

Reeve scooped up Avelina and her dog – and vaulted over the blaze. It licked at his legs, searing them. He ignored the pain and charged into the hallway. Avelina gasped as he deposited her on the floor. 'Get out!' he ordered, pulling her with him towards the stairs. 'Now!'

This time, she moved. They clattered down the steps. More people were evacuating the building. Reeve and Avelina went with them, finally reeling out into the street. The sudden cold came as a shock. A new siren grew louder – an approaching fire engine.

Reeve guided Avelina clear. Another check of the growing crowd. No sign of Locke. The Operative had taken the sensible course of action and long departed. The police car probably had cameras fitted; his presence might be recorded. Arsonists often hung around to watch the results of their actions.

'Are you okay?' he asked, suppressing a cough. He could taste smoke as well as smell it.

Avelina couldn't hold back a racking cough of her own.

'Yeah, yes,' she managed to reply. 'Thank you. My God, thank you.' She hugged her dog, trembling with a sudden release of adrenalin. 'But – my flat! Everything I had was in there.'

Reeve realised Locke's plan and silently cursed himself. He should have seen it coming. Idonia Foss had to be in the same place as the Operative's ghost target. And Avelina would now almost certainly move back into the family home. She might have fought with her mother, but she didn't seem to actively detest her. Parental concern would override any personal disagreements.

He kept the revelation to himself, though, not wanting to remind Avelina of their argument. He still needed both Fosses to stay in Munich to draw in Locke. Instead, he stepped back as the fire engine arrived. 'You'll need to talk to them. The police too, probably. I don't want to get involved.'

Avelina looked up from Peppo. Her eyes were briefly questioning, then she nodded. 'Okay. I understand.'

'I'll meet you later, when you're finished. Back at the coffee house. Okay?' Another nod. 'All right. I've got to go. I'm . . . sorry about your flat.'

Avelina managed a weak smile. 'I still have the most important thing from it.' She raised Peppo higher. 'Thanks to you.'

Reeve acknowledged with a smile of his own, then disappeared into the crowd.

CHAPTER 19

Idonia Foss's house was in northwestern Munich. Reeve surveyed the neighbourhood from the taxi. Big, expensive houses and apartment blocks on tree-lined streets. The car drove along the bank of what he at first thought was a river. It turned out to be arrow-straight – a canal. The water's surface had frozen, a few brave souls walking on the ice.

'The Nymphenburg Canal,' Avelina told him. 'It leads to the Nymphenburg Palace.' She pointed west. 'You could see it from here if it wasn't snowing.'

Reeve looked anyway. A bridge crossed the icy channel several hundred metres away. Beyond, the canal disappeared into the winter's grey haze, only vague distant shapes visible.

He had met Avelina again over four hours after they'd separated. Dealing with the authorities had been stressful for her. Dealing with her landlord, more so. He was furious about the fire – and that she had an unauthorised pet. She was equally angry at his callousness, only caring about his property, not her life. Reeve managed to calm her down. His rescue of Peppo had wiped away her angry doubts about him. The subject moved on to what came next. Avelina, somewhat reluctantly, accepted that she would have to move back in with her mother.

Whether Idonia would agree, they were about to find out. The taxi turned down a side street halfway along the canal. 'Nice house,' said Reeve as the cab stopped. The large residence stood in a spacious plot, mostly hidden by trees.

'I suppose,' Avelina replied with a shrug. She paid the driver, then exited with her only luggage: a bag of dog food. Peppo jumped out with her. Reeve followed. He checked the house as they came through the gate. A visible alarm, but no cameras.

Avelina rang the doorbell. 'I have a key,' she told Reeve. 'But Mother was not happy the last time I let myself in. She had changed the alarm code; I couldn't turn it off.'

'Do you know why she changed it?' A specific threat, or just a general precaution?

'No. Reynold suggested it.'

'Reynold?'

'Reynold Netz. The company's head of security. Mother sometimes gets threats because of our military contracts. He handles them.'

Reeve nodded. Probably the big guy in the suit he had encountered at Foss headquarters. Before he had a chance to ask more, the door opened.

Idonia Foss stood before him. Even on a Saturday at home, she was dressed quite formally. She reacted in surprise at seeing Avelina, then gave Reeve a suspicious look. Did she recognise him from the other day? 'Theo—' she began, before quickly retracting the name. Instead she addressed Avelina in German. Avelina's reply included a word Reeve knew: *Feuer*, fire. Idonia reacted with shock and concern. She stepped back to let Avelina enter, then eyed Reeve with caution. Her daughter's explanation did not fully mollify her, but she still gave a wary nod. Reeve came in. Idonia's expression turned to distaste as Peppo followed him inside.

She spoke to Reeve. 'My friend doesn't speak German,' Avelina said.

Idonia switched languages without missing a beat. 'I see,' she told Reeve. 'Then thank you for rescuing my . . . child.'

'He's rescued me twice now,' said Avelina. 'I was attacked the other night. He scared them away.'

More alarm in her mother's eyes. 'You were *attacked*?'

'I'm okay. It was some drunk assholes on the way home from the nightclub.'

'Oh. So you were dressed like . . .' Idonia's lips pursed as she regarded Avelina's clothing.

'I'm *always* dressed "like",' Avelina shot back, indicating her outfit.

'Which is perhaps why you were attacked. You know, modesty applies to men as well as women.'

Avelina's response was an irate burst of German, before turning back to Reeve. '*Anyway*, he has something important to tell you. It's important to both of us. But first – where's your phone?'

Idonia glanced over her shoulder. 'In my office.'

'Okay, good. Because I think you've been bugged.'

'Bugged?' Reeve noticed Idonia's hand go to her watch, seemingly unconsciously.

'Both of us. Somebody's hacked our phones.'

Reeve had expected disbelief or mockery, but instead

Idonia nodded. 'I had wondered if that might happen. But why would anyone bug *your* phone?'

'Is there somewhere we can talk?' Reeve asked. 'With no phones or electronics.'

Another nod. 'The library. Come with me.'

Idonia turned and walked down the hall. Stairs at the end led up and down. On the wall was something Reeve couldn't at first identify: a long metal rod. It had pride of place, as if it were a piece of art. But it appeared purely functional, mechanical.

Idonia did not stop to satisfy his curiosity, however. She descended the stairs. Below was a large, quiet room with deep red carpeting. The walls were lined with dark wooden bookcases. Beyond French doors, snow-covered steps led up to the rear garden. 'We can talk safely in here,' she said, turning on a lamp. 'Now what . . .'

The change in lighting gave her a better look at Reeve. She paused, eyes narrowing – then popping wide in recognition. 'You were outside our building the other day! You tried to get to my car.'

'I was,' Reeve admitted. 'I was trying to warn you. But your security wouldn't let me get near you. So I made contact with Avelina instead.'

His use of the female name brought a millisecond's flicker of disapproval from Idonia. But it vanished as she spoke. 'So. You have found both of us. What are you warning us about?'

Reeve took a breath. 'You've been targeted for assassination by a British covert agency called SC9. It's trying to destroy your business merger to protect British arms interests.

You know about the serial killer attacking trans women in Munich?'

'The . . . Bondage Killer.' She sounded faintly embarrassed at using the sensationalist name.

'He's actually the assassin, a man called Harrison Locke. He intends to kill you both. You would die as apparent collateral damage – in the wrong place at the wrong time. But Avelina is what's called a ghost target. The victims are decoys; *you* are the real target. The serial killer is just a cover to hide the political motive.'

Idonia was silent for a long moment, expression unreadable. Finally, she spoke to Avelina in German. Avelina's reply seemed positive, genuine. Another contemplative pause, then the elder Foss turned back to Reeve. 'I knew the merger would make me some powerful enemies. But enough to kill me?'

'SC9 has killed hundreds of people. They were all considered threats to British interests. And usually, the assassinations were made to look like accidents. SC9 is very good at covering its tracks.'

'And how do you know this?'

'My name's Alex Reeve. I used to be one of their agents – an Operative. But they thought I was a traitor, and tried to kill me. So now I'm trying to stop them.' He paused to see how Idonia would react to the revelation. But whatever her feelings, she kept them veiled. 'If I catch Locke before he reaches you, I can expose SC9,' he went on. A glance at Avelina. 'Save the lives of anyone else they've targeted.'

'Do you have any proof of this?' Idonia asked.

'No. All I can do is ask you to trust me.'

'Hmm. Their being British does make sense, I admit.' Reeve waited for elaboration, but none came. 'So, what should we do? The obvious action would be to increase our security. Perhaps leave Munich. But,' her gaze intensified, 'I suspect that is not what you are going to propose.'

'No,' he replied. 'Like I told Avelina, if you do that, SC9 will change their plans. They always have a backup.'

'So they would murder innocent people – then just walk away if things change?' Avelina shook her head. 'That's . . . horrible. Insane.'

'I know.' It *did* seem like a major commitment on SC9's part, Reeve thought. More involved and long-term than a typical operation. Had something changed at the agency?

He had no time to mull further on the question. 'The merger will be completed in the next few weeks,' said Idonia. 'After that, there will surely be no point in assassinating me? The deal will be done.'

'I don't know,' said Reeve. 'Will you be the boss of the new company?'

'I will be chief executive, yes – but as the head of a board. All the other bosses of the individual companies will have seats. If I am . . . removed, someone else will take over. The new company will not be affected.' She went to the French doors, looking thoughtfully out at the snow-covered garden. 'The serial killer strikes once every two weeks, I believe.'

'Yes,' Avelina told her. 'If he follows the pattern, the next attack will be on Friday.'

'So if we are not here, his plan is ruined. By the time of the next attack after that, the merger will be complete. We should go to the lodge,' she said to Avelina.

'If you do that, Locke will kill another ghost target,' Reeve insisted. He didn't know if that was true. It was what *he* would do in the same circumstances. But he had no way of knowing who Locke would target. His only chance of intercepting him would be lost . . .

Idonia seemed to spot his desperation – but before she could speak, Avelina cut in. 'No, we can't let that happen! It could be someone I know – one of my friends.'

'I can protect you both,' Reeve said firmly. 'I promise. I know how SC9 work. I know *Locke* – and I can beat him. SC9 doesn't know I'm here. That gives me the advantage.'

'I should still increase my security,' said Idonia. 'I have done it before, so it is not unusual. If I really am being bugged, they will know that. In fact,' she went on, 'I did it after you tried to reach me in the street.'

'Did you say anything that could be used to identify me?' he asked.

'No. Reynold might have given your description to the police. But would that be enough?'

'I don't know. Is Reynold an ex-cop?'

'No, he was in Luftwaffe intelligence before going into security.'

'Then probably not.' Reeve thought back to the encounter outside the Foss building. He had been wearing his beanie hat, covering his hair. Would a description of his face be enough for SC9 to identify him? On balance . . . no. White, around thirty, lightly bearded, British accent: they would be the most obvious descriptors. But SC9 had no reason to think he was in Germany. Even less to think he was actively hunting them. Until now, *run and hide* had been his strategy. They wouldn't expect that to change.

'Then I will increase security,' Idonia declared. 'Reynold can arrange for a bodyguard to stay at the house. I have done that before,' she told Reeve. 'So it will not seem too unusual. And Theo, you—'

'*Avelina*,' came the irate correction.

Idonia continued as if nothing had happened. 'You can of course stay here too, until you find a new place. I will deal with the insurance and all the other matters for you.'

Avelina begrudgingly accepted the help. 'Thank you.' She looked at Reeve. 'What about Alex? Where is he going to stay?'

'I've got a room in a hostel,' Reeve replied. He was well aware he couldn't afford it for much longer, but said nothing more.

'No, no,' said Avelina. 'Are you joking? Stay here! There are five bedrooms. I think one of them has never even been used.'

'I'm sure it has at some time,' Idonia said with an indulgent cluck.

'No, I don't want to be in the way,' said Reeve.

'You won't be,' Avelina assured him. 'If Mother can have a bodyguard stay here, why can't I?'

He began to feel uncomfortable. 'I'm not your body-guard.'

'You've saved me twice – I think that counts. And isn't it better to be a bodyguard than an assassin? Besides, Locke needs me here for his plan to work. That's why he set fire to my flat, yes? If you are already here, you will be ready for him.'

'Th— that is right,' added Idonia. Reeve suspected her stammer was because she had been about to call Avelina 'Theodore'. 'It would make sense for you to stay. And, I do not want to be rude, but . . .' She looked him up and down. 'It would give you a chance to clean your clothes.' *And yourself*, was the unspoken postscript.

Reeve reluctantly agreed. 'Okay. But that means SC9 can't know I'm here. Your phone, and probably your computer, will have been compromised. So you can't talk about me if you have your phone with you. I can't even be in the same room as it – the cameras will be active.'

Idonia nodded. 'That will not be a problem. I have used electronic security measures before. Never in my own house, but if that is what is necessary . . .'

Reeve turned to Avelina. 'The same applies to you if you get a new phone. SC9 can hack it without you even realising.'

'So I can't have another phone for a *week*?' she said.

'Surely you can survive for a week without a phone?' suggested Idonia. Avelina's horror-struck expression implied otherwise.

Reeve half-smiled. 'I can show you how to shield it if you need to. But it's easier just to have some simple rules. If I'm with you, your phone can't be. Keep the cameras covered, and try to muffle the microphone. If it can't see or hear me . . . nor will SC9.'

'And then you can catch the killer,' said Avelina.

'And then I can catch him,' he echoed. She smiled, reassured.

'I will call Reynold about the bodyguard,' said Idonia. 'And don't worry. I will be discreet. I will say I was disturbed by the crazy man from the other day. Which is true – but not in the way anyone listening will think.'

'Okay,' said Reeve. 'In that case, tell him Avelina is moving in because of the fire too.'

'Why?'

'GCHQ will hear – and pass it on to SC9. If Locke knows she's coming here, he won't need to surveil her. That means less chance of him seeing me. Now, if *I'm* staying here, I need to get my stuff from the hostel.'

'I'll come with you,' said Avelina.

Reeve didn't want the company, but couldn't see a way to refuse. Not least because he couldn't afford a taxi. 'All right. We'll be back soon,' he told Idonia.

She nodded. 'And Alex . . . thank you.'

'Thank me when I stop Locke,' was his reply as he exited.

Avelina followed him out. They ascended the stairs to the hall. Reeve regarded the gleaming metal piece again. It was about a metre long, each end clearly meant to attach to something else. The chunky top resembled a component of a universal joint. 'Do you know what that is?' Avelina asked him.

'Looks like part of a car.'

'It is. It's what made the company's name, back in the seventies. This is from the very first batch. My grandfather invented a new precision casting technique. It wasted less metal as flash, which saves money. It won us a contract to supply BMW with parts. That gave us the success to expand. Unfortunately . . .' A sigh. 'We expanded into weapons. First we made precision parts for other companies. Then, after Mother took over, we made the weapons themselves.'

'And you don't approve.'

'No. And now, with the merger, we are just going to make even more . . .' She regarded the casting glumly, then turned away. 'Okay, let's get your things.'

CHAPTER 20

Reeve remained on alert during the trip to and from the hostel. He didn't know how long GCHQ would take to pass on the news about Avelina. Locke might be watching the Foss house.

If so, he was not doing it from the street. Most of the nearby parked cars were covered in overnight snow. Those that weren't, were unoccupied. No watchers on station. He felt fractionally more at ease. SC9 was powerful, but not omnipotent. It only drew upon human resources from other agencies when absolutely necessary. People had the annoying habit of asking *why* they were spying on civilians.

No refunds were on offer at the hostel, so he decided to keep his room. A fallback hiding place might be useful. He packed some clothes, then he and Avelina returned to the house. Another check of the street before he exited the cab. None of the cars had moved, and all were empty. All the same, he kept his baseball cap on and head low. Only when he was inside did he relax.

Idonia met them in the hall. 'I left my phone in the office,' she said. 'Which feels strange. Almost as if I'm missing part of my body.'

'That's why spy agencies go to so much trouble to hack

them,' said Reeve. 'People take them everywhere with them – talk completely freely.'

'I know.' She fiddled with her watch band. 'You become dependent upon them without even thinking they might betray you.'

'Yeah. By the way, do you have any landline phones? Anything with a microphone can be used against you.'

'One in the office, another in the living room. My bedroom has one as well. I can unplug them if you want.'

Reeve thought for a moment. 'Just the one in the living room. If they're all unplugged, someone might get suspicious. Just remember not to say anything about me if you're in the room with one.'

'Of course.' She turned to Avelina. 'Th . . .' Avelina tensed, ready for another confrontation. Idonia paused, then continued: '*Mein kleiner Vogel*, could you show Alex to the third bedroom?'

'I can, *Mother*,' was the tart reply. Avelina led the way to the stairs. 'This way, Alex.'

Reeve followed her upstairs, carrying his pack. 'What does *kleiner Vogel* mean?' he whispered.

'Little bird,' she replied. 'It's what she called me when I was small. It's probably all she'll call me from now on. She knows I won't answer to Theo, and she'll never use my proper name.'

'She might just need time to get used to it.'

'She's *had* time. It's been two years. She doesn't *want* to get used to it.' She opened a door. 'Anyway, this is your room.'

Reeve entered. By the standards of the rest of the house, it was modestly sized. It was still bigger than his parents' room in his childhood home, however. The furniture was old-fashioned and formal. But it was a warm bed, so he couldn't complain. A door led into a small en suite bathroom. 'Thank you.'

'Make yourself comfortable. Would you like anything? Coffee, tea?'

'Coffee, thanks.'

'Okay. We will have dinner later. I'll see you soon.' She backed out, leaving him alone.

Reeve sat on the bed and took stock. This was not how he had envisioned his hunt for Locke. Being so close to SC9's targets posed a definite risk. But it was better than freezing in the street. And the prospect of an actual meal was a welcome surprise.

The situation was what it was. He just had to make the best use of it.

The promised dinner came quite late, at almost eight o'clock. Reeve was hungry enough to know he would eat whatever was put before him. All the same, he was disappointed by the menu. *Abendbrot*, Avelina explained with amusement, was not the main German meal of the day. That usually came at lunchtime. What arrived was a small helping of bread and cheese with a couple of sausages. Peppo took up position underneath his owner's chair. 'Don't worry,' said Avelina. 'I'll get you some more if you're still hungry.'

'Thank you,' said Reeve. He waited for Idonia to start, then attacked his own food.

While he ate, Idonia and Avelina conversed in German. The tone soon became tense, in a repressed way. He guessed

Avelina's gender choice was the elephant in the room. Idonia had a glass of red wine with her meal. The drink was finished before the food.

Avelina gave the empty glass a mocking look. 'We should speak in English. Alex seems a bit left out.'

'I'm fine,' said Reeve said, not wanting to be drawn into any family drama.

'No, of course, you are right,' Idonia told Avelina. She poured herself more wine. 'It must be hard being in a country where you do not know the language.'

'I get by. And lots of people speak English.'

'Perhaps if lots of English people spoke German, you would not have had Brexit?' She chuckled. 'Such a shame, for a friend to become a rival.'

'Mmm.' Reeve nodded noncommittally. Political debate joined family drama on his to-avoid list.

Idonia either took the hint or lost interest, instead turning back to Avelina. 'Oh! The *Münchner Wirtschaftsstipendium* ball is tomorrow, by the way.'

'The Munich Business Fellowship,' Avelina translated for their guest. 'Yes?'

'The invitations arrived two weeks ago,' Idonia went on. 'I had considered bringing Stefan as my guest. But he had an invitation of his own.'

Avelina's expression became quizzical. 'So . . . you want me to be your guest?'

'No, you received an invitation as well. They must still have you listed as being part of the company. I assumed you wouldn't want to go.'

'Why not? It's a bit stuffy, but the food is always good.

And there are usually interesting people to talk to. Like your new friend.' A suggestive smirk. 'Or . . . new *boy*friend?'

Idonia waved her hands in a dismissive gesture. 'No, no, no. Nothing like that. But he is very charming.' Her mouth twitched into a brief smile.

Avelina's curiosity edged towards suspicion. 'Then if you don't want me to go, why tell me about it?'

'I'm not sure if you *could* go. The invitation was addressed to Theodore Foss. And you have turned your back on him, after all.' Idonia's smile became that of a tennis player scoring the winning point.

Avelina stared at her for a moment – then broke into angry German. Her mother responded in kind. Reeve kept his eyes on his plate, hoping they would soon finish. But the argument just rolled on. 'Then maybe I *should* go,' Avelina eventually said, in English. Reeve looked up; the language switch was obviously aimed at him. 'I'll bring Alex as *my* guest. How about that?'

'I don't—' Reeve began.

Idonia spoke over him. 'I will *not* have you embarrass me in public! Not in front of my friends, or my business partners.'

'I won't embarrass you, *Mother*. Why would you think that? I will be the perfect guest. I won't say anything that could possibly make you look bad.'

'It has nothing to do with what you *say*,' Idonia hissed. 'You cannot go looking like . . . that.' She jabbed a manicured finger at Avelina's outfit.

'I won't be dressed like this,' was the cutting reply. 'I need to get new clothes anyway. These still smell of smoke.'

'That is not what I mean.'

'I know *exactly* what you mean,' Avelina snapped. 'But if you're embarrassed by the way I look, that's your problem, not mine. I didn't become the real me just to annoy you. Not everything is about you, Mother.' She looked back at Reeve. 'So, do you want to come, Alex? As my unofficial bodyguard, I mean – not anything else.'

Reeve had by now finished his food. He sat back, eyeing escape routes. 'I don't think that would be a good idea.'

'Well, I *am* going,' Avelina insisted. That provoked another bitter burst of German from her mother. Volleys flew back and forth across the table.

Reeve had finally had enough. He stood. 'If you'll excuse me?' he said. 'Thank you for dinner. If you don't mind, I need a shower. Then I'll probably go to bed.'

'Of course.' Idonia's tone was icy, but the cold was aimed at her child.

'Good night, Alex,' said Avelina. Reeve nodded to them both, then exited. The argument resumed behind him.

He shook his head as he climbed the stairs. Being drawn into other people's personal issues was something he'd never been comfortable with. Assassins and spies, life-and-death situations, he could handle. This? Not his field of expertise at all.

He reached the bedroom and undressed, looking forward to his first shower in days.

Locke answered his phone. 'Yes?'

'We just had confirmation.' Maxwell, calling from London. 'Our friend's kid had a fire in their flat. They've had to move back home.'

'Oh dear.' Locke's lizard lips tightened slightly, approximating a smile. 'What a shame.'

'Just thought you should know. Anything else happening?'

'No, everything is as it should be.'

'Good.' Maxwell rang off.

Locke lowered the phone, gazing out at the snowy street beyond his apartment. The plan had worked as predicted. Theodore Foss could have moved into a hotel rather than back to his mother's. But losing all his possessions to the blaze would be a psychological blow. Locke guessed – correctly – that he would want comfort, familiarity.

All the pieces were now in their correct places. He just had to wait a few more days to make his move.

CHAPTER 21

The promised bodyguard arrived at the house on Sunday morning. His name was Leopold Steber. Reeve assessed him. Ex-military, like his boss Netz. In his early thirties, solidly built, but with a lithe swiftness beneath the muscle. His expression gave little away, but his eyes were sharp and observant. He was probably Netz's protégé; protecting the company's head was a job for the best.

Steber, Reeve knew, was giving him the same kind of assessment. Who was the house guest in grubby, well-worn clothes? Idonia had vouched for him, but beyond that said little. The rule of not discussing him near phones also drew confusion. But it was accepted. The bodyguard was well-trained, and followed orders.

Protecting Idonia was his primary responsibility. That meant, Reeve realised with resignation, doing the same for Avelina had landed on him. Idonia was working in her office, so Steber would stay nearby. Avelina had other plans for the day, however.

'I need new clothes,' she told Reeve as he ate breakfast. 'Everything I had was in the flat. So we need to go shopping.'

He couldn't help noticing the plural. 'I thought German shops all close on Sunday?'

'They do. But where do I work?'

'A clothes shop.'

She beamed at him. 'And I have the key. I'll need to go to somewhere else as well, though. Zwei Zwei doesn't really sell anything suitable for a formal event. But I have a friend who owns a good place. We should find something there.'

He couldn't let it pass without comment this time. 'You said "we" again.'

'I know. I want you to come tonight. Which means you'll need suitable clothes as well.'

'I don't think that's a good idea.'

'I'm not going to stay locked in this house for a week, Alex,' she said. 'I was invited to the party tonight, so I'm going. And I don't care if it annoys my mother,' she added before he could reply. 'This is who I am now. She needs to accept that. Anyway, if I'm going, you need to come too.'

The prospect was not appealing. 'Steber's going with your mother. He can watch you.'

'He won't leave her side. I know how Reynold's people work. And come on,' she said, voice turning encouraging. 'You've been in hiding for months. It will do you good to get out. Free food, champagne, a string quartet. You'll like it! You don't have to talk to anyone if you don't want to. I'll just tell them you're my guest and leave it at that.' She eyed him – correctly guessing his thoughts. 'And don't worry. If anyone thinks you're my boyfriend, I'll say you're not. I know you're a one-woman guy. Connie is lucky, that seems to be quite rare.' She smirked. 'It's funny how many married guys come on to me . . .'

Reeve took the opportunity to change the subject by

picking up his empty plate. 'Okay, I'll go with you to the shops.' He headed into the kitchen. 'I'm not promising any-thing for this evening, though. I still think it's a bad move.'

'It's a social event for Munich's business leaders,' Avelina said, following. 'The Bondage Killer is not going to be there! I know – you're worried about being seen. You will be fine, trust me. It is not the sort of thing where people take selfies. There is an official photographer, and he always asks before taking a picture. You just say no, or move away.' She thought for a moment. 'If anyone asks about you, we can use a fake name. Do you have one?'

'Leo Martin,' he replied.

'That was quick. I guess you do. Okay, when you are ready, shall we go to the shop?'

Reeve reluctantly nodded. 'Yeah. Let's get it done.'

Rather than take a cab, Avelina led him westwards along the Nymphenburg Canal. 'We can get a tram into the city,' she said. 'And I wanted to show you the Nymphenburg Palace. That is where the event is tonight.'

He was not especially interested, but let her do so out of politeness. She brought him to a bridge and went halfway across it. The frozen channel below led towards appropriately palatial buildings a few hundred metres away. 'The palace is much bigger than what we can see from here,' she explained. Trees blocked the view on each side of the canal. 'There are whole wings to the north and south. But you will see them tonight. The party is probably in the Hubertussaal. It was the last time I went.'

Reeve nodded, still with no intention of going. They

continued to the south bank. A tram stop was not far down the street. A tram soon arrived. They rode it into central Munich, a change taking them to Glockenbachviertel. Avelina led the way to Zwei Zwei. She unlocked the door and entered, deactivating the alarm. Reeve followed her inside, relieved to be out of the cold. The anorak Avelina had lent him kept him dry, but was not especially warm.

'Now, what do I need?' said Avelina, switching on the lights. 'Everything!' She started to prowl the aisles, picking out garments. They were her usual alternative, look-at-me style.

'Are you sure this is okay?' said Reeve. She might work here, but simply helping herself felt wrong.

'Don't worry. I'll pay for everything. I still have all my cards.' The selection process took a tedious half-hour, but finally she went to the counter. All the items were put through the register, then she paid by credit card. 'All right. Now I have enough clothes to get through the week,' she said, packing everything up. It took four bags to fit them all. 'I still need something for tonight. But my friend's shop is not far away. I'm sure he'll have something for me. And for you.'

'I'm not going,' Reeve reminded her.

She grinned and made a record-scratch sound. 'Like in a movie,' she said, on his bewilderment. 'You know, when someone says, "I'm not doing that"? And then you cut to them doing that.'

'This isn't a movie,' he pointed out.

'It should be,' she said. 'Although . . . it would be quite a nasty one. A lot of innocent people have been murdered. So perhaps not.'

'I'll make sure it has a happy ending,' said Reeve.

She picked up the bags and went to the door. 'Your happy ending would be you finding Connie, yes?'

'Yes.' He said it almost with a sigh, as if the prospect was slipping away. 'It would be.'

'It can happen,' she assured him. 'Just stop this man Locke, and then . . .'

'Yeah.' The mere thought of Connie brought back his melancholy. He sighed, this time for real. 'Okay,' he said, not wanting to think about it. 'Where's this other shop?'

It was, as Avelina had said, not far away. The outfits it offered were very different from Zwei Zwei's selection. Dummies in the window wore a wedding dress and dinner suit. Avelina knocked on the door. 'I phoned him before we left the house,' she said. 'He said he would be here.'

A brief wait, then the door unlocked. A reed-thin man in a grey silk shirt opened it. 'Avi!' he cried, embracing her. They kissed on both cheeks, then spoke in German. The man gave Reeve an inquisitive glance.

'*Das ist – Leo*,' Avelina told him. 'He does not speak German, I'm afraid.'

The man smiled. 'Oh, good. I can practise my English! Hi, Leo. I am Frideric.'

Reeve shook his hand. 'Hi.'

'Come in, come in. It is cold outside!'

The visitors entered the shop with relief. Frideric closed the door. 'Now, Avi, you want to borrow some clothes?'

'That would be great, thank you,' Avelina replied.

He gave her an exaggerated look of warning. 'And this time you will keep them *clean*, yes?' To Reeve, he added:

'I let her borrow a dress once. It came back with chocolate on the front. *Chocolate*.' He tapped indignantly at his chest to show the position of the stain.

Avelina raised a hand. 'I promise.'

'Good. So, let us find you something.'

'And for Leo too,' she said. Reeve shook his head. She ignored the gesture. 'Something smart.'

Frideric examined him. 'He has a nice build. Strong, an athlete. He will look good in anything. Lucky man! I am sure I can find something. But what about you?'

She smiled. 'Show me what you've got.'

Reeve found himself struck by a familiar boredom. Connie was no clothes horse, but even she sometimes took time to try different outfits. His mother had often done the same when he was a child. So now, as then, he sat, waiting impatiently for them to finish . . .

It struck him that he was now completely unconsciously accepting Avelina as a woman. The old Alex Reeve – and definitely Dominic Finch, his birth identity – wouldn't have done so. Connie had changed him more than he'd realised.

Except Connie wasn't here. If anyone had changed him on this subject, it was Avelina herself. Interesting. His mind wandered down the new path. A cover identity so convincing it became real? That was the goal of every deep-cover agent. Except in this case, the subject had no intention of changing back. It wasn't unknown: spies sometimes went native, switched sides. Which would make them a target for their own side.

Just like him. Luckily, SC9 didn't know he was here. That

thought made him wonder about Locke. The next attack by the Bondage Killer would be in five days. Maybe he should use that time to start a more active search for him. His theory that Locke's cover might be medical still seemed sound. He was a trained surgeon, and liked to maintain his skills. Could he be at one of Munich's hospitals? How many did the city have? He would have to ask Avelina—

'Leo!' Speak of the devil. She called out from the shop's rear. 'Can you help me?'

'What with?' he asked, standing.

'I want your opinion.' Frideric emerged from the entrance to the changing area and gestured to him. He shrugged and walked over.

The shopkeeper stepped back with a theatrical wave at a cubicle's closed curtain. 'Avi,' he said. The curtain swept open.

Avelina stood beyond, one arm outstretched in a diva-ish pose. She smiled at him. 'What do you think?'

Reeve took in her outfit. It was a dress of some shiny, silk-like material, purple-blue in colour. His first thought was that it looked like a ballgown, the skirt long and flowing. Her shoulders were bare, revealing a couple of tattoos on her upper arms. Avelina gave him an expectant look. He wasn't sure what he was meant to say. 'It . . . goes with your hair,' he managed.

'And . . . ?' She waited a moment, then tutted. 'Oh, come on. You must have an opinion.'

'I don't know. I don't really have one.'

Avelina frowned. 'Why? Because you still think I'm a boy in girl's clothes?'

'No, because – because I'm not *interested* in clothes.' Frideric gasped at his statement in affected horror. 'You wear what you need to fit in.'

'I don't care about fitting in,' Avelina snorted, with a slight pout. 'I choose clothes that express who I am. This?' She twirled in place, the dress swishing around her. 'It's not my usual style. But it is an expression of my personality. I like to be free, to be feminine – but also to be noticed.'

'Well, it'll do that,' said Reeve.

'Unlike your clothes.' She gave his entirely functional ensemble a critical eye. 'If you were just being yourself, not needing to stay unnoticed . . . what would you wear?'

It was not a question he had given much thought. Certainly not recently. 'I don't know.'

'Okay, what would you wear for Connie?'

He didn't reply at once, brow furrowing. 'I don't know,' he said again.

'Really?'

'I just wore . . . whatever. She never said that she liked one thing over another.' Avelina and Frideric exchanged amused looks. 'What?'

'Oh, she would do,' Frideric chuckled. 'She was just waiting for you to ask what she liked.'

'You don't know her,' Reeve protested, feeling defensive.

Avelina sensed his discomfort. 'We're only joking,' she said apologetically. 'But what did Connie like? How did she dress?'

Reeve hesitated, thinking. Connie flashed through his memory. He could remember her face clearly, places they had been together. But her clothing . . . 'She dressed in –

185

casual stuff?' was the best he could manage. It was as if his mind had blurred out what she wore. That was alarming. He was a trained observer; those details should have been immediately available. So why—

Of course. His training taught him to recognise threats, targets. Connie was anything but. With her, he'd felt safe – and his mind had stopped taking notes. No wonder he'd become sloppy, made mistakes . . . almost been caught. And until now, he hadn't even realised he'd *made* an error, never mind why.

Avelina was about to say something, but again picked up on his state of mind. 'Anyway,' she said, 'this is what I'm going to wear.'

'No chocolate, please,' Frideric said in a stage whisper.

She gave him a mocking look, then turned back to Reeve. 'What about you? What are you going to wear?'

He blew out his cheeks in annoyance. 'I told you, I don't want to go.'

'Sometimes, you have to do things you don't want to. I would think you of all people know that.' She smiled. 'So come on. Choose something.'

Frideric leaned back on one foot, hand cupped thoughtfully to his chin. 'I have the perfect outfit.'

CHAPTER 22

'Frideric was right,' said Avelina. 'It is the perfect outfit.'

'I'm not sure about that,' Reeve replied. But he had to admit his reflection in the bedroom mirror looked good.

Frideric had provided him with a tuxedo. The only time he'd ever previously worn one was for an army squadmate's wedding. That had been lumpy and ill-fitting, a cheap rental. This, however, could have been tailored for him. He turned to check the suit from different angles. It still looked good. Thoughts of James Bond came unbidden into his head. He suppressed a smile. The reality of being a government assassin was considerably less glamorous.

The only thing not right was the bow tie. Again, the only time he'd worn one was for the wedding, years before. Back then, he'd needed help to don it. His attempt this time was lopsided, amateurish.

Avelina noticed it too. 'Oh, your tie. Do you know how to fasten it?'

'No,' he admitted.

'You're lucky – I do. Here.' She moved behind him, reaching around his shoulders. 'I would sometimes go to formal events with Mother. She made me wear them. A fifteen-year-old in a bow tie – I looked ridiculous! But I still remember how to fasten the knot.' She undid, then refastened the tie. 'How is that?'

Reeve checked it. 'Perfect. Thanks.'

She withdrew. 'And how do I look?'

He turned to face her. She was wearing the dress from Frideric's, now accessorised with jewellery. He assumed it belonged to Idonia. Her colourful hair was tied high. 'Good.'

A small smile. 'Is that the best you can say?'

'It still goes with your hair.'

She laughed. 'It's okay. Don't worry. I *feel* good, and that's what matters. Now, are you ready to go?'

'Almost.' Reeve picked up his jeans and rooted through the back pocket. He transferred what he found to the rear of his suit trousers.

'What's that?' Avelina asked.

'Just something useful.'

She looked dubious. 'Remember to take it out after, okay? Frideric won't want to find garbage in his clothes.'

'I will, don't worry. Now I'm ready.'

They left Reeve's room and went downstairs. Steber was waiting in the hall. Avelina asked him a question in German. He responded by indicating Idonia's office. 'Ach, even now she can't stop working,' Avelina sighed. Her eyes then widened in alarm, and she questioningly mimed holding a phone to Steber. He shook his head. 'Good. I just realised, if your friends hear me talk in English, they might get suspicious.'

'It's easy to make a mistake,' said Reeve, nodding. 'I made one before, just one, and they found me.'

'Is that when you had to leave Connie?'

'Yes.'

'Then I will try really hard not to make any more.'

The office door opened. Idonia emerged, wearing a formal, almost severe black and burgundy dress. She regarded Avelina and Reeve with surprise. 'Oh. You both—' Avelina raised a hand in warning. Idonia flinched, then shut the door behind her. 'Sorry. I forgot.'

'It's okay,' said Reeve. 'If your phone's on the desk, it probably didn't pick it up.'

'Your phone *is* on the desk, isn't it?' asked Avelina pointedly.

Her mother bristled. 'Of course it is. Charging. I deliberately let it run down during the day. I thought it might seem strange otherwise if I didn't bring it with me tonight.'

Reeve nodded. 'Good thinking.'

'But as I was about to say, you both look . . . good. A tuxedo suits you,' she told Reeve. 'Mind you, there are not many men it does not.' Her eyes went to Avelina.

'You have something to say, *Mother*?' came the challenging response.

'Not at all. Except that dress is a very pretty colour. It matches your hair.' Avelina grinned at Reeve: *Okay, you were right.* 'I would have preferred if you had asked before borrowing my jewellery.'

'You never minded when I was small,' Avelina replied.

'No. In hindsight, perhaps I should have realised . . .' Idonia addressed her bodyguard. 'Is the car ready, Leopold?' He reacted with surprise. It took her a moment to realise why. 'Oh. *Ist das Auto fertig?*' He responded in the affirmative. 'So easy to forget.'

'Let's go, then.' Avelina held out a hand, as if expecting

189

Reeve to take it. His reaction was less than amused. She grinned. 'That's okay. I'm a very modern girl. I can escort myself.' Still smiling, she led the way to the door, the others following.

Steber drove them the short distance in Idonia's executive BMW. The snow had picked up as night fell, the car's wipers working frenziedly. As a result, Reeve's first full view of Nymphenburg Palace was far from clear. But Avelina had been truthful about its size. All he could see was a seemingly endless wall of lights, every window ablaze.

The car followed several equally expensive vehicles heading for the north wing. Uniformed attendants directed them to a parking area. The BMW's occupants got out. All wore coats; Reeve's, though, was Avelina's utilitarian orange anorak. Even on the short walk to the door, it drew disapproving looks. 'I should have asked Frideric to lend you something nicer,' said Avelina.

To Reeve's surprise, Idonia spoke up for him. 'Nobody will notice after you take it off. They will just see a handsome young man in a tuxedo.'

Avelina couldn't suppress a sly grin. '*Finger weg, Mutter. Er ist mit mir.*'

Idonia shook her head and sighed. Reeve didn't know what Avelina had said – and suspected he was better off that way.

They reached the entrance. A marquee had been erected to provide shelter for those waiting. A man in a formal uniform checked each arrival's invitation against a list. Idonia reached him first, receiving an obsequious half-bow after her

name was found. Steber, as her plus one, was accepted without question. Personal security was apparently not uncommon
amongst Munich's business elite. They went inside.

Avelina and Reeve were next. The man gave the anorak a
sour look. Reeve opened it, revealing the tuxedo beneath.
Slightly mollified, the man extended his hand expectantly
towards him. Avelina took out her invitation from a small
handbag, waving it at him. 'Avelina Foss.'

The man stared at it, then looked back at her. '*Hier steht
Theodore Foss.*'

Avelina was silent for a moment – then erupted in anger.
Reeve only understood the occasional word, but could guess
what she was saying. The luckless functionary was being
accused of transphobia, ignorance, bigotry, and more besides.
But despite the verbal assault, he stuck to the letter of the
rules. '*Ihr Name ist* Avelina *Foss. Die Einladung ist für*
Theodore *Foss. Es gehört nicht Innen.*' He raised a hand,
palm out, to block her entry.

She glared at him, then yelled: '*Mutter!*' Idonia, who had
just given her coat to an attendant, looked back. '*Ich brauche
deine Hilfe bei diesem Idioten!*'

Her mother's irritated huff was audible even from outside.
She returned to the entrance, heels clacking on the polished
floor. Steber came with her, alert for trouble. Idonia quickly,
if reluctantly, explained the situation to the attendant. His
mouth pinched shut, but he nodded and returned Avelina's
invitation. Then he turned to Reeve, asking a question.

'Leo Martin,' Avelina said on his behalf. The man noted
down the name, then gestured for them to enter. She swept
angrily inside, Reeve following.

Idonia was displeased by what had just happened, prompting a muted, hissing familial exchange. Avelina broke it off with a disgusted sound and walked away from her. 'Can you believe that?' she said as she returned to Reeve. 'He wasn't going to let me in! Just because the invitation had my old name. Idiot!'

'He was just doing his job,' said Reeve, feeling some sympathy for the worker. 'How would he know you've changed your name?'

'So? He absolutely did not want to let me in once he realised I was trans.'

'That's not what I meant. He might not even have realised you *were*.'

She started to say more, then frowned. 'Well, I *do* look good tonight,' she muttered sulkily. 'He is still an asshole, though. And Mother . . . huh! I am so mad at her.'

'Why, what did she say?'

'She told him I was having a *phase* of dressing up like a girl. God! I can't believe I moved back in with her. She will never accept me for who I really am. What was I thinking?'

'You straight went to her for help, though,' Reeve pointed out. 'And she got you inside.' Avelina huffed and stalked away to check in her coat. He followed, smiling slightly.

The foyer was a high, airy room with a chequerboard marble floor. A broad staircase led upwards. Around thirty people mingled around its foot, but the guests were gravitating upstairs. The vast majority were over fifty, some considerably older. Avelina was the youngest person in sight by some margin. The only language Reeve could hear was German. He felt suddenly out of place, alone in a crowd.

Avelina gave her coat to a cloakroom attendant. 'Here, take that off,' she said. He handed over the anorak, getting a ticket in return. She regarded his tuxedo. 'Now you look much better. Not so much like a homeless man.'

'Is that how I looked to you?'

She raised a dismissive hand, still irked. 'What can I say?' She noticed Idonia heading up the stairs. 'Come on. Let's go to the main hall, get some champagne.'

They followed Idonia and her bodyguard. Another foyer above connected two busy rooms. The foursome entered the larger one, a long banquet hall with several elaborate chandeliers. A small stage was home to a string quartet. Reeve didn't know the name of the piece they were playing, but it was familiar. James Bond would have known, he imagined with a shrug of his tux.

Idonia stopped to talk to a group of people. Avelina continued past her to find a waiter with a tray of glasses. 'Here,' she said, handing Reeve some champagne before collecting her own. 'Best thing about the whole party. *Prost!* I mean, cheers!' She clinked her glass against his and took a swig.

Reeve sipped his own. He had never been a heavy drinker, but lager was the army standard. Connie had turned him around to wine during their time in Italy. The champagne was sweeter than he liked, but not unpleasant. He had no intention of getting drunk, though. He realised, with small amusement, that Avelina had got what she wanted. He had automatically gone into surveillance mode, watching the guests like a bodyguard.

Avelina was not limiting her own alcohol consumption. Her first glass was emptied in just a few minutes. A waiter replaced it almost immediately. She recognised someone and started talking to them, a small group soon forming. Reeve hovered on its outskirts, isolated by language. Avelina's glass gradually drained again. She was courting attention, enjoying being the centre of curiosity and intrigue.

He remembered from internet searches that she had featured in the news not long before. Numerous guests, men and women, came to chat with her. Were they genuinely interested in her change of gender? Or only because of her relationship to a powerful Munich businesswoman? Not understanding the language, Reeve found it hard to tell. But he did spot that some of the men had distinctly lecherous airs. Mostly older ones, from their clothing and watches very wealthy. Was it because Avelina represented something new and different? Or just power and entitlement expressing as lust?

It wasn't a line of thought he wanted to pursue. The same kind of unchecked power and entitlement had led to SC9's creation. Fuck/kill who you want, either way without consequences . . .

Unsettled, he looked for Idonia. He spotted Steber first, the bodyguard half a head taller than anyone around him. Like Avelina, Idonia was the focus of a group's attention. Also like Avelina, she was enjoying the drink, on at least her second glass.

His feelings of loneliness returned. He wanted Connie here, to help him endure the evening. The party was merely networking for the elite, friends of friends making useful connections. The long hall had an echo, turning all the laughter hollow, fake. He sipped his champagne again, more deeply. Where had Connie gone? Was she safe? He had taught her survival techniques, how to stay alive on the run. But that had only been a fraction of his own training. Was it enough? A grim pall, heavy as the snow outside, settled over him. He *should* have stayed with her. His decision had ended up wounding his heart, bringing only misery. And as for what it had done to *her* . . .

'Alex!' Idonia's voice. He looked around to see her approaching, smiling broadly – and slightly drunkenly. 'I mean, Leo,' she corrected in half-hearted apology. By now she had drawn Avelina's attention as well. She waved for them to join her. 'Both of you, come over here.'

'She looks unusually happy,' Avelina whispered to Reeve. 'Perhaps her boyfriend is here.' She excused herself from the group. Reeve followed with disinterest, still preoccupied by thoughts of Connie.

'Ah, good, good,' said Idonia as they reached her. 'This way.' She led them through the throng. 'Stefan just arrived. I would like you to meet him.'

Avelina giggled. 'Told you,' she said, nudging Reeve.

Idonia rejoined a cluster of guests, exchanging brief greetings. She asked a question; a woman gestured to one side. '*Ah, ja, danke,*' she said. 'Stefan!'

Reeve spotted the man she was addressing. Tall, blond, facing away from them as he spoke to someone. 'Stefan!' Idonia said again, touching his arm. He turned.

Reeve froze. He recognised the man instantly.

Harrison Locke.

CHAPTER 23

Locke faced him, also frozen, equally surprised. Then both men moved simultaneously—

The same instinctive move. Reeve brought his right hand to his chest, fingers sliding into his jacket. Locke did likewise. Again, they froze. Both were reaching for a concealed weapon. Reeve didn't have one. Locke didn't know that – so had paused his own movement. But did *he* have one?

Operative 61 wore a well-tailored tuxedo, similar to his own. It was possible he had a hidden holster beneath it. The gun inside would have to be small, slim. But it didn't have to be large to be lethal.

Locke's cold eyes gave him equal scrutiny. Coming up with the same result. No way to know for sure if the other man was armed. A standoff. How long would it last? If Locke really had a gun, he had no defence . . .

Idonia broke the moment, looking between them in confusion. '*Kennt Ihr euch?*' She repeated the question in English to Reeve. 'Do you know each other?'

Locke spoke first. 'Yes, we do,' he said. He had adopted an accent. Reeve wasn't sure which nationality, but it sounded Nordic. 'He was once a patient of mine. I operated on his arm.'

Reeve twitched at a phantom pain in his right forearm. Locke had caught him there with a knife slash during his escape from Mordencroft. 'Yeah,' he said. 'How's your shoulder? You were having some trouble with it.' He had paid his wound back with interest, using Locke's own knife. Then later, in London, had gouged the surgeon's sutured injury open again with his thumb.

Locke's eyes narrowed behind his large glasses. A disguise; Reeve knew he had perfect eyesight. Every Operative did. 'All healed now.'

Reeve nodded, his gaze still not leaving the other man. He wanted to say something like 'What a shame', but couldn't risk it. If he exposed Locke as a threat, and he *did* have a weapon . . .

Locke might gun down his primary target on the spot.

The guests' shock would allow him to flee the room before anyone could react. The gun would get him the rest of the way out of the building. A police manhunt would begin – but Operatives were trained to evade them. The chances were good that he would escape.

If he had a gun. Reeve still didn't know. But if he did, only Locke's own uncertainty was stopping him from using it.

He had to string out that uncertainty for as long as he could. His life might depend on it. As well as Idonia's, and Avelina's.

'Well, if you know each other, I don't need to introduce you,' Idonia finally chirped. 'But Stefan, this is . . . my child. Born as Theodore, but at the moment using the name Avelina.'

Avelina gave her mother a glare colder than the night

outside. Locke didn't react. He already knew his ghost target's background. 'Good to meet you, Avelina,' he said.

'And . . .' Idonia hesitated, still unable to call Avelina by her self-adopted name. 'And this is Stefan. Doktor Stefan Holke. Munich's new surgical superstar!'

Locke nodded modestly. 'I am just doing my job. Using my abilities to help others.'

Avelina had picked up on the tension between the two men. She gave Reeve a quizzical look. Then her eyes went to Locke. 'Hi, Stefan. Nice to meet you. My mother has talked a lot about you.'

'Nothing alarming, I hope.' Locke's mouth crinkled into a smile. It did not reach his eyes. He returned his full attention to Reeve. Both men's right hands were still raised, neither willing to be first to back down. In Reeve's case, maintaining the bluff. He still couldn't tell if Locke was doing the same. 'I was not expecting to see you here. What brings you to Munich?'

Reeve took a moment to reply. How much dare he reveal in front of the people he was protecting? 'The Bondage Killer,' he finally said. Locke's only visible reaction was the tiniest flicker of his eyes. 'I know who he is.'

'That is . . . interesting,' Locke replied. His hand slid slightly deeper into his jacket. Reeve did the same. But Locke's threat was not aimed directly at the other Englishman. The Operative gave the Fosses pointed glances. Reeve got the message. *Say anything more and I will kill them.* But . . . would he? *Could* he?

He could – if he had to. Even an unarmed Operative could kill an unsuspecting target in an instant. Reeve tensed, letting Locke see that he was ready to fight—

The Operative's hand retreated, slightly. 'I have actually just remembered something,' he said. 'While you are here, I should ask you about it. A medical matter,' he added, to Idonia. 'To follow up on my patient. So I must ask for a moment of privacy.'

Idonia was surprised, but nodded. 'Of course.'

'It will not take long. I will be back shortly.' He addressed Reeve. 'If you will lead the way to somewhere quiet?'

'After you,' Reeve insisted. Locke gave him another cold look, but started for the upper foyer.

'What's going on?' Avelina whispered as Reeve followed him past her.

'Tell you when I get back.' The Fosses exchanged uncertain glances.

The stairs were separated from the foyer by a solid balustrade. Locke led Reeve to an empty spot overlooking the stairwell. The two men stood facing each other, just beyond arm's reach. 'Alex Reeve,' Locke said. Despite his flat, unemotional voice, the name still sounded like a curse. 'You should have stayed in hiding.'

'You can drop the accent,' Reeve replied.

'My apologies.' No contrition was intended, and the accent remained in place. 'I'm maintaining my cover. It becomes second nature. As I'm sure you know from when you were Angelo Moretti in Italy.'

SC9 had discovered his false identity, then. He had expected it, but the confirmation was still unwelcome. It was another reminder that he'd been careless, sloppy. And it had cost him everything. 'Yeah, I remember. I was having a nice relaxing time there. You should have left me alone.' A harder edge to his voice. 'It would have been better for everyone. Especially the four Operatives I killed.'

'You brought it on yourself,' Locke reminded him. 'Looking for information about your father's early release from prison was a foolish mistake. It exposed your location. We would have found you eventually,' he added. Not a boast; a statement. 'But you would at least have had more time with Connie.' The tight little smile reappeared – this time with a hint of malevolent mockery. 'Where is she? I do hope she's well.'

Did that mean SC9 hadn't found her? Or was Locke taunting him, knowing she was dead? The latter thought filled Reeve with sudden anger. He forced it under control. 'So. You're the Bondage Killer.'

The Operative gave him a probing look. 'What brought you to that conclusion?'

'I'm not the only one who made a foolish mistake.' Locke drew in a breath, a flare of ire in his eyes. 'You left a calling card. Maybe nobody else spotted it, but I did. I know you. You're a perfectionist – but you're not as perfect as you like to think.'

'Nobody's perfect,' said Locke, but it was clear the criticism had stung. 'And what might this mistake have been?'

'I'll let you stew over that. But if I saw it, someone else will eventually.'

'*Eventually* will do them little good.'

'So Avelina's your next ghost target, huh? And you'll kill your real target, Idonia, at the same time?'

Locke stared calculatingly at Reeve for a long moment.

'You know, in training, the consensus was that you were not terribly bright, probably autistic. It seems we underestimated you.' His expression darkened. 'A mistake that will be easy to correct.'

'I'm going to stop you from killing them,' Reeve growled. 'I'm going to bring down SC9. And I'm going to expose Sir Simon Scott as the *real* traitor to the country.'

A flicker of surprise on Locke's face. 'Scott is dead.'

'What?'

'Tony Maxwell killed him.'

Reeve was thrown by the revelation, unsure how to react. 'What do you mean?'

'Scott took personal charge of the hunt for you in Italy. It went out of control. As you said, four Operatives killed, very publicly. Maxwell challenged him on it, and Scott removed him from his post. So he went to the UK intelligence chiefs for support. He claimed Scott's actions were a threat to British security.' Locke's lips curled, very slightly. Did he disapprove of what had happened? 'They agreed – so Maxwell shot him and ordered an immediate stand-down.'

Reeve's mind flashed back to events in Venice. Stone and Flynn had almost caught him . . . then unexpectedly withdrawn. Were they obeying Maxwell's order? 'So where's Tony now?'

'He took over as head of SC9. He was the one who assigned me to this operation.'

He gave Locke a startled look. 'Tony *approved* it?'

'He *devised* it.'

'The whole serial-killer cover? I can see a sick bastard like you coming up with that. Not him.'

'Believe what you will,' said Locke icily. 'Scott had another approach in mind. Something about political militants opposed to the arms trade, I believe. When Maxwell took over, he scrapped it and came up with this plan. He said I was ideally suited to it.'

'No, I can't believe that.' It was completely contrary to Reeve's image of Maxwell. His former mentor was a professional above all else. Get the job done, cleanly, efficiently. Quietly. This kind of sadistic showboating seemed utterly out of character.

'If you won't take my word for it, perhaps you should take his.' Locke reached towards his jacket. Reeve's right hand instantly snapped back into his own. 'My phone. Don't worry. I have no intention of starting a public firefight. Unless I have to.'

'Left hand,' said Reeve.

Locke let out a faint sigh, but obeyed. He fished out his phone. Several keypad presses before he dialled a contact; he was activating a scrambler. 'Tony, it's Stefan,' he said, when it was answered. 'I've unexpectedly run into a . . . mutual friend. Someone we haven't seen since last September.' He listened to the reply. 'Yes, that's right. Here.' He held the phone out to Reeve. 'He wants to talk to you.'

Reeve took the phone and retreated slightly, keeping a wary eye on the Operative. 'Hello?'

'Hello, Alex.' Tony Maxwell. 'The last time we spoke in person, I thought we had an agreement. Détente. You leave us alone, and we'll return the favour. For you and Connie.'

'Scott didn't go for it,' said Reeve. 'He tried to have us both killed.'

'He lost control of the operation. So I removed him. You would have been safe.'

'I didn't know that.'

'You should have figured it out. Do you think Scott would have let you get out of Italy? Out of Venice, even? He would have had every single Operative hunting for you, backed by MI6 and GCHQ. The only reason you and Connie aren't dead is because I *let* you live. I thought you were smart enough to realise that.' Maxwell didn't sound angry, just disappointed. That somehow stung Reeve more than any other criticism.

But he had greater concerns. 'You mean – SC9 wasn't looking for Connie?'

'No. Nor you. Like I said, I thought we had an agreement.'

A sick horror rose inside Reeve as he realised the full implications of Maxwell's revelation. If SC9 had stood down its hunt for him and Connie . . .

He had left her behind for nothing. They could have stayed together. They would have been safe.

But now—

Maxwell already knew where his thoughts were leading. The sounds of the party seemed to fade to nothing, leaving only his voice. 'But you broke that agreement, Alex. You've interfered in one of our operations. So now I don't have a choice. I have to declare you Fox Red again. You're a kill-on-sight target. And the same applies to Connie.'

'No!' Reeve barked, desperate. 'Leave her out of this.'

'I can't. And you know that. She knows too much about SC9 – thanks to you.'

The churning nausea rose higher, threatening to overwhelm him. Reeve battled to maintain his composure. Locke watched him intently. Had he guessed what Maxwell was saying? Would he risk blowing his cover to attack him? 'No,' he said, trying to turn the tables. 'You back down – or I'll release the stolen SC9 files to the media.'

But Maxwell was again ahead of him. 'No, you won't. Why risk your life coming to Germany to interfere with our operation? You could have exposed us from wherever you were hiding. I don't think you have Craig's phone any more, Alex.'

'I have his password. You *know* I do.' He had proved it by showing Maxwell pages from files detailing his past assassinations. 'I can give it to the media at any time. They already have the files; all they need is the decryption password.'

'That would expose *all* the files,' Maxwell countered. 'Every single one. Which would cause massive diplomatic damage to Britain. You think our allies would shrug off learning that we've assassinated their officials and politicians? You weren't willing to harm the whole country before. I don't think you will now. Alex . . .' A new urgent intensity, voice dropping. 'I gave you two chances already. This is your last. Leave Munich, *now*. Run. Go somewhere far off our radar, and never come back. And if you want to keep Connie safe, take her with you.'

'I *can't*.' The words erupted from him, unbidden, uncontrolled. He realised too late how much anger and despair was in the last. Maxwell inhaled, as if about to speak, then fell silent. The image of his face flashed through Reeve's mind. Expressions crossing it in rapid succession: surprise, calculation . . . *intrigue*.

He had just told the head of SC9 that Connie was alone, vulnerable. He had made her a target again.

And there was absolutely nothing he could do to protect her.

Another breath. This time, Maxwell spoke. 'It's your choice, Alex. I'll order Harrison to let you walk away. If you decide not to . . . well. Now, give the phone back to him.'

Numbly, Reeve did so, his mind a blur of conflicting feelings. What to do? He didn't know. Save himself, but sacrifice Avelina and Idonia? If he did walk away, would Locke let him go, whatever Maxwell's orders? He was still a threat to the Operative and his mission.

But SC9 could carry out their plan whatever he did. They would kill Idonia to end the merger, no matter what. And without a confession from Locke, he had nothing to prove his story. No proof that SC9 even existed. A crushing weight descended upon him. They had already won . . .

Locke spoke quietly into the phone. Answering Maxwell's questions. 'No,' said the Operative, regarding Reeve with clinical appraisal. 'I don't know, but likely.' Reeve guessed what he was being asked. Could he kill him right now without blowing his cover? Had Reeve told the Fosses about SC9, and the true identity of Doktor Stefan Holke? One more sentence from Maxwell – a command, not a question. 'Understood,' said Locke. His eyes never left Reeve, even as he ended the call and pocketed his phone.

Reeve felt adrenalin surge through his body. Fight or flight – he would do one or the other very soon. 'Going to try to kill me?' he asked, hand back inside his jacket. Maintaining the bluff until the last.

'Maxwell said I should let you leave,' Locke replied. 'If I were you, I would. Quickly.'

Bright colour amongst the guests caught Reeve's eye. Avelina had entered the upper foyer, looking for him. Locke realised who he had seen. 'You can't protect them,' he went on. 'Not them, and not Connie.' Reeve turned back to him, fury rising. Locke smiled. There was no humour behind it, only gloating. 'It doesn't matter where you run to. We *will* find you, and kill you. We will kill her. *I* will kill her. And enjoy it.'

'You sick *fuck*,' Reeve hissed.

His rage merely widened the repellent smile. 'What I've been doing to these freaks, here in Munich? That will be nothing compared to what I do to a real woman.' His lips widened far enough to reveal coldly grinning teeth. 'Like Connie.'

Reeve knew he was being goaded. But before he could stop himself—

His fist slammed into Locke's face.

CHAPTER 24

Reeve's blow broke Locke's oversized glasses. Blood spurted from the Operative's nostrils. Locke fell back against the balustrade. He had known the punch was coming – but still let it land. Reeve knew he should be asking *why*. But all he could do was stamp his heel down on the other man's chest. A woman shrieked, other voices nearby rising in alarm. Reeve kicked Locke again, harder. He gasped in pain.

'Alex!' Avelina shouted as she ran to him. 'Stop, stop!' He glanced towards her, seeing Idonia behind, then back down at Locke—

Someone tackled him, slamming him against the balustrade. He instinctively lashed out, cracking his assailant in the face with an elbow. The man stumbled back. But now more people were shouting, calling for help. Another man grabbed at Reeve's jacket and yanked him backwards. Locke's foot snapped upwards, catching him in the groin. It looked like a flailing, lucky hit. It was anything but. Reeve bent double, momentarily overcome by the sickening pain. By the time he recovered, a uniformed attendant was on him. The new arrival threw him to the floor and pinned him down. Reeve thrashed, but couldn't break loose from the knee on his neck. His breath rasped in his throat. Another man knelt on his legs, trapping him.

Avelina shouted in German. Reeve squinted up at her. She was trying to help him. But now more attendants had arrived, forming a cordon, ushering the onlookers back. Someone helped Locke stand. He wiped blood from his upper lip. A burst of frenetic, outraged German. His tone was shocked: *He just attacked me for no reason!* A couple of guests came to check on him – calling him by name. Doktor Holke was an invitee, known to the organisers. Reeve was not. It was obvious who they considered the instigator.

Avelina pushed through the cordon, crouching beside Reeve. 'He says you hit him – he wants to press charges! The police are already on the way.'

Considering the wealth and power of the party's guests, Reeve wasn't surprised. 'If they arrest me, I'll be killed,' he managed to rasp. 'SC9 will find me.'

Avelina rose and spoke urgently with Idonia. In turn, Idonia called out to an authoritative-looking man, engaging him in hurried discussion. The response was not positive, especially once Locke joined in. Avelina came back to him. This time, an attendant tried to block her. She leaned around him. 'That's the deputy mayor of Munich,' she told Reeve. 'He knows Doktor Holke – he wants you to be arrested.'

He swore silently. Locke had established a perfect cover, ingratiating himself with the city's upper crust. They would side with the man who seemed to be one of them. Reeve wouldn't be able to talk his way out of being detained.

His own plan had failed. Now the Fosses would have to take action to protect themselves. 'He's not Holke,' he hissed. 'He's *Locke*. He's the Bondage Killer.'

Avelina's eyes went wide. She sprang up and darted to her mother, pulling her away from Locke. The Operative watched coldly as she relayed in a whisper what Reeve had told her. Idonia gave Locke an uncertain, fearful look. He moved towards her – and she shrank back. Locke glared down at Reeve with a silent promise of retribution.

Commotion on the stairs, boots clattering up them. Two heavy-set male police officers arrived, asking what had happened. Avelina, then Idonia, spoke up first—

But were drowned out by the men. The cops immediately deferred to the latter group. The deputy mayor issued commands, ignoring Avelina's protests. 'They're going to arrest you!' she warned Reeve.

He already knew that, and was readying himself. The man kneeling on him shifted position to await police instructions. The weight on his neck eased—

He twisted his upper body sharply, catching the man off guard. His arm lashed up. The heel of his palm crashed against the German's jaw. His target fell backwards. The second man holding his legs tried to restrain him. Reeve managed to pull one foot free. He kicked out, catching him in the side. The man tumbled to the floor.

Reeve jumped up. Where were the—

Something smashed down on his right shoulder.

A baton. The cops were right behind him. Pained, right arm numbing, he tried to flee through the shocked crowd—

A sudden stabbing agony in his back – and he fell. He'd been shot by a Taser. Every muscle burned, locked solid, paralysed. Electrical pulses hit him in rapid succession, each more excruciating than the last. He had been subjected to

Tasers in his military and SC9 training. His mind had, perhaps out of trauma, wiped the memory of the pain they caused. Now it returned in full force. He couldn't even cry out, jaw clenched helplessly shut.

Feet clomped around him, shiny black boots before his face. The agonising pulses slowed – then cut out. He instantly slumped, muscles liquefied. Before he could recover, his arms were yanked behind his back. Cold metal closed around his wrists. Ratchets clicked – and he was handcuffed.

He was dragged upright, patted down. The only thing of note he was carrying was his wallet. It was extracted from his jacket pocket, flicked through. A small amount of money inside, no ID. One of the cops barked a question at him. Reeve blinked in bleary incomprehension. The words were repeated, louder. 'I don't speak German,' he tried to say. It came out as a breathless mumble.

Someone spoke with urgent authority to the cops. Reeve turned his head, fighting nausea. The deputy mayor. Avelina tried to interrupt, but was ignored. She called upon Idonia for help. But the elder Foss was shellshocked by what she had just witnessed. Or by what Reeve had told her. Locke lurked over her shoulder, watching him coldly. His presence alone was meant as a threat. *Say anything, and I will kill them . . .*

A bluff. It had to be. The cops were too close. And Reeve was now sure the Operative wasn't armed. That gave Avelina and Idonia a chance to escape.

If they took it . . .

The deputy mayor issued a final order. The cops pulled Reeve up and headed for the staircase. He looked back for Idonia, Avelina – and Locke. 'Holke is the Bondage Killer!'

he managed to shout. 'He's going to kill you both!' Enough people understood English to react with shock and alarm. The eyes of Munich's elite flicked towards Locke. Then Reeve lost sight of the trio as he was brought down the stairs.

He had done all he could to help the Fosses. Now, his priority was saving himself. Locke would report back to Maxwell as soon as he could.

And then, SC9 would come to finish the job they had started two years earlier.

Eliminate their rogue asset.

Avelina watched Reeve's departure with fear and uncertainty. What should she do? Go with him as a witness, and try to help? Get her mother to pay his bail? But a look towards Idonia gave her the answer. Holke – Locke – stood behind her. His gaze fell upon Avelina. For a split-second, his mask of urbane implacability dropped. The face of a cold, remorseless predator was exposed. Then the disguise snapped back up – but she had seen through it. She knew the truth.

And he knew that she knew.

A new fear hit her. More urgent – *primal*. She was being hunted . . . and the hunter was right there. For a moment she was paralysed, unable to breathe. Then she fought through it. 'Mother,' she whispered. 'We've got to go. Now.'

'I . . .' Idonia hesitated, regarding the other guests nearby. She didn't want to leave the event early. But self-preservation quickly overcame social niceties. 'Yes, you're right,' she said quietly. 'Tell Leopold to get the car.'

Avelina nodded. Steber was not far away. She spoke to him as her mother made apologies to her companions.

Idonia's farewell to Locke was strained. 'Idonia,' he replied, 'I can assure you that everything he said is nonsense. It wouldn't be professional for me to discuss former patients. But . . . I do not believe he is mentally stable.' He shook his head sorrowfully. 'I hope this unfortunate incident will not affect things between us.'

'No, no, everything is fine,' said Idonia. 'But – well, I'm a little shaken after what happened. A fight, violence, here? I'm afraid it's rather spoiled the party.'

Avelina touched her arm. 'Leopold's gone to get the car.'

'Good. I'm so sorry,' she went on to the wider group, 'but I have to go. I'll see you all again soon, I'm sure.' She said goodbyes. Locke was the last to receive one. He echoed it, with a cold, thoughtful expression.

'Come on,' Avelina muttered, leading her mother to the stairs.

'What are we going to do about Alex?' Idonia asked as they descended.

'I don't know. I really don't know.'

Locke watched the two women go. Once they were out of sight, he excused himself. His bloodied lip provided an obvious reason. He headed for the toilets – but stopped before reaching them and made a secure call.

'Yes?' said Maxwell, answering almost immediately.

'Reeve's been arrested,' Locke replied.

His superior's response was irate. 'I told you to give him a chance to leave.'

'He didn't take it.' Truth by omission, but Maxwell couldn't know that. 'He attacked me, and event security pinned him down. There are several VIPs here, so the police arrived almost immediately. Now that he's in custody, he can finally be eliminated.'

'I'll send Operatives to Munich to deal with him.'

Locke was surprised. 'I can handle it myself.'

'No. Did Alex blow your cover?'

'He accused me of being the Bondage Killer, yes,' was the reluctant reply.

'Just to the target? Or publicly?'

'Publicly. But I can still—'

'Your cover's blown,' Maxwell interrupted. 'Bug out, immediately. We'll switch to a backup plan.'

'That's not necessary.' Locke suppressed his rising anger. 'The targets have just left. I can still catch them at their home. It simply means accelerating the schedule.'

'It means completely wrecking the serial killer cover. And Alex has named you, specifically. If the Fosses are killed, you're automatically a suspect. That would lead to a full investigation. Walk away, *now*. That's an order.'

The Operative clenched his jaw. 'I understand,' he said. 'I'll leave immediately.'

'Good. I'll find out where Alex is being held. Someone else will deal with him. Call me when you're out of the country.'

'Understood.' Locke rang off.

Externally, he appeared calm. Inside, he was seething. Months of preparation, readying the perfect kill – and now it was all *wasted*?

No! He refused to accept that. He could still complete the mission. It would mean diverting from the Bondage Killer's established modus operandi, yes. But serial killers were, by definition, insane. They did not act rationally, and could kill driven by impulse rather than design. And while Reeve had accused him of being the killer, he *hadn't* publicly mentioned SC9. There was no overt political connection, no link to Britain. He could still ensure Idonia Foss never told anyone what Reeve might have revealed. He could even find the damn recording that British Intelligence were so keen to obtain.

If he acted quickly. If he carried out his assignment.

Tonight.

He continued to the bathroom and quickly cleaned his face. Then, without a word to anyone, he slipped from the party.

His final targets awaited.

CHAPTER 25

The police car headed through the dark, snowy streets towards Munich's centre. Reeve guessed he was being taken to police headquarters rather than a local station. The deputy mayor's involvement had made him a more important suspect. That was good in one respect. A longer journey gave him more time to free himself.

It was bad in another. Security would be much higher. If he didn't escape the car, he probably wouldn't escape at all.

He was in the back seat, hands cuffed behind him and seatbelt fastened. His muscles still ached, residual cramp from the Taser. But his shock-jangled senses had returned to normal. He took in every aspect of his surroundings. The car was a BMW 5 Series. The space in the rear was limited, both front seats pushed back. The two cops were each over six feet tall, and beefy with it. After securing him, neither paid him particular attention. He remained still, not giving them reason to do so. To their minds, he was going nowhere.

The car reached the far end of the Nymphenburg Canal and turned south. Reeve recognised the route. It was the one he had taken with Avelina to reach Idonia's house. The central railway station was only a few minutes away.

He doubted police headquarters was far from it.

He had to move now.

Reeve shifted slightly, easing his hands to one side. The movement was enough to draw a glance from the cop in the passenger seat. He fell still again. A moment, and the German looked away, satisfied he wasn't trying anything.

He was mistaken.

Reeve slipped two fingers into his back pocket. They probed, finally reaching its contents. A couple of crumpled receipts were the disguise for his real objective.

The piece of drinking straw he had prepared in Bled, days earlier.

He gripped the sliver of plastic between his fingers and slowly extracted it. *Careful, careful.* If he dropped it, he was doomed. With infinite care, he twisted his right hand around to reach his restraint. He had cut open the straw so it would fit into a handcuff's ratchet. He guided it in. The pressure of the metal against his wrist grew as the cuff was pushed tighter. It would get worse, he knew. SC9 had taught him the escape technique. The only way to free himself was first to *strengthen* his bonds . . .

He wiggled the straw, driving it further in, millimetre by millimetre. The cuff's edge ground into his wrist. Resistance grew the deeper his makeshift tool went. He felt the thin plastic flexing under the pressure. Only the straw's curvature kept it from bending. If it gave way, it would become useless. The discomfort of steel against bone finally became actual pain. He let out an involuntary grunt. Only faint – but the cop heard it and looked back.

Reeve froze. The officer regarded him with suspicion,

registering that Reeve's hands had moved. Had he guessed what he was doing? The trick was far from unknown. If he told the driver to pull over so he could check the prisoner—

A warning frown – then the cop turned away. Reeve contained his relief. Instead he concentrated on his task. The pain worsened as he kept pushing. The straw needed to completely cover the ratchet's pawl. Once it did . . .

The force crushing his wrist suddenly slackened.

The snippet of plastic had made it through. It now separated ratchet from pawl, releasing the pressure on the former. He raised his thumb and hooked it against the cuff, pulling. The steel restraint moved. A faint clacking as the ratchet's teeth bumped over the pawl. Reeve looked up – but the cops hadn't heard. The sound was drowned out by the *thwap* of the wipers.

He leaned back against the seat and forced the cuff fully open. The cushion stopped it from springing noisily apart. He brought his left wrist free and pulled out the straw. He would still need it to release his other hand. But not yet. His first priority was getting out of the car.

A message over the radio. The cops listened, one saying something. But it didn't concern them. The man in the passenger seat glanced at Reeve, then looked ahead again.

Reeve slowly moved his hand to his seatbelt buckle. A careful push of the release button. The belt came loose. He brought it across his front, then readied himself. A shift of his right foot, pushing his sole against the base of his seat. He needed as much leverage as he could get. A pause as the driver, on the left, brought the car around a turn. Pick the moment. Both cops were watching the road ahead—

Reeve lunged forward, propelling himself between the front seats.

He grabbed the passenger by the throat – digging the open cuff's point fiercely into his neck. Simultaneously he chopped his left hand hard to break the driver's nose. Hot blood splashed his wrist. Another ruthless strike, this time hitting the man's Adam's apple. The cop convulsed, tongue out, choking. One final blow with his balled fist – and the driver slumped in his seat.

The other cop clawed at Reeve's hand. Reeve squeezed harder. The German let out a strangled rasp of pain. He thrashed at his attacker's face – then fumbled for his gun—

Reeve punched him with his left hand. The blow was awkward – but still strong enough. The cop gasped, momentarily dazed. Reeve used that moment to grab the wheel and yank it hard to the right.

The car skidded, bounding over a kerb – at a lamppost.

Reeve pulled back just before impact and braced himself. The crash slammed him against the rear of the passenger seat. The cop himself was flung forward, the seatbelt catching him with a sharp jerk. The semi-conscious driver flailed like a rag doll.

Reeve fell back on to the rear seat. Even prepared, the collision had still shaken him. No time to wait for his head to clear, though. He had to get out. The rear doors would be child-locked; he didn't waste time trying them. Instead he scrambled over the front seats, thudding down on the centre console.

The cop on the passenger side was recovering. Reeve brutally elbowed him in the side of the head. The man cried out. Reeve grabbed the driver's door release and shoved it open. He hauled himself from the car, rolling out into snow. Onlookers gasped, stepping back nervously as he stood. He belatedly realised he was still in his tuxedo. The scene must have looked straight out of a movie.

He got his bearings, turning back towards the Fosses' house. If they had decided to leave Munich, Locke would have one chance to catch them. And Reeve would have one chance to catch *him* – and save them.

He broke into a run through the falling snow.

CHAPTER 26

Harrison Locke rented two flats in Munich. One was large and luxurious, in an upscale neighbourhood. The apartment of Stefan Holke, in keeping with a surgeon's income and standing.

The other was much smaller, barely furnished. That was of no importance to Locke. He had no intention of ever staying there. It was simply a bolt-hole, a place to store his equipment. He kept the Bondage Killer entirely separate from his cover identity.

He hurried up the stairs, head down, to the flat's entrance. He had never encountered any of his neighbours, and hoped not to start now. The narrow hallway was empty. He unlocked the door and slipped inside.

His phone chimed within seconds of his entry. The flat had been equipped with a motion-activated security system. If anyone came in, he would be alerted. Nobody ever had; he was merely being cautious. But he wanted a warning system in case the police found his lair.

He raised his phone, which recognised his face and unlocked. A quick tap and the security app opened. He saw himself on the screen, looking at his phone in infinite recursion. Another tap and the alert was cancelled.

Locke pocketed the phone and went into the bedroom. There was no bed, just a large built-in wardrobe. He opened it. His leather bag was inside, already packed and prepared. Everything he needed to complete his mission was within.

He quickly changed into more anonymous clothes. A tuxedo was on the conspicuous side. Once ready, he donned an overcoat and shoes. Neither had been worn before; both would be incinerated later. He was ready.

The Foss house was around ten minutes' drive away. Locke picked up his bag, then left.

Orders or otherwise, he would complete his mission tonight.

Steber led Idonia and Avelina into the house. Warning trills sounded. He opened the alarm panel and deactivated the system. 'If you'll wait here,' he said, 'I'll check the house.'

'Are you sure that's necessary?' asked Idonia as she locked the front door.

'Just being safe, Frau Foss.' He went to check the other potential points of entry, soon returning. 'All secure,' he announced, closing the library door behind him.

'Good,' said Avelina. 'I need to let Peppo out.' She hurried upstairs. Peppo had been left in her bedroom. She entered, and he dashed to greet her. 'Oh, good boy! Hi!' To her surprise, her mother had followed her to her room. 'Are you okay?'

'Shaken,' said Idonia, sitting on Avelina's bed. 'Stefan is really the Bondage Killer? I can hardly believe it.'

Avelina sat beside her. Peppo hopped up too, tail wagging.

'But he knew Alex, though. And Alex knew him. They were both shocked to see each other – I could tell.'

'So could I. Which only leaves two possibilities. Alex is trying to frame Stefan as a serial killer. Or . . .'

'He's telling the truth,' Avelina concluded for her. 'Stefan really is this Harrison Locke.'

'Yes. I know.' She rubbed her watch, thinking. 'Everything Alex said made sense. About the merger being a threat to British interests. And I've definitely made an enemy in the British arms industry. But enough to kill me for?'

'There are millions of euros at stake. Maybe even billions, if the merger is that big.'

'It will be.'

'That's a good reason to want the merger to fail. Will it, without you?'

Idonia nodded. 'Without me, there wouldn't *be* a merger.'

A glum silence followed, broken by Avelina. 'How did you meet Stefan in the first place?'

'Through the hospital's board of directors. They held a function a few months ago. The usual networking soirée. Stefan was their new star surgeon; they were showing him off. He'd just come here from Denmark. He was very charming.' Disquiet in her voice as she reviewed her memories of the event. 'He was . . . interested in me, right from the start. I thought it was because we sparked together. Maybe it was something else . . .'

Avelina put a comforting hand on her arm. Another quiet moment, then she stood, Peppo sitting up attentively. 'We need to get Alex out of police custody.'

'I doubt I have enough influence to get him off an assault

charge. Especially not after the deputy mayor got involved. I can pay his bail, though.'

'If he's still alive. Or if *we're* still alive.'

Idonia frowned, concerned. 'All right,' she said. 'I'll ask Reynold for more security. Then we'll go to the lodge – both of us. I can complete the merger from there if I have to.'

'Do you think that'll be safe?'

'It's five hundred kilometres away, in another country.' A sharp breath. 'God, I told Stefan about the lodge. I even invited him to it! And he's been *here*, in the house. If he really is the Bondage Killer . . .' She looked sickened. 'We have to go. Tonight. I don't feel safe here. At least the lodge is a long way from Munich. And I only told Stefan it was in Zermatt, not exactly where.'

'SC9 will know, though,' Avelina pointed out. 'And once you start making plans, they'll know where we're going.'

'Perhaps. But we'll have bodyguards to protect us.'

'What about Alex?'

'I'll do what I can to have him released on bail. Then I'll arrange for someone to bring him to the lodge.'

'Are we going tonight?'

'Given the circumstances, I think leaving as soon as possible would be a good idea. Leopold can drive us.'

Avelina nodded. 'Okay. I'll get my stuff. And Peppo's.'

Idonia pursed her lips as if about to refuse the latter, then relented. 'All right. I'll phone Reynold, then get ready.' She left Avelina to change out of her party dress.

Now free of the cuffs, Reeve ran through the Munich streets, breath steaming. Without a coat he was cold, but he forced himself not to feel it. Heavy snowfall whirled around him.

The foul weather gave him a small amount of cover. He was having to use side streets, lengthening his journey. Taking the most direct route would leave him exposed. He had already had to duck out of sight of police cars. He had attacked two officers; they wouldn't abandon the search.

About halfway to the house. He still had to cross the Nymphenburg Canal – a dangerous choke point. If the cops guessed his destination, they could trap him on the pedestrian bridge.

No choice but to risk it. He had blown Locke's cover. Either Operative 61 would bug out and let others perform the assassination . . .

Or he would finish his task ahead of schedule. Tonight.

If Locke were sane, he would do the former. There was no point taking unnecessary chances. But Locke was a psychopath. He hid his madness well, behind ability and urbanity. But it was there. Reeve had witnessed the rage burning behind his cold mask. Once it was unleashed, only one thing would contain it again.

The taking of a life. Or lives.

A siren gave him advance warning of danger. He slowed, hunching between parked cars. A police vehicle drove through crossroads ahead. Hunting for him. He waited for it to pass, then resumed his run.

If he didn't make it in time, Avelina and Idonia Foss would die.

Locke parked near the canal two streets from the Foss residence. His car would have been seen by traffic cameras en route. No matter; it wasn't registered to him. Like the second flat, the anonymous Volkswagen Golf had been provided by MI6. He had surveyed the area several times over the past months. This spot was not overlooked by CCTV cameras and had low foot traffic. Even on a clear day, he would have drawn little attention. At night, in a snowstorm, he would be almost invisible.

He collected his bag and exited the car. Head lowered, he made his way through the snow. Nördliche Auffahrtsallee, along the canal's side, would be the quickest way. It would also be the busiest, and he didn't want to be seen. Instead he took a more roundabout route to the Foss house. Lights on inside. Good; they hadn't fled immediately after Reeve's warning. A check of his surroundings. All clear.

He headed for his destination. Not the house, but the apartment building next to it. Another place he had previously surveyed. It had a vehicle entrance, and a side pedestrian gate. He entered the latter. No recent footprints in the snow. He walked down the path, leaving his own prints in his wake. The heavy snowfall would soon obscure them.

Locke stopped short of the apartment building. A tall bush blocked the view from its windows. Nobody inside could see him. He went to the wall adjoining the Foss property and peered over it. From here, he could see the rear garden. At least a foot of snow covered everything. He needed to leave the minimum trail to his point of entrance. One glance from a window could alert the targets to his presence. But he had already planned his approach on a visit to the house. Aerial photos and Street View's 3D mode had shown him additional detail. Once over the wall, he could skirt behind bushes to near the house's southwestern corner. From there, a basement-level entrance was only a few metres away. There were no lights above that part of the lawn. He could reach it unseen.

The house's alarm would have been deactivated when the Fosses returned home. He assumed the large, besuited man lurking near Idonia at the party was a bodyguard. A potential threat? Unlikely. Not against an Operative. Once he was removed, he could move on to his real targets.

A familiar tingle of anticipation began to rise at the thought.

He easily scaled the wall and dropped into the piled, virgin snow beyond. Bent low, he made his way around the garden. The traversal did not take long. His entry point was at the foot of semicircular steps cut into the lawn's edge. The basement room was dark. The windows above it were lit, but blocked by curtains. Nobody would see him.

Locke quickly crossed the lawn and descended the snow-covered steps. He shone his torch through the French doors into the room beyond. A library. Ideal; it was unlikely anyone would come in unexpectedly at this time.

He turned his attention to the doors themselves. His torch beam revealed a simple lock. He knew he could pick it. Less than a minute later, it was open. No alarm. He slipped inside, closing the doors behind him.

He stood still, listening. Faint sounds of activity from above. Heavy footfalls; the bodyguard? An inconvenience to deal with. But he had dealt with similar issues before. The man's death would, like Idonia's, appear to be collateral damage. Fallout from the Bondage Killer's objective.

Locke had already decided: to hell with Maxwell's orders. Once he started a mission, he completed it. He was not going to walk away from this one, not after all his work. He still had another assassination to carry out.

And he was going to enjoy it.

Quietly, carefully, he removed his coat and began to change into his medical coveralls.

Steber descended the stairs to the ground floor. Both his charges were packing everything they might need for the next several days. A trip to Switzerland? He hadn't expected it, but working in private security often brought surprise assignments. He didn't mind. He enjoyed travel, and besides, would earn a handsome bonus.

First, he needed to ready the car. He started down the hall towards the front door—

He paused. Why, he wasn't sure. There was just an odd feeling that something had changed . . .

Steber looked around the hall. His gaze finally settled on the door at the foot of the lower stairs. It was half-open. Hadn't he closed it? He was fairly sure he had. But he didn't think Frau Foss or her . . . *offspring* had been down there.

Should he raise the alarm? Not yet, he decided. He couldn't remember for sure if the door had been open or not. But it couldn't hurt to check.

He descended the stairs. The library was dark. He pushed the door fully open and switched on the light. Nothing seemed any different from when he had checked the exterior door earlier. Just paranoia, then—

He was about to turn off the light when he noticed

something. A discolouration on the carpet, by the outside door. A couple of steps closer revealed what it was. A damp patch.

As if someone had tracked in snow from the garden.

Steber opened his mouth to shout a warning—

No sound emerged. A hand clamped with terrible force over his mouth, pulling his head back.

The last thing he ever felt was a carbon-fibre blade slicing his carotid artery.

Locke kept hold of the bodyguard until he fell still, then carefully lowered him. He wiped his combat knife clean on the dead man's jacket, then resheathed it.

The threat had been removed.

Now it was time to find his targets.

CHAPTER 27

Avelina finished packing. Not that she had much to pack. Most of her possessions had been destroyed in the fire. Almost all she had were the clothes from Zwei Zwei. Peppo watched her from beside the bed. 'Oh! You'll need food,' she said. 'And a water bowl. It's a long drive. Come on, they're in the kitchen.'

She left her bedroom, the dog following. 'Mother!' she called as she descended the stairs. 'Are you ready?'

'I will be soon,' came the reply from Idonia's bedroom. 'Then I need to collect my laptop.'

'Okay. I'm almost done.' Avelina continued downwards.

She turned at the foot of the stairs to head for the kitchen. To her surprise, Peppo hesitated, sniffing, then went down to the library. 'Peppo! Where are you going? We don't have any dog books. Come!' The dog stopped at the threshold, looking back at her, then carried on inside. 'Okay, even my dog never listens to me,' she said with a sigh.

She entered the kitchen and found the biscuits and a bowl, then returned. 'Peppo! Come up here, I've got some food.' A rattle of the bag. 'Peppo, come on!'

No response. That was unusual. He never normally ignored food. Avelina descended the stairs. 'Peppo?'

229

Another rattle. She listened for a response. Silence. What was he doing? She entered the room and reached for the light switch—

Someone grabbed her.

A hand clamped painfully hard over her mouth, pulling her head back—

Pain exploded at the side of her skull, and everything went black.

Locke lowered his ghost target to the floor. He checked Foss was unconscious, then turned on the light. The bodyguard's corpse lay nearby, the still-twitching dog dead beside it. The animal's arrival had been an unexpected complication. Luckily, just as at the flat, it had been friendly. To its cost.

He rose, retrieving his bag. He needed to move quickly. Theodore Foss was still wearing female clothing, but had changed outfits, now dressed to travel. The family were preparing to flee Munich. He had made the right decision, then. SC9 would have had to reacquire them, potentially facing far greater security. This way, they would be the Bondage Killer's final victims. Any suspicions about British involvement would be drowned out by the media hullabaloo.

Locke took several plastic zip-ties from his bag. They were not in keeping with his usual MO, but time was critical. He couldn't afford to fiddle about with chains and buckles. Not yet, at least. Once he had what he needed, everything could be set up correctly. He rolled Foss on to his front and secured his arms tightly behind him. The young man groaned, starting to regain consciousness. Locke hurriedly took out a large ballgag and forced it into Foss's mouth. By the time he realised what was happening, the leather strap was fastened tight. Foss let out a muffled cry.

'Shut up,' Locke snapped, bringing the knife to his throat. Foss fell silent, eyes bulging in terror. 'Stand up. Make a sound and I'll cut your throat.' He hauled him upright. 'Upstairs.'

Foss saw the dead man and dog and moaned in horror. Irritated at being disobeyed, Locke struck him again with the haft of his knife. 'Last warning. Upstairs. Take me to your mother.'

He forced Foss up to the hall. 'Where?' he demanded in a harsh whisper. Foss glanced up the next flight. Locke put the blade to his throat and ascended with his prisoner.

Noises from a bedroom led him to his primary target. 'Leopold, is that you?' said Idonia Foss. 'Is the car ready? I'll just be a couple more minutes.'

Locke held her son tightly by his hair and kicked the door open. Idonia was putting clothes into a suitcase on the bed. She jumped, startled – then backed away in fear. 'Leopold! Help!'

'He's dead,' Locke said coldly.

Idonia stared at him. 'Oh my God. Alex was right. You *are* the serial killer!' Realisation behind her horror. 'But . . . I'm your real target, aren't I?'

'It's nothing personal,' he replied. 'But there's something I need first. The recording of Roger Glennmore. Where is it?'

'The recording—' Her expression became one almost of disbelief. '*That's* what you want?'

231

'Where is it?' he repeated. 'We know it's not on any of your computers, or your phone. So you keep it on something else. Another device, an SD card – whatever it is, you're going to give it to me. Or . . .' He brought the knife back to his captive's throat. 'I'll kill your son.'

'No, no,' Idonia gasped. 'Please, don't.'

'The recording,' Locke intoned. 'The recording! Where is it?' He raised the blade higher – and placed its point at the rear of Foss's cheek. The young man tensed. 'Last chance, Idonia.' He pushed the knife against his skin – and into it.

Foss cried out through the gag as blood ran down his jaw. Idonia screamed. Locke maintained the pressure, forcing the combat knife downwards. It carved through the flesh in front of Foss's ear. More blood spilled on to his neck.

'I'll tell you!' Idonia wailed. 'I'll tell you, *I'll tell you*! Please, don't hurt her! I'll give you the recording!'

Locke stopped his movement. He stared stonily at her for a moment. 'All right.' He drew the blade clear. Foss moaned.

'Let her go!' Idonia begged.

'The recording,' Locke said again. He brought the knife towards his prisoner's eye for emphasis.

Idonia regarded him in terror . . . then raised her left arm. 'My watch. The recorder's in my watch.'

Locke regarded it intently. Small, gold, expensive; a Cartier, if he wasn't mistaken. He wouldn't have imagined it was big enough to fit with a bug. But then, presumably, nor had the head of Xeneon. 'Is the only copy on there?' The knife's point remained at the younger Foss's eye.

'No, no,' Idonia replied, near-breathless with panic. 'By the bed, the base station?' Locke looked. On a small

232

nightstand was a thick metal disc connected to a power cable. He would have taken it for a wireless phone charger. 'It downloads recordings to an SD card overnight. I only keep ones that might be important. The watch asks me every hour if I want to keep what it's just recorded. It taps my wrist. If I tap it back, it deletes the last recording. Otherwise it keeps it.'

'Is that the only place you keep the recordings? No back-ups? No copies in a deposit box or with your lawyer?'

'No, no. I swear!'

'On your child's life?' He tugged at Foss's hair, bringing his head back – and exposing his throat. The blade's edge dropped again, resting against the bloodied skin.

'Yes.' Tears rolled down Idonia's cheeks. 'Oh, God, please don't. I'll give you everything.' She fumbled the watch from her wrist and tossed it on to the bed.

'The base station too,' Locke demanded.

She pulled out its power cord and threw it beside the watch. 'There. There they are. Those are the only copies, please believe me. You've got them all, they're yours. Now let her go, please. I'll give you anything you want. I have money, you can take it, as much as you want. If you want me to stop the merger, I'll do that too. Anything! Just please don't hurt her!'

A moment of consideration. 'That's a very generous offer, Idonia,' Locke said at last. 'If this were just about money, I would take it. But . . .' His face became ice-cold, deadly as a blizzard. 'This is not about money. It's about my mission.' A small, cruel curl of his lips. 'And I always complete my mission.'

* * *

Reeve ran along the north bank of the Nymphenburg Canal. The frozen waters stretched away towards the palace, its lights a haze through the snow. Could he have cut across the ice? It didn't matter now. He had made it over the footbridge unchallenged; the cops hadn't set a trap. Which meant they didn't know where he was going. He should be able to reach the Foss house.

Was Locke already there? He glanced up the side roads as he passed. A couple of cars had been recently driven, windscreens clear. Was one Locke's? Possibly. He wouldn't park right outside his target's home. But there was no way to know.

Not until he arrived. Penultimate street. He sprinted along the last stretch, breath burning in his throat. Around the corner. Lights in the house. Avelina and Idonia had come home – were they still there? He ran through the gate to the front door. Locked. Shit!

Knocking was not an option. If Locke was here, alerting him would be dangerous, if not deadly. He ran around the house to the rear garden – and saw footprints in the snow. Locke *was* here. The prints were fresh, sharply defined. Minutes old. Fear joined the adrenalised pounding of his heart. How *many* minutes? Was he too late?

No footprints leaving the house. Locke was still inside. He followed the trail down the steps to the library's door. No snow on the handle. He tried it. The door opened.

Steber's corpse was sprawled on the floor beyond. Beside it was Peppo's unmoving body. Blood had pooled around both. Human or animal, threat or harmless, it didn't matter to Locke. But where was he now? Where were his targets?

Reeve hurried up into the hall. Voices reached him from above. He didn't need to understand German to know the feelings behind them. Idonia, terrified, pleading; Locke, cold, impatient. He wanted something from her. This was her last chance to surrender it. Or . . .

Or he would kill Avelina. She had to be Locke's leverage. She was still alive – but not for much longer.

Reeve started up the stairs – then on impulse yanked the metal rod from its display. It was hefty, weighing several kilograms. Awkward . . . but any weapon was better than none.

He quickly continued upwards, footfalls as light as possible. Locke's voice grew louder. He was in Idonia's bedroom. The door was open. The Operative stood beyond it, back to him, clad in medical coveralls. He held Avelina in front of him, knife raised to her neck. '*Und ich erfülle immer meine Missionen*,' he said, his voice filled with triumphant finality—

Reeve charged, swinging his makeshift club.

Locke heard him coming. He started to twist away—

Too slowly. The steel rod struck below his right ear with a ringing thud. The Operative staggered. His knife hand flailed away from Avelina's throat.

Reeve saw her arms were tied behind her back. He pulled her away from Locke. 'Get out of here, run!' he yelled to the two women.

Idonia, shocked by his sudden appearance, took a moment to react. By then, Locke was recovering. Reeve pushed Avelina through the doorway and drew back his club to strike again—

Idonia fled for the landing – passing in front of Reeve. He had just started his swing, hurriedly arresting it. She cleared the room. He resumed his attack, but had lost momentum.

And now Locke's knife was raised, slashing at his hands—

Reeve jerked his left hand from the metal spar. The knife clanged against the metal. If it had caught him, it would have severed his tendons. But Locke wasn't finished. The blade swept upwards, biting into the flesh of his right hand. He cried out, pain costing him his grip on the car part.

But its swing had enough force behind it to keep moving. Locke lurched back as the hunk of metal hit his chest. It dropped to the floor between the two men. The Operative barely snatched a foot clear as it landed with an echoing bang.

Reeve saw he was off-balance and attacked again. He delivered a flying kick to the assassin's stomach. Locke gasped, propelled backwards into a window. His head hit one of the panes. The glass broke, shards raining on to the sill. He pulled away – and snarled in pain as a razor-sharp spike tore his cheek.

The two men faced off. Blood oozed down Locke's forehead from another cut on his scalp. It reached his right eye, forcing it shut. He wiped it with his free hand, but each pulse sent more crimson down the same path. Reeve shifted to Locke's right. If he could attack while the Operative's sight was impaired—

Locke realised what he was doing and went on the offensive. The knife thrust towards Reeve, again, a third time. He was forced to retreat towards the bed. Locke drove another stab at Reeve's face. He jerked backwards—

Snatching the duvet from the bed.

Reeve flung the covering at Locke, scattering the objects on it across the floor. It flopped down over his head and out-stretched arm. Locke batted it away, knife hand emerging—

Reeve grabbed his wrist.

Locke tried to break loose. Reeve slammed bodily into him, knocking him towards the window. The duvet fell to the floor as they struggled for supremacy. Reeve was stronger. Time spent carrying logs had built up more muscle than wielding a scalpel. He bent Locke's arm back, trying to force the knife from his grip.

Locke realised the danger. His free hand had been clawing at Reeve's face. It now tugged at the Operative's coverall. Reeve knew the move could only be for one thing. A gun. Locke groped inside his protective overgarment, fumbling for a hidden holster—

Reeve swung and powered his knee at Locke's groin. The older man tried to dodge back, but hit the wall. The blow found its target, bending him double. Reeve twisted his wrist around – and slammed the knife down on to a dresser. Its point stabbed deeply into the lacquered wood. Before Locke could respond, he elbowed him in the face. The Operative stumbled sideways along the wall, releasing the knife. It remained standing, buried in the dresser's top.

Reeve moved to grab it – but saw the other man reach inside his coverall. He whipped back towards Locke as he drew a gun—

Reeve's fist pounded into his left eye. A targeted attack; his right was still gummed shut by blood. Blinded, Locke swung the gun at him. Reeve snapped up an arm to block it. Their forearms thudded together. Locke pulled the trigger.

The shot was almost deafening inside the room's confines. Reeve felt the heat of the muzzle flash on his face. He grimaced, but kept up his attack, delivering a left hook. It was clumsy, but still hit Locke's cheek, rattling him. Before he could recover, Reeve grabbed his gun arm and forced it upwards. Another ear-splitting retort as Locke fired again. Plaster showered over them from the ruptured ceiling.

Reeve smashed Locke's hand against the edge of the window frame. The gun clattered to the floor behind Reeve. He turned to locate it—

Locke lashed out. A move borne of blind desperation, but it paid off. His fist caught Reeve's jaw, snapping his head sideways. The Operative yanked his trapped arm free. A furious kick knocked Reeve back towards the bed . . .

And the gun.

Locke wiped his bloodied eye, spotting Reeve – then his knife. He darted to grab it—

Reeve dropped and snatched up the pistol as Locke yanked the knife from the dresser. The SC9 agent instantly knew he would lose the confrontation. Instead he whirled – and dived through the window.

Reeve fired, but hit nothing as his target fell. Shrill clinks of glass from outside – then a heavy thud. He jumped up and rushed to the wrecked window. If Locke was wounded, he could capture him—

No such luck. Idonia's bedroom was directly above the house's rear porch. Locke had landed in thick snow – and immediately rolled into cover below. Reeve leaned out, hoping to catch him. Which way would he run?

A grunt of exertion – and Locke moved. Reeve had guessed

he would go left, staying beneath the overhanging bedrooms. He guessed wrong. By the time he realised his mistake and turned, Locke was at the house's corner. Reeve lined up a shot – but the Operative was gone. 'Shit!'

Locke was limping, though, hurt by the fall. He could still catch him. Reeve ran from the bedroom and charged downstairs.

He reached the hall, about to head for the front door. A cry of 'Alex!' stopped him. He hurried through the dining room. Avelina and Idonia were in the kitchen beyond. 'Are you okay?' he asked, reaching them.

'Yes,' Avelina replied, breathing heavily. Blood from a deep cut ran down her cheek and neck.

Idonia was severing the zip-ties with scissors. 'What about you?' she asked, looking fearfully behind Reeve. 'Where is he? We heard shooting!'

Reeve raised his newly acquired weapon. 'I'm all right. I'm going after him. Call the police, then get out.' He ran from the room.

Idonia strained to snip the final zip-tie. Avelina pulled her arms apart with a gasp of relief. 'My God, my God,' she said, embracing her mother. Idonia returned the gesture. Then Avelina drew away. 'I've got to help him,' she said, heading for the door.

'No!' Idonia cried. 'It's too dangerous!'

'The police will arrest them both – and SC9 will kill Alex.' Avelina rushed into the hall. It was already empty; Reeve had gone. Ignoring the pain in her cheek, she grabbed a coat and raced in pursuit.

CHAPTER 28

Reeve spotted Locke's trail the moment he left the house. The Operative's footprints were clear in the pristine snow. He followed them to the street. They angled south – towards the canal. He sprinted to the intersection.

Locke had gone east, running as fast as he could on his injured leg. Reeve raced after him. The other man was roughly a hundred metres ahead. Shooting him from that distance was possible, but risky. Reeve needed him alive. Without a confession, he had no real ammunition against SC9, only hearsay.

But the gap was closing quickly. Even if Locke had been unhurt, Reeve knew he was the faster runner. He would soon be close enough to make a precise shot to wound, not kill.

Locke passed the first side street. A glance back, seeing Reeve in pursuit. He swerved to weave between the trees lining the street. Reeve pounded after him, drawing closer. Would he duck down the next street, or keep going? A snap-shot fired on the run would almost certainly miss. He would have to stop to aim accurately. But would he have time?

The Operative reached the next street. He seemed about to cross it and continue onwards. But Reeve knew what he himself would do in the same situation. He slithered to a halt, whipping into a firing stance—

Locke abruptly changed direction. Reeve had been right – the Operative was turning up the side street. He fired. But Locke had expected it, diving across the sidewalk. Reeve's shot cracked over him. He hit the pavement, scrambling from sight around the corner.

Reeve cursed and charged after him. If the shots fired at Idonia's house hadn't alerted neighbours, that one would. This was a wealthy area: the cops would soon arrive.

He neared the corner. No protective cover to peek from; it was an ironwork fence, not a wall. Snow-swathed bushes blocked his view of the next street. Would Locke run or fight? He would only have a split-second to react. He readied the gun and whisked around the corner—

A VW Golf peeled out from the roadside. Reeve glimpsed a familiar face at its wheel. He fired three rapid shots. Holes burst in the windscreen, the glass crazing around them. The Golf swerved, bounding over the kerb.

Coming right at him.

Reeve turned to run—

The VW slewed across the snow, out of control. It hit Reeve from behind and bowled him painfully up on to the bonnet. He flailed his free hand, catching one of the wipers. Metal tore at his skin. He clung on as the car spun across Nördliche Auffahrtsallee towards the frozen canal—

It hit a lamppost. The Golf swung violently around. The wiper snapped. Reeve was flung from the bonnet. He landed on a low metal fence. The impact felt like being hit across the back by a baseball bat. The gun flew from his hand and disappeared into the nearby snow. He tumbled down a small slope to land hard on the icy waterway below.

The VW flattened the little fence, sliding tail-first down the incline after him—

It hit the ice – and broke through.

A rush of freezing water rolled over Reeve's legs. He gasped, trying to scramble clear. But the surface under him was breaking up. Before he had gone a metre, it gave way – and pitched him into the canal.

His first contact with the water had been a shock. This was the electric chair. The chill paralysed him, punching his heart, collapsing his lungs. All sensation was swallowed by an overwhelming abyss of cold. He sank deeper—

His clawed hands caught a ragged fracture in the ice. The touch crackled through his nerves, restarting feeling. Restarting thought. He had endured this before. Endured, and survived. He could do it again. Just *remember* . . .

Memories came back to him. Arctic survival. Special forces training, in Norway. An instructor had shoved him bodily into a hole in metre-thick ice. If he didn't get out on his own, he would fail the course. He had to—

Breathe.

A sharp gasp, forcing air into his lungs. His body desperately told him to keep breathing, faster and faster. He fought the urge. Hyperventilating would make things worse. Instead he held his breath, fingers clenching at the crack in the ice. It held firm. He pulled himself closer and started to drag himself up—

Locke grabbed his hair.

The Operative's hand closed, tearing at his roots. Reeve

let out a choked grunt of pain as his head was pulled back. The VW was half-submerged, front end still on the slope. The driver's door was open. Locke squatted at the hole's edge. His combat knife was in his other hand. 'This reminds me of two years ago,' he said. His voice was level, but there was venom behind it. 'I had my knife at your throat.'

Reeve tried to break loose. The grip on his hair was too tight. Any action other than holding position caused him to slip deeper into the frigid water. Locke leaned closer. 'Time to finish what I started.'

He brought the blade to Reeve's neck, finding the main artery—

A gunshot echoed across the canal.

Locke turned, shocked. Reeve managed to look sidelong – and saw Avelina a few metres away. She had come down the little embankment on to the ice. The gun was in her hands. It was pointed skywards; now, she lowered it. Aiming at Locke. 'Let him go!' she cried, voice tremulous.

'Shoot him,' Reeve rasped. 'Just shoot him!'

But he knew Avelina couldn't do it. He was trained to end human lives. She was vehemently opposed to violence. The gun wavered.

Locke released Reeve's hair. He dropped back into the water, cold punching his upper chest. The Operative rose and faced Avelina. He raised the black knife higher. 'Shoot him!' Reeve cried again. If she didn't, Locke would kill them both—

Flashes of light on the bridge to the west. Strobes. Locke saw them too. He looked in the other direction. More blue pulses on the canalside road. The police were coming.

The Operative hesitated, shooting a dark glance at Reeve – then ran for shore.

Avelina watched him go, unsure what to do. 'Shoot, shoot!' said Reeve in desperation. She broke through her uncertainty, tracked him – and fired.

But missed. The round smacked against a tree as Locke ducked behind it. He hared away towards the side street, using the tree as cover. By the time she moved to reacquire him, he was around the corner.

She stared after him – then dropped the gun and hurried to Reeve. 'My God! Let me help you out.' She crouched by the hole and held out an arm.

Reeve grabbed her wrist. 'Careful,' he warned, barely able to speak through chattering teeth. 'Don't slip.'

'I'm okay. I used to skate on this.' She took his weight and eased backwards. Reeve used his other arm to pull himself higher. With Avelina's help, he brought one soaked leg on to the ice's edge. She pulled him clear of the water. He rolled over, shivering. 'Oh, God, you're freezing!'

'Help me up,' he gasped. She did so. 'I can't stay here. If the police—'

'I know,' she cut in. 'I'll send them after Locke. You need to get inside, fast.'

He wrapped his arms around his upper body, trying to warm himself. She hurriedly removed her coat and gave it to him. 'I've still got my hostel room.'

'Okay. Good.' She pointed south, across the ice. 'Go to the other side. It should be thick enough to walk on. Keep going until you reach Amulfstrasse, and catch a tram to the station. I'll find you at the hostel later. Now go!'

'Thanks,' he managed to wheeze, before setting off. His feet were leaden blocks, thunking against the frozen surface. Blowing snow swirled around him, the wind as sharp as Locke's knife. He could feel his body heat sapping through his wet clothing. But he had to keep moving.

Not just to escape the police. His body wanted to rest, to sleep, just to *stop*. If he did, he would die. Keep going. Keep going. Never stop running. A glance back as he drove himself onwards. The first police car had reached Avelina. She was safe – for the moment.

Now, his own survival took priority. He reached the canal's far bank and scrambled up the slope. A road led southwards not far away. He headed for it, vanishing into the snowy night.

Locke staggered into his bolt-hole, locking the door behind him. He had escaped the police only by luck. A second later in vaulting a wall, and he would have been seen. He had slipped through gardens, eventually getting clear. He disposed of his protective outer garments in a bin. A taxi brought him back to his secondary apartment.

He took stock. Returning to his main residence was now out of the question. The Fosses would have told the police about him, the bodyguard's death corroborating their story. Stefan Holke was now wanted for murder. That cover identity was blown.

He had others, of course. But his face was known to the authorities. He could disguise himself, to a degree. But that had never been his strong point as an Operative.

He was a social chameleon, not a physical one. The police would be looking for him at public transport terminals. And they would be watching his home; he couldn't get his other car. How to get out of Munich?

More importantly, where would he go?

That question could wait. Pulsing pain reminded him of more urgent matters. He went to the bathroom. A bruised face glared back from the mirror. Reeve's assault had left his nose and upper lip swollen and purple. He had used melted snow to clean his bloodied face before getting the taxi. The deep glass cut had not closed, though, red rivulets on his cheek and neck. The smaller wound on his scalp had stopped bleeding, but stung like dripping acid.

Those were just the most visible injuries. He was still limping from the fall, hip aching. Even with a cushion of snow, a twelve-foot drop hurt. He also had smaller cuts from his dive through the window.

But he was alive. Still functioning. Still an Operative.

Still able to complete his mission. It was now not just an assignment. It was personal. Reeve had *humiliated* him. Reeve, and a woman, and her deviant son. A hot wire of anger burned deep inside him. He had killed others for less.

He would kill them too.

A cupboard contained a well-stocked medical kit. He retrieved it, then painfully stripped off his snow-damp clothing. A rapid, professional survey of his wounds. Then he set to work. Tweezing out glass fragments, cleaning cuts, stitching lacerations.

He used no anaesthetic. Instead, he let the various shades

of pain heat the wire, fuel for his fury. He *would* kill Reeve and the Fosses.

After he had made them suffer.

CHAPTER 29

Idonia looked out from the BMW's rear window. A call to Netz had brought him to the house with alacrity. Her security chief was now acting as her driver. After dealing with the authorities, she and Avelina had come to find Reeve, as promised. 'Is this really the place?'

Avelina picked up on her hint of disdain. 'Why, did you think he'd be staying in the Mandarin? Alex might have dressed like James Bond, but he doesn't have an expense account.'

'I suppose not. Do you know which room he's in?'

'No, but I know the name he's using. I'll find him.' Avelina opened her door. 'Maybe drive round the block while I'm in there. It feels safer to keep moving.'

Idonia nodded. 'I know exactly what you mean.'

Carrying a fleece, Avelina exited. The 7 Series drove off. She looked around. It was after three in the morning, the streets all but deserted. Locke, if he somehow were here, was staying out of sight. The mere thought of the Operative gave her a chill beyond anything from the weather. Her gloved hand instinctively went to the bandage in front of her right ear. The wound beneath it still stung, a low but burning itch.

She entered the hostel. A night porter regarded her

suspiciously. She asked for Leo Martin's room. To her relief, it was occupied. She went upstairs and cautiously knocked on the door. 'Alex?'

She heard a bed creak, then the door opened. Alex Reeve stood beyond, wrapped in a blanket. His face was pale, dark shadows under his eyes. An adhesive bandage covered the cut on his hand. 'Oh my God,' said Avelina, slipping into the room. 'Are you okay?'

'Been better,' was Reeve's curt reply. 'Hypothermia. I'll recover.' The single bed was piled with more blankets. A warm nest to help him survive the night. He peered at her bandaged cheek. 'What about you?'

'We went to the emergency room. They gave me stitches. Mother is okay physically, just shocked.'

'What did you tell the police?'

'The truth: that Locke is the Bondage Killer. Stefan Holke, I mean – that's who they're looking for. They asked about you, of course. I didn't tell them much. I said you rescued us, had a fight with Locke, then chased him.'

'Okay.' Reeve sat on the bed, gathering his strength. 'Sorry about your friend's tux, by the way,' he said. The ruined tuxedo was draped over the room's little radiator beside Avelina's loaned coat.

'Frideric will never lend me anything again,' Avelina replied ruefully. 'Listen, Mother and I – we're going to our ski lodge. We started packing before Locke arrived last night. You should come with us.'

'Where is it?'

'Zermatt, in Switzerland. We were going to drive, but now Mother's arranging a helicopter.'

Reeve gave her a half-smile. 'Must be nice having money.'

'It doesn't seem to buy us safety, though. Locke killed our bodyguard. And Peppo.' Emotion surged within her. The awful memory of seeing Steber's body – and the thought of her lost companion. She fought to control it. There was far more pent up behind that she didn't want to release. 'But – but that's what we're doing. You don't have to come with us, but . . . we would like you to.'

Reeve retrieved the clothing he had left in a drawer. 'I won't be able to get into Switzerland. I don't have a passport. They'll check, especially if we're flying in.'

Avelina gave him the fleece. 'Mother can take care of that.' The certainty in her voice drew a quizzical look from the Englishman. 'She's in the car outside. Are you coming?'

He considered the offer. 'Yes – for now,' he finally said. 'I don't know if I'll go as far as Switzerland. But I'll admit, I'm interested in what your mum thinks she can do for me.'

'She knows a lot of important people. Some of them owe her favours.' She helped gather Reeve's few belongings as he dressed. 'Are you ready?'

'Yeah.' A glum look as he donned the fleece. 'Your coat's still wet inside. And I left the other one at the party.'

'We'll buy you a new one. Whatever you need.' She touched his arm. 'You saved our lives, Alex. It's the least we can do.'

A faint smile. 'Thanks.' He turned to leave. 'Okay. Let's go.'

Avelina went to the kerb to wait for Idonia while Reeve lurked in the hostel's doorway. To his relief, the BMW soon arrived. They quickly got in. '*Geh ins Büro*,' Idonia ordered Netz, before turning to Reeve. 'Alex, thank God you are all right. You *are* all right, I hope?'

'I'll live,' he told her.

'Ah. A stoic.' She smiled at Avelina. '*Ein Stoiker*. Like your father. He would never admit to feeling less than totally healthy either.' Avelina gave her a little smile in return. 'Now, have you been told what we are going to do?'

'Yeah. You're going to your place in Switzerland.' Reeve didn't comment on her awkward, roundabout phrasing. Even after the evening's horrors, she still couldn't call Avelina by her chosen name. 'What did you tell the police about Locke? Did you mention SC9?'

'I told them you said he was a British agent, trying to destroy the merger. Did they believe me? I don't know. But I have friends in government who *will* listen, even if the police do not. This is now a matter of national security. I still have the recording of Roger Glennmore threatening me. It will go to the proper people, do not worry.'

Reeve straightened in alarm. 'Where's your phone? You don't have it on you right now, do you?' If SC9 were listening—

'It is in the trunk,' Idonia assured him. 'And Reynold had the car checked for bugs. We can talk freely.'

'Good.' He relaxed, slightly. 'Where are we going?'

'My office. Reynold called in extra security, so we will be safe. There are some . . . arrangements I will make for you. Then afterwards, we can fly to Zermatt. Reynold and his security team will come with us. They are former special forces soldiers who are trained to protect VIPs. And we still have you, of course.' A small smile.

'I'm not sure how much use I'll be,' Reeve said dolefully. 'I didn't catch Locke. He'll have bugged out, and SC9 will switch plans. I can't predict what they'll do next.'

'But you still know them better than anyone,' Avelina pointed out. 'Maybe you don't know what they will do. But you *will* spot them when they do it.'

'Hopefully not too late to do anything about it.'

'We have faith in you,' said Idonia. 'You saved us. And I will help you in return.'

Said help, on arriving at the Foss Präzisionsmetall head-quarters, began with Netz taking Reeve's picture.

'You said you didn't have a passport,' Avelina told him. 'Mother can fix that.'

'How?' Reeve asked as Netz left the room with the camera.

'As a weapons manufacturer, I have many contacts in the government and intelligence services,' said Idonia. 'Reynold does too. You will have a genuine German passport by tomorrow.'

Reeve still had misgivings. 'Not the best cover. I don't speak German.'

'Nobody is perfect. Now, while we wait, I am sure you will want some food.'

'I would, yes.' His freezing dip in the canal had drained his body almost to the point of collapse.

'We have a small executive dining room here. I don't know what food we have, but eat whatever you want.'

'Thanks.' He gave Avelina a brief smile. 'It really *must* be nice having money.' She grinned back.

The selection of available food was limited, but Reeve

didn't care. In his current condition, quantity and calorific content were all that mattered. He wolfed his way through two helpings of Käsespätzle, a cheese and pasta dish. Avelina sat with him, watching in amusement as the food disappeared. 'I think you needed that,' she said.

'I did,' Reeve agreed. He washed it down with a third cup of rich, hot chocolate. He still felt the after-effects of the punishing evening, but his strength was returning. 'Aren't you having anything?'

She shook her head. 'I'm not hungry.'

'It might be worth it even if you don't feel like it. You could be feeling delayed shock. You got cut; your body reacts to that.'

Her hand went to the bandage. 'No, I'm okay. But thank you.'

'For what?'

'For caring. For protecting me. Both of us. I'm sorry you didn't catch Locke.'

'Yeah, me too.' He kneaded his forehead, exhausted – and not just physically. 'I don't know what I'm going to do now. If anything, I've made things worse.'

'Because SC9 know you're in Munich?'

'More than that. I interfered in one of their operations. Now they'll hunt me with everything they've got.'

'But they were doing that anyway.'

'That's just it.' He slumped back in his seat. 'They *weren't*. I didn't know, but SC9 has a new boss. Someone I used to think of as a friend. Who actually helped me even when the rest of SC9 was trying to kill me. He called off the hunt for me and Connie. He was thinking, "If he doesn't bother us, we won't bother him." Only . . . I *did* bother them. By going after Locke, I made myself SC9's number one target. With Connie as number two. I don't know where she is. They don't either – but they'll find out. They have all of British intelligence backing them. Sooner or later, they'll track her down. And I won't be able to protect her.' A despairing sigh. 'She would have been *safe* if I'd done nothing. But I've just signed her death sentence.'

'No. You haven't.' The intensity of Avelina's statement made Reeve look up. She gripped his hand. 'She isn't dead yet, and nor are you. And nor are *we*. Without you, Locke would have murdered me, and my mother. You changed things. And you can *keep* changing them. You can save yourself, and Connie too. You just have to keep fighting. You just have to *not let them win.*'

Her confidence in him boosted his spirits – briefly. But then the reality of the situation weighed him down once more. 'Easier said than done. They've got all the resources. I've got nothing.'

'You've got us,' Avelina offered.

'Thanks. But I don't know how far that will get me.'

'Perhaps further than you think.' Idonia had entered the dining room behind him. 'I have something more that could help you,' she said. 'A contact: a friend of mine. They are a . . . a *facilitator*, is perhaps the word. They put people with certain skills in contact with others who need those skills. They can find you work. Very well-paid work.'

'I'm not a mercenary,' Reeve replied, instinctually uncomfortable at the thought.

'You do not have to be. I have never used mercenaries,

soldiers of fortune. But sometimes, I have needed people with . . . special talents. People who it was best not to put on the company payroll. So I called upon my friend to find them for me.'

'Corporate spies?' Avelina asked, her tone less than approving.

'Amongst other things. But that is not important. This is about Alex.' Idonia turned back to Reeve. 'My friend has many other friends, a lot of connections. A lot of *resources*. I heard what you were saying. You are looking for someone important to you, yes?'

'Yes.'

'He can help you find them.'

'If I work for him.'

'Not for him. For his clients. People like me. People who can be very thankful for the help they receive.' She gave him a beseeching look. 'If someone wants you dead, isn't it better to have friends and money?'

'I've already tried the alternative, so yeah,' said Reeve. 'I'll think about it.'

'Do. Please.' She gestured towards the exit. 'Perhaps sleep on it. I have turned a couch in my office into a bed for you. There is a shower in my private bathroom as well. We cannot leave until you have your passport, so you may as well rest.'

'Thank you.' He'd tried to sleep at the hostel, but had been racked by shivers. 'What about you two?'

'Mother wanted to book into a hotel,' Avelina said, with a glimmer of sardonic amusement. 'I persuaded her to rough it, just for one night. There are more couches in the conference room.'

Reeve managed a faint grin. 'I'm sure you'll survive.'

Idonia showed him to her office. The plush sofa looked more comfortable than most beds he'd used recently. He thanked her; she left. Burrowing under layers of new, clean blankets, he was asleep in seconds.

CHAPTER 30

Locke jolted awake. His first emotion was anger; he hadn't meant to sleep. He had too much to do. But performing emergency surgery upon himself had drained him. He checked the time. Almost six in the morning. Damn it! He'd been out for over four hours. Four hours in which his targets were free to flee . . .

He rose from his chair. Bruises ached, cut skin stinging. The lacerated side of his face burned at the slightest movement. His medical equipment was hospital grade; he had repaired himself as best he could. There would still be a scar, though. That was unwelcome. Operatives relied to a degree on being unremarkable, anonymous. A facial scar was distinctive and memorable. That could affect future assignments.

If there *were* any future assignments. He'd meant to call Maxwell after completing his surgery. He had to report his failure – and persuade Maxwell to let him continue. He was confident he knew where Idonia Foss would run.

He made the call, hoping to catch Maxwell asleep, off-guard. That didn't happen. 'Yes,' came the reply, almost immediately.

'It's me,' said Locke.

'Where are you?'

'My backup location.'

'Why are you still in Munich?'

'I needed medical attention.'

'Did you involve anyone else?' Wariness in the question.

'No, I took care of it myself.'

Silence on the line for a moment. Finally, Maxwell spoke again. His voice was level, controlled – but with cold anger behind it. 'I told you to leave after you met Reeve. Why did you disobey a direct order?'

'Because I could still complete the mission.'

'And did you?' From his sharp tone, he already knew the answer. GCHQ had doubtless been monitoring Munich's emergency channels.

'No,' Locke admitted. 'Reeve intervened. Somehow he escaped from the police.'

'He escaped from the police because he's an Operative. You should have expected that. Which is why I told you to get out. The plan was blown. If you'd left, all the authorities would have had was a mystery. Now they have survivors, witnesses.'

Locke felt his anger rising again at the dressing-down. Maxwell was patronising him, treating him like a raw recruit. 'I'm well aware of that, Tony. I was merely trying to salvage months of deep-cover work. The merger can still be stopped, if—'

'That's not your concern any more.' The interruption felt like a physical slap to Locke's face. 'We're switching to the fallback plan. Stone will carry it out.'

'*Stone?*' A rare surge of open emotion – in this case, pure contempt – filled his voice. 'You're handing the mission over to a thug like *Stone*? After all the time and effort I've put into it?'

'This is about the job, not your ego,' Maxwell said coldly. 'I'm handing the mission over to someone who'll get it done. Someone who will obey orders.'

'I can still make the kill,' insisted Locke, jaw tightening in fury. 'Idonia Foss will leave Munich now, yes. But I'm certain she'll head to her own property, somewhere she considers safe. Which means her ski lodge in Zermatt. I can be there this afternoon. And I can finish this as planned.'

'The serial-killer cover story is already wrecked. Reeve told the Fosses about SC9. After your botched attack at the house, they told the authorities. GCHQ picked up chatter about allegations of British involvement. And not just what the Fosses told the police. Idonia has friends in high places. She's already started talking to them.' A deep, irritated breath. 'I don't suppose you located the recording?'

'Actually, I did.'

'And do you have it?'

It took Locke a moment to force out the reply. 'No.'

'No,' Maxwell echoed. 'So Idonia still has it. And she can – she *will* – give it to the authorities.'

'I know where it is,' said Locke. 'Her watch is the recorder; its charger is the base station. All her recordings are stored on it. She will undoubtedly take them both with her. They're the most valuable things she has. They can be recovered, if I act quickly.'

'No.' The word slammed down with the weight of a millstone. 'For you, this ends now. Get out of Germany and return to London. That is an *order*.'

Locke did not answer at once, trying to control his anger. He also knew what he wanted to say might destroy him. Not merely his career as an Operative; it could end his life. But it had been on his mind for months, the idea growing, metastasising . . .

It had to be said. No matter the risk. 'You ordered us to stand down from hunting Reeve in Venice, Tony. That was a mistake, and it's now cost us dearly. I will not allow that mistake to be repeated.'

Maxwell's voice brimmed with danger. '*You* will not allow? Who the hell do you think you are, *Harrison*?'

'I'm an Operative,' was the curt reply. 'I do what needs to be done for my country. Idonia Foss must die; I will make sure that happens. And I will make sure Alex Reeve dies as well. Don't try to stop me.'

'If you think I'm going to let you—'

It was Locke's turn to interrupt. 'What are you going to do, Tony? Declare me Fox Red? With the other intelligence agencies all breathing down your neck? First Reeve, then Parker, now me – a third rogue asset under your watch. That wouldn't look good for you. It could make it look as if you're losing control of SC9. Just as it did for Scott when you killed him.' He went to the window, staring out across the darkened city. 'I'm going to carry out my assignment, Tony. If you have a problem with that, you can talk to me afterwards. But I *will* get this done. By this time tomorrow, Foss and Reeve will be dead. And I'll have your precious recording.' Before Maxwell could answer, he terminated the call.

CHAPTER 31

Maxwell lowered his phone, trying to keep his fury in check. So, it had finally happened. He'd expected a challenge to his leadership ever since he removed Scott. SC9's former head had controlled the agency for over thirty years. SC9 was based on his proposals, run according to his dictates, even now. Systemic inertia was a hard thing to overcome.

But Scott's looming, unavoidable shadow meant he also still had his loyalists. Locke had finally revealed himself as one. Despite his suspicions, Maxwell had to admit his open defiance had come as a surprise. But personal trust in an individual did not come easily to a psychopath. Locke's fealty was to the agency that allowed him to indulge his urges. And he had spent eighteen months as an Operative under Scott before Maxwell replaced him.

What to do now? Locke was, infuriatingly, right: declaring him Fox Red would not play well. With MI6 and the other agencies watching closely, he couldn't afford to appear weak. Having another Operative go rogue would be regarded as exactly that. However secret he tried to keep the order, it would eventually leak. Ryford-Croft and the others would involve themselves soon after.

He couldn't use SC9's own assets to deal with Locke,

then. Nor any from the wider community of British Intelligence. There were other options. Favours owed by contacts in other countries, or employing mercenaries. But using them ran their own risks. The timing was an inescapable issue. Idonia Foss survives an assassination attempt by an alleged British agent. Said alleged agent dies a violent death a short time afterwards. However many denials he issued, eyes would turn upon him.

Which was the last thing he wanted. He needed to maintain secrecy for personal reasons as much as institutional . . .

The answer came to him. In some way, he knew, it had been there from the start. He'd just wanted to eliminate all other options first. It was the most risky – yet, paradoxically, the least. The only danger would come if he was ever connected to it.

He would take every precaution to ensure that did not happen.

He was already up, and dressed. Knowing things had gone wrong in Munich, he had stayed awake, awaiting updates. Locke's call had followed a drip-feed of information via GCHQ. He left his study and went to the hall. Footsteps clattered behind him. 'No, you stay here,' he told Molly, the yellow labrador. She had been the youngest of Scott's three dogs. Scott's last words were a plea for their welfare. Maxwell felt obliged to live up to his word and look after them. The other two, both valuable pedigree animals, had been re-homed. Sentiment had brought Molly with him. Who could resist a smiling young lab?

Not him, apparently. Molly merely stood there, wagging her tail expectantly. She knew from his attitude that he was about to leave. 'Oh, all right, then,' he said, finding her lead.

This early in the morning, the roads were quiet. The drive took under twenty minutes. Bartleby House was a dour brick warehouse alongside a railway line. Molly at his side, Maxwell let himself in, locking the door behind him. A check of the electronic security system. No heat-sources on the three upper floors: no intruders. He wasn't surprised. This was as uninteresting a facility as could be imagined. Which was why SC9 was now based there.

He marched through endless musty aisles to a flight of steps in one corner. They descended to a door. Its keyhole had no key. Anyone trying to pick the lock would receive a lethal surprise. Maxwell instead flipped up the entire lock-plate to reveal a keypad. He tapped in his code and waited. Seconds passed, during which he was scrutinised by numerous security systems. Finally, locks clunked. He opened the door and passed through, Molly trotting with him.

Another door blocked the end of the short concrete passageway. This had a biometric lock, installed after he took control of SC9. A black glass panel scanned his finger-prints. Green light: approved. He entered.

SC9's subterranean headquarters had once been a wartime bunker. Maxwell had ordered the walls of drab institutional green repainted in less oppressive colours. His staff might spend long periods, potentially days at a time, down here. He knew the personnel roster, so was not surprised to find only one person present. 'Morning, Susan,' he said.

'Morning, Tony,' replied Susan King. She was older than him, one of Scott's original batch of Operatives. Maxwell had kept her under close scrutiny after taking over. However, his assessment of her had been correct. She was loyal to the country, to SC9, rather than a specific agency head. He had kept her on as his de facto number two. She was efficient, capable and organised. And she literally knew where all the bodies were buried. Some, she had put there herself. 'You're in early.'

'Something came up. Easier for me to handle it from here.'

'And you brought Molly! Hello, lovely!' She cooed over the labrador, who responded with a thrashing wag of her tail. 'Do you need anything?'

'A coffee would be great, thanks. Oh, and the latest red files.'

'I'll bring them to you.'

'Thanks.' Maxwell headed for a door at the room's rear. The main office could accommodate a dozen desk-bound Operatives, but was never that busy. The most he'd ever needed at one time was seven.

Right now, the fewer Operatives present, the better. He entered his private office, putting his phone into the security box by the door. All SC9 devices were regularly checked for spyware. But had it been hacked, undetected, the Faraday cage would block all signals from it. Molly lay down under his desk as he sat and logged into his computer. The latest updates regarding ongoing operations came up. All were secondary to the events in Munich. No new developments there. The police were still searching for Dr Stefan Holke – aka Harrison Locke. 'For fuck's sake, Alex,' he muttered. He'd given his former protégé every opportunity to stay off the radar. Instead, he'd come crashing back into SC9's affairs as visibly as he could. Locke was, of course, deniable. Every

Operative was, their new identities constructed to protect the State if they were caught. But doing so required work, consumed resources and time.

And if Reeve were caught, if he openly told the world about SC9 . . .

Again, everything was deniable. But SC9 had barely dodged a bullet when Craig Parker tried to expose its stolen files. That Reeve alone had stopped him was an irony not lost on Maxwell. But now, Reeve was a threat. He had interfered in a mission. Told a target of SC9's existence and purpose. Maxwell couldn't risk his telling others. Not any more.

King knocked, then entered with a cup of coffee and a folder. 'Do you need anything else?'

'Not for now, thanks,' he replied. She nodded and exited, closing the door behind her.

Maxwell opened the folder. The 'red files' were regularly updated lists of contact information obtained on foreign agents. Home addresses, phone numbers, emails. They were considered so valuable, their distribution was only physical, not electronic. Strictly need-to-know. The paper they were printed on was dark red, to make photocopying impossible. Systemic inertia again, Maxwell mused. A phone camera could capture the pages and make them legible with ease. But that was the way things had always been done, so . . .

He switched on his desk lamp. Black text on red might defeat photocopiers, but was scarcely easier for humans to read. He flicked through the pages until he found those concerning Russian assets. He knew the name he was after was on the list. He had seen it in prior updates. But had GCHQ's ceaseless electronic trawling identified his current details? Spies got through phone numbers like most people got through tissues—

There was the name. Most recently updated . . . two weeks prior. His personal number could still be valid. The red files only included contact details active within the past month. Past information was archived, but mostly for completionism. Agents rarely went back to old numbers.

He contemplated his computer. Should he check the subject's last known location? His plan would fall apart at the first step if he were in South America. But he decided against it. Better that there was no possible electronic trail. He wrote the number on a Post-It, and pocketed it. Then he stood and went to a filing cabinet. He unlocked it and opened a drawer. Inside were three boxed pay-as-you-go mobile phones. Different makes and models, from various suppliers. The common feature was that they and their cheap credit had been bought in cash. He unboxed one at random and put it in his pocket with the note.

There was no rush. Even with the time difference, it was still morning in Moscow. He began the day's actual work, drinking his coffee. Only after half an hour did he decide to make his move. He took something from a desk drawer and stood, signalling Molly to follow. She jumped up. He took her lead and left his office. 'Just giving Molly a quick walk around the block,' he told King. 'Back soon.'

He left the building. It was still dark, the weather cold and damp. Better than the freezing blizzards hitting Munich, though. He walked down the street, surreptitiously checking if he was being followed. He wasn't. All the same, he followed a twisting path down various side roads. Finally satisfied that he wasn't being tailed, he halted in an alley. He tapped the number from the red file into the phone and dialled it.

He used the wait for an answer to ready the object from his desk. An electronic voice-changer, little more than a toy. It would alter the pitch of his voice and mask it with a robotic-sounding rasp. But he knew from tests by GCHQ that was enough to confuse voice recognition. He just needed to avoid using common phrases to prevent a tempo match.

Since he wouldn't be speaking in English, that would not be a problem.

The call was finally answered. Maxwell was relieved; he'd started to worry the number had been abandoned. '*Da?*' Wariness in the Russian's voice. Who was calling him from an unknown phone?

'Garald Kazimirovich Morozov,' said Maxwell through the voice-changer, in Russian. 'I can tell you where to find Alex Reeve.'

A startled silence, followed by caution. 'Who is this?'

'It doesn't matter. I'll give you Reeve's location – if you agree to kill him.'

A low, menacing chuckle. 'Nothing would give me greater pleasure. What do you want in return?'

'Just Reeve dead, and anyone with him. There will be another Operative there. Kill him too.'

'You do not ask for much, do you?' said Morozov with mocking sarcasm.

'Do you want Reeve dead?'

'After what he did to me? Yes.'

'Then that's the deal. Are you interested?'

A pause. Maxwell had never met Morozov, but had read

his file. A cunning, dangerous man, the Russian equivalent of an Operative. The difference was in their relative degrees of subtlety. Operatives usually – not always – worked to make their kills seem like anything but targeted assassinations. Assassins from Russia's Directorate S, however, were much less discreet. Killing the target was one thing. But they also wanted those around them to know exactly *who* did it, and *why*. A very, very blunt warning, using very, very blunt methods. Victims of Directorate S were disproportionately prone to falling from high windows. More often than not, the windows would be closed at the time.

A subtle man could be blunt when the situation called for it. Maxwell was gambling that the reverse was a harder call. He knew Morozov had every reason to hate Reeve. He had killed several of the Russian's men. Wounded him severely enough to cause him to be reassigned from field work. Would the opportunity for revenge be enough to overcome his suspicion?

Apparently so. 'I . . . am interested, yes,' said Morozov. 'Where is he?'

'He'll be in Zermatt, Switzerland, some time today,' Maxwell told him. 'At the ski lodge of a German woman called Idonia Foss. You'll be able to locate it from her file; the SVR will have one. We won't speak again. Goodbye.'

He ended the call. Within seconds, the phone was dismantled. He started back to Bartleby House, dropping pieces down widely spaced drains.

Despite having taken every precaution, he felt a knot of foreboding. He had just technically committed treason. GCHQ would have automatically intercepted the call.

Reeve's name had been removed from GCHQ's active watch list two months earlier. Maxwell's order, slipped through amongst numerous other requests; part of the ill-fated détente. But a known *Sluzhba Vneshney Razvedki* agent being called from London would ring alarm bells. Russia's Foreign Intelligence Service topped the list of enemies of the British state. Someone at GCHQ might remember Reeve as a person of interest. And the call had been made only half a mile from SC9's headquarters . . .

All he could do for now was ensure his defences were in place.

CHAPTER 32

Garald Kazimirovich Morozov held his phone for a moment, thinking. Then he stood and marched to his office's door. 'Boris,' he called, gesturing. 'A minute.'

Boris Maximovich Pervak rose from his desk and shambled to him. The skinny, pasty young man would not have made much of a field agent. He was, however, an excellent technician and computer hacker. The SVR was always on the lookout for such people. It had given Pervak the option of three years in its service. The alternative was one year of bullying in regular military conscription. Pervak had happily accepted the offer. He had now been with Directorate S for five years, with no intention of moving elsewhere. Locating targets for others to kill was, it turned out, his calling.

'What can I do for you this fine morning, Garald?' Pervak asked. Grim smiles from both men; it was ten below freezing outside.

Morozov closed the door, then held up his phone. 'I just got a call from someone claiming to know the location of Alex Reeve.'

Pervak's unruly eyebrows shot up. 'Reeve? The Brit? The one who . . . ?' He glanced at his superior's right hand.

Morozov nodded. 'Yes.' Reeve had smashed his hand in a

car door during his escape. The Russian's injuries had cost him his forefinger, his middle finger now only partially mobile. Despite Morozov's best efforts, he had not been ambidextrous enough to pass the fitness tests. Field work was no longer an option. So he had been 'promoted' to an administrative position in Moscow. All well and good for his career, but . . . he missed the travel. And, he had to admit, the excitement. He had been good at his old job. There was something uniquely rewarding about making a perfect kill – and getting away with it.

He passed the phone to Pervak. 'I want you to trace the call. Find out where it came from.'

'SCS will have a recording. Probably a trace as well.' The Special Communications Service was Russia's electronic intelligence agency.

'I know, but I want to keep it in-house for now. Can you do it?'

An immodest shrug. 'Of course I can. Give me ten minutes.' Pervak smirked, then left the office.

He returned seven minutes later. 'Got it,' he said, entering without knocking. Morozov forgave the breach of protocol. He tolerated the nerd's eccentricities and social clumsiness – to a point. Pervak put the phone on Morozov's desk. 'The call came from London. An area called Bermondsey, doesn't mean anything to me. You?' Morozov shook his head. 'I was only able to pinpoint it to within about two hundred metres. There's nothing of intelligence interest nearby.'

'That doesn't mean anything,' said Morozov. 'We're dealing with SC9 here. They hide themselves very well.'

'Maybe not well enough, if someone's found Reeve.'

271

'Reeve's not in SC9 any more. They've been trying to kill him for two years. I'm wondering if someone in SC9 wants us to do their job for them.'

'You think it's a trick?'

Morozov gave the younger man a broad, unsettling grin. 'Of *course* it's a trick. You should know that by now. You can never trust the British. No, maybe SC9 are trying to clean house. That shootout in Venice, four months ago? You saw the news footage. Reeve was involved. The people after him were probably Operatives. The whole thing turned into a very public bloodbath. So now, SC9 are trying to finish the job – without getting their hands dirty.'

'So they tell *you* where to find Reeve,' said Pervak, nodding in understanding.

'Exactly. They think I'll want revenge, and will run straight to Switzerland to find him.'

'And will you?'

The disturbing grin returned. 'Well, yes! I'm not passing up the chance to catch Reeve. But I'm not going alone. And I'm not going to be their stooge, either. Reeve will die – eventually. But he'll die *here*. We'll extract everything we can from him. Including the password to Craig Parker's files. And we'll capture the other Operative our mysterious friend mentioned too.'

Pervak frowned. 'He wants you to kill another Operative? Maybe this guy isn't from SC9 after all. It could be someone trying to set us against them.'

Morozov shook his head. 'I thought about that. Nobody else knows. Not unless someone else infiltrated SC9 even deeper than we did.'

A small laugh. 'It'd be funny if every single Operative turned out to be planted by another agency.'

'Well, that's the ultimate goal, isn't it? Get your own man in at the top of the other side. But no, I don't think that's what's happening here. I suspect there's some internal politics going on. Our friend sees a way to get rid of Reeve *and* a rival. I'm happy to do that – but on *my* terms. We'll capture them, bring them back, and squeeze them like lemons. *Then* we kill them. And let the British know how we caught them. That will drive them berserk. There's nothing like a good mole-hunt to turn their intelligence community upside down.'

'And while they're backstabbing each other, they don't have time to look at us.'

'You're getting the hang of this, Boris Maximovich,' said Morozov. He stood. 'I need to talk to Grishin. While I'm gone, start prepping for an operation. Find out which men we have available in Central Europe. And arrange transport for me, fastest possible means. A private flight, if necessary. I intend to be in Switzerland by this evening.'

Pervak was surprised. 'You're going on a field op?'

Morozov held up his ruined hand. 'Reeve did this to me. I'm going to make him pay for it. In person.'

An impromptu personal appointment with the head of Directorate S was not easy to arrange. Even Morozov, a long-serving and trusted officer, had to wait outside his office. After over thirty minutes, his secretary finally ushered him in. 'Morozov, sir,' she told the man inside.

Pyotr Viktorovich Grishin did not look like a feared spymaster. Short, portly, balding, he more resembled an accountant or lawyer in some dull specialist field. He never bothered to correct anyone's mistaken impression. Underestimating him was an error many had made, but few had survived. He had run Russia's Illegal Intelligence department for over a decade. One of its tasks was to plant deep-cover sleeper agents in other countries. That side of the work required patience and subtlety.

The other side was where agents like Morozov came in. 'Ah, Garald Kazimirovich,' he said, dismissing his secretary. 'What brings you to me at short notice?' He gestured for his visitor to sit.

Morozov did so, then got straight to the point. 'Alex Reeve.'

There was no need for further explanation or consultation of files. Grishin had a memory as efficient as any computer. 'The SC9 Operative.'

'Yes. I know where he is.' He quickly summarised the unexpected phone call. 'I would like permission to capture him – and this other Operative.'

Something resembling a wry smile creased Grishin's cheeks. 'You know this is of course some kind of trap.'

'Of course,' Morozov replied, with faint humour of his own. 'But I read the file of this Idonia Foss. She is the head of a German arms company. She's currently leading the merger of several small European companies into one larger one. Which would make her a target for SC9. Removing her at this stage would cause the merger to collapse. British conglomerates like Xeneon would be perfectly placed to buy up the pieces.'

'So Foss is the other Operative's target. Why would your

contact, assuming he is from SC9, sacrifice him?'

'Internal politics, a power play, would be my guess. After the fiasco in Venice, maybe the British have put someone new in charge. But the old boss still has his loyalists. My mysterious friend may be trying to remove a rival.'

'Hmm.' Grishin nodded, then sipped from a china cup of mint tea. 'SC9. The British mystery box. Even after getting a man inside, we do not know enough about it.'

'Which is why I want to go to Zermatt. In overwhelming force. Our caller probably expects us to send a team of three or four. I'm thinking six or seven. I checked the location of Foss's ski lodge. It's outside the town, isolated. We use a sniper to stop anyone who tries to run. The rest of the team is an assault squad. Storm the building, capture Reeve and the other Operative – and kill anyone else.'

Grishin gave Morozov a look over the top of his glasses. 'You would do SC9's work for them?'

'It occurred to me that stopping this merger is in Russia's interests too. We have our own arms industry to protect. We don't need some upstart rival competing with our businesses.'

A faint grunting sound that could have been a laugh. 'You are starting to see the bigger picture, Garald Kazimirovich,' said Grishin. 'You will go far.'

Morozov chose his next words carefully. 'I only want to go as far as Switzerland for now.'

Grishin's glasses dipped again for another, more intense, stare. 'You want to go back into the field?'

'In a tactical command role, not direct combat. I don't need a trigger finger to issue orders. But I *do* need to be there.'

He leaned forward in his seat, gaze matching Grishin's intensity. 'I want to capture Reeve myself.'

'I understand your feelings,' said Grishin, after a moment. 'Your logic . . . not so much. You are emotionally involved, Garald Kazimirovich. You know as well as I that is not a situation we encourage.'

'I know. But I *need* to go, sir. Not just for myself, but for the men Reeve killed in Italy. I need to make sure he does not escape again.'

'And for him to know that *you* caught him?'

The only answer Morozov could give was a small nod. Grishin leaned back thoughtfully. 'Very well,' he said at last. 'Make a list of your requirements. I will authorise them.'

'Thank you, sir.' Morozov stood, about to leave.

A pudgy finger rose in warning, stopping him in his tracks. 'Do not make any mistakes. One Operative killed your entire team in Italy. This time, you are facing *two* Operatives.'

'Who seem to be facing each other,' Morozov pointed out. 'With luck, they won't notice us – until it's too late.'

'Then may all your luck be good.' The finger wagged in dismissal. Morozov exited, filled with a new sense of purpose.

And an old, much-missed sense of anticipation. The hunt was on.

This time, Alex Reeve would not get away.

CHAPTER 33

Reeve awoke sharply at a knock on the door. He sat up, briefly confused by his unfamiliar surroundings. Then memory returned. He was in Idonia Foss's office. The grey light of day seeped around the blinds. Almost ten in the morning. He hadn't meant to sleep for so long. Pure exhaustion had decided otherwise. 'Yes?' he mumbled.

The door opened. Idonia leaned in. 'Alex? Are you awake?'

'Yeah, yes. Just give me a minute.' She withdrew. Reeve rose and quickly dressed. 'Okay, come in.'

Idonia returned, this time accompanied by Avelina. 'Alex, how are you feeling?' asked the latter. 'Are you okay?'

'I'm . . . surviving,' was the best he could manage. Sleep and food had helped, but he still felt weakened, pained.

'We are all surviving,' said Idonia. 'Thanks to you. Here. A token of my thanks.' She handed something to Reeve.

He regarded it in surprise. 'A passport?'

'As promised. I told you I had friends in the government.'

Reeve flicked through the document. His own face looked back from inside it. Photoshop work had been done to clean him up, remove his bruises. The holder's name under his picture was Daniel Gant. The passport's anti-counterfeiting measures were in place; it appeared completely genuine. It probably was. All nations maintained a stock of 'blank' identities for their intelligence services. They needed only the new user's photograph for activation. SC9 could similarly call upon MI5 for fake, yet authentic, British identity papers. They would rarely be provided so quickly, though. Especially not as a favour. 'German efficiency. Thank you. Will it work?'

'I have been assured so. With money and the right connections, anything is possible.'

Avelina smiled sarcastically. 'Wouldn't it be great if that were used to make the world a better place?'

'No one can make things better for everyone,' Idonia replied, faintly hectoring. It was apparently a topic they had debated before. 'All we can do is make things better for some.'

'And try not to make thing worse for the rest,' was the pointed rejoinder.

Idonia drew in a tired breath, then turned back to Reeve. She gave him a large envelope. 'There is more paperwork in there. For social security, that kind of thing. There is also a pre-paid debit card. I have put twenty thousand euros on to it.'

Reeve blinked. 'Thank you. That's . . . very generous.'

'You saved my life. *Our* lives. If you need more, just ask.'

'Thank you,' he said again.

'Now, I have arranged a helicopter to Switzerland. We will be there around one o'clock.'

He nodded. 'What about security?'

'Reynold has three men, the specialists I told you about.

They have all worked for the company before; they can be trusted. One of them is also our helicopter pilot. If there is any trouble in Zermatt, he can fly us out.'

'When do we leave?'

'Whenever you are ready.'

Avelina held up a paper bag. 'I got you some things you might need. Toothbrush, toothpaste. I bought you new clothes as well. I remembered your sizes. I thought you might like some clean things.'

'I would, yes. Thank you.'

Avelina smiled again. 'They're in the boardroom. I'll get them for you.' She left the room.

Reeve checked the bag's contents. 'Have you heard anything about Locke?'

'Not yet,' Idonia replied unhappily. 'The police are looking for him. Nobody has seen him, though. Might he come after us again?'

'If he was following standard procedure for an Operative, no. If a mission is blown, you walk away, immediately.'

'But he came for us at the house even after you exposed him.'

'Yeah. So I don't know what he might do next.' He wondered how Maxwell had reacted to events. Surely he would have ordered Locke to bug out after the events at the palace? That led to a concerning thought. Was Locke acting against orders? He had tried to complete his mission once, even when the situation demanded withdrawal. Would he now double down?

No way to know. All he could do was take protective action. Leaving Munich was a good start. He looked around as Avelina returned, carrying two large shopping bags. 'Here,' she said, offering them to him.

'Thanks.' He noticed a boxed iPhone in one bag. 'I don't need that.'

'Oops, that's mine,' said Avelina. She plucked it out. 'Don't worry,' she added, on his critical look. 'I paid cash for it. I won't activate it until we're in Zermatt. And I won't use it around you. Okay?'

'I *knew* you couldn't go a week without a phone,' said Idonia, teasing.

Reeve reluctantly nodded to Avelina. 'Okay. I'll make you a Faraday bag for it, though.'

'A what?'

'Shielding; layers of plastic and foil. It'll stop it from being used as a bug.' She nodded. 'I'll clean up, then we can go.'

'All right,' said Idonia. 'We will see you soon.'

Reeve acknowledged, then went into the bathroom to get ready.

Locke raised his head at the sound of a car pulling into the driveway. He had been lurking in the house's side porch for almost an hour. Under normal circumstances, he would have expected his target to arrive forty minutes earlier. It must have been a busy shift.

He waited until he heard the car's door close before standing. His footprints on the snow-covered drive were clearly visible. He needed to show himself before the target called the police. Sure enough, as he rounded the house's side its owner was staring at the trail. Someone had arrived, but not left. Confusion would become alarm in moments—

'Gerhard,' said Locke. The pained rasp in his voice was only partly faked. Dr Gerhard Hitzfeld looked around at him. Locke waited for his hospital colleague's reaction. Surprise or shock would be understandable. Fear would mean Hitzfeld had been warned about him. Which would it be?

Surprise – becoming shock as Hitzfeld saw his bruised face. 'My God! Stefan, what happened?'

'I was attacked,' Locke told him. He made a show of being unsteady on his feet. Hitzfeld hurried to help support him. 'Muggers, robbers, I don't know. I ran from them. This was the nearest place I knew.'

'Jesus! Let me get you inside. You must be freezing.' Hitzfeld brought him to the front door and unlocked it. 'Here, come in.'

'Thank you.' Locke's gratitude at entering was at least partially genuine. The house's interior was agreeably warm.

Hitzfeld closed the door and disarmed the security system. Locke reached inside his coat. 'What happened?' the German asked. 'Someone at the hospital said the police were looking for you—'

Locke whirled and drove his combat knife up into Hitzfeld's lower jaw. The diamond-sharp point punched through skin and tissue and bone into his brain. The Operative grabbed Hitzfeld with his free arm, then twisted his knife wrist. Wet crackling noises came from inside the German's head. Locke felt him convulse – then go limp. He yanked out the blade and let go. Hitzfeld collapsed to the floor, eyes wide.

Locke assessed his handiwork. At its angle of entry, the knife should have bisected the hypothalamus. That in itself would cause massive trauma to the autonomic nervous system. His twist to deliver further damage had finished the job. The blow was not immediately fatal; Hitzfeld was still twitching. But his brain was effectively destroyed. He wiped the knife clean, then re-sheathed it.

A rapid search of his victim. Car keys, wallet, phone. He took the first two and discarded the last. The wallet held over a hundred euros in cash, and several credit and debit cards. Locke had his own financial reserves, but these would still be useful. Maxwell might cancel the cards of his backup identities.

He made a breakfast of poached eggs, preparing himself for the journey. Then he collected his gear from the side porch and got into the German's Mercedes. His destination was entered into the satnav. Five hundred kilometres; in present conditions, nearly a seven-hour drive. Curiously, the route stopped short of Zermatt itself, at somewhere called Täsch. Was the road blocked? He took out his smartphone; a burner, bought weeks earlier. SC9 didn't know about it, so shouldn't be able to track him through it. A rapid check. No, the road wasn't closed, although recent snowfalls had been heavy. It turned out that Zermatt simply didn't permit cars on its streets. Electric taxis were the only motorised transport allowed.

It didn't matter. He could get a taxi or train to the town from Täsch. From there, he would take a cable-car, then proceed on foot. SC9 had given him the location of Foss's lodge weeks before. It was at the resort's furthest edge, two hundred metres from the nearest building. Idonia Foss liked isolation.

As did Locke. It meant nobody would hear the screams.

He started the car and began his long journey to Switzerland.

CHAPTER 34

The helicopter flight from Munich to Zermatt took less than three hours. That was even with a stop at Zurich airport. Despite being surrounded by the European Union, Switzerland was independent from it. Treaties allowed for free travel, but air passengers still needed their identities confirmed. Reeve hid his tension as the Swiss customs official examined everyone's passports. The ink was metaphorically – perhaps literally – barely dry on his newly issued document. He watched as it was passed through a hand-held scanner . . .

And returned. Everything was in order. He knew better than to show any external signs of relief, though. Instead he waited for everyone else to be checked. There were six others with him. Avelina, Idonia and Reynold Netz. The pilot and lead bodyguard was a lean-faced blond man called Curt Beckmeyer. His two associates were Trost Miltner and Konrad Thorner. Both were burly and crop-haired; the biggest difference was that Thorner was bearded. Each had their own papers approved, then returned. Reeve finally relaxed as the official walked away. Beckmeyer spoke to air traffic control, and the chopper resumed its journey.

The Alps rose below as the helicopter headed southwest. For the first time in a seeming eternity, Reeve saw the sun in blue sky. He suspected the break in the weather would be fleeting, though. More clouds loomed beyond the peaks ahead. He made the most of it, enjoying the view.

'There's the Matterhorn,' said Avelina after a while. Reeve saw one particular peak standing above the others around it. It was an almost cartoonishly perfect triangle, capped with snow. 'Zermatt is about seven kilometres from it.'

Idonia, meanwhile, was engaged in an intense German discussion with Beckmeyer. The pilot, in turn, debated with someone over the radio. Whatever the subject, it eventually seemed to end in Idonia's favour. She listened to a reply over the headphones, then smiled. '*Bring uns direkt zur Skihütte,*' she ordered. Beckmeyer made a small course adjustment.

Reeve was able to deduce the English translation. 'We're going straight to the ski lodge?'

'Yes,' Idonia replied. 'Usually, we would have to land at Zermatt heliport and take the cable-car. But I received special permission to fly directly to the lodge. I told them about our security concerns. It also helps that I am friends with the mayor of Zermatt,' she added smugly.

The helicopter continued onwards, gradually descending. Ahead, Reeve saw what he assumed was Zermatt. The town spread across a flat-bottomed valley, the Matterhorn towering over it. He spotted the heliport at Zermatt's northern end, colourful aircraft parked in the snow. A railway line ran past it into the town proper. But his own ride continued onwards, sweeping over a cable-car line heading uphill. Two lines, he realised, running parallel. Enclosed gondolas carried people up and down both routes.

'The cable cars go to Furi,' Avelina piped up. She indicated buildings higher on the mountainside ahead. 'You can take other lines to the different ski routes from there. Or you can carry on up to the Matterhorn.'

'There's a cable-car to the top?' Reeve asked, surprised.

'Not the top.' She pointed off to the left, but he couldn't pick out which specific feature she meant. 'It goes to a smaller peak, to one side. But it's still high up. The view is amazing on a good day. And you can even go inside a glacier.'

'Cool.'

Avelina grinned. 'Did you just make a joke?'

'I didn't mean to, but . . . I suppose,' he said, half-smiling. 'How long before we land?'

'Only a few minutes,' said Idonia. 'I can see the lodge.'

It was her turn to point. Beyond the small village of Furi, buildings were scattered up a tree-speckled hillside. They became more widely spaced the higher they went. The last was roughly a hundred and fifty metres below the hill's summit. He saw a path winding up through the snow towards it. But the track didn't stop there, rising to the crest of the slope. He followed it—

And saw the Foss family's ski lodge beyond.

It stood at the start of a relatively gentle treeless expanse. The building was a striking mixture of traditional and modern design. The roof was steep and overhanging to mini-mise the build-up of winter snow. The windows below it, though, were floor-to-ceiling glass. A stark contrast to the little shuttered windows on the other buildings below. Either they were exceptionally well insulated, or Idonia's heating bills were enormous.

He took in the rest of the structure. Three floors, by the

look of it. Clad in wood, but probably with a concrete or steel frame to support the glass. It appeared luxurious, expensive. What about the surroundings? The path continued past it. It led to a cable-car station on the plain. He saw a gondola slowing to pass through it. His mind automatically stored the information: *escape route*. There was nothing else in sight higher up other than cable-car pylons, though. He looked back at the hillside. The tree line was roughly a hundred metres below the lodge. Under that, the pine forest was dense enough to provide cover. If it could be reached. One hundred metres through thick snow was a lengthy enough run to leave him vulnerable. Especially to an Operative . . .

He tried to assess more of the landscape. Cable-car lines off to the left, a steep-sided valley beyond them. But then the chopper changed direction. Reeve looked back at the lodge as the aircraft arced towards it. A perfectly flat square of snow stood on the building's far side. A helipad. Wry amusement. Idonia hadn't taken advantage of her influence on the spur of the moment. She'd already used it to get her retreat built in the first place.

The helicopter descended. Its downwash blasted concentric ripples of snow from the pad. But the covering was still thick enough for the skids to disappear into the whiteness. The aircraft touched down with a thump. Miltner seemed especially relieved to be back on solid ground.

Reeve looked back at the lodge. He'd assumed its roof was symmetrical on both sides. The reality was different; the building was wedge-shaped. The wall facing him rose vertically to the roof's summit. Its upper section, almost half its total height, was glass. The top floor's southwestern wall was a giant window, a balcony running its full width. A glance in the other direction told him why. It gave a completely unobstructed view of the Matterhorn.

'What do you think, Alex?' asked Idonia, seeing his interest.

'Nice place,' he replied. 'Must be a hell of a view from inside.'

'It is. From this side you see the Matterhorn, from the other down to Zermatt. There is probably no better in Switzerland.'

By now Beckmeyer had secured the helicopter from flight and powered down the engines. He unfastened his seatbelt. The passengers followed his lead and began to disembark. 'So what's the plan?' Reeve asked.

'My men will check the house first,' said Netz. 'None of the security alarms have been triggered, but it is a precaution.'

'What security does it have?'

'The only entrances are at ground level, at the other side. They are covered by cameras and motion sensors.'

Reeve noticed a weather-shielded camera at the lodge's corner watching the helipad. 'Is there a panic room?'

'No, but the top floor has only one way up to it. It can be defended. My men have all had counter-terrorism training. They will hold off any intruders.'

'What about weapons? Is everyone armed?'

'Yes,' said Idonia. 'There is a gun cabinet. I made sure it was stocked with enough weapons and ammunition for everyone. Well, except you,' she added to Avelina. 'I know you do not approve of guns.'

'I still know which end the bullets come out of,' Avelina replied spikily.

Everyone exited the helicopter. Beckmeyer checked the aircraft while Netz and his other two men trudged to the lodge. Reeve tugged up his new coat's zip. The sun was out, but the temperature was still well below freezing. He surveyed his wider surroundings. 'So you've got your own cable-car station?' he said, gesturing upslope.

'It's not only for us,' said Avelina, amused. 'It's called Aroleid – it's a stop for skiers and hikers. It's not as convenient as it looks. You can only get on or off if you're heading up from Furi. There is no downward stop.'

'So how do you get down into Furi from here?'

'You ski, of course,' said Idonia, as if the answer were obvious. 'Can you ski?'

Reeve had trained extensively in his military career. 'Yes.'

'Good. We have skis and boots in the lodge. There should be something that fits.'

'What about supplies? How long can you hole up if you need to?'

Idonia looked puzzled; Avelina translated his question into German. 'Ah, I see,' Idonia said. 'There is enough for probably a week. I had the caretaker bring more supplies this morning. But if I can persuade my partners to accelerate the merger, we will not need them. Once the merger is complete, there is no point in killing me. Correct?'

'In theory,' said Reeve. 'I think Locke's still a threat, though. He might try to kill you again – and me too while he's at it.'

'Why would he take that risk? Especially now people know the serial-killer story is not real?'

'Because he's a psycho,' was his blunt answer. Neither of the Fosses appeared reassured by it.

A voice called in German from the lodge. Reeve turned to see Netz on the top-floor balcony. A panel of the expansive glass wall was open to act as a door. 'The house is clear,' said Idonia, relieved. 'We can go inside.'

Reeve led the women to the lodge. Beckmeyer stayed at the chopper, still going through his post-flight checks. The bodyguards' trail led around to the building's northeastern face. A large, overhanging porch roof provided shelter for two doors. 'That door is for the ski room,' said Idonia, passing the larger entrance. 'We will go in here.'

A security camera stared down at them as they reached the second door. Idonia opened it and went inside. Warm air immediately hit Reeve. The caretaker had turned on the heating as well as stocking the pantry. They kicked off snow on a large mat, then hung up their coats. 'The ski room is through there,' Idonia said, indicating a door. 'There are showers, and a sauna too. If you like that kind of thing.'

'Never tried it,' said Reeve.

'Maybe you should,' offered Avelina. 'I use it some-times when I'm here. It's relaxing when you're in the right mood.'

'Don't think I'll be in a mood to relax until we're all safe.'

'Nor will I,' said Idonia. She led the way up a curving wood-panelled staircase. 'All the bedrooms are on the next floor. There are six, enough for twelve people. I assumed you would want privacy, so you have one for yourself.'

'Thanks,' said Reeve. 'I don't need anything special, though.'

'That is hard to avoid, I'm afraid. All the bedrooms are very nice.' They reached the next floor, the stairs bringing them to the middle of a hallway. Doors lined both sides. Idonia opened one. 'You can have this one.'

Reeve took it in. Even the king-size double bed appeared a little lost in the large room. Panoramic windows overlooked Zermatt in the distance. Walk-in wardrobes occupied one wall, with a door to an en suite bathroom. A large flatscreen television was mounted at head-height beside the entrance. 'It's nicer than my hostel room,' he said. 'Thanks.' He went to the windows. A snow-shrouded balcony was outside, partially covered by the overhanging roof. He regarded the landscape beyond. His attention instantly went to a couple of people walking towards the lodge. Threats? Probably not: they appeared middle-aged, and were following a well-defined trail. 'Is that the path from Furi?'

Idonia and Avelina joined him. 'Yes,' said the former. 'It's quite steep in places, but not dangerous.'

'Where does it go?'

'It's a hiking route,' Avelina told him. 'It goes to Aroleid station, then on to Schwarzsee. You can walk all the way to Trockener Steg in good weather.'

Reeve had no idea what those places were. But he was more concerned about the path itself than its destination. 'Wait, you built your private retreat right next to a public footpath? There isn't even a fence?'

Both women gave him odd looks. 'No,' said Idonia at last. 'That just . . . isn't done.' The very concept of enclosing the land around a mountain house seemed alien to her.

'So random people can walk right past your front door? Okay,' he said, realising he was taking a very British attitude to property boundaries. 'Well, at least you've got cameras, so you can keep an eye on them.' He turned away from the view. 'Six bedrooms, and seven people? Who has to share?'

'The bodyguards will work in shifts, so someone will always be awake,' said Idonia. 'Okay, I will show you the rest of the lodge.'

She led Reeve and Avelina from the bedroom. Another flight of stairs headed upwards. These were narrower, three right-angled turns along the ascent. Reeve looked up, seeing an open space above. Netz had been right; the stairs should be defendable. Against one or two intruders, at least. A larger force making an open assault would be another story. But would Maxwell take that approach? The last time SC9 went in heavy, in Venice, it had ended in disaster . . .

They reached the top floor, emerging in its centre. Idonia had saved the most impressive part of the tour for last. Most of the level was a single huge room with a steeply vaulted ceiling. The towering full-width window indeed gave a spectacular view of the Matterhorn. Smaller, but still tall, dormer windows cut into the roof provided overviews of Zermatt. The room itself, while open, was demarcated into different sections. A luxurious lounge before the high window. In one corner, a gleaming stainless-steel kitchen adjoined a dining area with a long table. Smaller, more intimate clusters of armchairs and coffee tables were dotted about. The only enclosed areas were in the corner across from the kitchen. Reeve guessed one door led to a bathroom. Another opened into a glass-walled room with blinds. Set into one wall was a large stone and metal fireplace. 'Here we are,' said Idonia proudly. 'The Grand Hall. I have had many good times here with friends.'

Avelina headed for the kitchen. 'Let's see if Gunther restocked the wine racks. Oh, he did!' She crouched to examine various bottles. 'Chateau Margaux. You should give him a raise, you know.'

'Gunther is paid more than adequately,' was the faintly snippy reply.

'You say that about all your staff, Mother.'

'What do you think, Alex?' asked Idonia, changing the subject.

'I like it,' was Reeve's polite answer. In truth, it represented a level of opulence beyond his comprehension. The only similar place he had ever been was a drug lord's London mansion. Idonia's tastes were less gaudy, but still more about show than comfort. The last place he had lived with Connie was a small flat in Umbria, Italy. The entire apartment could have fitted inside this one room. But he knew which he would rather be in. Was that all wealth amounted to in the end? Just . . . *more* of everything? Could anyone really distinguish a fifty euro bottle of wine from one costing five hundred? Or five thousand?

Avelina noticed his antipathy and changed the subject. 'So are we allowed to leave the lodge?'

Netz entered from the glass-walled side room, which Reeve assumed was Idonia's office. 'You can go outside, yes. But you must have someone with you.'

'We have only just arrived, and you want to go out already?' Idonia asked Avelina.

'It might be the only chance I get,' Avelina replied. 'I checked the weather forecast. There's going to be a blizzard this evening.'

'Would a blizzard cut off Zermatt?' Reeve asked thoughtfully. 'Shut down the railway and cable cars?'

'The cable cars, yes,' Idonia told him. 'They stop them if the wind is too strong. The railway, I don't know. I have known it to be closed in very bad weather. It depends how long the blizzard lasts.'

'What about the roads to Zermatt?'

'There's only one road,' said Avelina. 'They try to keep it ploughed. But if it's a bad storm, it gets blocked very quickly.'

'That might be to our advantage. If nobody can get into town, nobody can threaten us up here.'

'Unless they're in Zermatt already.' Avelina's face filled with dismay as she considered her own words. 'Do you think anyone is?'

'I don't know. How long would it take to drive here from Munich?'

'Six or seven hours,' said Idonia. 'It would depend on the weather. Could Stefan – I mean Locke – be here already?'

'I don't know. But we need to be prepared,' said Reeve. He turned to Netz. 'Idonia said one of the bodyguards will always be awake?'

'At least one, yes,' said the security chief. 'They will work eight-hour rotations. You and I will also be here. I assume you are willing to help protect the Fosses.'

'I am,' Reeve told him. Avelina smiled in gratitude. 'Where are your CCTV monitors?'

Netz indicated the glass-walled room. 'There are screens in Frau Foss's office. And there are more in the utility room on the bottom floor.'

'Okay. So anyone walking along the track past the lodge is a suspect. If they get close, keep an eye on them until they move well clear.' A thought came to him. 'How well will the CCTV work in a blizzard?'

'The cameras have infra-red,' said Netz. 'Even in the worst blizzard, you can still see for ten metres.'

'And what about the motion sensors?'

'They cover the two doors on the ground floor. They are both under shelter, so snow should not affect the sensors. If anyone comes to the doors, they will be seen.'

'And there are no other ways in?'

'No,' said Idonia. 'The bedrooms facing Zermatt have balconies, but they are too high to reach.' She indicated the door in the glass wall. 'I do not think anyone could climb up to the balconies on this floor.'

'They would have to be Spider-Man,' Avelina added.

All the same, Reeve went to see for himself. He opened the balcony door and stepped out. The cold air wrapped spikily around him. Below, the helicopter stood on the pad, rotors still. The path wound through the snow towards the cable-car station. Rocks occasionally poked above the white blanket, but otherwise there was no cover. He looked down over the railing. A sheer wall of glass, wood and concrete dropped away below. Satisfied, he returned indoors. A brief check of the windows as he closed the door. Triple-glazed, with a faint gold tint to the inner panes. Not to provide shade, but to reflect heat back inwards. Such large panels would have been toughened to some degree as well. Three layers wouldn't stop a bullet – but might deflect it.

He kept that thought to himself as he turned back to the others. 'All right. I think the place is as secure as you can make it. But keep the ground-floor doors locked at all times. Are your guys going to do regular patrols?' he asked Netz.

'Of course,' said the German. 'They will make reports by radio.'

'Good. So I guess now we wait and see if anything happens.'

'I'm not sitting around doing nothing,' Avelina insisted. 'There'll be time for that when the blizzard arrives. Before then, I want to do *something*. Alex, why don't you come out with me?'

'Where to?'

'We could ski down to Furi and catch the cable-car into Zermatt. Or go to the Matterhorn,' she said, more animated. She pointed at the towering mountain. 'We can take the cable-car at Aroleid, then the Matterhorn Express at Trockener Steg. I can book the tickets on my phone.'

Reeve was not keen on her plan. 'If you use a credit card, SC9 will know where you are.'

'I am sure they know anyway,' said Idonia. 'I did not pay for the helicopter rental in cash. And SC9 must know I own this place. It is hardly a secret. There was a magazine article about it last year.'

'Come on, Alex,' Avelina said imploringly. 'You might not get another chance to do it. And no offence to Reynold's men?' She gave Netz an apologetic look. 'But you are the person I most trust to look after us. After all, you promised. I know I will be safe with you.' She smiled at him.

Reeve felt suddenly uncomfortable with the praise. 'I do my best,' he said lamely.

Avelina picked up on his shift in attitude. But before she could comment on it, Idonia spoke to Netz. 'Do you think it is safe for them to go out, Reynold?'

'With what you have told me about Mr Reeve?' Netz replied. 'I would say yes.'

'Good,' said Avelina. 'Then what do you say, Alex? Do you want to go down to Zermatt? Or would you like a trip to the top of a mountain?'

Reeve considered the offer. 'The mountain,' he said at last. 'Why not. You only live once.'

She smiled. 'Hopefully for a very long time.'

'Yeah,' he replied. His own smile lacked humour. 'Let's hope.'

CHAPTER 35

Once they were ready, the trek to Aroleid cable-car station did not take long. Even with fresh snow, enough hikers had followed the route to carve a path. Once there, a gondola soon arrived, a box of blue-tinted glass. The upward-bound cars slowed to a crawl through the station, doors open. Reeve and Avelina simply stepped aboard before they closed again. Reeve surreptitiously assessed the other passengers. Two men with skis, around twenty, both speaking German. Unlikely to be Operatives – too young. All the same, he kept a wary eye on them. It didn't take long to realise they had no interest in him, only Avelina. Even layered against the cold, she still looked feminine. An inner smile. Would they still feel the same if they knew more about her? Another thought overrode that one: either way, it was none of his business.

Unless they *made* it his business.

Luckily, neither skier was inclined to do so. The journey's first stage, to the large station of Trockener Steg, took about fifteen minutes. Having recently viewed the Alps from a helicopter, Reeve was initially unimpressed by the view. But the relative calm and quiet of the ascent gradually won him over. The mountain peaks had a stark beauty different from anywhere else he had experienced. And, as Avelina pointed out, that was only half the journey.

The cable-car for the second leg was larger, able to take more passengers. They shared it with half a dozen others, putting Reeve on edge. There was nothing to suggest they were anything but sightseers. Even so, he paid more attention to people than scenery. His tension did not ease until Avelina pointed out their destination. A blocky mountain peak, draped in snow, stood ahead. At its left side, a smaller wedge of rock clawed higher into the sky. Even from a distance, a dark archway set into it was visible.

'The Klein Matterhorn,' Avelina told him. 'It's the highest cable-car station in Europe. Three thousand eight hundred metres, something like that.'

Reeve couldn't help but view it from a tactical perspective. 'And the cable-car's the only way down if there's trouble.'

It was an observation, not a question, and she picked up on it. 'Do you think there might be trouble?' She lowered her voice. 'Even if SC9 know we came up here, how would they get here so fast?'

'They wouldn't,' he admitted, after a moment's consideration. 'And it's too public. If an Operative tried anything here, there'd be too many witnesses.' He surveyed the approaching mountain and cable-car terminus. It couldn't help but remind him of the old war movie *Where Eagles Dare*. 'If they escaped in the cable-car, the cops could just stop it. They'd be waiting at the lower station when it restarted. And I wouldn't fancy free climbing down.'

She gave him a bright smile. 'So you can relax, yes?'

His response was a brief half-grin. 'For now.'

The cables steepened on the final stretch, wind swinging the gondola. One of the other passengers let out a nervous gasp. But the car rumbled through the last pylon and levelled out. 'Enjoy your stay at Europe's highest mountain station,' said a chirpy recorded voice. The car swept into the concrete archway and slowed. The more nervous travellers expressed their relief.

Reeve and Avelina exited. He had already noticed the thinning air during the ascent. Running had kept him fit enough to handle the diminished oxygen level. Even so, he still felt an unsettling light-headedness. His companion, though, wobbled as she walked for the exit. He caught her by the arm. 'Are you okay?'

'Oh, *ja, ja,*' she replied. 'Yes. I haven't been up this high for a while.' She drew in a few deep, slow breaths. 'I will be okay. But thank you.'

'No problem.' He waited for her to straighten, then they continued. A rock tunnel led out of the station. He paused to examine a sign: a map of the summit's attractions. His alert level suddenly rose as he realised his assumption had been wrong. The cable-car *wasn't* the only way down. There was a second aerial tramway; to where, he didn't know. And even this high up, there was a ski run. An Operative with the right gear could make a very rapid exit indeed . . .

Calm. Calm. Avelina was correct. SC9 couldn't possibly have arrived ahead of them. That would require not just omniscience, but teleportation. That didn't rule out the possibility of someone following them up. But . . . would they?

Knowing that Maxwell was now in charge of SC9 changed

things. His former mentor was a planner. He thought in the long-term – and had taught his students to do the same. Yes, improvisation in response to changed circumstances was a necessary skill. But despatching someone to a mountaintop on a spur-of-the-moment pursuit felt . . . *desperate*. The kind of desperation which saw four Operatives die in Italy. That had ultimately seen Scott forcefully removed from the agency he created. It didn't feel like something Maxwell would do—

'Are *you* okay?'

Reeve realised he was staring at the map, lost in thought. 'Yeah, sorry,' he told the curious Avelina. 'So where are we going?'

'This is the Glacier Palace,' she said, indicating an icon at the map's far end. 'We can go there, then look at the view?'

'Sounds good.' They set off again. Reeve glanced back towards the cable-car station. Another gondola had arrived, more visitors entering the tunnel. Were any of them Operatives, hunting him? *No*, he told himself firmly. There was being cautious, and there was being paranoid. He knew from experience that Operatives could be sent into the field quickly. But not *this* quickly. It had taken Flynn and Stone over twelve hours to reach him in Italy. To reach him *and Connie*, he corrected himself, with a twinge of guilt. How had he not automatically thought of her as well? But he had left Munich only a few hours earlier. It was unlikely anyone could catch up before evening. By then, he would be back at the ski lodge. A defendable location, and he now had backup. He allowed himself the rare luxury of feeling safe.

For the moment.

Avelina led the way. The Glacier Palace required extra payment to enter; she took care of it. The attraction didn't quite live up to its name, more bunker than palace. Narrow tunnels had been cut through the ice into various chambers. Avelina was more impressed than he by the ice sculptures each contained. He was, however, quite taken by two carved wolves. It didn't take much self-reflection to realise why the imagery had drawn his eye.

The tunnels quickly felt claustrophobic, though. He was relieved when they exited and headed for the viewing platform. A spectacular vista greeted them at the top of the steps. Snow-capped mountains surrounded them, sawtooth peaks rising above the horizon. The view would have been breathtaking even had the air been thicker. 'That's Italy down there,' said Avelina, pointing south. 'And that's the Matterhorn.' She indicated a peak to the northwest. 'A lot of people don't recognise it from this angle.'

'It looks different,' Reeve agreed, breath steaming in the frigid air. Avelina drew her new phone from the Faraday bag Reeve had made. He left her to take pictures and went to a quiet corner of the platform. The tourists' chatter faded as he gazed into the distance. The cold here was different from that in Bled and Munich. It was deeper, but less damp. Somehow that made it more bearable. He looked southwards, towards Italy. The last place he had seen Connie. Where he had *abandoned* Connie. He closed his eyes, letting the chill wind wash over his face. The world dropped away, leaving him alone with his dark thoughts . . .

'What are you thinking?' Avelina said quietly. Reeve opened his eyes. He hadn't realised she'd come to him.

Various nondescript lies popped into his head. But almost to his own surprise, he answered with the truth. 'I was thinking about Connie. Actually, about what you asked me in Munich.'

She gave him a look of faint confusion, not remembering. 'What was that?'

'In the coffee shop. You asked me if I was going to find her again after I exposed SC9. I never gave you an answer. But I've been thinking about it a lot. Since I . . . since I didn't catch Locke.'

She moved closer, lowering her voice. 'What do you mean?'

It took an effort to force out the words. 'I've fucked up,' he admitted. 'I've made things worse – for me, and for Connie. Now SC9 won't stop hunting me until I'm dead. And Connie too.' He put his elbows on the rail to support himself, shoulders sagging. 'They could locate her and kill her,' he said, with an exhalation of misery. 'And I wouldn't even know about it.'

Avelina put a gloved hand on his arm. 'You could protect her if you went back to her.'

'I'd have to find her first. And she could be anywhere in Europe.'

'But my mother's friend might be able to help you. And you've got money and a passport now – you can travel.'

'That's not the issue.'

'Then what is?'

He took a deep breath before replying, still staring across the mountains. 'I'm sure I could find her eventually, now I've got some resources,' he said. 'But if I did, then . . .' He hesitated.

'Then what?' Avelina asked.

'I don't know if she'd want me back. She might not want to see me again. I'm – I'm *afraid* she won't forgive me for leaving her.'

She regarded him with sympathetic eyes for a long moment. Then: 'I'm amazed.'

It wasn't the response he had expected. 'Why?' he asked, confused.

'The one thing in the world that scares you is *that*? Seeing the woman you love again?'

'I love her, but she might not love me,' he protested. 'Not after what I did to her. I abandoned her! And for . . . for *nothing*! We would have been safe – *she* would have been safe – if I'd stayed with her. But I didn't. I left her. She might hate me now.'

'She might,' said Avelina. 'But she might not. Don't you want to know?'

'Yes. But—'

'But nothing,' she cut in sharply. 'You don't have to stay on the same path in your life, Alex. You can *choose* to change it, like I did. I was fucked-up, until I realised what I had to do to fix myself. Maybe you can fix yourself too. You just need the willpower to do it. And I don't believe that you don't have it. Not after everything I've seen you do.'

Reeve remained silent. Avelina's words stung, but they had also hit home. 'Look,' she went on, more softly, 'I know what it feels like. Facing someone you love who you *know* doesn't like something you've done. But . . . you have to do it. You can't just hide from them because you're afraid of what they might say. I was shit-scared when I first went to my mother as . . . as me. And she *didn't* like it; I knew she wouldn't. But . . . you know?' She looked back in the direction of Furi. 'Maybe that is changing. It wouldn't have, if I had just stayed away. If Connie still loves you? You have to know. I would have to. You'll have money, you'll have resources, you'll have friends who can help. You can find her.'

'I don't have friends,' he said.

Her hand tightened on his arm. 'Yes, you do. Whatever help you need to fix things, I'll give it.'

Reeve turned towards her. She smiled up at him. His own smile in return was smaller, but genuine. 'You're right,' he said, nodding. 'I have to find her. But after you and Idonia are safe, okay?'

'Well, I didn't want you to run off after her right away,' she replied, teasing. Then her expression changed.

Reeve followed her gaze. There had been an anvil-like bank of dark, heavy cloud off to the southeast. It was now closer, rolling over a line of peaks. 'Is that the blizzard?'

Avelina nodded. 'That will reach us in a couple of hours. We should get back down.'

'Not going to argue with you there.' He had been outdoors in heavy snows in Bled, but this looked on another level entirely. They both started back towards the cable-car station.

CHAPTER 36

Reeve's vague unease rose in inverse proportion to the altitude as the cable-car descended. He wasn't sure why at first. He and Avelina were nearing Aroleid station when the answer came. The ski lodge was visible ahead near the crest of the hill down to Furi. He realised why he was unsettled. The gondola was the lodge in microcosm: a glass-walled cage. Once inside, there were few ways out. He hadn't personally checked all escape routes from the ski lodge. Netz's men seemed competent and confident, but that perhaps wasn't enough . . .

'Is something wrong?' Avelina asked. 'You look . . . intense.'

He decided not to burden her with his concerns. 'I usually do,' he said, with faint humour. 'Just checking the area. I want a better look around when we get back to the lodge. How long will that take?'

'Not long. We get out at Furi, then catch another car back up to Aroleid. Ten, fifteen minutes.'

He nodded, then looked back. The towering cloud bank had risen higher, as if pursuing them. Ahead of it, the clear sky was turning a vaporous grey. The weather would soon change, for the worse.

The cable-car reached Aroleid. As Avelina had told him, only upward-bound gondolas stopped there. Theirs swept over the station and continued downhill. Zermatt spread across the valley floor ahead, Furi a closer spattering of buildings. Reeve surveyed the forest below. The valley he'd noticed from the helicopter was off to his right. Was that a bridge across it? He logged the information in his mental database. The more he knew about the local area, the more secure he would feel.

The rest of the journey took only a few minutes. Reeve took in his destination. Furi's largest structure by far was its sprawling cable-car station. Several lines radiated outwards from it, heading up into the snowy peaks. A traditional wooden building was next-largest, a hotel or restaurant to his left. Other, smaller cabins were widely dispersed around it.

The gondola rumbled into the station, swaying as it slowed. To the right, the interconnected buildings were concrete; left was a blue glass annexe. Reeve glanced into it. Unused gondolas hung from a snaking track inside. He guessed all would be attached to the cables at the height of tourist season.

'We're here,' said Avelina as the doors slid open. She hopped out of the slowly moving car, Reeve following. 'We go around to the other side to ride back up to Aroleid.'

They walked through the station. Most people were heading back to Zermatt in advance of the blizzard. A shout drew Reeve's attention. A man in hi-vis stood on an upper-floor walkway, calling to an engineer below. 'We came down at the right time,' said Avelina, listening to him. 'The wind's getting stronger. They'll be stopping the cable-cars soon.'

They headed through the station to the upward-bound platform. Nobody else was ahead of them. They waited for an arriving car to disgorge its couple of passengers, then boarded. Chains and spinning wheels pulled it along a track before it reattached to the cable. A burst of speed, and it glided upwards.

Behind, another gondola slowed and opened its doors. Only one passenger emerged. He stepped out, surveyed his surroundings, then headed for the exit. The cold wind struck him as he neared it. He tugged his hood over his blond hair, covering a bandage on his right cheek.

Harrison Locke had arrived.

He strode out into the open and looked uphill, following the line of the cables. A steep hill rose before him, a path winding past trees and cabins. At its top, he knew, was Idonia Foss's retreat. He could have ridden the cable-car, but opted to move on foot. He wanted to see the ground, find the escape routes. Not for himself. To discover where *Reeve* would go.

Not that Locke had any intention of giving him the chance.

He shrugged his backpack higher on his shoulders, then started his trek up the hill.

In the valley below, a red-and-white train arrived at Zermatt station. Over forty people disembarked. Many carried skis as well as ordinary luggage, ready for a winter sports vacation. The more experienced dubiously regarded the sky beyond the Matterhorn. A storm was coming; the slopes would be closed. Only the very brave or very foolish would go out into a blizzard. But they were here now, so all they could do was see it through. They dispersed into the town, heading for their hotels.

One group, however, kept walking.

There were seven of them, all men. Anyone paying attention might have noticed that their outerwear was identical. They might also have noticed that while all bore large packs, none had skis. But Zermatt's residents and visitors had their own concerns. Nobody gave them more than a fleeting glance.

The men marched to the town's cable-car station . . . and continued past it. Furi was visible on the hillside above, a stiff hike through the snow. None were concerned by the journey. In training, they had been dumped in the Siberian wilds in the middle of winter. The helicopter that left them had flown on to land fifty kilometres away. If they hadn't reached it in twenty-four hours, they would have failed the test. And, quite probably, died. That knowledge had given them a very strong incentive to succeed. The walk ahead here was nothing by comparison.

The man in the lead paused, listening to a public-address announcement from the station. 'They're going to stop the cable-cars soon,' reported Garald Morozov. A few of the Russian's men weren't fluent in the local languages. Their skills lay in other, more deadly areas. 'That's good for us. It cuts off one of our target's escape routes.'

'One of ours, too,' noted a man called Zagoskin.

'They only go *up* the mountain from the target zone,' Morozov reminded him. 'We didn't bring skis. Or were you planning to escape in a toboggan?' Muted laughter from the others. 'All right. We have roughly a four-kilometre trek through snow, uphill all the way. I want to be there in . . .' He checked his watch. 'Ninety minutes.'

'Lead on, sir,' said another agent, Gorovov. More amusement from the SVR team.

Morozov willingly accepted the challenge. 'Follow me, then.' His voice became as cold as the surrounding air. 'Let's get these British bastards.'

His men straightened, filled with resolve. They resumed their journey at pace, heading for Furi.

From behind a rock, Locke observed the ski lodge through binoculars. The building's clean, modern lines appealed to his sense of aesthetics. He was more interested in its internal layout, though.

The lowest floor had two doors, and no windows visible from his position. Were there other potential points of entry on the far side? He suspected not. He had spotted the helicopter parked behind the lodge. Footprints led from it around the building to the doors. If there were a rear entrance, the passengers would have gone straight to it. There might be windows, but the ground floor was probably the lodge's utility area. No need for a view from there.

The next floor up, beyond easy reach, had balconies overlooking the valley behind him. Bedrooms, most likely. He knew the sleeping areas weren't on the top floor. That had windows on both sides, and he had glimpsed silhouettes moving around. One shadow looked very much like Idonia Foss. The others, he couldn't identify. There were at least three men in the building, though. Hired security – and perhaps Reeve.

He had time to keep watching and find out. There was no way to approach the building unseen in daylight. But nightfall was not far away – and nor was the impending blizzard. It was no longer merely on the horizon, but towering over it. The clouds dwarfed even the Matterhorn; they would soon swallow the mountain. The snowstorm would be intense.

Locke was ready for it. Wilderness survival wasn't his speciality, but it had still been part of his military training. He could endure an evening in the snow. Especially if killing Reeve was his reward.

He continued his watch for a while, formulating a plan. Then he retreated downhill into the woods. Once the blizzard arrived in full force, he would move. Before then, he had preparations to make.

CHAPTER 37

Avelina scratched the back of her neck beneath her hair. 'I'm going for a shower,' she announced, standing.

Reeve was at the dining table in the Grand Hall, eating a sandwich. 'Okay,' he said. Miltner, on a sofa reading something on his phone, acknowledged in German. Avelina glanced at Idonia's office, but her mother was talking to Netz inside. She shrugged and went down the central stairs.

Reeve looked towards the Matterhorn – or rather, where it had been. The peak had disappeared behind a threatening wall of cloud. The mountain was less than four miles away; the blizzard would soon be upon them. Nobody would be going out for a while.

He finished his food and washed the plate, then went to Idonia's office door. It was ajar, she and Netz still involved in a discussion. He tapped on the glass. Idonia looked around. 'Alex? Do you want something?'

'Can I talk to you for a minute?'

She seemed about to say she was busy – then changed her mind. A brief exchange with Netz, who nodded and left the room. She gestured for Reeve to take his place. 'I'm not interrupting anything important, am I?' Reeve asked.

'We were discussing security issues relating to the merger. They can wait a few minutes,' Idonia replied. She had donned slightly more casual clothing, a black cashmere sweater over her blouse. 'How can I help you?'

'I've decided to take your advice.' She gave him a questioning look. 'About contacting your friend. You're right; I'm better off with connections and resources. And like you said, I have . . . special talents. People might pay me to use them.' He registered her flash of unease. 'Don't worry. I'm not planning to become an assassin-for-hire. I have *other* talents.'

'Good, good,' she said, with subtle relief. 'My friend is anyway not in that line of work. At least, that I am aware.' A faint smile. 'I will find you the details so you can contact them.' She took a black leather address book from her handbag. Reeve noticed her watch and its base station on the desk beside it. 'What changed your mind?' she asked as she leafed through the book.

'Avelina persuaded me.'

Idonia nodded. 'Theo was always good at convincing people to do the right thing.'

'*She* hasn't managed to do that with everyone, though.'

She paused at the pointed comment. 'I know what you are going to say, and why,' she said at last. 'And, you are right. It is not for me to decide how . . . my child lives their life.' A faint sigh as she realised she had avoided using a pronoun. 'My child. Theodore. Who is now Avelina. That is – *her* choice.' The pill was bitter, but this time she swallowed it. 'That is something people can do now, and I have to accept that. But in my mind, Theo will always be . . .' She leaned forward, one hand to her mouth as if hiding her expression. 'My little bird,' she said, a quaver of emotion behind the words. 'My beautiful baby boy. Who I should have spent more time with when he was younger. Because I'm never going to see him again, am I?' Her voice almost broke on the last words. 'He is – *she* is Avelina now.'

'They're still the same person,' said Reeve. 'Different clothes and hair don't change that. Or even a different name. I wasn't always called Alex Reeve. But just changing my name didn't change who I was.' A pause, then: 'It took someone else to do that.'

She lowered her hand, looking up at him. 'Your girlfriend.'

He nodded. 'Connie. Yeah.'

'Theo—' She clenched her lips in exasperation at herself. '*Avelina* told me about you and her. That you had to leave her behind, to protect her.' If Idonia knew the full truth, she was keeping it to herself. 'But you still love her, don't you?'

'I do,' he said. 'And I want to find her, to let her know that. That's why I decided to contact your friend. If they can help me, then I'll do what it takes.'

Idonia glanced at the address book, as if she had forgotten it existed. 'Yes, of course. Sorry.' She found a particular page, then picked up a pen and notepad. 'I will write it down for you.'

'Thanks.' He waited for her to do so, then took the proffered paper. He read the information, memorising it – then to her surprise tore up the sheet. 'It's okay. I have a good memory.'

'I hope you do,' she replied, with a little amusement.

'Would you like me to send an email as an introduction? Then they will know to expect you to contact them.'

'Yes, but don't use any names. Keep it short, not much detail. SC9 and GCHQ will still be monitoring you,' he explained on her questioning look. 'Just say I'm . . . an associate. I'll write a letter to contact them myself.'

She gave him an approving nod. 'Once this is over, it could be the start of a new life for you.'

'Or a way to get back my old one.' That came out, unintentionally, in an almost wistful tone.

'I hope you do,' Idonia told him.

'Thanks.' He stood. 'I'll let you get back to work.'

'Okay.' She drew in air as if about to say more, but no words emerged. He waited. Finally, she spoke. 'If we didn't make weapons . . . none of this would have happened, would it?'

'SC9 wouldn't have targeted you if you only made car parts, no,' said Reeve.

'Hmm.' A glass door led to a small balcony overlooking the valley. She gazed out at the darkening sky beyond it. 'Avelina left the company *because* we make weapons. She tried to convince me to go back to what we used to do. Perhaps I should have listened.'

'There's still time.'

'The train is already moving,' she said, with resignation. 'There is a lot of money, a lot of jobs, aboard it. If I pull out, everything comes off the rails. Not just for my company, but all the others.' Another sigh, deeper. 'All the years I have given to the company, all the effort. It cost my marriage – it has almost cost my child. I put my work before my family. Now, I am wondering if I made the wrong choice.'

'You should tell Avelina that, not me.'

'I know. I know.' She leaned back in her chair, still gazing out at Zermatt.

He guessed she wanted to be left alone, and started for the exit. 'Do you want me to get Reynold?'

'No, not just now. I will talk to him again later.'

'Okay.' He left the office. Netz was talking to Miltner across the room. He gestured to Reeve: *Does she want me?* The Englishman shook his head. Netz looked puzzled, but nodded.

A while later, Avelina returned. She had changed clothes, wearing a colourful jumper and pink jeans. 'Hi,' she said, greeting the room's occupants.

Reeve was about to reply when Idonia called from her office. 'Avelina?'

Avelina looked towards the door in surprise. '*Ja?*'

'Come in here, please. I would like to talk to you.'

The glance Avelina gave Reeve told him she was expecting conflict. She went to the office, her mother meeting her at the entrance. A brief, silent face-off – then, to Avelina's surprise, Idonia hugged her. Avelina was momentarily startled, but then returned the embrace. Idonia spoke quietly to her in German. Whatever she said produced a huge, emotional smile from her child. 'Oh, *Mama* . . .' Avelina replied, tears beading in her eyes. Idonia smiled back, then both women went into the office.

Reeve watched through the glass as they hugged again. Then he turned away, letting them share the moment in private. The circumstances that had brought about the reconciliation were awful. Yet it had still happened – and he had played some part in it. That brought an unexpected swell of . . . satisfaction? Happiness? Whatever the exact emotion, it was a positive one. *You did something good.* Connie's voice. He hoped the real Connie would approve.

If things worked out, maybe he would be able to ask her in person.

'*Oh, jetzt fangt's an,*' said Miltner. Reeve looked around. The German stood at the tall window. Snow had started falling outside a short time before. Now, a swirling, almost solid wall of it rolled towards the lodge. Within moments it arrived, the impact practically physical as flakes hit the glass. For the first time, Reeve heard the wind even through the triple-glazed panels.

Netz checked an app on his phone. 'It is forecast to last all night,' he reported.

Reeve joined Miltner at the window. The whirling blizzard had drastically curtailed visibility. He could only just make out the helicopter. 'Will the chopper be okay parked there?'

'Curt told me it will, and he knows what he is doing. We will not be flying anywhere for a while, though.' Netz chuckled faintly. 'I do not think we will even be *walking* anywhere. But that is good; we will be safer. Nobody will come all the way up here in this.'

'I wouldn't bet on that,' Reeve replied, his tone matter-of-fact.

Netz looked unsettled, then picked up a walkie-talkie to check in with his team. Beckmeyer and Thorner responded promptly. 'Everything is good,' he announced. Reeve nodded – then stood and started for the stairs. 'Where are you going?'

'Just seeing for myself,' Reeve replied. He went downstairs to begin a security patrol of his own.

CHAPTER 38

Locke picked his way back to the rock he had used as an observation point. The snowfall was so heavy, he needed a handheld GPS unit to find it. Once there, he put the device away and wiped snow from his goggles. The lodge was barely fifty metres away. Despite that, he could only see its lights, not the building itself. The blizzard's disorienting swirl obscured all detail.

He hunched down, wriggling his gloved fingers. Even in layers of Arctic-grade clothing, he was still uncomfortably cold. But he would not have to endure it for much longer. He extracted the binoculars from his pack. No choice but to raise his goggles to use them. Whirling flakes immediately stung his eyes, the chill clawing at his exposed skin. He quickly peered through the field glasses.

The ski lodge leapt closer. The top floor was brightly lit from within. A lower room was also alight, though curtains had been drawn. He checked the doors. Nobody had been outside recently. The tracks that had been there were already half-erased.

He looked back at the upper floor. Someone walked across the room within. Idonia. If he had a sniper rifle, he could eliminate her right now. But that was Deirdre Flynn's area of expertise, not his. And the moment was already gone. She passed out of sight, sitting down. He would have to deal with her in person, not through a telescopic sight.

But that had been his intention all along. And the anticipation of doing so was rising.

Redonning the goggles was a relief. He put away the binoculars and raised the GPS again. Coordinates had already been entered. He had solidified a plan during his wait in the woods. Twenty metres northwest of the lodge, the ground fell away sharply, soon becoming a cliff. It was not a direction from which anyone would approach the building.

Which made it ideal for his purposes. It would take him a while, especially in the current conditions. But the GPS would guide him. His route was a spiral around the lodge, wide at first before tightening. It would take him to the north-western cliff. He would stay low, just below the lip of the slope, out of sight. At the closest point to the building, he would ascend. The security cameras covered the path up from Furi, and – he presumed – the helipad. It seemed unlikely any were aimed at the cliff. If they were, he would adjust his plan. But he was confident that would not be necessary.

He began his journey. The GPS was in one hand, a sturdy tree-branch in the other. He had broken it from a pine during his wait, carving it to the shape he needed. It now resembled a long walking stick, or staff. But it was more than a trekking aid.

It was his key to the ski lodge.

He had taped a red-lensed torch to the GPS unit. Its ruby glow would be hard for others to spot – almost impossible in the blizzard. But it was enough for him to see his way. He tromped through the rising snow, circling relentlessly towards his target.

The total distance he covered was only a few hundred metres. But it took him over twenty minutes in the freezing darkness. He sidestepped carefully across the slope until his GPS warbled. He was in position.

He pocketed the device and used the stick to make a slow advance uphill. The lodge came into view above. He was exactly where he had intended to be: directly facing its side.

Cameras were now his concern. He retrieved the binoculars again, scanning the building. A cluster of cameras was backlit by the glow from the interior lights. They overlooked the helipad and the rising plain beyond. None pointed towards him. As he'd expected.

Nobody would see him. It was safe to proceed.

Locke advanced, boots biting through the snow to find traction beneath. It did not take long to reach flatter ground. He was soon at the lodge itself. He shone his torch across its wall. No windows on the lowest floor. There were some on the next storey, but well beyond reach. No way in there.

He moved towards the lodge's northernmost corner. The roof's slope was broken by the balconies outside the bedrooms. But not even an Olympic gymnast could leap high enough to reach them. Not without help.

Help was what he had spent his time making in the woods. He hefted the branch. Its thick end had been carved into the shape of a hook. Locke had tested it in the forest. It would support his weight . . . and let him climb up.

He judged the height of the balcony's edge. It was reachable, just. He would have to jump as high as he could.

Shrugging off his pack, he readied himself, then sprang upwards, arms at full stretch. The stick's hook clonked against the balustrade – but didn't catch. Locke landed, dislodged snow falling on to him. He held in a curse and tried again. This time, the staff found a grip.

Arm muscles straining, he hauled himself upwards. Despite his best efforts to be silent, his feet thumped against the wooden wall.

Reeve sat in an armchair in the Great Hall, thinking. About Connie – but also about himself.

He had a notepad on his lap, a few sentences hesitantly written, then crossed out. How best to introduce himself to his potential future employer? And what kind of work might need his skills? As he'd told Idonia, he had no intention of becoming a paid assassin. Connie would *definitely* never forgive him for that. In which case, what else could he do?

He ran through options in his head. Bodyguard, obviously; he was more than capable of that. Infiltrator; undercover work, playing a role, had been his speciality even before SC9. Courier, combat tutor, hostage rescuer—

A walkie-talkie squawked. Beckmeyer answered, Avelina and Idonia looking up from their meal. 'Miltner,' Beckmeyer told them. 'He thought he heard a noise downstairs. He's going to look.'

Reeve stood. 'It's okay,' he assured the two women, who regarded him with apprehension. 'I'll check.'

He went to Idonia's office. Netz was at her desk, working on a laptop. 'I heard,' said the German as Reeve entered. They went to a monitor on a counter in one corner. The screen showed feeds from the lodge's CCTV cameras. Several may as well have been showing static. The one covering the doors was clearer, sheltered from the swirling snow. Both entrances were in full view of the infra-red camera. 'No fresh prints,' Netz observed.

Reeve looked more closely at the other images. He made out the helicopter on its pad in one. Its rotors flexed in the wind. There was no sign that anyone had been near it, though. The tracks left by its arriving passengers were all but gone. He focused on the ground in the other feeds. Again, there were no footprints.

Netz went to the door and spoke reassuringly in German. One last look at the monitor, then Reeve returned to the main room. 'Did *you* see anything?' Avelina asked him.

'No,' he replied, returning to his seat.

'But . . . ?' she went on, probing. 'You have that serious face again. Do you think something is wrong?'

'I don't know.' The answer was truthful. He hadn't *seen* anything concerning, but . . . 'What kind of noise did Miltner hear?' he asked Beckmeyer.

The pilot relayed the question over the radio. 'A banging sound,' he said on getting an answer. 'It has stopped now.'

'It might have been something blowing in the wind,' said Idonia. She did not sound convinced by her own suggestion.

Netz gestured at Beckmeyer, who raised the walkie-talkie again. 'Thorner?' he said. '*Vergewissern Sie sich, dass dort unten alles in Ordnung ist.*' An acknowledgement quickly came from the other bodyguard.

'They will both check,' said Netz. 'It is probably nothing, but let us be safe, yes?'

'Yes, definitely,' Avelina replied.

Netz nodded to Idonia and went back into the office. She hesitated, then returned to her meal. Avelina gave Reeve an uncertain look. 'I'm sure it's fine,' he told her. 'It *is* windy out there.'

'Okay.' One last glance, and she went back to her own food.

Reeve picked up the notepad again. He had never written a letter to a prospective employer in his life. Even when he joined the army, he had simply walked into a recruitment office. Despite Idonia's advance contact, he still had to get his introduction just right.

But an interloping thought kept interrupting. Nothing had been banging in the wind before. So why would something start – and then stop? Should he investigate for himself?

He held back the urge. Miltner and Thorner seemed capable. Besides, he didn't want to step on any toes. He turned his attention back to his task.

Three glass-walled bedrooms opened on to the large balcony. The furthest from Locke had the curtains drawn, low light inside. The other two were dark. He went to the nearest, moving around the balcony's edge to minimise his footprints. The door had a common type of lock. He knew he could pick it, even in gloves. He took out his tools and set to work. The lock soon surrendered. He quickly slid open the door and ducked inside.

The Operative was already on full alert. He tugged down his coat's zip and drew a gun. It had a suppressor, but he only intended to use it if absolutely necessary. No gun was completely silent. Unlike a knife.

He crept to the inner door and listened intently. Footsteps beyond; someone descending stairs to ground level. Locke had unavoidably made noise as he climbed the wooden wall. To anyone inside, it would have seemed to come from the lowest floor. One of the bodyguards was investigating.

Locke kept listening. Somebody else was still on his floor. He heard a door open, faint steps on carpet. Another guard, checking the rooms. Had the man already checked this one? He risked opening his door a crack. A hallway beyond, doorways and a staircase on the opposite side. The furthest entrance was open, a light on within.

He closed the door. A few seconds later, he heard someone else do the same. Heavy steps, then another room was opened. The bodyguard was coming towards him, checking each bedroom in turn.

Locke holstered the gun and drew his black combat knife. He would ambush the approaching man when he entered. Next, the bodyguard downstairs. That way nobody could surprise him from below. Once they were dead . . .

He would find his targets.

Reeve was having little luck with his letter. How the hell to phrase something like this? *You don't know me, but Idonia Foss gave me your details. I'm a former British assassin looking for freelance work. Can I have a job?* Direct, and accurate, but he doubted it would be the best way to introduce himself.

A rattle of cutlery brought him out of his thoughts. Avelina and Idonia had finished their meal, Avelina collecting their plates. He belatedly realised it had been a few minutes since Beckmeyer's radio call. Neither Miltner nor Thorner had replied, to his knowledge. Beckmeyer himself was now in the office, speaking to Netz. Reeve put down the pad and went to the doorway. 'Did your guys find anything?'

Beckmeyer broke off from his discussion with sudden concern. 'No, they haven't reported in.' He snapped up his walkie-talkie. 'Trost, Konrad. *Hast du etwas gefunden?*' No reply. 'Miltner, Thorner. *Wo sind Sie?*'

The radio remained silent. Netz stood, his own alarm rising. He spoke urgently to Beckmeyer, then both men exited the office. Reeve joined them. 'I need a weapon,' he said. 'Where are the guns?'

Idonia answered, worried – and faintly embarrassed. 'In a locker . . . in the utility room. Downstairs.'

'Oh, great.'

Beckmeyer drew an automatic from his shoulder holster. 'I will find the others,' he said, heading for the stairs.

Netz went to his employer. 'Idonia, stay with me,' he said.

'Alex, what's happening?' asked Avelina, scared.

'I don't know,' he replied, starting after Beckmeyer. The German hurried down the stairs. 'Wait here until I—'

Two flat metallic *clacks* echoed from the stairwell. Reeve recognised the sound instantly. Suppressed gunfire. A heavy thump as a body fell, a gun clattering down the stairs. Then someone rushed up them – but it wasn't Beckmeyer.

Locke.

CHAPTER 39

Reeve was caught in the open as Locke reached the top of the staircase. The assassin's gun fixed on to him—

Then whipped sharply around as Netz grabbed for his own concealed weapon. It didn't clear its holster. Locke fired. The bullet slammed into Netz's left shoulder. The security chief spun and crashed to the floor. Avelina shrieked in fear, Idonia so shocked even sound was beyond her.

Locke advanced, gun returning to Reeve. 'Drop your weapon,' he ordered. The Danish accent was gone, his original clipped public-school tones back in place.

'I'm not armed,' Reeve replied.

The Operative assessed him with cold eyes. 'I suppose not. You would already have drawn it. Move back, over there.' He indicated an armchair a couple of metres from Reeve, who cautiously retreated towards it. Locke went to the groaning, writhing Netz. The German's gun had dropped to the carpet beside him. Locke kicked it away, then regarded Idonia and Avelina. They cringed back in instinctive fear.

Reeve tried to draw his attention from the two women. 'I'm surprised to see you here.'

'Clearly.'

'I thought Maxwell would have told you to bug out.'

'He did.' Locke turned back towards him. 'I'm here against orders. I dislike leaving a job unfinished. And also,' his cold, reptilian eyes narrowed, 'I was not going to let you escape.'

'A personal vendetta? Not your style.' *Keep him talking*, Reeve thought. He was already scanning the room, locating cover, anything he might use as a weapon. A large sofa was off to one side. If he could dive behind it, he might be able to reach the kitchen area. A block of knives stood on a counter . . .

But Locke knew what he was thinking. Reeve's retreat had not been straight, instead subtly curving closer to the sofa. 'That way,' he said, with a small twitch of his gun. Reeve reluctantly sidestepped towards the chair. 'I have developed a personal dislike of you. That is not conducive to a long and happy life.'

'So what are you going to do? Torture us like those people you killed in Munich?'

Locke shook his head. A small smile formed on his lips. Somehow, that was more chilling than his usual emotionless mask. 'No. You've actually taught me a valuable lesson, Reeve. About putting results before perfection and personal pleasure. I'm simply going to kill you.'

The gun's muzzle locked unshakingly on to Reeve's chest—

One of the windows overlooking Zermatt shattered.

All three sheets of glass in the pane disintegrated. A dark metal cylinder burst through the crystalline cascade and arced down into the room. Reeve knew instantly what it was. A stun grenade. Trained instinct took control; he dropped, palms covering his ears as he closed his eyes. Locke reacted identically – but couldn't protect his right ear without dropping his gun—

The flashbang detonated. The noise hit Reeve like a punch. The darkness behind his eyelids flared as if lightning had struck in front of him. But his senses were only jarred, not obliterated. The smashed window had dissipated some of the blast outside. The flare subsided. He opened his eyes, already scrambling back up.

Locke had chosen protection over keeping his weapon – but too late. He hadn't quite shielded his right ear before the flashbang exploded. The Operative clutched his head in dizzied agony. Reeve looked around. Avelina and Idonia had both fallen, caught by the mind-hammering detonation. To his surprise, Netz had managed to cover his ears despite his injury. The former military officer had also been saved by his training.

Who fired the stun grenade? SC9? Reeve didn't know. But he had to deal with the closest threat first. He rushed to Locke and snatched up his gun. Locke blinked at the movement – then his eyes focused and snapped on to his enemy.

Reeve was already aiming the gun down at his head. His finger tightened on the trigger—

Loud reports from below. Not more flashbangs, but the doors being blown open. The new attackers were assaulting the building. Shouts reached Reeve from outside. He knew the language. Russian.

A shock colder than the wind blowing through the broken window. Someone had yelled his name.

It wasn't aimed at him. It was a command: *Find Reeve!*

The newcomers weren't after the Fosses. They were hunting for *him*, personally.

Not just him. The leader bellowed another order. 'And find the other Operative! If you can take them both alive, do it!'

Reeve snapped his gaze back to Locke. 'I know you speak Russian. Did you hear that?'

Locke was breathing heavily, still recovering. But he managed to reply. 'I did.' His mouth tightened into a snarl. 'Maxwell! He was the only one who knew I was coming here. He sold me out to the Russians!'

'He sold us *both* out.' Reeve hesitated, knowing the danger of what he was about to do. But there was no choice. 'If we don't fight them together, we'll both die. Or worse.'

'Agreed,' Locke snapped back. 'We work as a team. For now.' He did not need to add that the alliance would be short-lived. Both men knew they would be mortal enemies again the moment the threat was over.

Another hesitation – then Reeve reached down with his free hand. Locke gripped it. Reeve pulled him up—

The sharp clamour of automatic weapons came from below.

Morozov's team hadn't been able to obtain plans of the ski lodge's interior. Their assault was by necessity improvised. But every man involved was well trained in breaching buildings. Two had taken each door, small shaped charges blowing both locks simultaneously. They kicked them open and rushed inside.

The pair entering the larger door, Zagoskin and Litke,

found themselves in an unlit room. Both had tactical flash-lights mounted on their weapons. They advanced, sweeping the beams around the dark space as Morozov shouted orders outside—

A man in a suit stood in a corner.

Zagoskin reacted instantly. He unleashed his weapon on full-auto. The suited man's torso erupted in bloody explosions. Litke fired his shotgun, blasting a plate-sized hole in the defender's chest . . .

But he didn't fall.

'What the fuck?' gasped Zagoskin, ceasing fire. Both men stared in bewilderment at the bullet-riddled man. Their target was already dead, throat cut. He hung by his collar from a hook on the wall.

A door to one side was thrown open. The two Russians whirled – then eased as they saw the other entry team of Gorovov and Minin. 'We're clear, clear,' Zagoskin assured them as their weapons found the shredded corpse. 'This asshole was already dead.'

'The other Operative,' said a stern voice from the exterior entrance. Morozov. He switched on the lights. 'He's here to kill Reeve, and everyone else. The others, I don't care about. But I want Reeve *alive*. If you have to kill the other Brit to ensure that, do it. Now find him!'

There were two more doors in the changing room. Zagoskin and Litke hurried to check them. The other pair returned the way they had come. 'Stairs through here,' Gorovov shouted back to his companions. 'Going up!' He and Minin pulled down their hoods for better visibility, then ascended, guns raised.

* * *

Reeve helped Netz stand, quickly assessing his shoulder wound. Painful, bloody, scarring – but not fatal. The bullet had torn through muscle rather than smashing bone. His arm was still mobile. 'Keep pressure on it if you can,' he told the German. 'We have to get out of here.'

'Help Frau Foss,' said Netz, fumbling in a pocket for his phone. 'I will call the authorities.'

Reeve went to Idonia and Avelina. The younger Foss was already recovering, blearily sitting up. 'What happened?' she said.

'Stun grenade,' was Reeve's curt reply as he aided Idonia. 'We need to move.'

Netz let out an exclamation of surprise. 'I can't get a signal,' he said, holding up his phone. 'But I made a call earlier—'

'They're jamming us,' said Locke.

Both Avelina and Idonia reacted with fearful shock as they saw him standing behind Reeve. 'Someone else is after us,' Reeve explained. 'Russians. They want us *all* dead.'

Netz retrieved his gun and went to the balcony door. 'We have to get to the helicopter. The balcony has a fire ladder; we can climb down.'

'The pilot's dead,' Reeve reminded him, with an accusing glance at Locke.

'I can fly it. Enough to reach Zermatt, even in this.' Netz opened the door—

The back of his head exploded in a shower of gore and splintered bone.

* * *

Beyond the helipad, a Russian named Malyutin lay in wait. Literally: he was on his front, a sniper rifle on a bipod before him. The team was using Western guns, his a Heckler & Koch G28. If anything went wrong, there would be little to link its members to Russia. The weapon was fitted with a thermal sight. It could pierce the swirling snow as easily as a light drizzle.

The lodge was a different matter. Contrary to Hollywood's depictions, thermal cameras could not penetrate walls, or even glass. The towering windows on the building's south-western side were as opaque as concrete. Malyutin was relying on his own eyes to see inside. Details were hard to make out through the blizzard. But he could see enough to spot movement near the balcony's entrance.

He switched back to the thermal sight, readying his weapon. The crosshairs were fixed upon the centre of the door, its frame standing out clearly. He waited, waited . . .

The door opened. A tall male figure stood within, a ghost in white and shades of grey. Malyutin had already seen that the man did not match Alex Reeve's description from Morozov. A fractional shift of aim, and the crosshairs found the figure's head—

He fired. The rifle kicked in his hands. At this relatively close range, the bullet reached its target practically instantaneously. A hot spray burst from the man's head, and the white ghost fell.

The sniper wore a radio headset under his hood, throat mic beneath his camouflaged balaclava. 'One target down on the southwestern balcony,' he reported. 'Nobody else'll be coming out that way.'

* * *

Idonia screamed as Netz's corpse collapsed in the doorway. 'Reynold!' Avelina stumbled back from the horrific sight.

Reeve had no time for sympathy. Instead, he found concealment. The shooter had to be higher on the plain to get a firing angle. He was probably also using a thermal scope. A conventional sight would be obscured by the blizzard—

An escape plan formed. 'We'll have to jump down from the other balcony,' he said urgently.

Avelina had belatedly dropped, pulling her mother down with her. Locke was also in concealment behind a chair. 'There might be another sniper,' he replied.

'The ground's lower – no good angles from there. I think there's only one sniper, covering the helicopter.'

Locke considered it. 'Probably correct,' he admitted. 'I couldn't see much of the upper floor from below. If we reach the woods, we'll have cover.'

Reeve addressed the two women. 'Get on to the balcony. Jump down to the next floor when you get my signal.'

'Why do we wait?' asked Idonia, voice quavering in shock from Netz's death.

'They're sweeping the building. If they see you, they'll kill you. We need to clear the way for you.'

'I don't have a weapon,' Locke pointed out with dry sarcasm.

Reeve glanced at Netz's corpse. The German's gun was still in his hand. If he tried to recover it from the dead man, the sniper would kill him. He looked around the room – then hurried to the stairwell. No bullets punched through the panoramic windows in his wake. His guess was right; the man out on the plain couldn't see through the glass. The sniper was there to prevent anyone from escaping. A glance down the stairs. Beckmeyer's body was sprawled below. No sign of his gun. It had probably fallen down to the landing. Descending to search for it was too risky with attackers in the building.

Instead he continued on to the kitchen. He reached for the largest blade in the knife block – then changed his mind. He yanked open cutlery drawers, finding a hefty meat cleaver. 'Here,' he said – tossing Locke not the cleaver, but the gun.

Avelina gasped. 'Oh, my God! Do you trust him?'

'I trust his survival instinct,' Reeve replied, moving to the top of the staircase. Heavy footsteps and barked Russian reached him from the floor below. He picked out one urgent report: *Another body here!* Locke's handiwork, either Thorner or Miltner. 'They're coming,' he warned. 'Avelina, Idonia, get outside. Quick! Locke, cover me.'

The Fosses scurried into the office. Avelina impulsively pocketed the recorder's base station as Idonia opened the balcony door. They cringed as a snow-laden wind rushed in. 'We'll freeze!' Avelina protested.

'You'll have to manage,' Locke snapped as he went to the top of the stairs. Reeve rounded the balustrade surrounding the stairwell and looked down. Nobody in sight – yet. But they would appear in moments. A shout from below, further away: *Ground floor clear!* At least two assault teams. They were following a pattern. Secure each floor in turn, then go up to the next.

That way, nobody above them could escape.

The Fosses disappeared on to the freezing balcony. Reeve

perched on the balustrade, readying his weapon. 'First floor clear!' a Russian yelled, close by. 'Moving up!' Shadows swept across the lower landing – then a figure entered the stairwell. Heavy coat, SCAR-SC compact submachine gun in gloved hands. The man looked up to check for threats—

Reeve was already plunging down at him. The bang of his landing and the *chunk* of the cleaver cracking bone were simultaneous.

But Reeve had hit the Russian's gun as he dropped, knocking him off-balance. He fell on to the steps. The invader crashed limply down on top of him. He was dead, almost a kilogram of stainless steel buried in his skull.

Reeve struggled to get free. The cleaver wasn't the only thing weighing down the Russian. The man wore a backpack and had body armour beneath his coat. He forced the corpse higher – but another man was now at the staircase, gun raised—

It took the Russian only a split-second to know his partner was dead. He fired as Reeve ducked. The armour on the corpse's back and shoulders stopped the burst of bullets. But the gunman started up the stairs to find a clear line of fire.

Reeve tried to haul the dead man higher to shield his head. But the corpse's feet caught on a step. Where was Locke? The Operative should be covering him – had he been betrayed already? The Russian rose into view, mouth an angry snarl. His SCAR came down—

Two shots from above. The attacker lurched back. But the rounds had hit his chest, centre-mass – and been stopped by his armour. He swung his gun up at Locke, higher on the stairs.

The dead man's weapon was sandwiched between Reeve and the corpse, pointing downwards. The Englishman grabbed it – and held down the trigger.

The gun was set to full-auto. Muzzle flare burned his shin, hot gas from the ejection port searing his hip. But the barrel was clear of obstructions. The Russians had body armour – but it *only* protected their bodies. Madly spraying rounds smashed into the second man's legs, shattering bone and shredding flesh. He screamed and fell backwards on to the landing.

Reeve twisted and forced the corpse off himself. The other Russian was down – but still a threat despite his injuries. He struggled to sit up, bringing his gun to bear—

Reeve fired again. This time, he could aim. A shorter burst of bullets hit the Russian's groin, ripping up into his abdomen. The man slumped like a stringless puppet, blood gushing from the entry wounds.

'Messy,' was Locke's acerbic comment as he descended the stairs. He skirted around Reeve and the first dead Russian. 'Hurry up. More coming.' He reached the landing and headed along it.

Gun in hand, Reeve stood, about to follow – then noticed something on the corpse's shoulder. A small disc-shaped object with a transparent top. He knew what it was. A beacon, flashing invisible pulses of infra-red light. On a thermal scope, it would flare brightly every few seconds, impossible to miss. A way for the Russians to identify themselves to their sniper even through a blizzard. He plucked it from the dead man's coat and pocketed it before following Locke.

He passed the spiral stairs to the ground floor. Two men were running up them.

The leading Russian saw him – and aimed his shotgun.

CHAPTER 40

Reeve ducked and ran as the shotgun swung at him. A hole the size of a football exploded in the wall just behind him. He hurtled to the end of the hallway. Locke had entered Idonia's bedroom. For one chilling moment he thought the Operative was going to shut him out. But then Locke withdrew to let him past, slamming the door behind him.

Both men knew better than to stay near it. Reeve dived behind the bed, Locke jumping sideways as the shotgun blasted again. A ragged oval ripped open in the door. The gunman ran closer and unleashed two more shots. One blew a second hole in the door, the other tearing through the wall beside it. The latter was barely a foot from Locke. He flinched as flying splinters struck him.

The room was unlit, but now shafts of light stabbed through the smouldering holes. Reeve peered over the bed, seeing Thorner's body in a corner. He met his killer's gaze. Locke raised his gun and gestured questioningly towards the ruptured wall. *Can I shoot through the hole?* Reeve shook his head. The Russians' body armour made firing blind near worthless. And if the Operative crouched to take a sighting, he would be seen – and shot.

Locke frowned. Then he regarded the television mounted

by the door. Its power lead was partly visible, looping down before running into the wall behind it. He grabbed the cable and yanked sharply at it. It ripped loose from the television's case.

Reeve had no time to wonder what he was doing. A dark shape slipped past the holes in the door. The man with the shotgun. His companion scurried across behind him. Reeve raised his stolen SCAR. In the chaotic rush, he hadn't had time to check its remaining ammunition. A glance at the magazine: NATO-standard 5.56 millimetre. Square box, not curved – only twenty rounds. The Russians hadn't expected much resistance.

He wasn't sure how many rounds he had unleashed on the stairs. Well over half. He would have to use the remainder carefully.

But he would *have* to use them. The man with the shotgun braced, about to kick open the door . . .

Then paused.

Reeve knew why he was hesitating. The men he was hunting had already killed two of his team. He didn't know exactly where his targets were. If he burst into the room, he would be unbalanced – vulnerable. He instead shifted position, reaching for the door handle. The second man prepared to spray the room with bullets. The handle turned—

Locke thrust the ragged end of the power cord against it.

A blue flash and sharp electric snap – and the man outside jerked backwards. His glove, dampened by snow, made a perfect conductor. He reeled into his companion, knocking him back, then fell.

Reeve took advantage of the confusion. He aimed where

he hoped the second man's head was and fired. The bullet punched through the wood. A crack from outside as it hit the wall. Shit! But he couldn't have missed by much. Someone let out a startled gasp.

Locke darted to the hole in the door frame and sent two rounds through it. The second man stumbled out of sight with a winded grunt. The bullets had hit his body armour. The uneven clump of his footsteps became a hurried run as he fled for cover. Locke yanked open the door and sent another round after him. But the Russian had reached the stairwell and dived clear.

The electrocuted man was sprawled on the floor at the Operative's feet. Locke finished him off with a shot to the face, then glanced back at Reeve. 'Time to go.'

'Yeah.' Reeve slid open the balcony door.

Zagoskin crouched in the stairwell, recovering his breath. The two bullet impacts felt like sledgehammer blows to his chest. But the body armour had done its job. 'Litke's dead,' he reported. From his cover he could see Minin's corpse, blood pooling around it. 'Minin too. I haven't seen Gorovov, but he's probably down as well.'

Morozov swore in his earpiece. 'Have you seen Reeve?'

'Yes. The other Operative's with him; they're both armed.'

'Where?'

'First floor, northwest corner.'

Another curse. 'I'm coming in.'

Reeve stepped outside. The cold wind sawed at his exposed skin. There were footprints in the snow: Locke's point of entry. He crossed the balcony and looked cautiously over its edge. Lights were now on below, illuminating the snow beyond the lodge.

An armed man stood some ten metres away, looking towards the entrances. Reeve brought up his gun—

The man spotted the movement. He started to raise his own weapon – then realised Reeve was already finding his target. He ran for the lodge as Reeve fired. Two rounds smacked into the snow behind him. Reeve tracked him and unleashed two more shots. The man lurched, hood ripping open with a burst of down. But the bullet had only clipped him. He ran on, reaching cover below.

Nobody else was visible on the ground. Reeve looked up at the higher balcony. 'Avelina! Idonia! Jump down, quick!'

The two women appeared above. Their hair and clothes were already encrusted with snow. 'We haven't got coats!' Avelina said through chattering teeth as she climbed down.

He helped her to the balcony. 'Nothing we can do about that.'

Locke reached the door as Reeve assisted Idonia's descent. 'How many outside?'

'None on this side. I think they're all in the lodge except for the sniper. Keep them busy while we get down.'

The Operative hurried back to the bedroom door. Shouts in Russian came from the hallway beyond. The man in the stairwell peeked out from his cover. Locke fired, forcing him back. 'Okay, go,' he called to Reeve.

'Come on,' Reeve told the Fosses. Avelina climbed over the balustrade first. Reeve gripped her wrists and lowered her as far as he could, then let go. She hit the ground with a thump. 'You okay?'

'Yeah, yeah,' she gasped, standing. Reeve aided Idonia over the balcony and sent her after her daughter. Her landing was harder, producing a cry of pain. Avelina looked towards the open doors in fear, but nobody had heard.

'Locke!' Reeve said before dropping down himself. By now, Avelina had helped Idonia stand. 'We've got to get to the woods,' he said, gesturing downhill.

'We'll freeze if we stay out here,' Idonia protested.

'It's that or get shot. Stay with me.' He led the way at the best speed he could manage through the snow. Locke jumped down from the balcony and yomped after them.

Where was the sniper? Still guarding the helicopter – or moving to cover the other side of the building? Reeve didn't know. But the thought triggered a memory. He dug into his pocket, finding the infra-red strobe. It had an adhesive patch on its back. He pushed it against his shoulder, hoping it would hold in place. It did, though didn't feel firmly attached.

It only had to stay there until they reached the woods. 'Stay on my left side!' he shouted to his charges, indicating with his arm. 'Use the lodge as cover for as long as you can!' They would be exposed before reaching the trees, but not for long. If he could delay the sniper from firing, even for a few seconds . . .

Morozov reached the first floor, his Glock handgun readied. No sign of Zagoskin – but the fates of other team members were immediately apparent. Minin was dead at the foot of more stairs, blood pooling around him. At one end of the hallway was another corpse, face a mangled mess. He only identified it as Litke when he saw the shotgun beside it. 'Where are they?'

Zagoskin emerged from the room beside Litke's body. 'Four sets of footprints on the balcony. Looks like they've jumped down to the ground.'

The thud of boots on the spiral stairs announced Shilovsky's arrival. Morozov rounded angrily on him. 'What the fuck are you doing in here? You're supposed to be watching the outside!'

Shilovsky gave him an unfriendly glare. 'I got shot, *sir*,' he snapped, showing the rip in his hood. Blood glistened on his neck.

'You've been *scratched*,' Morozov growled, before speaking into his headset. 'Malyutin! Targets are out of the building – watch for them!'

Beyond the helipad, Malyutin acknowledged the command. He raised the rifle and slowly swept it from side to side. The thermal sight revealed what was hidden by darkness and whirling flakes. Amorphous dark grey shapes drifted across the scope; snow-shrouded trees on the hillside below. Nothing hotter, though. So where—

A bright running figure came into view from behind the building. Malyutin quickly fixed the crosshairs upon it – then saw the flash of an infra-red beacon. Someone was pursuing the targets. He quickly scanned the ground around his teammate. Nobody else in sight. The man was angling to the right – had his quarry got so far clear already? More trees blurred across the scope as he searched for them. But still nothing stood out against the cold grey background. 'Where are they?' he asked. 'I can see one of us chasing them, but there's no—'

Morozov angrily cut him off. 'What? We're all in the building!'

'But I can see a beacon—' This time, Malyutin broke off by himself as realisation hit. He whipped the G28 back across to locate his target. The running man had reached the slope's lip, lower legs obscured. The crosshairs found his back—

His target dropped – a split-second *before* he pulled the trigger. The rifle jolted. Malyutin steadied it, then looked back through the sight. The man had ducked the moment he reached cover. A faint pale swirl rose from where he had been: hot breath. He was still alive.

A frantic sweep back to the left, scouring the space beyond the building. Another hurrying figure appeared, already halfway over the top of the slope. Smaller than the first – a woman. He targeted her—

Again, he was too late. A second person practically dived to pull her down out of sight. 'Shit!' he growled, before activating his throat-mic. 'Lost them, I repeat, I lost them. They got over the edge of the hill.'

Morozov listened with rising fury to the sniper's message. 'Fuck!' he snarled, pounding a fist on the banister. Zagoskin and Shilovsky looked on, concerned. Their leader did not have a reputation for taking failure well. An angry exhalation, then: 'All right. Shilovsky, that helicopter – can you fly it?'

'Yes, of course,' came the reply. Shilovsky had been a Russian army pilot before joining the SVR.

'Even in this weather?'

An immodest, almost mocking chuckle and shrug. 'Yeah.'

Morozov nodded. 'Malyutin, meet Shilovsky at the helicopter. I want you two to find them from the air. Zagoskin, you're with me. We'll follow their trail on foot. Again, if we can capture Reeve alive, do it. Now let's go!'

The three Russians ran back down the stairs to begin the hunt.

CHAPTER 41

'We're almost there,' said Reeve encouragingly. Avelina and especially Idonia were struggling to keep up with the two Operatives. The steep slope was made even harder to traverse by knee-deep snow. 'Keep going, we can make it.' The first trees were a dozen metres ahead.

Locke looked back. Only the lodge's uppermost floor was visible, windows aglow through the blizzard. 'They *must* be following us by now. How many rounds do you have left?'

'Not many. You?'

'Seven, and a spare magazine. You take the rear. You have more range.'

'And you have more bullets,' Reeve replied firmly. He had no intention of leaving Locke alone with the Fosses, even while ostensibly allied.

Locke made a dismissive sound, but slowed slightly to let the women pass. Reeve kept going, finally reaching the edge of the woods. What little light there was in the open dropped to nothing. He slowed, feeling his way forward. The Russians would soon catch up if they were reduced to this pace—

'Alex!' Avelina called from behind him. 'Where are you?'

'Here, over here,' he said. 'Follow my voice.'

'I can do better – I'll follow your tracks.' A light came on, bright enough to make Reeve squint. He realised it was the torch on her new phone. He held in a bark of criticism; she had just blown his night vision. But what was done was done.

Instead, he signalled for her to join him. She did so, Idonia with her. 'You know the area,' he said. 'How do we get down to Furi without being caught in the open?'

'There isn't really a way,' Avelina replied. 'The trees stop before we get anywhere near the cable-car station. Although . . .' She aimed her torch diagonally down the slope. 'If we went across the—'

'They're coming!' Locke warned sharply.

Reeve looked back. His vision was recovering. Between the trees, he spotted two bright lights coming over the crest of the slope. 'Go where you're going,' he told Avelina urgently. 'We'll catch up.' He and Locke retraced their steps to the limit of the trees as the Fosses moved on. Reeve readied the SCAR. The Russians were roughly sixty metres away, but it was hard to be sure. The swirling snow made judging distances tricky. 'Ready?' he asked Locke.

'Of course,' was the cold reply.

Reeve lined up his sights. He couldn't see the man holding the torch at all, only its light. He fired a single shot. Two rounds cracked from Locke's pistol. Both lights dropped sharply to the ground. Were the Russians hit? But then the torches went out. Locke fired again, but Reeve knew the SVR agents would be rolling clear. They had only been clipped, if they had even been hit at all.

'Let's go,' said Reeve. Both men hunched down and weaved between the trees after the Fosses. Their caution was justified a few seconds later as automatic fire crackled from the slope. Bullets thunked into wood, explosions of snow dropping from the drooping foliage. But none struck close to the Operatives.

Avelina had turned down the brightness of her torch. It was now a pale will-o'-the-wisp ahead, dancing through the woods. Reeve and Locke soon caught up. 'Where are we going?' Reeve asked Avelina.

'There's a bridge,' she replied. 'It's called Hängebrücke – it goes over a canyon. There are paths on the other side. One of them goes to the cable-car station, with trees almost all the way.'

'How far is it?'

'From here? I don't know exactly. It's half a kilometre from the lodge, maybe, although the hill's steep in places.'

'Can you make it?' Reeve's question was addressed to both women. He could tell Idonia was suffering more than her daughter from the cold.

'I think so,' Avelina replied.

Idonia's response was more uncertain. 'I – I will have to, won't I?'

'You can do it,' Reeve assured her. 'I'll help you. All we have to do is keep going until—'

He broke off as a new sound cut through the wind. A deep, thunderous rumble, mixed with a high-pitched whine.

The sound of a turbine engine powering rotor blades. The helicopter.

Malyutin had taken sniper shots – successfully – from helicopters before. Those, however, had been military, designed for such purposes. The civilian AgustaWestland AW119 was built to keep its occupants cocooned inside the cabin. He was perched sideways on the rear seat, wedging the door open with one knee. Not a comfortable position, nor a safe one. The lap belt didn't extend far enough to hold him properly. The best he could do was loop it around his right leg. He was under no illusions that it would save him from a fall.

The thought made him more determined to finish the job quickly. The helicopter rose above the ski lodge. Shilovsky, piloting, switched on a spotlight. The beam stabbed through the blizzard. Even that intense light barely revealed the trees lower down the slope.

Malyutin had a clearer view. He swept his thermal scope over the woods. Somewhere in them were the fugitives. The sooner he found them, the sooner he could be back on solid ground. 'I can see the forest,' he shouted into his headset. 'No sign of them yet.'

'They're there,' Morozov replied, voice barely audible over the engine's roar. 'They fired on us. We're following their tracks. They're heading right, roughly east.'

Shilovsky was also listening to the radio exchange. 'Changing course,' he warned the sniper. Malyutin braced himself as the AW119 slowly wheeled about. The strong wind was buffeting the aircraft, forcing its pilot to be extra-cautious.

'I can't see the woods,' Malyutin complained as the helicopter turned. The open door now obstructed his line of sight. 'I need you to fly sideways if I'm going to get a shot.'

'You want a hot towel and champagne too?' was the sarcastic retort. But Shilovsky brought the aircraft back around, sliding it towards the forest.

Malyutin resumed his sweep. The rotor downwash batted at his rifle, but he didn't yet need to hold it stable. All he needed was a flash of heat in the scope—

There! A flicker of white amidst the cold grey. He snapped the gun on to it, scanning the surrounding area. 'I see them!' he reported. More bright flashes appeared through the snow-draped foliage. The targets were on the move.

'Take the shot if you can,' Morozov ordered. 'Shoot to wound, if possible. I still want Reeve alive. We'll finish the others on the ground.'

'I'll try, sir.' Malyutin had no intention of handicapping himself. If he wounded anyone, it would be because the conditions had prevented a kill. 'Shilovsky, they're at your two o'clock, about two hundred metres. Bring us above them so I can get a clear shot.'

Shilovsky changed course again. The helicopter bore down upon the fugitives.

'Chopper's coming in!' Reeve warned the others. The spotlight was pointing downhill, but moving across the slope, straight for them. The helicopter was flying sideways – so the sniper would be leaning from its flank. 'Avelina, Idonia – stay close to the tree trunks. It'll give you the most cover.' The sniper's thermal sight couldn't penetrate the snow-covered trees. But it *could* pick out body heat through even the smallest gap. Reeve had previously used thermal sights himself to spot hidden targets. In such cold surroundings, any exposure through concealment would shine like a star.

The women kept going, Locke following. Reeve stopped, putting a trunk between himself and the helicopter, and removed the SCAR's magazine. His fingertip found cold, curved brass inside its top. There was at least one round still in it. He pulled it out. Nothing popped up in its place. The mag was now empty.

He reloaded the bullet. Counting the round already in the chamber, he had two shots. There were at least four Russians pursuing them. And there was also Locke to consider. Grim-faced, he clacked the magazine back into place and set off again.

Malyutin briefly raised his eye from the thermal scope. Spill from the spotlight illuminated the forest below. The trees thrashed in the chopper's downwash, dislodged snow swirling into a miniature hurricane. He looked back into his sight. There had been intermittent glimpses of his targets as the helicopter descended.

Now he could see them more clearly.

Flailing branches kept obscuring them, but he still made out at least three people. The nearest, the man with the stolen beacon, ducked behind a tree. Smart move: the trunk would provide protection from a bullet. But he couldn't stay there. 'I see them,' he told Morozov. 'Close on our position – we'll lead you to them.'

'On our way,' was the brusque reply. Morozov sounded as if he was running, hound chasing the hare.

'How far away are they?' asked Shilovsky.

'Eighty metres, if that,' Malyutin told him. 'Keep on this course – we're coming straight at them.'

He readied himself, muscles tensing to steady the rifle as he searched for targets.

* * *

Reeve slogged through the snow to catch up with Locke. Avelina's light was dimly visible ten metres ahead. She and her mother were following his instruction, weaving closely around the trees. The ground became steeper, more treacherous. 'What were you doing?' Locke demanded.

'Checking my ammo.'

'And?'

'You've got as many mags as I have rounds.'

'I see.' Was there an edge of satisfaction behind the Operative's otherwise flat voice?

Reeve didn't have time to dwell on it. The helicopter was closing. 'How far to the bridge?' he called to Avelina. The noise of the approaching chopper forced him to shout. The blizzard's gusts were being overpowered by something more constant, more threatening. The AW119 was driving a freezing, fuel-reeking gale ahead of itself, blasting the trees.

Stripping away their frozen covering.

Clumps of snow showered over them as branches shook overhead. Idonia gasped as one hit the back of her neck. Both women were shivering, hopelessly underdressed for blizzard conditions.

Idonia drew ahead as Avelina slowed to reply to Reeve. 'I'm not sure. We still have to go under the cable-car and across a ski run. But we must be very close to them now.'

'Have the trees been cleared under the cable-car?' Locke asked urgently.

Reeve answered before Avelina could search her memory. He had noted it from both the helicopter and the cable-car ride. 'Yeah. It's not wide, but we'll need to cross open ground.'

'Be ready to take fire—'

A startled shriek from ahead – as Idonia slipped and tumbled down the hillside.

Reeve lost sight of her in the darkness. 'Idonia!' he yelled. He started after her, only almost to fall himself. The ground beneath the snow was littered with loose stones and broken branches. 'Are you okay?'

Avelina also shouted after her mother in German. '*Ja*, yes,' came a winded reply from downhill.

Locke changed direction, angling towards Idonia. 'I'll get her.'

Avelina gave Reeve a fearful look. 'You can't leave him alone with her!' she hissed.

'I know,' he replied. 'But we've got to keep moving.' They continued on, rounding a few more trees—

Their cover vanished.

They had reached the cable-car line. The trees beneath it had been cleared for maintenance and emergency access. The gap was roughly thirty feet: ten metres. That distance could be crossed in a few seconds in normal circumstances. Through snow, on steep, detritus-littered ground, not so quickly.

Reeve looked downhill. Another light appeared. Locke had a torch. The red circle of its beam found Idonia, sprawled on her back in a snowdrift. She was about forty feet below Reeve and Avelina. 'Get her up!' he told Locke. 'We've got to—'

More snow pelted him. He looked back – as light swept

over them. Not from the spotlight, but reflected off the snow-covered trees. The helicopter came into view, fierce rotor downwash pushing away the branches concealing Reeve. It jittered and jinked as its pilot held course against the pounding wind. A black hole gaped in the aircraft's side – an open door.

He couldn't see the sniper. But the Russian would be there.

Gun at the ready—

Reeve grabbed Avelina and dived. A high-pitched whip-crack passed right behind him. Reeve scrambled behind a tree trunk, shielding Avelina with his body. Another round smacked into wood. Shattered bark fragments rained around the pair. Avelina cried out in fear.

Reeve tensed, ready to run. But no more shots followed. The pine was thick enough to stop the sniper fire.

Which meant the Russian would find new prey.

Malyutin swore. He had lost his targets behind a tree.

So move on. There were others.

He swept his sight over the slope. A band of ground running up it was empty of trees. The cable-car, he realised, seeing lines angling steeply upwards. Nowhere to hide beneath them, and the downwash was swatting the branches aside—

White against the dark grey.

Two figures. One moved as if sensing that he had been spotted, darting for cover. The other was struggling to stand. A woman.

It made no difference to the SVR assassin. He had killed

men, women, children with the same detachment. The cross-hairs found the middle of her chest—

The white shape vanished. The same wind revealing his targets had blown more branches in front of them.

He took the shot anyway.

Idonia finally got to her feet. She started to run across the hillside. The helicopter was coming straight for her. But if she could reach the forest beyond the cable-car line—

She couldn't.

Blood and torn flesh exploded from her thigh as a bullet ripped through it.

CHAPTER 42

Reeve heard Idonia's scream even over the helicopter's thunder. As did Avelina. '*Mama!*' she wailed, jumping to her feet—

Reeve pulled her back down. 'If you go to help her, you'll die.' Soldiers knew that sniping those trying to help the wounded breached the rules of war. That didn't stop it from being common practice. SC9 actively taught it as a means to force a target to leave cover.

So would the SVR.

Another scream, this a drawn-out wail of agony. Avelina struggled to pull free. 'They're going to kill her! You promised you'd protect us, you *promised*!'

Reeve clenched his jaw. An Operative would leave her. The mission came first. But he was no longer an Operative. He had already failed Connie; he couldn't fail the Fosses as well. But leaving cover would expose him to the sniper. Unless—

He rose and readied his gun. Two rounds left.

He had to make them count.

'Stay here,' he told Avelina – then he rushed out into the open.

The helicopter was barely twenty metres away, just above

357

the treetops. He saw the void of the open door.

Movement within, a faint glint of light off metal. The sniper had seen him.

And was taking aim.

Reeve threw himself sidelong. Snow spattered his face as the sniper's round hit the ground beside him.

The Russian would already be reacquiring him. Reeve whipped up his own weapon and pulled the trigger. No time to aim. A snapshot was all he could do. If he got lucky, if he hit the sniper . . .

He didn't. Faint red sparks spat in the darkness. The round had struck the fuselage. Only inches from the open door, but it may as well have been a mile. Now he only had one bullet left. And the sniper was already recovering—

A shrill from the engine – and the helicopter rose sharply. The pilot, reacting defensively to the bullet impact. He had no way of knowing the shooter was down to his last round. Reeve glimpsed frantic movement in the doorway. The sniper hadn't expected the sudden climb.

He would have lost his aim—

Reeve gripped his SCAR with both hands and took aim himself. Not at the open door, but the cockpit. Beckmeyer had sat in the right-hand seat when he flew them from Munich. Survival now hung on the Russian pilot doing the same . . .

He fired.

Last shot – but it hit home.

The AW119 lurched, veering sideways away from him – then started to turn. The spotlight flashed across the snowbound trees. Reeve glimpsed a figure slumped in the starboard pilot's seat. A hole was punched in the Plexiglas beside it. The turn became a spin, the aircraft losing height—

Its rotors clipped the treetops. The topmost branches were scythed off – then the blades hit thicker wood below. Carbon fibre shattered. The crippled helicopter reeled towards the ground . . .

Heading for Reeve.

A moment of shocked paralysis – then he charged back uphill. '*Run!*' he bellowed. Avelina was equally stunned, only breaking into motion as he reached her. The helicopter spun down behind them—

It hit the ground. The smashed rotors carved into soil, the fuselage cartwheeling in a shower of disintegrating metal. Malyutin was flung out and crushed beneath it. The tail boom tore away at its base and tumbled along behind. Reeve dived to flatten Avelina into the snow. An axe-like *thud* as part of the tail rotor slammed into a tree beside them. Avelina screamed.

But the chaos was far from over. Flames erupted inside the engine compartment. A fuel tank ruptured, flammable vapour escaping, finding the fire—

The helicopter exploded.

It bowled across the hillside, leaving a trail of burning debris and liquid flame. More mangled wreckage smacked down like meteorites. Reeve brought both arms up to shield the back of his head, Avelina beneath him. Something jagged and heavy struck his hip. He yelled, but the sound was drowned out by another explosion. The AW119's flaming carcass slithered across the clear-cut swathe of forest. The deep snow in the open finally brought it to a halt.

Reeve raised his head. He now had no difficulty seeing his surroundings. Fires lit the woods, a crackling wall stretching across the slope below him. Chunks of burning machinery were strewn all around. He pushed himself off Avelina. His hip ached as if struck by a hammer. He groaned, then sat up. 'Are you all right?' he asked.

She was panting, in the throes of a fear-fuelled adrenalin rush. 'Yeah, yeah,' she said between breaths – before rolling sharply on to her side. 'My mother! We have to help her!'

This time, Reeve agreed. The helicopter's destruction would give them respite, however short. He helped Avelina stand. 'Come on.'

They skirted pieces of fiery wreckage, only to be halted by the trail of blazing fuel. Reeve assessed it. High and fierce, the heat intense enough to warm his freezing skin. It would burn them even if they made a running jump through it. They would have to go around—

Movement through the lashing flames. Locke, emerging from cover below. 'Locke!' Reeve called. The Operative looked uphill and saw him. 'Get Idonia! We need to keep moving – they'll be here soon!' He glanced back the way they had come. No sign of their pursuers' torches. But they were probably already running to reach the crash site.

Locke raised a hand in acknowledgement, then continued into the open. Squinting through the fire, Reeve finally spotted Idonia. She lay on her side, hands clutching her thigh. The snow around it was dark with blood. Alarm rose. Had the sniper's bullet ruptured her femoral artery? If so, the chances of saving her on the run were almost zero. 'Check her leg!' he shouted to Locke.

'I do know what I'm doing, Reeve,' was the arch reply. Locke reached Idonia and crouched, shining his torch over her. He raised his free hand as if about to examine the wound . . .

Then paused. He turned his head, looking back up at Reeve and Avelina. Without shifting his gaze, he drew his combat knife from inside his coat.

'Shit,' Reeve gasped. The alliance was over; Locke was about to complete his objective. But there was nothing he could do. Even if he hadn't dropped the SCAR, it was empty. There was no way he could reach Idonia in time. 'Locke, you fucking piece of shit, no!'

'*Mama!*' Avelina wailed as she realised what was about to happen. '*Bitte tu es nicht, nein!*'

Idonia stared in horror at Locke – then looked past the fire for her daughter. '*Avelina, ich liebe dich – jetzt lauf!*'

Locke regarded his victim with clinical precision . . . then drove the knife into her throat.

Avelina screamed as he slashed the blade outwards, severing Idonia's trachea. Blood gushed on to the snow. A sickening shock rolled through Reeve's body. He had failed.

But he was already moving, grabbing Avelina's arm and dragging her with him. 'He'll kill us next! Go!' A glance through the flames. Locke stood, switching the knife to his left hand.

His right drew his gun—

Reeve ducked, pulling Avelina lower – and changed direction. Cracks of gunfire echoed across the slope. But Locke was shooting blind through the wall of fire. Reeve heard bullets whip past, but none hit. 'Keep going!' he told Avelina. 'Into the trees!' He angled to pass behind the smashed fuselage. Rounds struck metal with sharp clonks of impact. But the helicopter's remains blocked Locke's line of sight.

Beyond it, though, the tree line was still a few metres away. Reeve hauled Avelina with him, running as fast as they could across the gap. The shooting stopped; Locke's magazine was empty. But he had another, quickly reloading. Reeve and Avelina reached the trees as he fired again—

The bullet hit wood just behind them. All Operatives had to attain minimum standards of marksmanship. But Locke, Reeve remembered, had been at the lower end of their training intake. All the same, he didn't stop, weaving between the trees. Another couple of shots lanced after them. None came close.

'How far to the bridge?' he demanded. Avelina didn't reply. 'Avelina! I need your help – how far to the bridge?'

'Not – not far,' she stammered. Her voice was weak, shaken. 'The ski run is just below. There is a path to the bridge.'

The hillside slope became steeper. Reeve raised Avelina's arm higher so her phone would light the way. They scrambled down a rocky embankment on to a clear lane through the forest. 'There,' said the young German, pointing. Reeve saw a space between trees on the track's far side. They hurried towards it.

Locke's eyes narrowed in exasperation as he lowered his gun. Reeve and Theodore Foss had reached cover. He shouldn't have missed them from this range! Annoyed at himself, he started after them—

A shout from behind. He looked back into the woods. Torchlight flickered between the trees. The Russians were approaching. Higher up the hillside; they would emerge above the line of burning wreckage.

That meant they would see Reeve and Foss's tracks, not his. He could wait for them to pass, then follow. If they killed his targets for him . . .

It would be disappointing. The anticipation of rendering Reeve helpless before slicing open his throat had been rising.

But he could live with it.

He changed course, angling into the woods below the wreckage.

'Fuck!' exclaimed Zagoskin as he and Morozov reached the AW119's burning remains. 'You think anyone's still alive?'

'Not from this,' was Morozov's curt reply. He had witnessed helicopter crashes before. From low altitude, without a fire, survival was possible. *With* a fire . . .

He turned his attention back to the tracks they were following. He didn't need his powerful Maglite torch here. The footprints were plainly visible, lit by the flames. 'Two of them went this way. Where are the other two?'

'Down there.' Morozov looked in the direction his subordinate was pointing. A body lay downhill, a woman. Blood soaked the snow around her. 'Who did *that* to her?'

'The other Operative.' So his suspicions were correct. There was some sort of factional war within SC9. Reeve was being hunted by an Operative, who had been betrayed by another. Good. A weakened, in-fighting SC9 could only be to Russia's benefit. Serve the bastards right for what they had done to his countrymen. He turned back to the footprints. Both were men's sizes. He had read up on Idonia Foss during the train journey to Zermatt. Her son was some sort of cross-dressing pervert. He might try to look like a woman, but he couldn't shrink his feet. 'Follow the tracks, and we'll catch up. I still want Reeve alive.'

Both men resumed their run, crossing the clear-cut ground beneath the cable-car line. 'And the others?' asked Zagoskin.

Morozov gave him a cold glance. 'Kill them, of course.'

CHAPTER 43

Reeve and Avelina hurried down the winding path. The slope undulated, rocks and roots hidden by snow threatening to trip them. Reeve stumbled on one, Avelina barely catching him. 'Are you okay?' she asked.

'Yeah,' he replied, recovering. The phone's light caught her face; streaks of frozen tears glistened on her cheeks. He set off again, Avelina with him. 'What about you?'

'I – I don't know. It's too much, I . . . can't think about it.' She shone the torch ahead to guide them through a bend in the narrowing path. 'We're nearly there.'

Over a small rise, down into a snow-filled dip – then the forest opened out.

Reeve winced as a freezing wind hit his face. In the trees, they had been partly protected from the blizzard. Now it struck back with full force. The black abyss of the canyon lay before him. The bridge was a slim line of metal disappearing into the darkness. It was suspended by cables, which moaned and creaked alarmingly in the gale.

He went to its end. The structure was narrow, just enough space for two people to squeeze past each other. Steel grillwork decking, chain-link mesh protectively enclosing the space under the handrails. The low light only revealed a few metres of what lay ahead. Even that was enough for him to see the bridge swaying in the wind. How bad would it be halfway across? 'How wide's the canyon?'

'I'm not sure,' said Avelina. 'About a hundred metres?'

'And how *high* is it?'

'About a hundred metres?'

Reeve held in a sarcastic retort. A dangerous crossing, and from it a fall would be lethal. But they had no choice. 'Okay, let's cross it,' he said, glancing back—

Lights flashed between the trees behind them.

Avelina saw his sudden alarm. 'Is it Locke?' she gasped.

'The Russians.' They were approaching, quickly. A rapid decision. 'Go across,' he told Avelina, backtracking over their footsteps.

'What about you?' she asked in surprise, and concern.

'I'm going to stop them. Go on!' he added more forcefully at her hesitation. She gave him a worried look, but started across the bridge.

Reeve retreated until he was under a tree. He grabbed a branch above and pulled himself up into the dense, snow-covered foliage.

The lights drew closer.

Morozov hurried down the path, kicking up snow. He flicked the heavy Maglite at the ground to check the tracks, then up again. So far no lights had been visible ahead. Even if the fugitives had a phone torch or similar, they were keeping it low. Sensible, to avoid being seen – but it would force them to pick their way forward. With more light, the SVR men could move much faster.

Something ahead other than snow and trees. A dull reflection off grey metal. 'There's a bridge here!' he said. The footprints in the snow led right to it. He increased his pace.

The blizzard returned in all its power as he reached a cliff-edge. Shielding his eyes against the biting snowflakes, he shone his light at the crossing. A narrow suspension bridge, flexing and swaying in the wind, stretched away before him.

Someone was staggering across it.

Morozov raised his gun. But he knew from bitter experience that his left-handed aim was not up to the challenge. He needed to get closer. 'Come on!' he shouted back to Zagoskin as he stepped on to the bridge. 'We've got them!'

Reeve hung from a tree branch, hunched up tightly. The evergreen's foliage and covering of snow limited his vision. But he could see enough to spot the Russians' torches drawing closer – and passing.

The leader called out to his companion. Reeve recognised the voice. Morozov. He had seen Avelina on the bridge. A knot of tension in his gut. If he took a shot—

But the SVR agent instead started after his quarry. What about the second guy? The other light was still at the terminus, shining down at the snow . . .

Moving back towards him.

The man had noticed something that Morozov, in his eagerness to catch Reeve, had overlooked. There was only one set of footprints on the bridge. Reeve tensed, readying himself. The light swept back and forth across the ground – then up—

Reeve swung, bursting from the tree – and kicked the Russian in the chest.

Both his feet made solid contact. The SVR man reeled backwards. One heel caught a rock. He tripped—

And fell over the edge.

He screamed as he dropped – then the cry was abruptly cut off. The smack of bone on rock was audible even over the wind.

Reeve had landed on his back. He rolled upright and went to the bridge. The only light now came from the two torches upon it. One weak, one strong.

The latter was gaining on the former.

Morozov had been forced to holster his gun to grip the handrail. The wind tore at the bridge, swaying it violently. The movement was not merely a simple swing. It was simultaneously bouncing and twisting, the effect sickening. Each step along the metal walkway required effort to stay upright.

But he was gaining on his targets. He brought up the Maglite in his right hand. Its intense beam found the younger Foss ahead. No coat, or even gloves. The blizzard would be freezing him, draining his energy. The Russian was closing the gap.

The realisation spurred him forward. The further he went, the more severe the bridge's demented shudder became. He was nearing its middle. A sudden, brutal jolt threw him sideways against the handrail. He clutched it more tightly, battling to stay upright until the wind subsided. Breathing heavily, he shone his torch ahead again. Foss had fallen, clutching at the chain-link. Morozov tilted the beam higher. Nobody beyond. The rest of the bridge was empty. Where was Reeve?

A glance back. Nothing but darkness behind him. Where was *Zagoskin*?

He turned and brought up the Maglite—

A man was following him across the bridge. But it wasn't his comrade.

'Reeve!' The name escaped Morozov's lips in a steaming burst, whipped away by the gale. He hooked his right elbow around a stanchion and fumbled for the gun. Another powerful gust shook the bridge, steel clanging and wailing. He almost dropped his Glock, just managing to clamp his fingers around it. He was sure he could beat Reeve, even with his damaged hand. But he still wanted the advantage the gun gave him. The Brit wouldn't escape him this time.

If he could capture him alive, as planned, good. But the situation might not permit that. It only took the Russian the briefest moment to decide how to proceed.

If he had to kill Reeve . . . so be it.

The light warned Reeve that his hope of catching Morozov unawares was ended. He broke into a run, hands outstretched at guardrail height. The bridge's swaying grew worse as he approached the centre. One palm brushed along the rail to steady himself. He lowered his head to minimise his target profile, squinting into the beam. He couldn't see Morozov through the glare – but had to assume he was taking aim—

Muzzle flash, the gun's crack almost drowned by the wind. Reeve heard the bullet whip past to his right. The bridge's movement had thrown the Russian's shot off target. But the closer Reeve got, the less likely he was to miss.

The torch shifted, Morozov changing position. Refining his aim—

Reeve ducked still further – as a gust struck the bridge like a physical blow. The wind screamed past him, flying ice particles slashing at his exposed skin. He reeled and grabbed the handrail. The dazzling beam jittered crazily away from him. Morozov had been sent staggering too. The decking rocked and twisted underfoot like a fairground funhouse. He forced himself onwards. Morozov hadn't recovered yet, the torch pointing down into the ravine. If he could reach him before he did—

The bright beam swung towards him, a lighthouse warning of death rather than life. Reeve kept going, feeling the bridge sway again. He rode with it instead of fighting it. The swing sent him against the chain-link – and again Morozov missed.

By less than before. The snap of displaced air was louder. The next shot would find him.

If he let it.

Reeve forced all his remaining energy into a sudden burst of speed. He crossed the final few metres to the Russian. Morozov swept the gun at him—

Reeve swung his right arm. It caught Morozov's forearm, knocking his wrist against a stanchion. Morozov made a sound of pain. Reeve seized his opportunity and drove his elbow at the other man's hand. It caught the gun and sent it whirling into the void below.

Reeve spun to press his attack, left elbow pounding the Russian's sternum. Morozov's coat and armour absorbed most of the blow – but he still grunted sharply. Reeve stabbed his fingers at the other man's eyes—

Morozov ducked, turning. Reeve's attack found only his hood. The heavy Maglite smacked against the side of the Englishman's skull. Reeve lurched, dizzied. Before he could recover, the Russian struck him again, harder. Reeve stumbled against the bridge's side, chain-link clattering. The torch rose again – then hurtled down for a third, decisive strike.

Reeve desperately threw an arm up to block it. He succeeded – partially. The torch only caught his face a glancing blow. But it was enough to make pain erupt in his nose, blood flowing. Then the Russian forced his forearm against Reeve's throat – and pushed.

The breath was trapped in Reeve's lungs as his airway was cut off. He tried to retaliate. But Morozov kept pushing, bending his upper body over the guardrail. Metal ground into his back. The SVR agent's left fist slammed into Reeve's side with hammer-blow force. Then again, and a third time. Only a choked rasp escaped Reeve's mouth.

Morozov leaned closer. The torch beam bounced off snow on the handrail, illuminating him. Reeve saw he was missing his right forefinger, middle finger unnaturally stiff. Then the broad-jawed Russian grabbed him with his left hand – and lifted.

He was going to throw him over.

Reeve kicked. But Morozov was pressed against him, restricting his movements. His waist slipped over the guardrail. Morozov tipped him back over the deadly void below. 'I promised I would kill you for what you did in Italy,' the Russian growled. 'Now, it's time!'

He shifted his left hand, tightly gripping the material of Reeve's trousers. Reeve struggled, but the other man lifted him higher, higher—

And shoved him over the edge.

Reeve clawed desperately at the chain-link with one hand – and Morozov with the other. He caught the neck of Morozov's coat. The SVR man had been leaning forward for leverage. The sudden jerk, Reeve's full weight behind it, pulled him over the guardrail. Both men fell—

Reeve's shoulder crackled as he caught himself. The chain-link rattled and strained, a fastener snapping. The fence buckled – but held. Morozov managed to snag the cable supporting the top of the wire mesh . . .

With his damaged right hand.

The two men hung helplessly, shock and fear overpowering all other responses. Then their survival instincts kicked in. Reeve looked up. He could see nothing; the Maglite had fallen into the ravine. He groped upwards with his free hand, finding the chain-link.

Feeling it judder. Not from the wind. Morozov was dangling beside him, to his right.

His instinct was to climb. But training took over. To survive, he had to fight. Only one man would make it back on to the bridge. And Morozov would know that too.

Reeve pulled himself higher – then twisted his lower body and kicked out. He couldn't see his opponent, but still scored a solid hit. Morozov gasped. Another kick, then Reeve reached up for a higher handhold. His fingers found the mesh's support cable. It trembled as Morozov shifted position, about to attack. Reeve was ready. He swung back as a boot lashed at him. It caught his thigh. A hard, painful impact – but he withstood it.

Then struck again.

Another swing, back at Morozov – kicking as high as he could. The Russian had caught the chain-link with his left hand. Reeve's boot slammed into it. Bones broke with a gruesome snap. Morozov roared in pain. He lost his hold, dangling only by his weakened right hand.

Panting, straining, Reeve hauled himself upwards. Another kick at Morozov, then he reached the guardrail. He dragged himself over and crashed down on to the walkway.

A second to catch his breath, then he stood. He could hear Morozov's panicked exertions as he tried to find new grip. Reeve reached out blindly, feeling the other man's hand clenched around the wire. He stepped back—

And smashed his heel against it.

An agonised shriek – then the bridge jolted violently as the weight on it abruptly reduced. The scream faded to nothingness below.

Reeve grabbed the handrail to steady himself, then looked along the crossing. Through the blowing snow he saw a faint light. Avelina. She was almost across. Breathing heavily, he hurried after her, Morozov already forgotten.

CHAPTER 44

The wind remained as strong, but the bridge's gyrations eased as Reeve neared its end. He stepped onto solid ground with relief.

Darkness surrounded him. Not even Avelina's phone torch was visible. He crouched, but couldn't pick out any tracks in the snow. 'Avelina!' he shouted. Had she fallen, or was she hiding?

The latter. 'Alex?' A scared voice from a few metres away. He cautiously moved towards it. The torch came on, revealing Avelina behind a tree. 'Oh my God! Are you all right?'

'Yeah.' He realised his cracked nose had bloodied his face. 'It's not serious. Are you okay? Can you keep going?'

'I think so.' She wrapped her arms around herself, shivering. 'I thought I was going to freeze on the bridge. It's a little better in the trees.'

'We've got to keep moving. I took down the Russians, but Locke's still out there. Where's this path to Furi?'

The mention of Locke spurred Avelina into motion. 'This way.' Reeve followed. They picked their way uphill. 'Oh! I just thought,' she exclaimed after a minute. 'They were jamming our phones at the lodge. But now we're away from it, I can call for help!'

'Try it,' said Reeve. Man-portable cellular jammers had ranges ranging from dozens of metres to a kilometre. What had Morozov's team brought?

He had his suspicions, and they soon proved true. 'It's still not working,' Avelina said in dismay, regarding her screen. 'I can't get a signal.'

'We'll have to keep going until we're out of range.' They continued up the slope, reaching a picnic area. Chunky wooden benches rose from the snow. Paths led off in different directions. 'Which way?'

She pointed left. 'Over there.'

They continued past a snow-draped seesaw and tyre swing. The path widened still further. 'Does this go straight down into the village?' Reeve asked.

'Not straight. It's quite winding. But it will get us there.'

'How long will it take?'

'I don't know. I walked this way with my mother a few times, but there was less snow . . .' She trailed off, shivering again. This time it was not solely from the cold. 'My mother,' she said with a sob. 'Oh, God. He killed her. He killed her!'

'I'm sorry,' said Reeve. He felt not just sympathy, but a deep shame at his failure to protect Idonia. The Operative's betrayal had been inevitable.

Anger rose inside him. He had failed Idonia. But he was not going to fail Avelina. A new, burning determination. Locke would not get off the mountain alive.

'She – she tried to protect me,' Avelina said quietly. 'Just before . . .

Reeve remembered Idonia had shouted something in German. 'What did she say?'

'She said, "Avelina, I love you. Now—"' Her voice broke. '"Now run." She finally accepted me as who I am. And then, and then—' She started to sob, shoulders shaking in grief.

Reeve put an arm around her. The gesture was as much to keep her moving as for comfort. The path curved sharply to the right. The wind picked up as they neared the bend. Few trees ahead; they were exposed on steep mountainside. Somewhere in the darkness was Furi, but its lights were lost in the blizzard. He guided her onwards through the freezing storm.

Locke reached the far side of the ravine. Even for the calm, unemotional Operative, the crossing had been stressful. But more so for Reeve, he'd seen. Four sets of footprints led to the bridge. Three went across. The confused knot of a scuffle halfway over. Then only two made it to the other end. Reeve had taken care of the Russians for him.

Now all he had to do was follow the remaining tracks to finish the job.

A degree of caution was needed. One Russian had been ambushed, thrown or kicked over the cliff. Locke removed the red filter from his torch to brighten the beam. He kept a measured pace, enough to spot any irregularities in the footprints. But there were none. Reeve knew he was armed. His targets were trying to escape, not attack.

A snow-smothered picnic area formed a ghostly tableau in his torchlight. The tracks went left. He followed them. Before long, the path curved rightwards. He narrowed his eyes as the stinging wind gusted harder. His torch revealed that the path traversed a steep, rocky slope. Presumably it zig-zagged downhill—

A light below.

Reeve and Avelina made their way down the switchback path. The going was relatively easy; it was a well-trodden hiking route. Maybe it would not take long to reach Furi—

A flash at the edge of Reeve's vision. He turned – and saw a light higher on the hillside. He pulled the startled Avelina with him. 'Move!'

Gunshots echoed off the rocks as they scrambled into the trees below the path. A round thwacked into a trunk just behind them. '*Scheisse!*' Avelina yelped.

'Keep going,' said Reeve. 'Use the trees for cover.' The firing stopped. Locke had lost sight of them. 'If we stay on the path we'll be exposed. How much does it zig-zag? Can we take a shortcut downhill?'

'I don't know! I remember that it goes along the edge of the ravine, then down a hill towards Furi. We . . . we might be able to,' was the best reply she could manage.

'Turn up the torch so we can see better.'

'But he'll see us.'

'I'll shield you. You find a way down.'

Avelina looked back at him unhappily, but adjusted the torch. The low glow became brighter, illuminating the way ahead. It was still a far cry from the intensity of Morozov's Maglite. Reeve glanced uphill. No sign of Locke through the trees.

But he knew he was coming for them.

The slope became steeper. Avelina scrabbled down it,

gasping as she slipped. Reeve reached for her, but she had already caught herself. 'We'll have to climb down,' she warned. 'It's turning into a cliff.'

'I'll help you if you need it,' he replied. Another look up the mountainside. A flicker of light in the blackness. Locke was also cutting down the slope rather than following the path.

She started a hesitant descent of the rocks. Reeve crouched above, waiting for her to get clear before following. He flexed his fingers, trying to force blood to flow through them. He had warmed them under his arms whenever he could. Now, though, they would be exposed – and he had no idea for how long. If they went numb while he was still climbing down a cliff . . .

He had no choice but to take the risk. One last squeeze of his fingers, then he went after Avelina. 'How are you managing?' he called to her.

'I'm okay,' she replied. 'It's steep, but I can do it. There are a lot of footholds.'

'Good. Just keep going.' He was already right above her, but forcing her to move faster could be disastrous. He concentrated on finding firm holds for his own hands and feet. A glance down. Avelina's torch lit only the area directly beneath her. He couldn't tell how far they had to go. It could be five metres – or fifty—

Her light suddenly waved crazily. She shrieked as she slipped – then jarred to a halt a metre below. Loose stones clattered into the dark. 'Avelina!' Reeve shouted.

'Ah! Oh, *scheisse*!' she cried, pained. 'I hit my leg on a rock. Shit, fuck!'

'Are you okay? Can you still move?'

'Yes, yes. I'm good.' She aimed the light downwards. 'I think I see the path!'

Through the whirl of snowflakes, Reeve spotted flat ground below. 'Get down there, quick.'

She descended, with some pained gasps. Reeve clambered sideways and jumped down. He wavered on landing, but kept his footing. They had reached another leg of the path. 'Here, I'll help you.'

He aided her down the last couple of metres. Avelina gratefully made landfall. 'Thanks.' She shone the light at her leg. Her jeans were torn, blood on her shin. 'Oh! It hurt, but I didn't realise it was that bad.'

'Can you walk on it?' Reeve asked.

A couple of experimental steps. 'Yes.' They set off again. Reeve saw that Avelina was limping, but she was able to maintain pace. It did not take long before the wind picked up again. She shone the light ahead as they reached a tight curve. The tops of trees thrashed before them, the blizzard's force worsening. 'It's the ravine,' she said, sounding relieved even through her breathless shivering. 'Furi isn't far away now. We just follow the path down into the village.'

'Then let's get there,' he said as they rounded the bend. 'Mobiles might be jammed, but not landlines. There should be one at the cable-car station. You can call for help.'

She picked up on his wording. 'What are *you* going to do?'

'What I should have done at the lodge. Or even back in Munich. Kill Locke.'

'But he has a gun.'

'It won't make a difference.' The anger in his voice deterred Avelina from further questions. Instead she pressed on through the snow.

The path narrowed as they went along. A steep rocky bank rose to their right; there was nothing to their left. Avelina kept the light on the ravine's edge for guidance. 'Nearly there,' she said. 'After we go under the cable-car, there are some fields.' She flicked the torch upwards, searching for the overhead lines. 'We cross a bridge and we are in the village. The station is straight—'

A monstrous blast of wind roared up from the ravine, hitting them head-on. Reeve halted and hunched down, blinded by sharp flecks of ice. The gale's force still made him stagger. Avelina gasped, stumbling back—

She stepped on a loose stone beneath the snow. Her injured leg buckled. She reeled sideways – and went over the edge.

Reeve lunged to catch her. He snagged her jumper, slowing her – but the overstretched material slipped from his frozen hand.

Avelina's scream echoed from below as she slithered down the steep slope. A shrill of pure terror as she fell into open air – then the cry cut off.

Reeve crawled to the edge. 'Avelina!' He could now see nothing. The German's phone had either landed in deep snow or broken. How far had she fallen? He had no idea how deep the ravine was at this point. On to hard rock, a drop of ten feet could be fatal. A drop of thirty feet almost certainly *was* fatal. 'Can you hear me? *Avelina!*'

Nothing but the howl of the wind. Then—

'Alex!' Her voice was faint, filled with pain. 'Help me, I'm here. Help me!'

Reeve swore under his breath. What should he do? She had survived the fall. But there *was* a fall, and if he followed, he might not be so lucky . . .

But he had made a promise. He wasn't going to leave her to die – or to be murdered by Locke. He looked back along the path. No sign of the Operative's torch. He swung his legs around to start his descent.

The rocky gradient he found beyond the path was steep, but not sheer. He eased himself down it, feeling stones and grass under the snow. Avelina called his name again. 'I'm coming,' he told her, concentrating on finding footholds. How far below was she? The ceaseless wind made it hard to judge from her voice. He kept descending. Fifteen feet, twenty. The slope became steeper the lower he got. At some point, it would become vertical—

'Alex!' The cry was clearer this time, not far below. 'Where are you?'

'I'm coming down! Keep talking so I know where you are. Are any bones broken?'

'I don't know. It – it hurts when I try to move my leg.'

The rockface disappeared from under one of his probing feet. He had reached the fall. He kept lowering himself, clinging to the best handholds he could manage. His lower body was now over the edge. 'Okay. I'm going to drop down. How deep is the snow?'

'I'm not sure, but – quite deep. I'm in a snowdrift. Sixty, seventy centimetres, perhaps?'

About two feet. A landing cushion – but not much. At

least his entry to the fall would be controlled, unlike hers. 'All right. Here I come.'

He braced himself, legs bent against the cliff – and jumped clear.

A surge of instinctual fear at his drop into dangerous darkness—

He hit the ground. Snow exploded around him. The rocks beneath the drift were sharp, uneven. He pitched forward, landing on his front. Frigid ice hit his face and neck. He gasped at the sudden enshrouding cold, then pushed himself upright. His touchdown had been jarring, but not outright painful. 'Avelina, I'm down. Where are you?'

'Here.' He followed her voice. She was not far away. He reached out, finding her lying on her back in the snow. 'Oh, thank God.'

'I'm going to sit you up. Tell me if anything hurts.'

She took a few deep breaths. 'Okay. Do it.'

He took hold of her upper body and carefully raised it. She let out some strained grunts, but managed to sit upright. 'I'm okay, so far.'

Reeve shifted position. 'All right. You need to stand up. I'll help you. Ready?'

More preparatory breaths, nervousness behind them. 'Yes.'

He straightened, bringing her with him. She was almost upright when she cried out in pain. 'Oh, *Gott*! That hurts, it hurts!'

'Where?'

'My leg, my left ankle. Oh!' She almost fell against him.

It could be broken, Reeve realised, but there was no time

to check. 'We've got to move. I'll support you.' He went to her left to take the weight off her foot, then looked for her phone. No light in the darkness around them.

But there was one above.

Locke advanced down the path as quickly as he dared. A steep drop lurked to his left, and he was fully exposed to the wind. Several severe gusts had already staggered him. One mistake, and he could go over the edge . . .

The footprints ahead jumbled together – then vanished.

He halted, raising his gun as he swept his torch around. Was Reeve waiting in ambush? But there was nobody there. A closer examination, and events revealed themselves. The prints already suggested that Foss was limping. He had been hit by the wind, stumbled – and fallen from the cliff. Reeve, it appeared, had climbed down after him.

Locke cautiously neared the edge and shone his light downwards. Snow had been scraped from the steep rocky slope beneath him. The ground below was beyond the beam's range, though. Were his targets dead at the bottom of the ravine? Or had they survived – and were now escaping from him?

He had to see for himself. If he didn't, he might never reacquire their tracks. Furi could not be far away now. He pocketed the gun and torch, then began to follow Reeve's trail downwards.

CHAPTER 45

The river running through the ravine had frozen. Reeve supported Avelina as they made their blind, hesitant way across. The ice creaked and moaned beneath them – even cracking a couple of times. But it did not break.

The smooth surface under the snow eventually gave way to rocks. Reeve relievedly guided Avelina up the riverbank. 'We made it. We're on the far side.'

She made a little sound of pain as she hobbled beside him. Reeve didn't think her ankle was broken; she could take some weight on it. But it was badly sprained, possibly suffering a hairline fracture. Without his help, she would struggle even to walk. Moving at any speed was out of the question.

He looked back as they reached trees at the top of the slope. Only one thing was visible in the snow-swept blackness behind them. A single point of light, stark, cold.

Tracking them relentlessly.

Reeve shifted his hold on Avelina to ease the stress on her leg. 'Locke's following us. We need to move faster. Where's the village?'

Her voice, when she replied, was weak. The frigid conditions and her injury had drained her. 'We *must* be almost there. The river goes right past it.'

He groped through the trees, peering ahead. Only darkness lay before them. Another glance back. Locke's torch was obscured by the woods, but he would be gaining. All the Operative had to do was follow their tracks. Was there any way to ambush him? Not without leaving Avelina, and with her wounded leg she would be extremely vulnerable—

She straightened, suddenly finding new energy. 'I can see lights!'

Reeve looked – seeing tree trunks silhouetted against a hazy grey glow. The pair increased their pace and emerged into the open, the wind hitting them again. But something started to become visible through the blizzard. Large, blocky shapes, powerful lights shining down from them . . .

The cable-car station.

They headed across rough open ground towards it. Another look back. Locke's light bobbed as its holder started to run. 'Shit! He's coming.' Reeve pulled Avelina with him through the snow. She gasped in pain, but he kept going. If Locke drew close enough to target them before they reached cover, they were dead.

The station loomed ahead, taking on form through the swirling snow. The lights illuminated the area outside its entrance; the building itself was unlit, deserted. Reeve headed for the main doors – then saw they were closed. He changed direction. By necessity, part of the structure was open so the cable-cars could travel through it. He brought Avelina to the turnstiles for the Aroleid line. She made a startled sound as he effortlessly lifted her over the barrier. Where was Locke? The torch was nearing the station. Still following their trail towards the doors – but that would soon change.

Reeve vaulted the turnstile and quickly moved with Avelina into the building. The snow on the floor thinned, then disappeared. No more footprints for Locke to follow. He looked around. The station's interior was dark, only emergency exit signs illuminated. But he remembered the layout from earlier in the day. A walkway overlooked the concourse area. It probably led to offices – where there would be telephones—

A harsh metallic rattle from his left, close by. He spun, alarmed – but it was just gondolas shaking in the wind. The low lights glinted off glass and metal. They were beside the 'garage', ranks of empty cars suspended from the winding rail. Reeve led Avelina towards them. 'Hide in there,' he told her.

'Where are you going?' she asked, afraid.

'Upstairs, to find a phone. I'll make sure Locke knows where I've gone to draw him away from you.'

'Can't we use the cable-cars to get down to Zermatt?'

'I doubt I'll be able to start them without a key or a code. But even if I could, Locke would stop them – or reverse them. You stay hidden until I get back.' She hesitated. 'Go on, quick!'

She reluctantly limped for the hanging gondolas. Reeve started in the other direction – then noticed lights nearby. A control panel was mounted on a support pillar. He looked up. The cable-car track was right overhead. A large horizontal yellow wheel marked the start of the route's upper leg. The cable looped around it. Points allowed cars to join or leave the cable, or continue straight up the mountain.

A red light glowed above a prominent switch on the panel.

He pushed it. The light turned green – and the mechanism above came noisily to life. Wheels spun and chains clattered in the track, ready to pull gondolas along. But the cars' only movement was their slow, pendulous shivering. Presumably a separate system moved them through the garage.

The sound would serve to distract Locke, though. He glanced towards the open entrance. The Operative wasn't yet in sight – but couldn't be far away.

The thought spurred him on. He jumped over barriers and hurried into the concourse. How to reach the upper floor? No stairs or ladders were visible in the sparse lighting. But a vending machine glowed nearby – beneath one end of the walkway. He ran to it and clambered on to its top. The walkway's railing was within reach. He hauled himself upwards. A dim light beyond glass revealed a window, a door near it. He tried the latter. Locked. He went to the window and hit it with his elbow. It took a couple of hard strikes to break the double-glazed pane. A shard tore through his clothing, cutting him. He winced, but took the pain, climbing up on to the sill. The rest of the glass fell and smashed as he kicked it out. The way clear, he ducked into the room beyond.

Locke heard the singing clash of glass hitting concrete as he entered the station. He snapped his torch towards the sound. The beam swept across the empty concourse. No broken debris in sight. He remembered from his arrival that there was an upper floor. Reeve was probably searching for a phone to call the local authorities.

They couldn't help him. The winds were too strong to use the cable-car line to reach Furi. The only way here was on foot. A forty-minute trek even in the best conditions. In a blizzard, probably double that.

His task would be over in minutes. He brought the torch beam back to the floor ahead. Some snow had blown into the building, but it soon faded to nothingness. His quarry's footprints disappeared with it.

But not entirely. The snow was gone, but Reeve and Foss had still left damp traces on the concrete. He followed them until he neared the clattering machinery overhead. An attempt at distraction, undoubtedly. A closer examination of the fading trail. A change of direction, both turning towards the parked gondolas. Then Reeve reversed and headed for the concourse . . .

Locke stopped, sweeping his torch across the lines of stationary cars. He already knew from Foss's tracks in the snow that he was limping, badly hurt. Reeve had probably told him to hide while he went upstairs. The gondola garage was the obvious place to do so.

Pursue Reeve first, or Foss? The latter. If Reeve had a gun, he would have used it by now. He was not an immediate threat. Kill the pervert first, then concentrate on Reeve's long-overdue death.

He readied his gun, then entered the garage to begin his hunt.

The pain in her ankle was excruciating, but Avelina remained crouched between two gondolas. The cars hung in little trains of between four and eight from the overhead track. They swayed in the wind gusting through the building, creaking and rattling.

Another rank of cars was between her and the entrance. She saw Locke enter, a distorted figure through panels of curved, tinted glass. He stopped, shining his flashlight around the station – then entered the garage.

Avelina held her breath in terror. She could barely walk; running from him was impossible. All she could do was hide. But it wouldn't take him long to search the storage area. She dropped lower as she heard his footsteps over the noise of the machinery. Her ankle burned, wounded bone and muscle silently screaming. It took all her willpower not to join in.

Locke's light flicked along the other row of gondolas. Their doors were all closed, the cabins inaccessible. The beam dropped, checking the floor in the gaps between the trains. It found nothing. The footsteps resumed.

Drawing closer.

Avelina fearfully peered into the car shielding her. Locke's torch shone through the others in front of it. The Operative was a distorted shadow behind his light. She ducked her head, holding in a gasp of pure terror. Her mother's killer was just metres away. Boots on concrete, nearer, nearer, the torch getting brighter—

Another light came on.

Locke halted sharply as something changed in his peripheral vision. He looked back between the hanging gondolas. A room on the upper floor was now illuminated.

He retreated for a clearer view of the rectangle of diffuse light. A shadow slipped across a wall beyond it.

Reeve.

* * *

Reeve found a telephone in an office. He used it to call the Zermatt police. But he already knew they would arrive too late to affect events. He told them about Idonia Foss's murder – and that her child was still in danger. Then he hung up. He had to get back to Avelina before Locke found her.

He quickly returned to the room where he had entered. Cold-weather gear hung on hooks; that would be useful when he had to leave. He went back to the broken window, about to climb out—

Fire exploded in his right arm.

CHAPTER 46

Reeve cried out and fell back into the room. He overcame his shock, realising what had happened. He'd been shot!

He flattened himself beneath the window as two more rounds impacted above him. A hurried check of his arm in the low light. His sleeve was torn, blood glistening within the ragged hole. But the wound was only shallow, a pencil-wide line across his biceps. The pain subsided to a stinging burn. He cursed himself for his carelessness. He had not closed the room's inner door on his return. In his rush, he'd forgotten to switch off the hallway lights beyond. He had been silhouetted in the window as he tried to exit.

If Locke were a better marksman, he would be dead. He couldn't afford another mistake.

Staying low, Reeve scurried back to the door. The switches for the hallway lights were outside it. He closed his eyes and turned them off. The room plunged into darkness. Before Locke's vision could adjust, Reeve rushed to the window and dived through it.

He landed hard on the walkway, thudding against the railing's base. A new flare of pain in his wounded arm. He ignored it, rolling back towards the window – as more bullets struck above him.

* * *

Locke moved into the concourse, gun aimed at the window above. A dark figure appeared in it. He fired – seeing a puff of blood. Reeve fell back out of sight. The Operative kept his weapon raised. Had he got him? Was he dead?

The light went out. Damn! Not dead – which meant he would try to save Foss. Locke waited for any movement above . . .

A faint blur – then a thump as his target hit the railing. Locke opened fire, the gunshots echoing piercingly through the concrete building.

Avelina couldn't see what was happening, her view blocked by the ranks of cable-cars. But fear overpowered reason. She heard a shot, Reeve yelling in pain – then more gunfire. *He's hit*, her panicked mind told her. *He's down – he's dead. You'll be next. You have to run. Run!*

She knew she *couldn't* run. But the terror of being trapped was overwhelming. She pushed herself upright and desperately staggered towards the garage's open end—

Agony erupted in her ankle. She screamed and fell against a hanging gondola. It swung, pitching her to the floor. The car rolled along the track and crashed against its neighbour.

Locke heard the cry and metallic bang that followed. He ceased fire and glanced back into the garage. Foss had left hiding – probably trying to run.

His target was not going to escape. Not now.

He looked up at the walkway again. Reeve had flattened himself on the floor, the concrete protecting him. No way to shoot him – but it also meant he was pinned. If he dropped down to the concourse, he would be exposed . . .

Locke darted back into the garage. He cut between the ranks of gondolas to intercept his prey.

Reeve had also heard Avelina fall. The shooting stopped. What would Locke do? Concentrate on him – or go after his wounded target? He listened, trying to pick out any sounds over the rattling machinery—

Footsteps. Running.

He risked raising his head. A glimpse of Locke as he passed the illuminated control panel. The Operative reached the parked cable-cars and turned between them.

More movement further away. The glow of an emergency sign revealed a couple of gondolas swinging on the rail. Not merely rocking in the wind; something had hit them. Avelina. The exit was not far beyond. She was trying to escape.

Reeve realised he couldn't reach her in time. Not if he dropped down into the concourse. He would have to jump barriers, round the ranks of cars . . .

But there was a more direct route.

He sprang up and ran to the walkway's railing. Not along its length, but at its end. He vaulted on to it – and made a flying leap at the cableway.

A maintenance gantry ran above it. His fingers caught a support girder. He swung from it, free hand clawing for higher grip—

The chain clattering inside the machinery snagged his sleeve.

His arm was yanked sideways. He tried to pull loose. His

sleeve stretched, but remained entangled. His hand was being pulled towards the spinning wheels—

Reeve twisted, muscles straining – and his overstressed sleeve ripped apart. He snatched his hand clear, its back brushing cold steel. No time for relief. He pulled himself up on to the gantry. The storage area opened out before him, the rail a winding maze. Avelina was somewhere at its far corner.

Locke was heading towards her.

Avelina limped to the end of the train of cable-cars. The freezing wind hit her again as she neared the station's open end.

But she couldn't get to it. She had to cross an open space and climb over the turnstiles. She would be completely exposed. And now she couldn't go back. Locke was somewhere behind her. Closing in—

Light swept over her through the glass of the last gondola.

Locke moved between the lines of cable-cars, shining his torch into them. He was almost at the far end of the rail. Foss had to be hiding close by – there was nowhere else for him to go—

The beam found a huddled shape, colours that didn't belong. Behind the final gondola in the furthest rank.

The figure ducked. But the hunt was over. Locke reached a gap between two cars and started to squeeze through. Only one more row of gondolas separated him from his target.

The glow of Locke's torch revealed his position to Reeve. Only metres from Avelina.

Crossing under the rail between two gondolas—

Reeve dropped down at the hanging train's other end – and hurled himself at it.

The cars clashed together, lurching along the track. Locke had not yet cleared the gap. He was slammed between the two gondolas, the breath pounded from his lungs. Both gun and torch fell from his hands.

The first car swung back at Reeve. He jinked clear and ran. If he could reach Locke before he recovered—

The other cars recoiled from the impact, rolling backwards. Locke stumbled out from the gap. Reeve rushed at him, jabbing at his eyes. But the Operative, while winded, was not helpless. He jerked his head away to take the strike against his cheek. The two men collided. Locke reeled back. 'Run!' Reeve yelled to Avelina. 'Get out of here, go!' He drew back his fist for another attack—

Locke snatched out his combat knife.

The light from the fallen torch picked out the black blade's edge. Locke's face was briefly bisected by its shadow. Then he lunged, stabbing at Reeve. The former Operative darted in retreat. The knife rushed at him a second time. Reeve leapt clear through the gap between the gondolas. The blade's tip sliced through his clothing and cut a thin line across his back. Locke started after him, but paused, searching for his gun. It was lost in the darkness. He briefly debated his options – then pursued.

Reeve slipped through a space in the next rank of cars. The barrier separating the garage from the embarkation area blocked the way beyond. He swung himself over it. Locke rushed up behind him. The *swoosh* of the slashing knife was audible even over the machinery above.

Reeve ran towards the station's open end. The glow from the exterior lights lit the way. A thick pillar marked one end of the cableway's mechanisms. An access ladder was mounted on it. He scrambled upwards, not wanting to face the blizzard's teeth again. Locke was right with him, swiping the knife at his Achilles tendon.

He jumped up. The blade clanged against a metal rung just beneath his foot. He lashed out, kicking backwards. The blow made contact. Locke lurched away with a sound of pain. Then fury drove him after his enemy.

Reeve reached the ladder's top, finding himself back on the maintenance gantry. Machinery ground away ahead of him. He advanced along the narrow catwalk. Maybe there was something he could use as a weapon. A metal bar, tools, anything—

There was nothing. The cableway's workings were neat, clean, ordered. Swiss. And now Locke was on the gantry with him, advancing. Reeve turned. The Operative was a silhouette against the blizzard outside. The blade was readied in his outstretched hand. Reeve retreated – until a girder obstructed his way. Locke thrust the knife—

Reeve whipped up his right arm to deflect it away. Before Locke could react, he sent a left jab at his face. His knuckles pounded into the other man's cheek. Locke re-coiled. Reeve made a grab for the knife. But Locke was ready, twisting his wrist to flick his weapon sideways. The carbon-fibre edge caught the heel of Reeve's palm. Flesh ripped, hot blood running on to his wrist. Reeve gasped, jerking back.

Locke drove the knife at him again. This time he scored a firm hit.

Reeve yelled as the blade stabbed into his biceps. He instinctively tried to pull away – thumping against the girder. His feet slipped on the metal catwalk. Before he could catch himself, he crashed down on his back.

Locke loomed over him, knife raised. The bloodied point hovered over his neck. Searching for the precise spot to make the kill—

The delay was less than a second. It was too long.

Reeve grabbed the Operative's arm – and with all his strength, shoved it sideways.

Into the machinery.

The chain caught Locke's thick coat sleeve. Before he could react, his hand was drawn into the whirling wheels. He screamed as his fingers were crushed against the knife's hilt. Then the hilt itself sheared apart with a crack. The blade clattered down beside Reeve as Locke was dragged over him. He grabbed it – and drove it up hard into Locke's chest.

Another scream, this one wet and gurgling. Reeve clamped his other hand around part of the gantry. The machinery relentlessly hauled Locke onwards – but the knife stayed put. Its black edge sliced through skin and muscle and the organs beneath. Blood and stomach fluids sluiced out, splashing across the concrete floor below. Locke kept screaming – then was pulled around the rail curving towards the garage. He fell from the walkway, but his hand was still trapped. His torn intestines spilled from his eviscerated torso, trailing behind him.

Panting, Reeve sat up. Locke was still being carried away from him by the machinery. Then his smashed hand jammed at the end of the active section of track. He dangled there, gasping and twitching, before finally going limp.

Reeve stared at him for a long moment, then crawled back along the catwalk. He still held the broken knife. No point leaving the murder weapon for the police. He climbed down. 'Avelina!' he called. His voice sounded shockingly weak in his own ears. Where was she? Concern rose. Had Locke reached her before him—

'Alex!' Another feeble voice, from the garage. He shakily made his way back into it. A light danced between the glass gondolas. Avelina, holding Locke's torch. She limped to him, casting the beam over his body – and recoiled. 'Shit, shit! Oh my God!'

He realised he was covered in blood. 'It's not mine,' he managed to say. 'Most of it.'

She glanced around fearfully. 'Where's Locke?'

'Back there. Dead, don't worry.' He jerked a weary thumb over one shoulder. 'I called the cops in Zermatt. Someone'll be here to help you soon.'

'Me? What about you?'

'I need to go. I just killed a man; they'll take me in for questioning. And then SC9 would send more Operatives after me.'

She gripped his wrist. 'No – you can't just leave me!'

'I'll stay with you as long as I can. And I'll wait nearby until I know you're safe. But I have to go.'

Avelina bowed her head. 'I . . . Okay. I know. I'm sorry.'

'So am I.' He put a hand on her arm, guiding her around the gondolas. 'Come on. There's a first-aid station upstairs. I'll fix you up.'

She aimed the light at him again, seeing his wounds. 'I don't think I'll be able to help fix you.'

A faint smile somehow forced its way on to his face. 'Don't worry,' he told her. 'You already did.'

CHAPTER 47

Avelina Foss took a deep drink of water to counter her dry mouth. There was nothing it could do to aid her nervousness, though. Today was something she had wanted to delay. But it had to be done. Postponing it would not be fair to the people whose lives her decision would affect.

She stood and limped across her mother's office. *Her* office, she corrected forcibly. Two weeks had passed since the terrible events in Zermatt. Her mother's funeral had been four days ago. It had nearly broken her. But she knew she had to go on. Like it or not, she now had a responsibility to others. No more running away from what she had to do.

One of her office's doors led directly to the conference room. She took a deep breath, then went through. Those already inside rose in respect. 'Thank you,' Avelina said quietly. They watched as she took her seat at the head of the table. The attendees consisted of three groups. One was Foss Präzisionsmetall, GmbH's few external shareholders. They had only a minority stake in the company; Avelina had inherited the controlling interest. Another was senior members of management and the workforce, including the union representatives. Their jobs would be directly affected by her decision today. The last represented the other arms manufacturers involved in the merger. They were doubtless hoping she would continue as her mother had intended.

They would all leave the meeting disappointed to various degrees. She hoped some would see the upside of what she was about to tell them.

All eyes were now on her. She knew what they were thinking. Those that already knew her: *She's not Idonia. She doesn't know what she's doing.* The others: *This freak, this pervert, wants us to take him seriously? We can run rings around him. He doesn't have a clue.*

Both groups were in for a surprise. Avelina knew exactly what she was doing. She had had many differences of opinion with her mother. But she had always learned from her.

She belatedly realised that she had unconsciously chosen to *look* like her. Serious business required a serious appearance. No punky miniskirts or high-heeled goth boots today. Instead she wore an Armani suit. A ladies' design, of course, with a knee-length skirt. Her hair was still coloured, but tied back in a neat pony-tail. She was not going to compromise her own identity, even for this. Her mother had finally accepted her as she was. That was what mattered.

'Thank you for coming,' she began. The words sounded reedy; she cleared her throat. Some of her audience took that as a sign of nervousness. Avelina could see their expectancy, their feeling they were about to walk all over her.

Time to prove them wrong. 'As you know, I'm the new managing director and majority shareholder of Foss Präzisionsmetall, GmbH. The circumstances through which that happened are awful. I'm very grateful for the sympathy you've all shown me.' Murmured commiserations around the table. 'Thank you again. Now, I'm going to get directly to the point.'

She straightened in her chair, sitting taller. 'Effective immediately, the company will transition out of arms manufacturing. All orders already taken will be fulfilled. But no new ones will be accepted.' A susurrus of shock around the room. 'The sales team will target our original core market: precision parts for the auto industry. That division of the company will be expanded. All arms division machinery and systems that can be transferred to it, will be. The rest will be sold off at the best possible price.'

One of the older managers spoke up. 'You're closing the arms division? But that's almost eighty per cent of our business! You can't do that!'

Avelina fixed him with an unblinking stare. 'I can, and I am. As I said, there will be a transition period. I want to minimise job losses as much as possible. However, anyone who has a problem with the company's new direction . . . is free to resign.'

Her eyes remained fixed on the man. He looked away first. 'You don't know what you're doing,' he muttered.

'You'd be surprised,' she told him.

Another man, from the Spanish alliance partner, had a question. 'How will this affect the proposed merger of our companies?'

'It will end it,' was her blunt, prepared reply. More shock from the attendees. 'At least, as far as Foss Präzisionsmetall's participation is concerned. The other parties are free to continue as they wish. But Foss will no longer make weapons.

So it would be pointless for it to join a weapons-making consortium. Wouldn't you agree?'

The Spaniard clearly did not. 'There will be lawsuits over this,' he said darkly.

'I'm sure there will,' was Avelina's firm reply. She regarded each of the others in turn. 'Now. Are there any more questions?'

CHAPTER 48

Tony Maxwell faced the three men across the oval table once more. He knew the meeting's purpose this time. After weeks of scandal, Roger Glennmore, head of Xeneon, had been forced to resign. The recording of his attempted blackmail of Idonia Foss had been publicly released. Foss's company had withdrawn from the merger – but the controversy hit Xeneon's share value hard. It had been unable to capitalise on the weakened state of the other companies involved. An American-led consortium took advantage instead. The whole affair was a major blow to the British arms industry.

And now, the UK's intelligence heads intended to scapegoat him for it.

Maxwell smiled inwardly. He was ready for them.

Aubrey Ryford-Croft of MI6 opened the inquisition with a recap of events. SC9's involvement was pilloried at each step. 'An operation that was an appalling failure in every respect,' he concluded. 'Badly planned, and botched in the implementation. As a result, the national interest has been damaged. Xeneon had to buy back its own shares to prevent a partial American takeover. A huge amount of money, wasted. Xeneon's credibility battered. Really, the worst possible outcome. For which somebody,' he gave

Maxwell a cold look, 'must be held responsible.'

Maxwell didn't flinch. 'You're right,' he said. 'Somebody *must* be held responsible. And I'm looking at them.'

It was not the response the three men had expected. Justin Stockley of MI5 blinked, then bristled with indignation. 'Don't you even think about trying to deflect—'

'Let me lay out exactly what happened, Justin,' Maxwell interrupted firmly. 'Simon Scott instigated SC9's operation. After his death I continued it, believing it in Britain's strategic interest. From SC9's perspective, the mission was a success.'

'A success?' hooted GCHQ's Michael Barwell. 'I'd hate to hear your definition of a failure.'

'I'm coming to it,' Maxwell replied, undaunted. 'But SC9's target was eliminated, and the merger collapsed. That was the objective. It's not SC9's fault Roger Glennmore was stupid enough to let himself be recorded. Nor is it SC9's fault that MI6 and GCHQ couldn't do their *fucking jobs*.' The angry expletive shocked the others – as intended. 'Idonia Foss had a recording, and you couldn't find it. The two most expensively funded intelligence agencies in Europe, and you couldn't find it! How many field officers do you have in Germany, Aubrey? How many supercomputers and hackers do you have, Michael? But neither of you had the *balls* to take the direct action necessary. Instead, you palmed it off on to SC9!'

Before the other men could respond to his tirade, Maxwell stood, planting both hands on the table. He glared down at them as he continued. 'I'll remind you that SC9 is not an intelligence agency. We are not spies. We are *assassins*. We kill people who threaten the interests of the British state. And we are very good at it.' His tone became still darker, more threatening. 'That is, when we are not being sabotaged *by our own side*. Your bullshit bureaucratic infighting caused this, Aubrey. Yours too, Michael, Justin. You saw this as a chance to expand your fiefdoms, to take over SC9. And my mistake was to let you try it. SC9's charter grants it total independence. *Total*. I shouldn't have allowed you to compromise that. And now we've seen the result. One of my Operatives is dead. He was distracted by a task that wasn't his responsibility. Simon would never have allowed it, and nor should I. Well, it will *not* happen again.' He stood up straight. 'SC9 has a job to do. I suggest that in future, you let it do so without interference. Because I will not allow the failures of others to damage my agency again. I hope I've made myself very clear.' He turned away and started for the exit. 'If that's all, I'll get back to my work.'

He had estimated a fifty-fifty chance that outrage would prompt a response. He was ready for it. Any arguments they might throw back at him had been predicted, counters prepared. But he reached the door without a word from behind.

They would begin once he was past the soundproof barrier, he knew. The three men were not used to being challenged. They would be angry, affronted. They might even consider knee-jerk retribution. That would be . . . unwise. He'd hoped his implied threat was impossible to miss.

Even without their taking any immediate action against SC9, there could still be problems. But Maxwell was up for the fight. *Be firm. Be resolute. Be ruthless.* He would follow his old boss's mantra to the letter.

If that meant retaliation against anyone who threatened what was now his . . . so be it.

Maxwell left MI6's riverside headquarters, but did not immediately return to SC9. He had another meeting on the Thames.

This was considerably more public, and circumspect. There was a possibility that Ryford-Croft or Stockley had him under observation. Slim, but considering events, non-zero. So he used his experience in spycraft to minimise the risks. If there were any watchers, they were hanging well back. Too far away to monitor his meeting – or even realise it had happened.

The Thameside path opposite the Houses of Parliament was always busy at lunchtime. It was a favourite spot for tourists. The small parks at each end were also popular with workers wanting to eat outdoors. Maxwell walked briskly through the crowds. The man he was here to meet was ahead, moving slightly less quickly. He drew alongside him, eyes fixed forwards. 'I made my case,' he said quietly. 'Hopefully they're smart enough to leave SC9 alone. I wouldn't want to have to escalate matters.'

'Good,' replied his contact. 'We're very happy with the outcome. Xeneon being knocked out let our interests step in. Things couldn't have gone better.'

'And my money?'

'In your Swiss account. Under your false name, of course. Make sure you remember to show the right ID.'

Maxwell didn't smile. The clandestine exchange was already becoming dangerously long. 'Anything else?'

'Not now. We'll be in touch in the usual way when we need you again.' The American slowed slightly to let him draw ahead.

Maxwell continued on, ascending the steps up to Westminster Bridge. His contact continued along the riverside beneath it. He turned east, heading for Waterloo station. He could now return to SC9. As he had told the intelligence chiefs, he had work to do.

Not all of it was in the interests of the nation. Some was entirely in his own.

The journey back to Bartleby House took around forty minutes. Maxwell had taken the Tube, then walked an indirect route. Partly so he could buy lunch; he was genuinely hungry. But also to check if he actually was being tailed. As far as he could tell, he wasn't. That was something, at least. If somebody *did* start following him, he could be pretty sure who had sent them.

Susan King greeted him as he cleared the second security door. 'Afternoon, Tony. How did the meeting go?'

'As well as could be expected,' he replied, with a half-smile. 'Anything new I should know about?'

'I've sent you some operational status reports. They're on your computer. Oh, and there's an eyes-only document for you from Six. It's on your desk.'

'Thanks.' He headed for his office. As promised, a plastic envelope awaited him. It was printed with a complex, repeating pattern. An anti-tamper system. Any stress would cause the ink to change colour. He checked both sides of his delivery. All the ink was black, as it should be. It turned a warning red at one end as he ripped the seal. A single sheet of paper was folded inside. He extracted and read it.

A long, thoughtful pause as he considered what he had just learned. Then he rose and went to the door. 'Susan?' he called. 'I need you to book me a flight.'

CHAPTER 49

Avelina Foss brought her car into the house's driveway and pulled up. The winter's snow had, thankfully, finally melted. Spring was not yet here, but at least the most bitter cold was over. She got out and started for the door—

'Hi.'

She flinched and halted. The events of the previous month had scarred her, nightmares always lurking. Until the merger was confirmed as terminated, she had employed round-the-clock bodyguards. Even now, there was the residual fear that SC9 might still want her dead.

But the man who slipped through the automatic gate as it closed was no enemy. Alex Reeve stood before her. His dark hair was now bleached blond. He looked tired, grim – but no longer exhausted and weather-beaten. Whatever he had been doing, there had been a roof over his head. 'Alex!' she exclaimed, before looking around in alarm. 'Is it safe for you to be here? What if someone's watching the house?'

'They aren't,' he said, with certainty.

'What are you doing here?'

'I wanted to make sure you were okay. I read about you taking over the company – and what you did. That was brave of you. It would have been easier just to carry on with the merger.'

'I know. And obviously that's what Mother wanted to happen. But . . .' She sighed. 'I couldn't do it. I was opposed to the company making things that would be used to kill people. And after what happened, I was even more opposed. Maybe it was the wrong decision. It's already cost the company a lot of money, a lot of business. But . . . I had to be true to myself.'

Reeve nodded. 'I don't know anything about running a business. I can't say if it was right from that point of view. But it was right from yours – and that's what matters.'

A small smile. 'Thank you.'

They walked to the house's door, stopping outside. 'So are you okay?' Reeve asked. 'Physically, I mean? I did what I could to patch you up in Zermatt, but . . .'

'I'm good,' she assured him. 'My ankle is almost better. I will be able to start wearing high heels again soon!' They both grinned, briefly. 'Everything else is . . . fine, I suppose. I have some scars.' Avelina indicated her cheek. A raw pink line marked where Locke's knife had cut her. 'They will heal. On the outside, anyway. The ones on the inside . . . I don't know how long they will take.'

'It can be a long time,' Reeve told her gloomily. 'I know that for myself. My mum, she died when . . . my dad murdered her.' Her eyes and mouth widened in shock. 'I still don't think I'm fully past it. But . . . it doesn't hurt as much as it did.'

'I'm a long way from that,' she said, with a sad laugh.

'You *will* get through it. I wanted to tell you that.'

'Before you go again?' He nodded. 'Where to? And what have you been doing since Zermatt?'

'Staying out of the way, mostly,' he said. 'I know you said you'd protect me with the Swiss police—'

'I did,' Avelina cut in. 'I told them you'd saved me from Locke and the Russians. They seemed to accept it.' An ironic laugh. 'I suppose they listen more to trans people when they're from a rich family.'

'Thanks for doing it. But I went back to the lodge to get my passport and stuff. After that I hid in the woods until the next morning, then walked down to Zermatt. Caught the train out of town, and just kept my head down. Waited a few days for the heat to ease off, then left Switzerland.'

'Did you come back to Germany?'

'No, France. I can speak the language. But I came back here to see you.'

She nodded in gratitude. 'So what are you doing next?'

'I'm going to do what your mum suggested. Talk to her friend – see if they have any work for me.'

'Are you sure that's the best thing to do? I mean, you have a new German identity now. You could get work here.'

'*Ich nichten sprachen Deutsche.*'

She pretended to wince at his appalling grasp of her language. 'Point taken.'

'Besides, your mum was right. Her friend will have contacts, resources. I'll need them to find Connie.'

'Oh – you're definitely going to look for her?' A hint of excitedness entered her voice.

He nodded. 'After what you said on the Matterhorn, yeah. I *was* scared about seeing her again – in case she rejected me. But she might not. And I still love her. I've got to know whether she still feels the same. And if she doesn't . . . if there's anything I can do to change that. But if I don't find out, I'll always regret it.'

Avelina smiled, then stepped closer and wrapped her arms around him. 'You go and find her. And if you ever need my help for anything, call me.'

'Thank you.'

A lengthy pause, then she released him. 'Well,' she said, slightly awkward. 'Do you need anything from me *now*? Money, transport?'

'I'm fine,' said Reeve. He turned and started for the gate. 'Take care of yourself, Avelina.'

'You too, Alex. And . . . I hope you find Connie. And that she still loves you.'

His only response was a part-hopeful, part-rueful nod. Then he was gone.

CHAPTER 50

Pyotr Viktorovich Grishin had already read the after-action report in full. But he slowly pored over each page again, letting the man standing before him sweat. Finally, he looked up. 'And this is everything?'

'Yes, sir.' Boris Pervak had never dealt directly with the head of Directorate S before. He was not enjoying the experience.

'Why did it take so long to collate?'

'We, ah, we had to wait for the Swiss to complete their investigation. They're very thorough. And then we had to obtain copies of their findings. It took a while. They have pretty good computer security, for cops. And they're,' a nervous laugh, 'quite hard to bribe.'

'Indeed.' There was not the faintest trace of amusement on Grishin's face. He leafed back through the document, at a snail's pace. Pervak's nervousness expressed itself as a jiggle in one heel. He forced himself to be still at the spymaster's disapproving stare. At last, Grishin finished and carefully tapped the pages into a neat stack. 'This does not reflect well on the Directorate.'

Pervak realised he was expected to answer. 'No, sir.'

'Seven men dead, and nothing to show for it. The only

small mercy is that none can be confirmed as SVR agents. Otherwise, a humiliating failure. Somebody will have to pay.'

Pervak blanched. 'Y-yes, sir.' He waited with growing fear for the hammer to fall . . .

It dropped – but to his immense relief, not on him. 'SC9 and this rogue Operative of theirs caused this. It's time to take direct action against them.'

An enthusiastic nod. 'Yes, sir.'

'They will be under pressure at home. They've been specifically named in the German and Swiss investigations. That will set them scuttling like cockroaches. There's nothing these sorts hate more than being exposed to daylight. So we must take advantage of their panic. I want to see everything we have on SC9, everything Morozov's mole gave to us.'

'I'll start on it at once, sir,' said Pervak.

Grishin nodded in a clear gesture of dismissal. The young man turned to leave. 'Oh, and Pervak?' He froze. Each of Grishin's words was punctuated by a stab of his finger against his desk. '*Find. Alex. Reeve.*'

Maxwell stopped his car and checked the building across the road. It was the address MI6 had given him. Madonna Alta was a suburb of the Italian city of Perugia. This particular street was nothing to write home about. No houses, just blocks of flats. Half-hearted graffiti on the walls, the parked cars mostly several years old. High-density, low-income apartments.

The kind of place a person might live if they wanted to avoid notice.

He got out and crossed the road. His car had been provided by MI6 – as had the gun in his concealed holster. So far, Ryford-Croft and the others had not withdrawn support for SC9. If they did, he would deal with it however he felt necessary.

He entered the building and went up a concrete stairwell. The flat he was looking for turned out to be on the fourth floor. Not somewhere a professional would have chosen. No alternative exit routes: it was too high to escape via the windows. The only way out was by going through him.

That wasn't going to happen.

He found the right door and knocked. No response at first. Was the occupant at work? His information suggested otherwise at this hour, but it could be incomplete. Knowing that the other agencies were checking out SC9's priority subjects had made him cautious. This one had been deliberately low-profile. He wanted to keep MI6 and the others well away from it . . .

A sound from inside. He straightened, readying himself. The door opened.

Connie Jones stood inside.

They had met once before, on a London rooftop. Recognition in her eyes. Then shock.

Then fear.

'Hello, Connie,' said Maxwell.

She stepped back, afraid. One hand came up as if to slam the door on him. It never touched the handle. They both knew the Operative would reach her, no matter what. 'Oh, God,' she gasped. 'What – what do you want?'

'Just to talk. For now.' He looked her up and down. A

small twitch of his eyebrows. His information was *definitely* incomplete, outright cursory. Whichever junior officer had been assigned to investigate her had overlooked one rather obvious fact. Connie saw where he was looking and instinctively put a protective hand over her belly. She was visibly pregnant; Maxwell estimated five to six months along.

'Well,' he said, almost amiably, 'this complicates things. What *are* we going to do with you?'